TRUE LOVE

USA TODAY BESTSELLING AUTHOR
MJ FIELDS

Copyright © 2022 by MJ Fields

All rights reserved. No part of this publication may be reproduced, distributed, or transmitted in any form or by any means, including photocopying, recording, or other electronic or mechanical methods, without the prior written permission of the publisher, except in the case of brief quotations embodied in critical reviews and certain other noncommercial uses permitted by copyright law.

This book is a work of fiction. All names, characters, locations, and incidents are products of the author's imaginations. Any resemblance to actual persons, things, living or dead, locales, or events is entirely coincidental.

John Ross
m.
Maggie

Molly   Alex   Tessa   Kendall   Jake

R O S S

BLUE
VALLEY
SERIES

Josie Ross- Fields
div.
Troy

R O S S

Jack Ross
div.

Jasper *d.*   Jason *d.*   Jade

R O S S

Landon Links   *- div.* Kate
m.   Lucas
Audrianna

Alexandra   Ally

L I N K S

USA TODAY BESTSELLING AUTHOR

M J   F I E L D S

True Love Playlist

Dancing Queen - ABBA
Better Man - Pearl Jam
How's it Going to Be - Third Eye Blind
Shimmer - Fuel
I Don't Want To Miss A Thing - Aerosmith
Time After Time - INOJ
Wishlist - Pearl Jam
To the Moon & Back - Savage Garden
Gettin Jiggy Wit It - Will Smith
Landslide - Fleetwood Mac
Let's Go Crazy - Prince
Honestly - Stryper
Love Song - Third Day
Art In Me - Jars Of Clay
Blessed Be Your Name - Newsboys
What's My Age Again? - blink-182
Higher - Creed
Black Balloon - The Goo Goo Dolls
Out Of My Head - Fastball
Amazed - Lonestar

I Could Not Ask For More - Sarah Evans
Nookie - Limp Bizkit
Cruel Summer - Ace of Base
Wide Open Spaces - Dixie Chicks
Cowboy Take Me Away - Dixie Chicks
No Scrubs - TLC
Slide - The Goo Goo Dolls
My Own Worst Enemy - Lit
Brown Eyed Girl - Van Morrison
Moon Dance - Van Morrison
Crazy Love - Van Morrison

Click For The Playlist on Spotify

The Blue Valley Series
MUST BE READ IN ORDER

Blue Love
New Love
Sad Love
True Love

Forward

The Blue Valley series is not your typical love story. It is a journey through one's past ... maybe even a story resembling someone close to you. *It's our story.*

Tessa Ross has finally decided to give herself a break.
A break from her forced smiles.
A break from the **people she loves**.
A break to help her heart heal.
A break to **mend and regain the strength** that she once had.
A break to find herself again.
A break to **focus on the next step in her life journey**.
And so, she puts distance between herself, **Lucas**,
and **Blue Valley**, returning to her family's house in **Cape Cod,** a place that she always loved and felt loved in.
Will it lead her home to seek comfort in those she loves, or will she see that home has always been with her?

Warning: Highly Emotional!

This book contains volatile characters in real-life situations
that may be triggers to some readers.
This was love, not a fairy tale…
until it became one.

*PLEASE NOTE: this series was previously released as The Love
series (MJ's very first works) and has been through a complete rewrite,
which consists of a change from narrative to first person/ dual POV
and forty thousand words worth of new content.*

To The Reader

PLEASE NOTE:
This series was previously released as The Love series (MJ's very first works released in 2012-2013) and has been through a complete rewrite, which consists of a change from narrative to first person/ dual POV and forty thousand words worth of new content.

Warning: *Highly Emotional!*
This book contains volatile characters in real-life situations that may be triggers to some readers.

The Rearview Mirror

Chapter One

I watched in the rearview mirror as Blue Valley became smaller and smaller with each passing moment that I say goodbye. *Goodbye to a future that is no longer.* I knew this would happen someday—that I would leave. I prepared for it, accepted it, only to have it thrown in my face. Blue Valley is home, always will be, but it is different for me now. *Quicksand.*

But then something happens. That something is the realization that view in the rearview is so much smaller than looking out the windshield.

I vow to myself that I am done looking behind me, because looking ahead … I can breathe without the ache in my chest causing me to never really … breathe when I look ahead of me, seeing everything there is to look forward to. That view doesn't get smaller. No, it gets bigger. It becomes clearer. And so, I keep looking forward.

We shouldn't spend our lives looking in the review, and that was exactly what I was doing, looking for something I romanticized—him and I forever—that it distorted reality.

I look beside me and smile.

"It's sunny, and seventy-five in Upstate, New York," I announce to my copilot, my soul, my rescued labradoodle, Leia, as we drive south on Interstate 81. That smile, that feeling of peace I felt when I made the decision to head to the Cape, to the house my great aunt Ann left to our family after her death, a place of peace and love.

Three loves. The first teaches what you want and need, *check*. The second breaks you so badly that you don't think you will ever want to put yourself through that again, *check times a million*. The third, I'm changing it up. My third love is me. I need to love my life, love myself ... anyway. And yes, it will be easier to do that away from Blue Valley ... at least for a little while.

Never will I ever allow myself to be consumed so much by another that I lose myself, *like ever.* I am doing it, finally taking a break from my life, the one I loved, but loved too deeply that it suffocated me.

Seven hours to go where I can plant my feet in the sand and hit the proverbial reset button.

All this self-talk, this hyping myself up, I'm using to drown out the doubt.

It's fine. I'll be all right.

I am.

I hit play on the tape player and my "Strong and Free" mix tape begins. How could anything be wrong with Abba's "Dancing Queen" blasting through four—okay, three speakers, since one no longer works—all around me?

9

I reach over and pet Leia, realizing she is in desperate need of a haircut.

"Sorry, girl. I should've thought about that last week, but we'll find a place; a doggie spa that'll make you the prettiest pooch on the Cape. Just, seriously, don't scare them. Then, after we get you all set, and I get myself sorted, too, maybe we'll fix up the Jeep. Well, at least make a regular appointment and start making us a priority."

Half an hour later, my phone rings mid-belt to "Respect."

I hit answer and say, "Hello."

Phoebe laughs as I turn down the radio.

"Hey, Phoebe. What's up?"

"Not much. What have you been up to? I haven't talked to you in a week."

"Just busy. You know, getting things sorted in 'Cuse, and, uh ... Well, what have you been up to?"

"Just hanging out. Have you talked to Lucas?"

Ouch.

"Alex mentioned he showed up, and I was, you know, just wanting to give you a reminder that I'm here ... anytime."

"I talked to him yesterday ... He's doing all right." *Delusional as always, but now he's alone in it.* "He seems to think he's going to change and fix us." I force a laugh then continue, "But that's why we're here. That among other things. But it is what it is."

"Hey, you know you didn't have to send me money. I know it wasn't your plan to call the wedding off."

"I knew if I didn't send it and tried to hand it to you, you wouldn't take it. But there was no way I would ever feel right with not having paid you all back for dresses for a wedding that is not happening. Plus, I thought I could buy them from you. You know, have a big party when I get home from my vacation. We certainly could use something to start the bonfire with."

"Vacation? Where did you decide?" Phoebe asks.

"I am actually on my way to Cape Cod. Leia and I are on 81, about to get on 88, heading to the beach house. No one is going to be there all month. I just need to get away, you know."

"Wow ... a month, huh? You sure you can afford that?"

"I don't have any bills, Phoebe." *Or anything else.* "I'm going to be fine. I've been saving for a year now, slamming the overtime lately, so I'll be fine for a few weeks, as long as I avoid too much retail therapy."

Silence.

"Phoebe, I am okay," I assure her. "Leia and I are going to get pampered and chill. Read. Run. All the good stuff. But, please, do not let my whereabouts find their way to *him*. He's not good, Phoebe, and I will admit that makes me stupid."

"I'm here for you. I know we haven't talked this week, but I have been thinking about you. I want you to know I love you, and I think you made the right decision," Phoebe says sweetly.

I give her sweet back. "Thank you. I know you're here. I know you're busy, too. Hey, if you need to get away, I'm just a seven-hour drive."

"Hmm ... with Alex in vet school and working on the farm, and me taking online courses, I just may take you up on that. But, you know ... I do have baggage."

"My niece or nephew are not baggage; they are a blessing."

"You should probably ask Jade, too," she suggests.

"Maybe we could make it a girls' getaway. You guys could swing by the farm and grab my gown and bring yours along. We could go out, all dressed up in them, and then come back to Aunt Ann's place and jump in the ocean." *My dream.* "You know, mess the dresses up. Maybe we could have Laura come up and take photos."

I nearly miss my exit while lost in planning.

"Hey, Phoebe, I have to start paying attention to where I'm going. I will talk to you soon, okay? And make sure no one knows. I need a few days."

Phoebe promises her lips are sealed. And, after we hang up, I rewind and crank Aretha.

Five hours and one traffic jam later, I am getting off I-90, the Massachusetts Turnpike.

Leia begins to get antsy.

"Okay, Leia, we need to pull off soon and find a place for us both to go to the bathroom and get you a drink and fill up the tank. Half an hour, tops."

I eject the tape then turn on a radio station, smiling when I hear a familiar and favorite voice. I crank up the radio and sing along with Eddie Vedder. Soon after that, I find a rest stop, get Leia out, let her do her business, clean up after her, get her settled back in, fill her travel bowl with water, and then head to the restroom.

Public restrooms disgust me. I remember Grandma always sprayed and wiped them down, then lined them while telling us about all the germs and diseases you could get if your backside touched the seat even for a second. So, I stand, hovering above the toilet. When finished, I flush the toilet with my foot then walk out and grab some paper towels. Putting them under my arm, I wash my hands, dry them off with the paper towels, and then use them to shut off the water and open the door.

"Love you, Grandma Mary and Grandma Martha. You taught me well," I whisper as I exit the building … germ-free.

It's nearing five p.m. when we are stuck in another traffic jam, and both Leia and I have had enough.

I look at the map while we sit and see we're about thirty miles from MA 25E then about half an hour to Chatham.

After we begin moving again, traffic isn't that bad, and I am glad we will still miss rush hour. I decide it's time to call home and let them know I headed out earlier than expected.

When Mom answers, I say, "Hey, Mom, we are about thirty miles from Ann's place."

"When did you leave?"

"I left about eight hours ago." I laugh.

"It's a five-and-a-half-hour drive," Mom states. "Did you run into problems?" She doesn't let me answer, she sighs. "Tessa, I know you love that Jeep, but you should have let Dad look at it—"

"Jeep's good. Traffic was backed up a couple times. Sorry I left early, but I decided to not sit around and wait until Monday. Can you text me the security code?"

"Of course. Please call me when you get there."

"Will do. Love you, Mom."

"Enjoy the Cape, Tessa."

I find the house, but it isn't exactly as I remember it from my last visit years ago, but Mom did say they hired a handyman to make some improvements. I just didn't know how extensive those improvements were, and I am only seeing the back porch and new shiplap siding.

"Maybe it's just the exterior, Leia," I say as I put the Jeep in park.

The parking lot is shared with the neighboring homes, so as I jump out with Leia, I hope that I got it right.

We walk to the door as I check the texts for the code.

I open the now enclosed back porch, which spans the

entire back of the house by I would guess eighty feet, and step in.

I look around and decide I like it. It will be the perfect and a secure space to put Leia's crate in when I need to run out and do errands. Honestly, I don't even think the crate is necessary, but I did lug it here.

"Wow, Leia, look at this. It's your own room."

She wags her tail happily as she sniffs around. When she comes back to me, she licks my hand and nudges it.

"You and Chewy would have been great friends, Miss Leia."

She nudges my hand again.

"Okay, okay, let's go explore."

I punch in the code, unlatch the security lock, open the door, and step inside.

Upon entering, I look around and see just how much the place has changed, yet I still feel the peace it has given me every time I have visited throughout my life.

I squat down and pet my girl. "You would have loved her girl, and she you."

The floors are now tiled in the enlarged kitchen to the left of the entry. To the right is a study where Ann's room used to be, which is smaller now, and the bathroom beside it has been made bigger. The entire floor plan has been opened. The kitchen has been updated with stainless steel appliances and white cabinetry and new granite counter-tops. The half wall has been removed, and in its place is a large island with a stovetop and small sink. On the opposite side is seating for four, and just beyond that is a dining table and chairs.

"They got rid of Aunt Ann's back porch, Leia, and used it as part of this addition and …" I turn the corner and look up. "Wow."

Cathedral ceilings and a two-story stone fireplace

stands tall at the end. On each side of it are two massive French doors facing the Atlantic. I walk to one set of doors, unlock them, and throw both sides open. "Amazing."

I step out onto the sand-colored stamped concrete patio spanning the length of the house and thirty feet deep. Adirondack furniture, a couple chaise lounges, and potted plants are scattered around, making it basically its own living space.

There is not a soul on the beach, private, and as beautiful as ever. Forty feet beyond the patio is sand and the entire area is fenced in with a white picket fence. To the left of the fence, a brick wall stands cold and harsh, a fortress … a warning, holding the neighbor's deck high above Ann's property.

"Let's go, Miss Leia. You're going to love this!" I kick off my sandals, hurry to the gate, and throw it open. Then I step out, dig my toes into the sand, and look beside me. "You wanna go dip our paws in the water?"

I stand with my toes in the wet sand, watching the sun set as Leia dances around the shore, not getting any closer. I take a giant step in and yell, "Jump in, girl!"

I laugh as I watch Leia leap into the water and splash around, barking and wagging her tail. She seems so happy to be here. All the splashing reminds me that I need to use the bathroom.

"Okay, Leia, let's go back for a bit, unpack, and get settled in, okay?"

When she follows me, right at my heels, I wonder who the hell decided to give up on her. When the thoughts, the emotions, get too heavy, I shake it off, latch the gate behind me, and then turn to look back at the water as the sun sets behind us.

I look beside me. "You and I are two lucky ladies.

Tomorrow is a new day, and you and I are going to make the best of it."

Inside, I decide to head upstairs and find four bedrooms, all with a nautical theme, and a master suite that is east-facing with floor to ceiling windows and a great view of the old lighthouse.

"We're calling this room," I tell Leia then run to the bathroom.

While washing my hands, I look in the mirror. My sloppy bun is now a floppy bun, and my mascara is smudged under my eyes. I quickly wipe it off, and when I turn my head slightly, I see light scarring from one of my senior year field hockey injuries.

I pull the elastic from my hair and let it fall. Then I run my fingers through my waves and consider cutting it all off as I massage my scalp to release some of the tension.

"Okay, girl, let's grab our stuff from the Jeep. I bet you're hungry, huh?"

Arms loaded, as I walk into the house, I see a black convertible sports car coming down the drive.

I set the suitcase and toiletry case on the counter then glance out the window to see the driver of the car hitting the steering wheel. When Leia barks, I look to see her dancing around her empty water bowl.

After filling it and setting it down for her, I hear a knock on the door.

When I open it, I have to look up to see past the broad chest to catch the face of the man filling the doorway.

We stare at each other for a few moments. Even with his eyes covered in aviators, he's … striking. Chestnut brown, messy waves of hair shape his chiseled face and square jaw.

"May I help you?"

"Do you drive the navy Jeep?"

I nod.

"I live next door, and I believe you're in my parking spot."

"I'm so sorry. I didn't realize—"

He clears his throat, interrupting me, and says, "Yours is the third and fourth spot to the left. The corner four are mine." He then quickly turns and walks away, loosening his dark charcoal tie.

"All right, I'll move it now," I call after him.

Unsure he heard me, I wait, and when he shrugs off his sportscoat, my eyes land on his backside. *Dear God.*

Never seen a more perfect ass. Never.

I reach in and grab my keys off the counter, tell Leia to stay, and head out.

Walking toward the Jeep, I see the neighbor sitting in his car, fingers impatiently tapping his steering wheel with one hand as his other runs through his hair.

Sliding into the Jeep, I wonder what he's hiding behind the aviators, and why, when it's almost dark, is he still wearing them.

Not my business, I think as I throw it in reverse and feel almost ashamed that I am actually checking out a man other than Lucas. I know all too well that I don't need to fill a void. I need to get strong again. I also remind myself that it's fucking ridiculous that, after nearly five months, I feel like I'm betraying something. Not him—he did that, not me, not my virtue, that's long gone—and then it hits me.

I feel that, in looking at another man, finding someone else attractive, I feel like I'm betraying ... love.

Well, screw that, I think as I park, kill the engine, grab some bags, hurry to the house, and see him doing the same. *If I want to fantasize about the god-like creature in the black Jag, I can.*

Vacationers

Chapter Two

Collin

alking into my house after being away for months, I didn't expect more bright-eyed vacationers next door. As a matter of fact, the owners had been really good about giving me a heads-up when weekly tenants would arrive, due to the fact I would have to get in contact with them when some group of high schoolers, posing as adults via their half-assed online application process, didn't catch it and left the outdoor firepit blazing near the gas grill that they didn't turn off that caught fire.

I wasn't being neighborly when making that phone call. I was pissed that it might have caused a fire that would have spread to my home while I was away. Since then, I have, unbeknownst to them, taken on the task of doing background checks on the tenants while I was away so when I was able to take a break and come back here, I would have something to come back to.

I liked the woman I dealt with enough, but *this revolving door was for the birds*.

I throw my keys on the entry table as I walk into my massive kitchen, a far cry from the minuscule but apt ones of the places that I have recently visited.

Opening the refrigerator door, I look to see what Joan, my housekeeper, prepared for tonight, thinking at least someone gets some use out of this kitchen while I'm away on business or doing long stretches at the hospital when I am in town.

I don't need what I have, but I've worked hard for it. At twenty-seven, I've accomplished all the goals I set for myself. After graduating high school at seventeen, I completed my Bachelors in two and a half years then went on to medical school and served my country while in the Navy. Since then, articles have been written about how I revolutionized the health care industry by inventing a drug that helps people with cancer deal better with the side effects from chemotherapy.

When I was approached by "big pharm" to buy it from me, the amount they offered caused me to ask questions. When asked to sign a legal promise that I would not discuss the drug, I looked much deeper into the company and was sent down a rabbit hole of research. Bottom line: they wanted to bury my findings because it would have caused them to lose money on many other drugs. Therefore, I declined, and then there was an attempt to strong arm me.

Fear is not an emotion I cower to. I was able to launch it successfully. Then, after that, I realized that the issue with this, and all the other nations of this world, was rooted in fear, so that has become my focus—empowerment. I now work in security and health for third-world countries, and I do it by working with the people, not their corrupt governing bodies. So, yes, I have worked hard enough to deserve its rewards, but a life of little causes me to force relaxation and pleasure in my life.

I have had relationships, but none that lasted any longer than two months. I make it clear to anyone I have ever touched that I will always put my studies and life's work first, and I have never wavered.

Sex is a necessity in my life. I knew this from the first time I had it and, like all things in life, I worked at it until I mastered it. I can please a woman quickly, and I make it my mission to make sure they are satisfied before I am.

After I realized women were not all how I had experienced— growing up with a monster— they become easy to figure out. They are drawn to me first because of my looks. Second, because of who I am. Third, because of a challenge, *one I do not set forth.*

I watched my mother, a drug addict, bring men in and out of our home. It was always the same: she would come home drunk or high with a new guy at least once a month. Those who stayed were there in the morning and would get breakfast and treated as if they were a king. This would last about a week, a month at the most but, eventually, there would be an argument, one always involving alcohol or drugs, and he would leave. She would sit on the couch for days, speaking as few words as she could, chain smoking and crying. The ones who came and left before dawn, not staying for breakfast, didn't have the same effect on her. She could function, and it was usually a tolerable week. Those times, when she acted like a real mother and not the woman who stumbled over herself to please a house guest, didn't last long. There were few who were ever asked to return. As soon as she had received what she was after, be it drugs or money, they were gone. And those are my *good memories.*

So, I avoid women who need to drink to partake in sexual activity. When they show signs of attachment, like wanting to stay the night, I remind them that I need to study or work. One might think this would drive women away, but it doesn't. I was made keenly aware that, that often brought on a challenge for them, which is preposterous. I have learned how to vet my partners.

I particularly enjoy evenings with flight attendants, as they always have places to go, and there is always a return pending. I also enjoy women I meet at conferences. And once in a while, the tenants from next door who come and leave within a week.

Tonight, it is Amber, a flight attendant who I have been in contact with for about a year. We work well together, no expectations. She is highly sexually driven, and especially appealing to the eye, with dark hair and legs that go on forever. She has not once asked to stay and can withstand several hours of activity before leaving and letting me know when she may be back in town again.

I always enjoy a visit with Amber, but tonight feels strange, and I know why.

The tenant from next-door.

There is something about her. She smiled at me when I was short. She wasn't rude like the natives and normal tourists who I have encountered lately. When she looked up at me, with haunting ocean blue eyes and full lips, I was at a loss for words, which never happens, ever. She's … beautiful.

The microwave stops, and I grab the plate of chicken parmesan. Eating, I try to figure out what it was that happened. I had yet to take in her hot, curvy body, round, perky breasts and ass, muscular legs, and long, blonde waves. It wasn't that. It was her eyes.

After eating, I decided to shower and forge forward with the evening's plans. It has been three weeks since a release, and I wanted to ensure that I was ready.

After my shower and throwing on a shirt and a pair of slacks, the doorbell chimes and I make my way to the door.

Standing before me, I take Amber in. She's wearing a black coat that hangs just above her knees, heels, and black stockings. With zero hesitation, I take her hand and kiss it as I walk her in, turn her, pin her against the wall, and pull the belt strap as she shrugs off the coat, revealing a black corset and garter belt that hold up the stockings. I spread her legs with my knee, and she moans.

"Always ready," I state.

She turns, sinks down to her knees, unbuttons and unzips me as she licks her lips, and then she hungerly devours my cock as I slowly move back. She crawls across the floor, and as I open the door leading to the deck, I offer a hand to help her up. She declines, and so I move us slowly outside.

Knowing this could take some time, since I just got myself off in the shower, and also knowing Amber loves to give oral, I lean back and enjoy.

She stops and looks up, pulling my dick from her mouth to ask, "Everything all right tonight?"

I look down and realize I'm still not fully erect. I take the back of her head and guide her forward. "It'll get there."

Shades

Chapter Three

It has been forever since I've allowed myself to drink. I was concerned I would make—or receive—a call, make a bad decision, one that would circle like a storm of momentary and dizzying love … no ecstasy, only to spit me out again. The fact that I didn't even consider it was cause to open a bottle and celebrate. And that celebration ended in the most exciting way possible— me falling asleep outside in an Adirondack chair, with my girl next to me.

I wipe away the sleep from my eyes and stare at the lighthouse. I watch as the light moves across the water, a beacon to keep those who may get lost …

Holy shit, and also, wow.

In the moonlight, I see the back of the neighbor's head as he looks up at the sky. His skin bare, sculpted like a model from a Gap ad, all long and lean and …

Shit again.

I nearly fall out of my chair when I see a woman pop up from behind the brick wall, startling Leia, who barks.

I drop to the ground and cover her doggy mouth. "Shh … girl. It's okay. Let's go inside. It's all right."

Trying to scamper into the house, I trip over the bottle of wine, and it rolls—loudly, I might add—across the patio as I drag a growling Leia toward the house. This causes the motion sensor to kick on the lights on the entire patio.

No freaking way, I think as I hurry toward the door.

When I glance up, the woman is running inside, laughing, and then I hear … that voice, say, "Goodnight."

I do not respond as I slide inside, shut the door behind me, and lock the damn door.

Goodnight? The audacity of that man! Seriously, on the deck with his neighbor thirty feet away!

A minute later, I hear a car start and pull out of the parking lot.

I grab a glass of water and chug it, chasing it down with two more. Then I head upstairs and fall into bed, laughing.

―――――

I wake, still dressed and feeling like shit, but when I see the sun rising, I roll to my side, pat the bed, and Leia jumps up, both of us watching it for a moment.

"Think we should spend our first morning here or get out there and run with the rising sun?"

She hops off the bed at the word *run*.

We'll be doing a whole lot of that.

Smiling, I force myself up, hurry to the bathroom, pee while rummaging through my bag to pull out a tee-shirt. It's one of *his*, an orange 'Cuse tee.

Tossing it aside, I make the decision to donate all the remnants of him.

———

D ressed in running shorts and a sports bra to tame the girls, I throw on a sweatshirt then look in the mirror as I brush my teeth. I then pull up my hair, wrapping it in a bun.

Since all hell broke loose, I've lost twenty pounds, but the girls, they've stayed put. *Thanks, Grandma Ross.* That may not have changed, but something has. I am no longer insecure about my body. And, right now, I will admit I look better now than I did in high school. Well, a tan would be nice, but a few good days in the sun should accomplish that.

Downstairs, I throw on my running shoes while Leia does her little tap dance by the door, excited to head out as I lace up. Then we head out the door.

Not a hundred yards from the house, I see … him … coming up from behind us and think, *What a way to start day one.* I pick up the pace, all just to avoid an awkward moment.

I see this going well—hope, anyway—until Leia begins barking her damn head off as she turns around and tugs on the extendable leash that I bought for when we run.

She tugs, I turn to tug back, and she jets left, tripping me. I end up ass in the sand.

"Good morning," the neighbor says with more than obvious amusement as he extends his hand, offering help.

"Yeah, you, too," I mumble as I stand, refusing his hand.

As I untangle my leg, Leia yanks the leash, and I start to fall again. Luckily, I right myself and quickly lunge to grab the leash, tripping over a huge piece of driftwood. Pain shoots through my ankle, but it only registers for a second, because within that second, warmth washes over my body in waves as arms wrap around me and lift me up before I faceplant into the sand.

Shocked at the feeling, I look over my shoulder, and he smiles down at me. That smile also sends waves of warmth, comfort, and … something else altogether through me as he asks in a compellingly voice, "You okay?"

Heat covers my face as he sets my feet on the ground, and I nod. "Yes, thanks."

Quickly realizing Leia isn't barking, growling, showing teeth, or at my heel, I look around and see her pretty far out in the Atlantic.

Sheer panic strikes when I see her swimming, which is a first—she normally splashes—farther and farther from shore. I jolt forward, and the pain in my ankle sears through me. However, I manage to not fall.

Then he moves past me, runs to the water's edge, kicks off his sneakers, tosses off his sweatshirt, and drops his shades.

I yell a warning as I get up. "Be careful—she may not react the way you expect!"

He's fast … so fast that he gets to her almost before I blink. I watch him grab her around the middle, and she doesn't freak out—unlike me—as they swim to the shallow water.

When they get to the shore, she shakes off as he takes off his shirt and grabs his sunglasses and sneakers. Then, when she begins barking and jumping around his feet, he bends down and pets her. A smile, as bright as the sun, etches across his beautiful features as he picks up the leash and tells her to heel before they walk back toward me.

Still somewhat in shock at Leia not freaking out on him, and in a bit of awe at … him, I shake my head as they approach. When I take a step and wince, he reaches out his hand to take mine. Then he bends and wraps my arm around his shoulders.

"Ever used crutches?"

I hold back a bark of a laugh and simply nod instead.

"Right now, there aren't any available, so you'll use me."

After a few steps, he sighs in semi annoyance. "I know you don't want my help, but you're going to have to take it." Then he wraps an arm around my waist, lifts me, reaches beneath me with the hand that holds Leia's leash, and carries me.

That feeling, that warmth, it's all-consuming, and my body tenses immediately.

Embarrassed by that, I close my eyes tightly, hating that I feel so comfortable in his hold.

When we get to the house, he lowers my legs but doesn't let my feet touch the ground. Then he opens the gate latch, walks all of us in, and closes it behind him.

"I think I can manage—"

"Then, how about not thinking and letting me deal with the situation?"

My ass hits the chaise lounge.

"This is gonna hurt, but has to happen."

"Wha—ouch!"

He pulls my sneaker off then my sock. And even though it hurts, I'm painfully aware that my toenails aren't polished.

He stands and quickly moves toward the doors that

leads into the house. The door that is locked. "I'm going to get you some ice. What's the code?"

Without hesitation, I rattle it off.

He walks in, and Leia follows him. If she trusts him, I know I can.

When he walks back out with ice wrapped in a dish towel, I hear my phone ringing from inside. He steps in, retrieves it, returns, and hands it to me.

As I open my mouth to say hello, he applies the ice to my ankle, and I wince.

"Damn that hurts," escapes my mouth before I even say hello.

"What's going on, Tessa? Everything okay?" my sister, Kendall, asks.

I miss her by a day. Guilt, pain, and the inability to keep up anymore overwhelms me enough to make my eyes burn, but I manage to choke out an, "Uh-huh," before the phone is taken from me.

"Hello. This is Collin. I live next door. Who am I speaking with?" He listens and nods. "Kendall, yes, that's me, your tenant—" Collin pauses and listens then turns to me and quickly away. "*Your sister* was going for a run and, long story short, she ended up on her bottom and twisted her ankle pretty—" He pauses again. "No, I'm sure it's not broken; probably sprained. I have some pain meds. Might make her tired, but should help—" Again, he pauses then says, "No problem. Here she is."

He hands me the phone and mouths, "*I'll be right back,*" pointing toward his house then leaving me alone to talk with Kendall.

I catch Leia following him. "Leia is follow—"

"She'll be fine." He reaches down and takes her leash.

"You okay?" Kendall asks, drawing my attention back

to where it should be and not watching the neigh—Collin … walk away with my dog.

"Hey, sorry."

"You okay, Tessa?"

"I'm okay. I'm just sorry that I mixed up the dates."

"You did not. I came home early to spend time with you."

That makes me even more emotional. "Seriously?"

"That's cool, right? Like you have to say yes since I am packing now then heading your way."

"No way?" I smile, even though she can't see me.

"I am in desperate need of a mani-pedi; you down for that?"

"Most definitely."

"Then everyone else will be coming up, too. I'm just trying to hurry so I can beat them. So, we'll chat soon, right?"

"Okay, see you in a few hours. Drive careful. I love you."

I thought I would be alone a few days to get settled, that they were coming up next week, but this is even better, actually.

As I move to set the phone down, I apply a bit too much pressure and wince.

"Easy," I hear that voice—*that voice*—and look up to see … Collin holding out two pills. "These will dull the pain."

I take them from him, and then he pulls a bottle from his pocket.

"These will relax the muscles and help with the swelling."

I take the bottle, too, and thank him.

"You going to take them?" he asks, crossing his arms.

I nod. "I will once I get inside and get squared away." I shrug. "Not real good with pain meds."

I expect him to leave, but he simply looks down at me.

"So, thank you for your help. I really appreciate it. My sister will be here in a few hours, and the rest of my family will all be here, as well. I'll warn you in advance; it won't be as quiet over here as last—" I stop and throw the pills in my mouth, just to stop the embarrassment I keep bringing on myself. Drinking down the pills, I clear my throat. "Feel free to come over and have dinner with us. You can bring your girlfriend, if you'd like."

His lips twitch up slightly, and then he takes a few steps to a chair and sits down, probably staying for the comedic value of entertainment I am giving, and Leia sits beside him.

"Thanks for the invite. I'll check my schedule."

I sit quietly, trying to figure out what to say next. Not one thing comes to mind.

"Sit back, take those other pills, and try to relax. Your ankle is swelling. I'll stay to make sure you're okay, help you inside, if need be, and check on you a couple times while you wait for your family." Leia rests her head on his lap, and he pets it. "Yes, and you, too."

Unable to read him, I seriously want him to take off his sunglasses so I can see his eyes, see if it's kindness or something else completely. But I also don't want to know if it's something else completely. He might even be better-looking, definitely more … refined than Lucas, not that, that matters, I suppose. Seriously, it doesn't, because I am so far from ready for a rebound that it's comical. Also, I know perfectly well rebounds are a farce, and I most definitely am *not* ready to start dating again. I don't even know how to go about that. Nor am I the one-night stand type—that I know of. Bottom line, he has a girlfriend, and I am falling in love … with me.

Unfortunately, I still want to see his eyes, and Collin

apparently wears sunglasses all the freaking time. Well, except when his girlfriend is around.

I decide to break the middle school stare off and look at the ocean.

After several painstakingly and uncomfortably long minutes, the drugs set in, and I wage war … and lose on keeping my mouth shut.

I turn back and look at him. "Would you like a drink? You could grab a beer out of the fridge."

"No, I'm good." He sits back and drinks the water that he brought over.

"I don't want to keep you from anything. I'm feeling better, thank you." Pain leaving, head … heavy.

"I think I'll hang out to see how those pills affect you. Wouldn't want to leave you here alone. You might try to get up and end up falling on your ass again." He smirks.

Damn, even his teeth are perfect.

Face hot, head heavy, eyes harder to keep open and focused, and mouth untrustworthy, I sit up to fight all those effects and do so ineffectively.

"How are you feeling?" Collin asks with true concern in his voice.

"Like crap," I blurt out.

Oh, I can't believe I just said that …

Shut up, shut up, shut up.

"I haven't drank in a while, and I feel like I've been doing shots. My ankle is throbbing, but I really don't care, and these clothes are bugging me. How are you feeling?"

Collin laughs softly as he stands. "I'm good. Sun's getting hot. I'm going to run home and grab a hat. Stay put."

I lay back in the chaise and watch as *that dog* follows him over again. I then close my eyes.

I wake when my foot is being lifted and something cool

is being lifted from my ankle. Then I nearly jump off the chaise when I see a white baseball hat, but my body doesn't allow that quick of a movement since I'm seriously messed up.

When he looks up, I see a Red Sox emblem on it. He looks younger, and yes … more appealing with that stupid hat on. Would look better if it wasn't the Sox, but whatever. Even gorgeous god-like creatures have flaws.

He holds up a bag of ice. "Just changing this out. Still pretty swollen." Then he sets it on my ankle, moves to grab something, and that something is a plate with fruits and cheeses on it. "You should eat something."

"You didn't have to go through all that troub—"

"I didn't. Just eat." He sets the plate down then moves back to his chair.

I grab some grapes and pop them into my mouth, watching him as he watches me.

Distance, I need distance from his intensity.

"I need to go inside for a minute," I say, pushing the ice off and standing—well, wobbling—which causes him to mutter under his breath as he stands.

I go slow, not that I have a choice to go any other way, and move from furniture piece to furniture piece, and then finally to the door, highly aware he's following me.

When I open the door, I nearly trip but catch myself. Go me. Then I manage to make my way to the bathroom.

When I look in the mirror, I am horrified at the sight of me—sleep in my eyes, makeup smudged, and the sloppiest of sloppy buns atop … well, sort of atop my head.

"Feeling good!" I yell. "All set, thank you."

I start a shower then think better of it, so I switch to a bath instead.

Perfect

Chapter Four

Collin

$\mathcal{I}$s she really doing this? Taking a bath when she's under the influence? This is partially my fault due to the fact that I gave her the maximum dose of muscle relaxers, not wanting to see her in pain, which she should be able to handle, but as she said she's, "*Not real good with pain meds.*"

I should be running back to my place and not looking back. I know damn well I could call Joan in to take care of this situation, yet here I stand, even though she fucked up my evening last night in a mind-boggling way.

The woman is frustratingly beautiful and naturally so. Her hair, those eyes, she's small, but has curves for days. All of that almost overshadows something else I've yet to uncover. I would guess an insecurity. She comes off as confident, but it's fragile.

I don't like that for her, and it is none of my business, *none at all*.

This morning, when I saw her heading out for a run, I decided I was going to get to know her a bit, see if she was a no-strings kind of woman, if she was down to play during her vacation. I'm safely assuming she's not.

When I hear her begin to splash around, I lean in to listen to make sure she hasn't fallen and, a few seconds later, the door flies open. Hair in a towel, another held close to her body, she expels minty fresh breath.

Making damn sure my eyes stay on hers—that are glassy—I ask, "You all right?"

"Oh, damn," she sighs, and then her full, pink lips tip up in the corner as she says, "Yep, just great." She tips her head back and the towel falls, the smell of lilac wafting from her long, thick waves as she shakes it out while running her fingers through it.

"Um … Collin?"

I nod, confirming that's my name still.

"Can I ask you for a favor?" She adjusts the towel so its wrapped tightly around her body. "Could you not look when I come out, please?"

I nod once. "Fine."

She then starts to hop on one foot, and yes, I can see it, even though I have done as she asked by looking away, and I did until this display. Then she begins to crawl up the stairs, on all fours.

For some reason, this annoys me a great deal, and I stalk toward her. "You need to just lie down and quit messing around."

When she looks over her shoulder and sees me coming toward her, she begins to laugh. It's airy, so carefree, so wholesome, and then she asks, "Really? I'm just trying to get some clothes on, buddy. If I'm annoying, maybe you should march your perfect ass home. Your girlfriend may not like you being over here, helping the clumsy chick in a towel from next door. I certainly wouldn't."

And beyond f*rustrating!* I think as I grab her up, turn her, toss her over my shoulder, and march my *perfect ass* up the stairs.

"Your stuff in the master bedroom?"

She laughs harder now. "Why yes, it actually is. It's this—"

"I know where it is," I interrupt that sound, that sound that makes me feel … something.

I drop her on the bed then look around for her clothing. I see a small, brown, beat-up bag and mentally note she will be gone soon. Unsure of what to do with that, I dig through the bag, toss a shirt, some more shirts, and search for a bra and panties. Finding them, I deduce that they aren't of the cheap variety, and that says something that I, as a self-appointed guardian of the inebriated—also the cause of it—should not be thinking about and head back to her where she sits, towel clenched like a woman in a church pew with fingers around her pearls and become almost irrationally frustrated at the contradiction that is Tessa.

I throw her shirt over her head, and she quickly puts her arms through the holes. Then I squat down with black, lace boy shorts in hand, and she starts to pull her feet up. Knowing damn well that will cause a peep show, I demand, "Don't." I ease her feet in the holes, and then do the same with the boxer-style shorts, pulling them both up to her knees. Then I stand. "I think you can get it from here." And I turn.

Voice mixed with annoyance and embarrassment, she snips, "Maybe I don't want to wear this!"

As soon as the words escaped her mouth, I turn and look down at her as she puts her hands over her mouth.

"You're being irrational, and I think you know this. Put them on … or I will."

She looks blankly at me and, being a man of my word, I pull her up and do just that.

After setting her back down, she quickly and defiantly stands, the towel drops, and she takes a step then begins to fall.

I scoop her up. "Never met a person whose sprain needed to be in a cast, but now I have." I deposit her back on the bed. "You're staying here, and you're going to rest. You're going to heal, so help me God, or I'll bend you over my knee and—" I stop when I notice her eyes get huge. "You're a pain in the ass." I pull back the covers and tell her, "Lie back." I half-ass tuck her in, and she gives me a glossy glare.

"Perfect ass, huh?" I shake my head.

"Yep, I'm sure you knew that already. I'm also sure I'm about to fall asleep. Could you do me one last favor?" she slurs, eyes softening, and I nod. "Take off those glasses. I haven't been able to see your eyes. You can tell a lot about a person from their eyes."

I oblige, and she smiles in a sad kind of way.

Then, as her eyes close, she mutters, "You're stunning."

I prop her foot up on a pillow and sit beside her, watching her chest rise and fall—strictly for medical reasons—and doing it unknowingly planting my *perfect ass* next to her.

I get comfortable while she settles in. When she rolls to her side, I lean down and try to fix her foot without disturbing her.

She whispers, "It's going to be all right now." Then she wraps her arm around my waist, and the heat hits hard, like a brand, and I freeze. The initial shock at this fades quickly, and the warmth spreads in a way that is calming and comforting and … confusing.

Feels good.

I shouldn't take this, allow this, but I do. I then use my foot to adjust hers slightly and sit back so that I can steal this moment then make my escape once she's out completely.

I adjust to the comfort, lean back propped on a pillow, breathing in lilac without trying, and she inches closer.

This is wrong, *but it's not.*

She moves in closer, and I close my eyes.

When my phone vibrates in my pocket, my eyes pop open, and I find myself lying on my side, arms tightly around her and even tighter, because she has her hands on mine, holding them against her body just as tightly.

Then the dog barks, and her body tenses, and I hear, "Who's a good girl? Who's a good girl? Miss Leia is! Did you miss Auntie Kendall? You gotta go potty?"

The door opens then shuts below us, and she turns and looks at me. Our eyes meet, and I simply ask, "Are you feeling any better?"

"My ankle still hurts, and my head is very foggy. How did we end up in here?" She releases my arms, and I move away from her and slide off the bed.

"You decided to take a bath and tried to make it up the stairs. I carried you because you were"—I stop from saying *a pain in the ass*—"not being a good patient. We got you dressed, and I helped you into bed. You passed out and grabbed my arm." Something about her face being shocked and the awareness causes me to go on. "You also talked about my perfect ass. I guess we both fell asleep until your dog barked."

She looks at me as she sits up, waiting for more. There is no more to give.

"That's it."

She nods and stands, and I grab her by the waist when she buckles.

"I'm good." She sets her hands over mine, and that searing heat hits hard again. She looks up, eyes big and questioning.

Unsure if she feels that same pain or she's still wondering how we ended up the way we did, I give her what I can. "If something happened between us, you'd remember; trust me," I say as that heat spreads to warmth … again.

She frowns a bit and nods. "Well, Collin, I thank you for helping me out. I'm sure it'll all come back to me. Sorry to waste your day."

I step back. "Let me help you get down the stairs."

"I can—"

"So can I," I cut her off.

When we get to the bottom, Kendall walks in with Leia. I remember Kendall from last summer. Her and some college friends came up.

Smirking, Kendall asks, "How're you feeling?"

Tessa gives her a stern look and snips, "Fine."

I look to her and say, "I'm sure it's not broken, or she would be in a lot more pain. I gave her pain meds that … well, made her a bit loopy, tired, and a real pain in the *ass*."

Kendall laughs. "That's not the pain meds … She's always been a pain in the ass."

Tessa scowls at me then her sister.

Kendall continues, "The family will be here in an hour or so. I stopped and grabbed some lobsters. If you don't have plans, you should come back and hang out tonight. That's the least we could do. You did take care of our little Tessa."

Younger sister.

"He may have plans."

"Thank you for the invite, but—"

"You've never experienced the whole family," Kendall cuts me off. "At the very least, it will be entertaining."

Tessa sighs. "Geesh, Kendall, give him some room for escape."

I look at Tessa. "That bottle of pills? Don't take more than one. You can take Motrin again now. I'm going to leave and see what my schedule entails."

I pull my phone out of my pocket and realize the battery is dead. I throw it on the charger then head to the bathroom. When I return, I see that I have three missed calls and several messages.

I thumb through them and see Amber's number. I send her a message.

- Something's come up, and I'm not going to be able to see you tonight.

Amber replies quickly, too damn quickly.

- Ok, I won't be back around for a month. Hopefully that we can "get together" again then. I hope you're feeling better. After being sent away last night before things even got started, I wonder if it was me or you were really ill.

I let the worry she's getting attached go and toss the phone aside.

That's it, uncomplicated and easy … just how I like it.

Then I boot up my computer, check my email, and see my itinerary for next month's trip.

I'll be gone for five weeks in Ecuador, training and helping at one of the small villages and hospitals I helped build and fund. I always love going away to new sites, seeing the progress, and occasionally running into old "friends." For now, a month at home hanging out sounds good, really good. I can finish up my next paper, and it will be published before I return from my next trip to Ecuador.

I sit back, run my hands through my hair, and rub my nose. I can still smell her scent on my hand. She's going to be a distraction in a big way. Then I get up and throw my shoes on, heading back out to finish the run that started all this to begin with.

Leia is barking at the gate, jumping around, when I walk out. When I get to the bottom of my stairs, I lean over the fence and pat her head. Then I see the girls.

"She loves you," Kendall calls out. "I think she wants to go with you."

"Sounds good, if it's all right with her." I nod to Tessa.

I see her face flush as she looks down and waves her hand dismissively. "Sure, her leash is on the fence post."

I grab the leash, open the gate, and Leia bounds out. I hook her up. "Be back."

Distraction

Chapter Five

Tessa

"You certainly are short with him when I was on the phone. What's up with that?" Kendall asks as soon as he's out of earshot.

"He's arrogant," I respond, hating the flush I feel on my face.

Kendall smiles. "He's next level hot. Might be the distraction you need right now."

"Kendall, really, I don't think so. Besides, I'm *more* than sure he has a girlfriend." I laugh to myself.

"No, Tessa, Collin doesn't *do* relationships," she states. "I've been here a handful of times and have only seen a couple women leave there. I asked about his girlfriend once, and he told me he didn't have time for those. Just occasional friends."

My jaw drops. "Are you one of them?"

"Seriously, Tessa? Did you just ask me that? Mom would have my ass, and yours, for even saying that."

"And you're trying to hook me up when you know it's wrong? Mom would have your ass for that, too." I laugh.

"Well, I just figured one of us should check it out and report back. You know, live vicariously through each other. And you're already tainted." She grins.

Kendall ducks, avoiding getting nailed by the pillow I just threw at her head.

"I don't think that's a good idea. I could kick your butt and run, and no matter how fast you hopped, you couldn't catch me."

We laugh.

"I'm going to unload the car. Will you be okay without me for a minute?" Kendall jokes as she gets up.

Leave it to me to get hurt while on vacation.

Leave it to my body to react like it's never been touched when he so much as put his hands on me … just to help.

Leave it to my heart—diseased as it is—to beat faster when he touches me.

Leave it to my mind to trick itself into believing he's something other than a man who wants a piece of vacation ass.

Leave it to my … soul to practically sing when I woke and he was still there.

Sick, needy, twisted … maybe it was me all along.

I hobble into the house to turn on the radio and open a window, and as I hobble back out, I grab a throw blanket from the back of couch to curl up in, because God help me, since getting out of that bed with him—with Collin—I haven't been able to get warm.

Kendall walks out and plops down at the end of the

chaise lounge. "You should be listening to playlists." She throws her thumb back to the house. "This is not good."

"Wasn't even paying attention," I admit.

"Oh, please." She cracks open the bottle of Motrin and hands me two, and then she pulls a bottle of water from her hoodie pocket and hands it to me. "You are the one who got me started on the whole music is—"

"We were young and naïve then." I smile sadly, hating that I made her believe in that nonsense even more than I did, apparently.

"Next song sets the mood for"—she pauses and shakes her head, smiling back just the same—"whatever I decide it does."

We wait like kids on Christmas morning, naïve as all get out for the song to change from "To the Moon & Back" by Savage Garden, and when it does, she closes her eyes.

"Don't you feel sorry for him, Tessa," Kendall states as "Landslide" by Fleetwood Mac begins. "He did this to himself, to you. But you need to let yourself feel the music, this song, summon your inner Stevie, okay?"

"She's been summoned," I assure her.

"Promise?" she asks

I nod, and she hugs me.

I wasn't going to do it, take another pill, but I really need one for the pain, and not just the escape, although that is side effect I'll gladly endure.

I run my hand down her hair, always so soft. I miss her, and although I love she's comforting me, I hate that she feels she needs to do that for me.

"You mind handing me those muscle relaxers?"

She lets go. "Just one?"

I laugh instead of cry. "Yes."

After I pop the pill, she sits beside me, and I move over

as I lift the blanket. "You must be exhausted from travel. Tell me about your trip?"

"It was amazing," she begins.

I hear Kendall talking and open my eyes, realizing everyone must be here. I make my way in and am greeted with a big hug, distanced by Phoebe's belly.

"This place is amazing!" She smiles.

As I show her around, Jake and his "not girlfriend," Sarah, arrive. Next is Molly, Cory, and Sydney, who runs and jumps on my lap as I listen to her tell me all about her trip here. I notice Kendall waving in the distance, and I know who it is she's waving over.

When he walks through the gate, Leia darts to him, and he squats down and gives her smitten behind attention.

"Damn," Alex says, sitting across from me. "Look at her."

I nod as Leia bounds on to the end of the chaise as if to lead the neighbor to me.

This feels awkward, but I'm sure it feels much more so to him.

I shield my eyes as I look up. "Thanks for taking her for a run."

He nods. "Should be good for the day."

All of a sudden, the volume on the radio shoots up, and my brother, Jake, comes running out, playing the air guitar. "Remember this concert, Tessa? You took me out of school my junior year to my first concert. Wonder if Mom and Dad know what a bad influence you were."

Then I hear Mom's voice from inside, "They do now."

I kiss Sydney's head. "You should go say high to Grandma Maggie and Grandpa John."

Then Jake steps forward, a warm, easy smile on his seriously handsome face, and holds his hand out to Collin. "Hey, man, I'm Jake."

"The baby of the family," Phoebe explains as she walks out and extends her hand. "I'm the sister-in-law and best friend to the injured."

He smiles and shakes her hand. "Collin. Nice to meet you both."

"Beer?" Jake asks.

"Sure." Collin nods.

I glance at Phoebe, and she arches an eyebrow. I do mine in turn, and she grins.

Kendall calls Collin over, and they disappear beyond the fence.

Thank God.

Mom and Dad walk out; Mom holding Sydney, and Dad lugging a huge cooler with Alex at the other end.

"Mags, where's this thing going?" Dad asks Mom as she leans down and kisses the top of my head.

Then she stands and turns. "Keep it close to the house. Salads and beverages are in there."

"A body or two, as well?" Alex jokes.

Mom looks back at him. "Not yet."

We all laugh.

"Sunset beach volleyball game?" Jake asks in a challenge.

They all bite, and I ... I pout.

I catch Kendall and Collin walking over, arms full of wood for a fire.

Dad starts the grill, while Jake, Sarah, and Kendall set up the volleyball net, and Alex and Collin start the fire.

Molly sits next to me with Sydney. "You're pouting."

"I'm worthless and jealous that I am missing out on volleyball."

"Well, then stop pouting and let's *wine*." She holds up a bottle.

"Let's."

It isn't lost on me that Collin, now free of sunglasses, looks over at me several times next the past hour, and it's also not lost on me that the way he looks at me makes it apparent he thinks he's going to be getting himself some. Unluckily for him, I'm buzzed yet aware, mainly because Sydney told me I was coloring outside the lines, and she wasn't wrong, so I switched to water.

I try my best not to love the ease he seems to have with my family. Hell, even Alex seems to like him, since he picked him for his team … and Collin, the neighbor with the kick-ass house who lives high above those surrounding his, doesn't seem so high and mighty at all.

I wonder if Ann's Joe sold because of what happened, or if he was one of those house flippers. I should ask Collin if he knows how to contact him. I would like to thank him for that day, as well as being kind to a quirky old woman with a huge heart.

As dinner is grilling, Alex, Phoebe, and Collin take to one side of the net; Jake, Kendall, and Cory take the other. Well, Phoebe doesn't really play; she just avoids the ball. Collin, well … he seriously can't get any hotter. Tan khaki shorts slung low on his hips and hitting his knees, white tee-shirt, white … backward ball cap.

"Pretty nice view … huh, Tessa?" Molly smiles.

"Great view," I respond before I even realize it.

Molly laughs, and I elbow her lightly.

Mom and Sarah set the large, wooden table, and then they bring the salads out of the house while Sydney and I color. Okay, Sydney colors while I watch "the game" that ends with basically Alex and Collin high-fiving like Goose and Maverick in *Top Gun*. Collin being Maverick, of course.

"Tessa." Molly laughs. "Did you hear me?"

Nope, I think as I look at her. "Sure, I'll take another," I answer, and she looks at me oddly. "Glass of wine. Isn't that what you asked?"

I knew she didn't, and so does she, but she gets up. "I'll get you one."

Returning with a glass of red, she sits. "Hey, Sydney, go help Grandma with the napkins?" As soon as Sydney leaves, she says, "Okay, real talk. How are you doing, Tessa? We were a bit shocked when we found you already left. Mom was really worried about you. So was I."

"I'm good. This is a great diversion—being away from everything—and now that you're all here, it's perfect."

Mom announces dinner, and Molly smiles. "We'll chat later." Then she stands.

Everyone heads in to wash up, and I wait my turn as I watch Collin walk toward the gate. He isn't gone long, but when he returns, he's no longer wearing a white shirt or hat. He's in a black, long-sleeved tee.

His eyes hit mine, and they soften. I should not like it, but I do, so I avoid it by getting up and slowly making my way inside.

After using the bathroom and washing my hands, I lean in and look in the mirror at my reflection. I got some color today, I think as I grab my toothbrush, brush my teeth, and then apply moisturizer in hopes to keep that color longer and not peel.

When I return outside, the table is full. The only empty spot left is between Sydney and Collin.

It's all right, I got this, I think as I slowly make my way to said spot.

Sydney smiles as she sees me coming, taps the chair beside her, and says really loudly, "Great view, Auntie Tessa."

Molly and I lock eyes and, thankfully, we don't bust up laughing. I manage to kiss the top of Sydney's head and say, "Sure is."

Collin stands and pulls out my chair before I have the chance to, and my face heats up as I say, "Thank you."

Molly gets up and hurries to the house, no doubt to laugh, and quickly returns with another bottle of wine. She quickly pours me a glass.

"Thank you."

Dinner is great. Everyone seems to enjoy themselves. Dad talks a lot about his new venture—organic farming—and mentions more than once that it's a busy time of the year. After several comments like that, I notice Mom kick him under the table. I can't help but giggle, knowing how uneasy he is about not being at the farm for even a minute at this time of year.

I notice that Collin's eyes are on me, in question. I simply look away and take a small sip of my wine. So much for taking it easy.

When dinner is about finished, Sydney yawns.

Molly looks over at her all nuzzled into my side. "Looks like someone is ready for bed. Say goodnight to everyone."

Sydney slides down and walks around the table, giving everyone hugs and telling them goodnight. When she reaches Collin and looks up at him, I take my last sip of wine.

"Night-night, Great View."

I begin to choke on that sip and stand to leave the table before I spit it all over everyone. I throw my hands in the air like we taught Sydney to do when something goes down the wrong way and finally stop sputtering.

"Good job, Auntie Tessa. You put your arms up like a big girl." She throws her arms around my legs to congratulate me on my big girl accomplishment.

"Molly, can I go in and turn a movie on for her?" I ask, not wanting to turn around and face him.

Molly nods, and I take Sydney's hand and limp toward the house.

And that's when I hear Dad.

"Well … that was uncomfortable." He laughs. "But I agree with Sydney, you are one handsome son of a gun."

I want to die.

Sydney is asleep in minutes, and I decide to stop hiding and head back out.

Alex is grabbing everyone a drink and jokingly puts one in front of our parents. He knows their two drink rule. Well, Mom's rule. Dad takes it and winks at her as she looks at him disapprovingly.

"That's for kicking me when I was explaining organic farming to Collin here." He kisses her cheek, and then slams—yes, Dad slams—his beer and stands.

He pulls out Mom's chair, grabs her hand, and pulls her up. "Make sure that fire's out. See you all in the morning." And that quickly, they're inside.

I sit next to Molly, leaving the space between Collin and me open. Molly fills my glass.

"Damn, Tessa, what's it like to drink again and not be the DD for the guys? You sure you can handle another glass? You're looking a little tipsy," Jake jokes.

"It's all right. Not necessary, but all right." I lift it up. "Can you go turn on some tunes, please?"

"What shall it be?" he asks.

"I don't care … just not sappy music."

"I have a mix tape." Kendall hops up and hurries in before Jake has a chance.

"Sounds great," I reply.

After attempting to help clean up, Collin insists he does it. Not to be outdone, Jake and Alex help out, while we females head to the patio area. Once done, they join us.

When the song "You Oughta Know" by Alanis Morrissette comes on, my brothers sit, looking at each other, and began making up their own words.

"*I want you to know that I'm sickened by you. I wish nothing but the worst for you,*" Jake sings.

"*An older version of me,*" Alex takes over. "*Is she big-chested like me?*"

"*Would she go down on you in a theater,*" Jake sings as he winks at Sarah.

Feeling buzzed and amused because this is the first time I've seen Alex drink more than one drink, and he's acting like … a Ross who's drank more than one drink, I join in, "*Does she speak red-neck and would she smoke your doobies?*"

Kendall takes over, "*I'm sure she makes a really excellent bar whore.*"

Collin blends right in, not singing but enjoying himself, looking relaxed even.

After a bit, Molly comes out with a Polaroid and asks, "Hey, can we get a group picture before any of you pass out?"

Collin offers to take it, and he snaps about ten photos. Then Phoebe grabs the camera and tells him to get in the shot.

It's like the parting of the red seas—all of my siblings move so that Collin has to sit pretty close. Phoebe immediately begins shooting. At one point, he moves my ankle so that he doesn't sit on it and asks me to move back until I am practically on his lap. So close that his back touches my chest. I throw up bunny ears behind his head as I leaned over his shoulder to make a silly face, and he turns toward me. We are nose to nose for what seems like forever.

"All right, Alex, time for bed, big boy," Phoebe says, breaking the ... whatever that was, and takes Alex's hand.

In seconds, Molly and Cory, Jake and Sarah, and Kendall follow suit, leaving us sitting there alone, uncomfortably close to one another.

"This is awkward," I whisper then word vomit. "It's nice, but awkward."

Damn those words flow too easily when I drink!

He just sits there, watching me as I basically squirm, and he's enjoying it immensely.

"You have a great family, Tessa. You all seem to enjoy each other's company a great deal." It's more a question than an observation.

"Yeah, they're pretty great ... most of the time," I joke.

Silently, we stare at each other, and the heat in my body temperature rises so quickly that I swear my clothes are melting off.

His smile says he knows it, too.

"You know, this has been the most fun I have had in years. My family is, um"—he pauses—"small and scattered around the world."

Again, in typical true me form, I open my mouth and out flies, "I think you looked like you were having a pretty good time last night."

He laughs, and it's deep and ... sexy. "That's one way to make the path to get rid of whatever obstacles are in our way."

"Sorry, I don't often drink, and this is part of the reason. I open my mouth and stuff just comes out. No control."

"You're two for two."

This confuses me, and yes, he sees that, too.

"Two nights you've drank. But I can obviously tell it's not your usual."

"Where is your girlfriend?" falls out, and I look away, scolding myself inside.

"We kind of went through this earlier. I don't have a girlfriend. By the shape you seem to be in now, I'll probably have to answer that question again at another time. So, listen up, okay?" He grabs my head between his hands and makes me look at him. "I don't have a girlfriend. Relationships are messy, and I don't have time for that. What I do enjoy is the occasional … no-strings kind of relationship. When I'm not working, I like sex for hours, days even. I like to give and receive over, and over, and over again. When I've had my fill and so has my partner, I can concentrate on work. I love to hang out with my friends, but only have time for a handful. And right now, I wish that I could throw you over my shoulder, take you over to my place, and have you over, and over, and over again."

My jaw drops as I stare at him, hoping he can't see that my body is literally pulsing … everywhere. But I'm pissed, too. If I weren't so turned on, I would slap him across the face right now.

I close my eyes in order to regroup then open them and slowly remove his hands from my head, but then I lean forward and push up on my knees, inching my way closer to him. I take handfuls of his hair, gently guide his head to the side, and whisper in his ear, "You couldn't handle it. I've been with the same man for nearly five years. I gave him everything over, and over again, wherever and whenever he wanted it." I allow my voice to get deeper. "I kept it hot."

His eyes penetrate mine, but I don't let them pin me.

"I just called off our wedding because he didn't know how to treat me. Sex … hot, dirty, loud, earth-shaking sex is just that. I wanted more, and he wanted everything but to return the respect I gave. I can be a whore in the bedroom, beyond what you can probably even bring yourself to ask your friends with no strings. As I sit here and see your excitement grow"—I look down at the bulge I purposely caused by saying all the things I knew he wanted to hear then watch his sky blue eyes darken and bite my lip for effect—"I can promise you this ... I'm not a no-strings kind of girl. I never will be. As hot as you are, and as lonely as I am, I'm telling you over, and over, and over again—no."

With that, I release his seriously silky, thick, amazing waves and shove him back as I stand, smiling to myself for setting freaking boundaries.

He stands in front of me, grabs me around the waist, and basically shits on those boundaries by tossing me over his shoulder. "You'll say yes, I guarantee it."

I squirm and try to get down. He doesn't let me as he walks toward his house.

"I will scream if you don't put me down now."

He smacks my ass, shocking me as he chuckles in amusement. "Oh, you'll scream, and moan, and yell my name." He spins around, changing directions and heading back to Ann's house. "But first, you'll beg, Tessa. I can promise you that. You'll beg me at least a handful of times before I unleash on you."

"And I can promise you, you pompous, arrogant ass, that you'll be on one knee in front of God and my family before that happens," I snap.

The light comes on, the door opens, and he sets me on my feet. I turn so I am face to face with Molly.

"She needed some help getting in. Goodnight, ladies." Collin then leaves.

"What the heck was that all about, Tessa?" Molly gasps.

"He's impossible. He drives me crazy."

Molly laughs as she steps back, and I walk in. "I get that. You guys looked at each other all night at dinner. Is there something you want tell me?"

"I'm going to bed." I limp toward the stairs, up them, make my way to the room, and crash in the bed next to Kendall, who sleeps like the dead.

When I close my eyes, it is his steamy blue intensity that I see.

And sleep … it comes hard.

Chapter Six

The next morning, I stand, waving goodbye to my parents from the parking area, and as they pull out, I see a Jag speed in.

I turn quickly to head inside when the car shuts off and Leia bounds past me.

He shuts his door and laughs, "Good morning." He takes her collar and brings her back to me.

"Thanks, Leia." I scowl at my less than faithful companion that is obviously all too taken with *the neighbor*.

Once in front of me, he squats down beside Leia and pets her. Then he looks up as he reaches for my freshly wrapped ankle. "Nice wrapping." He lightly fingers the ace bandage.

"Mom fixed me up before she left. She's a nurse," I say, gazing down at him touching me, trying and failing to ignore the warmth that spreads … everywhere, and step back.

Standing up but not stepping back, he pushes his sunglasses onto his head and asks, "That's wonderful. And, what about you?"

"I'm a nurse, as well. Just finished my degree."

"How long are you here?" he asks.

"I was going to stay for a month, but I have this really creepy neighbor who asks a lot of questions."

"I'll make sure to keep an eye out for him. What's he look like?" His lips, really … really nice lips, twitch up.

"Average height," I lie, since Collin is a good inch, maybe two taller than Lucas, who is six-two. "Okay build."

To this, he smirks.

"He's cute, you know … for a creepy neighbor. Pretty full of himself, though, which some women"—I point to myself—"find arrogance unattractive. And he is that. Actually, I'm not quite sure how his head fits through his doorway."

I hear Jake call from behind me, "Hey, man, are we still on for today?"

Collin drags his eyes from me. "Absolutely, I just went out and grabbed a few things. If you want to take this, I have a couple more bags to grab in the car."

Wait. What?

"Dude, is that a Jag?" Jake asks. "Sweet ride!"

"Thanks," Collin says.

As he hands Jake the bag under his arm, I step back. *Perfect time to escape.*

"Hey, Tessa, want to give me a hand?" Collin grabs my hand before I even have a chance to answer and pulls me behind him, glances back to see that I'm okay every few steps.

"I would love to," I say with exaggerated radiance but pull my hand away.

Okay, so this is how it's going to be now, even after what he said last night? Cool, I guess.

He pops the trunk and pulls out a vest. "I grabbed this for your niece to wear on the boat today. I didn't have any child-sized life vests onboard. Is it the right size?"

Confused, I nod, "Yes, but what boat? What's going on?"

"I lost a bet last night. I owe your family a boat ride around the Cape." He winks. Yes, winks.

Irritated by this, I hiss, "A bet? Seriously? What were my brothers betting you? That you couldn't get me in your bed last night?"

I start to turn, and he grabs my shoulders, stopping me. "I'm pretty sure your brothers don't seem like the kind of guys to pimp out their sister. It was the volleyball game. You need to get over this. I don't want you in my bed. You'd probably argue over how many orgasms I'd give you. Now, help me carry a few of these bags in."

Face hot as the sun, I turn from him and grab a couple bags.

I feel the heat of his body resonating off him as he steps closer and leans over my shoulder.

"Not my bed, Tessa. I want you here, like this from behind. I want you in the water with your legs wrapped around me. On my boat, in the middle of the day." He steps around me and grabs a twelve pack and a couple bags, saying. "But not in my bed."

Why can't I learn to keep my big mouth shut?

I can see how much satisfaction he is getting out of this, yet I follow him into his place with the bags.

His house is much different from what I expected. It's not a bachelor pad. It's clean and tidy. Not something I would expect from a man who lives alone. The appliances are stainless, and the countertops concrete. The floor is thickly planked hardwood that looks like an old barn floor. The walls are a dark gray, but with all the natural light flowing in from everywhere, it isn't gloomy at all. His home is a perfect mix of old and new. It's breathtaking. From the outside, you'd never expect this; you'd expect luxury log cabin, but not this.

He doesn't say anything as he pulls out coolers, and I help fill them. I notice he's bought the Swedish Hill wine I love, and he notices that I notice.

He winks. "Pretty good, huh?"

I elbow him. "Pretty sad, actually—trying to get me drunk. Not real confident in yourself, are you?"

I have to force myself to look away, and when I see Leia sniffing around his leather couch, I freak a bit. "Leia, come."

"See? That's why she likes me better." He saunters over, grabs a thick throw blanket, tells her to wait, covers the couch, and then nods. "Okay, girl."

Leia sits on the couch like a princess and looks past him and at me. I swear she rolls her eyes.

I scowl at her. "Traitor."

Then I hear a deep, rich, beautiful sound. Collin laughing.

Shit, and basically all but shoved in it, I think as I finish packing the cooler.

Collin grabs it up and walks to the wall of windows, pushing open the French door and stepping out. Leia hops off her throne and trots out after him. *Yep, she's a traitor.*

"If you all come through here and go under the deck, you'll come to a door. Go down the stairs, and you'll see the boat launch," he calls to who I assume is my family, also traitors … sort of.

I step out onto the huge deck and see a hot tub—custom made from flagstones—an outdoor kitchen—also custom—and a beautiful firepit. I walk to the side and look around, realizing you can see for miles up here. Everything including the entirety of Ann's yard.

I then notice him watching me, body relaxed, face soft, eyes … covered of course.

"Okay, Leia, let's get you home," I say, hoping she obliges.

She does.

Collin follows me over and walks … inside?

I ignore that because you obviously can't uninvite the invited. Well, not in books with vampires, anyway. Besides, he's as beautiful and probably as lethal to one's heart as one, too.

When he walks out with her water dish and sets it down, I feel as smitten with him as Leia does.

"You be a good girl." He pats her on the head as I add some kibble to her food dish. When he stands, he looks me over. "Gets chilly on the boat; you may want to grab a sweatshirt."

"Okay," I say with scary ease then walk in to grab one.

After I change, throw on a sweatshirt, and grab a couple extra in case anyone forgot one, I walk out into the porch.

"Feeling better, I see." He points at my ankle.

I nod. "Not babying it helps."

He holds the door open. "After you."

I walk out then stop and watch as he locks the door. "I'll follow you."

He smirks.

I roll my eyes, and he laughs that same laugh, and I decide that will make my list of top songs this week.

As we walk down the flagstone stairs, I look around. "This place ... every bit of it is stunning,"

"A lot of hard work went into it."

"Hey, I was wondering if you could give me the name of the realtor so I can find out who the owner was about five years ago."

He stops mid-stairway and looks back. "And, why's that?"

I shake my head. "My aunt owned the house, left it to my family, and she, uh ... well, I'd just like to send him a thank you card. He was a good neighbor to her."

"Hmm ..." he says, looking me over. Then the corner of his lips turns up a bit.

"Less creepy than the current resident." I roll my eyes.

He smiles as he turns and walks to the bottom of the stairs.

Turning the corner, my freaking jaw drops.

Then Jake laughs. "This isn't a boat, man; it's a freaking yacht."

"What's a freaking yacht, Aunt Tessa?" Sydney asks, and everyone snickers.

"It's a big boat," I explain as I take her hand. "And Uncle Jake has a potty mouth."

Collin walks over and squats in front of her, holding the life vest. "This is for you."

"Oh, wow, thank you, Great Vie—"

He laughs. "My name is Collin."

"But—"

"Hey, Sydney," Molly interrupts her—*thank God*. "Isn't it cool that Captain Collin got a Sydney-sized life vest?"

"What's a life vest, Captain Collin?"

I look at Molly, who winks, and I mouth, "*thank you*."

We cruise slowly out into the water and take in the breathtaking views of The Cape. As the afternoon sun gets hotter, I throw my hair up, put on my shades, loose the sweatshirt, apply sunscreen, and lounge next to Kendall.

"This *freaking yacht* is insane." Kendall sighs.

"I've decided I'm going to be one of those people who lives on a boat ... But first, I have to save enough money to buy one."

"We can go halfsies." She grins.

"Let's," I agree.

Chapter Seven

*L*ying there in a white halter swim top is a major issue for me. I knew it then, in a way, but I definitely know it now.

Fuck, I'm not even close to being ready for this stage in my life and, from what I'm gathering, she isn't, either.

Sydney is sitting in my seat, thinking she's driving, while Alex, Jake, Cory, and I toss in lines.

"So, what's up with you and my sister?" Jake asks, and the others snicker.

"That's a good question. I think she and I could be friends"—*and will be*—"but I get the impression that she's a hard sell on that, and I get that. So am I. I don't know her all that well"—*yet*—"so nothing is going on."

I listen to them talk about her—Jake selling her, Alex warning me off. I appreciate both of their input.

I learn that she recently called off her wedding and that she really did love the guy and gave him a million chances that both agreed he didn't deserve. I knew she just finished her degree and that she worked a ton.

"She's really vulnerable right now. A week from today, she was supposed to get married. I don't know what you're into, but don't mess with her emotions. She's amazing and has a heart as big as this ocean," Alex says, staring out into the water. "The next person who breaks it will end up at the bottom of it."

"I don't start something with anyone until I'm sure they know my work is a priority to me. I work hard and would never hurt anyone knowingly. Warning taken and respect given for being that to her—a protective brother. Not going to lie and say your sister isn't attractive and intriguing, but she is very different than what I look for in a woman. Regardless, she drives me a bit crazy in a way—"

Jake laughs. "We lived with her for eighteen years; we know all too well how crazy she can drive people. She drove our folks crazy for years. But no bullshit, she's all heart, and she gets a great deal of satisfaction out of helping and doing for others. And protective as hell, too.

"I remember, one day, she was driving out of the school parking lot when I threw a snowball. I hit the biggest guy out there, an honest to God accident. After seeing the kid grab me and push me down, shoving my face into a snowbank over and over, her crazy ass pulled over, blocking half the traffic, and ran in dress shoes and a skirt. She shoved him so hard that he fell into the snow. He jumped up as if he was going to kick her ass. She got nose to nose with him and said something about having a small penis and needing to feel like a big boy by shoving a kid less than half his incredibly grotesque size down. Then told him that if he ever touched me or any other kid and she found out about it, she would fuck him up. It was the most embarrassing moment of my life, but my boys thought it was hot. Before the cops came, she was grabbed by one of her friends."

Alex laughs. "Jade?"

Jake laughs. "Yeah, man. She dragged us to the old farm truck. Tessa was swearing like a sailor the whole way home, Jade telling her to get in the damn truck, me feeling like a pussy. Good times in Blue Valley. Growing up with sisters, our friends all had big ass crushes on all three of them, but Tessa wasn't sweet and quiet like Molly, and Kendall was young still. She gave as good as she got; often times better. We both got into plenty of disagreements when our boys would start talking about what they would like to do to them. Pissed me off and grossed me out at the same time." Jake laughs.

As the sun starts to dip west, the girls start to rouse. I overhear Phoebe telling her today has been a better day than the alternative. Tessa agrees. Apparently, today was her bachelorette party date.

Sydney certainly adores her—constantly hugging her, and she gives it all back to her.

The last story Jake tells—and his are far more light-hearted than Alex's—I notice her walking toward us, Sydney on her back.

She gets to us and asks, "What's so funny?"

"Top secret," Jake says then takes a sip of his beer.

"But rest assured, it's nothing to do with you or your crazy antics when you were younger." I wink.

She rolls her eyes, turns to her brothers, lips thinned out, and Sydney moves so they're nose to nose. "It's okay,

Aunt Tessa. Everything is fine. The sun is going down, and it's beautiful and a great view."

"All right you." Tessa swings her around and gives her a loud raspberry on her little cheek. "You're so lucky you're a beautiful, intelligent princess, or I'd feed you to the whales."

We eat dinner on the boat, and when the sun starts to dip further, we head back. By the time we dock, Sydney is fast asleep on Tessa's shoulder.

Everyone, myself and Tessa included, were able to relax and enjoy that day, something I'm not sure I've ever really done.

Once on the dock, Molly takes Sydney, and Tessa, chilled from no longer having her human blanket, grabs her sweatshirt and puts it on before she grabs the garbage bag and starts to help clean up. I like that about her, too—she doesn't expect to be pampered.

Her brothers grab the cooler, still full of beer and wine never even touched, and she and the girls grab the bags.

She looks at me before stepping off. "It's been a great day. Thank you so much, Collin."

"I had a great time. Hey, I could turn the hot tub on if anyone is interested? It'll take about half an hour or so."

Everyone agrees, Tessa included, and I pull the boat back inside and undercover.

I get the hot tub fired up and fill the ice buckets beside it with beer, wine, and water, which was today's beverage of choice, and look over to see Tessa through the kitchen window, putting together what I assume is a charcuterie board, as everyone else wanders over. Then I see her outside with Leia.

When she finally makes her way over, she has but one place to sit, and that is by me.

When she pulls off her coverup, Jake, the family smart ass, starts. "Bow chicka-chicka bow wow."

Both Phoebe and Sarah, who are sitting beside him, smack him.

When she gets in, I hand her a glass of wine.

"Thanks," she says, sliding into her seat.

"We're missing tunes, man," Jake says as he begins to stand.

I grab the remote from the ledge and ask, "Any requests?"

The girls want pop; the guys country. I simply hit play. Then the discussion about music starts.

I like this. It's different. Overwhelming a bit, but not in the way in which I've been accustomed to.

When "Take My Breath Away" comes on, Jake begins the shenanigans with changing the lyrics, and the chorus is changed to, "*Take my breasts away*," and they all laugh at him.

They talk about music and what the greatest bands of their generation are. They decide on Pearl Jam, Zeppelin, and even Counting Crows making the cut.

I am forced to intervene. "You're all missing some great stuff—Jazz, Blues, the instrumental pieces. True art."

Tessa looks at me for the first time. "Lyrics are an art-form. Poetry. Eddie—"

"Oh, here we go," Jake cuts in. "Fuck Pearl Jam. No greater song ever written than those penned by Garth Broo—"

"Oh God, shut up," Kendall cuts him off. "Have you ever even listened to U2?"

"Not on fucking purpose, that's for sure," he grumbles, and everyone laughs. This encourages Jake. "It's not always a beautiful fucking day, Kendall. Sometimes you're knee deep in shit, and that song coming on makes you want to get your shotgun out and blow your damn—"

"Oh my God, shut up, Jake," she cuts him off.

Tessa, now on her second glass, sinks down in the hot tub, eyes just above the water, and looks to Phoebe with pleading eyes.

Phoebe cuts in, "How about we—"

"Holy porn tub, Batman," Jake cuts her off when I flip on the hot tub lights.

Everyone laughs, including me, and then everyone starts to do what they do—destroy lyrics to every song that comes on. The more they drink, the crasser it becomes.

Tessa pulls her sunglasses off of her head and puts them on. "I come here for a relaxing time and this is what I get?" She says this joking of course, and they know this. Then Tessa becomes the crassest of them all. After a while, she leans back, rests her head, and soon, everyone else gets quieter.

When they decided to call it a night, they leave, and they do so leaving Tessa behind.

Perfect, she and I can chat.

"Would you like another glass of wine?"

She doesn't answer.

I remove her sunglasses. She is out, sound asleep.

I take the glass and finish the wine. Too sweet for my taste but not bad. I set the glass on the built-in console shelf behind me and watch her sleep.

Is it weird? Yes. But some may think it's odd to look at a piece of art for hours, too.

When she begins sliding toward me, putting her head on my shoulder, eyes open a sliver, a smile ghosts her lips then quickly disappears, I revel in it.

After a bit, she starts sinking down, and I pull her onto my lap slowly and easily.

She wraps her arms around my sides, and the searing heat spreads, and I revel in it, as well. She then rests her head on my chest, and I close my eyes, feeling the calming power she has over me, a man who doesn't ever feel calm. Without thought, I kiss the top of her head.

After this, I feel her move, her chest rising and falling faster, and know for certain she's waking. And yet, she doesn't make a move to pull away.

My dick, always controlled, begins to harden as she lifts her head and looks up at me. Her arms stay in the exact same place. Her back arching, causing her to press against my erection and she moans.

I lift her chin, stroking my thumb along her jawline as I look into her eyes, gauging the level of intoxication. Her eyes are enflamed, my own eyes burning right along with hers. I bow my head and run my nose against her cheek. Then I kiss her forehead and feel her body tremble.

I pull back, cautious of my control when it comes to this thing, this loss of self-control, unfamiliar feelings, time —all of that. Then, slowly and softly, again and again, I press my lips to hers, aware my heart is beating nearly out of control inside my chest. I tug at her lip, and she opens her mouth, an invitation for my tongue to explore hers. And I accept.

She tastes sweet, hot, addictive.

Gripping the edge of the hot tub, I don't allow myself to touch her, knowing where that will lead. She turns, straddling me, bows to my neck, kissing it, then down my chest, nipping at my nipple. My cock jumps as she tugs at it then licks and kisses lower and lower as she moves her hands up my thighs. When I see just her blazing blue eyes above water, and intent to keep going down within them, I react the only way I can.

I grab her hips and stand abruptly. When she starts to wrap her legs around my waist, I lift her higher and toss her over my shoulder before stepping out. Inside the house, I set her feet on the ground and grab two towels. I toss one over my shoulder and begin drying her back off immodestly.

She turns, looks down at my dick standing proud, and whispers, "Wow."

"Fuck," I hiss as I lift her up, walk to the couch, and sit down, bringing her down on my lap.

Sitting on her knees, hands on my shoulders, she is still looking down.

"Eyes up here, not down there." I lift her chin.

In the light, I can see I was a little off at her level of intoxication.

"Tessa, you're drunk, and I'm feeling no pain. We, as adults, need to make an adult decision. I know the view is great."

She presses her lips together and makes the prettiest puffy bow.

I look back up at her eyes. "It's pretty damn amazing from here, too. Unless you're ready to beg, I think I need to stop this."

"I like the kissing a lot, a whole lot. I'm absolutely *not* going to beg." She licks her lips in anticipation, and then she kisses me, and she does it a fuck of a lot less gentle than I went at hers.

I do not pull back, and I give it back to her just the same.

Tongues, teeth, lips, biting, sucking, fighting for control, and she doesn't relent, which is hell on me. Worse than that is when she starts rocking against me, and my dick feels that searing brand, that pain and pleasure, and I am sure I'm not alone.

I grab her waist, rubbing my thumbs up her tight and trim stomach, and then I lift her up and off of from me.

I stand quickly, adjust my dick, and run my hand through my hair. Readying myself to have a conversation … again, I look at her, and all that hardened, well-versed plan takes a shit all over my hardwood floor when I see her wide eyes, her swollen and nearly bruised bow lips.

"Collin, I'm a twenty-four-year-old—"

Knowing she's going to give consent and me not ready, which is so messed up, I grab her up, back to chest, and walk us into the bathroom, where I turn on the water and step into my shower.

"Need to cool off, now."

She fights—*oh man, does she fight*—trying to push past me, I don't move because I know we both need a cold shower, and when I've had enough, and I know she has, too, I walk us out, grab my robe, and put it around her.

She says nothing.

I wrap a towel around my waist, drop my shorts, and then walk into the master closet, grabbing some pajama pants and stepping into them. I then grab her some clothes and head back to the bedroom, setting a pair of drawstring shorts and a hooded sweatshirt on the counter and instructing her to put them on.

She turns, giving me her back, shrugs off the robe, drops the towel, and does so shivering. I watch her dress, desperately wanting her to do the opposite, but knowing this isn't right.

I take her hand and walk out to the kitchen, where I drop her hand, grab two glass bottles of water from my fridge, set them down, grab the Tylenol from my drawer, dump four in my hand, give her two, and toss the other two back. Then I give it to her straight.

"I don't do this ... the kissing, the holding, the talking. I don't do this." I motion to the door. "I don't hang out with family, and I don't take a minute to relax, let alone blow off an entire day. I work hard. It is all I need in this world. It works for me. I don't take time off, and when I do, it's forced. And I certainly don't feel drawn to some girl who's a mess emotionally."

Eyes to the ground, she says, "I'm sorry." And then she turns and walks out my door ... and I let her.

Awakening

Chapter Eight

Collin

a knock at the door takes me away from my morning paper, and I walk from my office to the back entry.

"Hey, Collin. Sorry, man, I didn't mean to wake you. We're leaving in about an hour and just wanted to say goodbye to you and, uh, Tessa?" Jake smirks.

Panic hits hard as I shake my head. "Tessa's not here."

We both take off out the door. First, we look in the parking lot and see her vehicle is parked in the same spot it has been since I was a dick and made her move it. Next, the deck, beach, and patio. She isn't anywhere to be found.

"Hey, I'm going to look around the house again."

Angry at myself for letting her walk out last night, and

wired because I haven't slept at all because she's in my head so deep that it now hurt, I tell him, "I'm going, too."

We look upstairs, and in the bathroom, all the bedrooms, even the fucking closets. Then we head downstairs and look around.

I throw two fingers in my mouth and let out a loud whistle, and Leia comes walking out of the study. I pat her head then quickly walk in to find Tessa curled up in a tight little ball with her knees to her chest inside the sweatshirt, the hood on her head, and drawstring pulled tight.

Jake and I look at each other, both relieved.

I grab the blanket off the floor that must have fallen off her and cover her back up. Then I walk out.

Kendall hands me a cup of coffee and says, "Thank you."

"I can't believe she slept in there of all places," Kendall whispers to Jake.

Jake shakes his head. "You're so superstitious."

"Why?" I ask, wanting that question to be answered, the one I have floating in my head, wondering if Tessa is that girl, but am terrified to ask because, deep down, I know it is.

"She does a great job taking care of others, but she sucks at doing it for herself. We have to go home today—all of us have to work—and it's doesn't seem right leaving her here alone," Kendall whispers.

"I'll be here all month. I'll watch out for her," I ease her worry.

"Thank you, man." Jake hugs me.

What is it with this family? I wonder as I pat his back.

"Oh, dammit!"

We hear Tessa from the study as she races into the bathroom, and then we hear the distinct sound of vomiting. Then …

"Stupid sweatshirt, stupid shorts," she hisses as they come flying out the door. "Stupid wine." She starts throwing up again.

I walk in and grab her hair, holding it back.

When she stops, she grabs enough toilet paper to wipe an elephant's ass and wipes her mouth.

"Thanks, Kenda—"

She stops when she looks back and sees me.

I let go of her hair and walk to the tub to start the shower. When I look back, she glares at me.

As I leave, I tell her, "It's warm this time."

Jake and Kendall stand there, along with everyone except Sydney. They all woke up when they heard her throwing up, yet oddly, not when we went into their rooms.

"She is in the shower now," I explain, and their jaws all drop. "I didn't look," I say, and they all laugh quietly.

Molly leaves, returning with clothes, as we all drink coffee silently.

When Tessa gets out and sees us all standing there, she rolls her eyes as she walks past us to the couch. "Bet you'd like to know whose toothbrush I used."

Sydney hops down the stairs then runs and dives on Tessa.

"I didn't use your toothbrush, my sweet princess."

"Tessa, you slept in there?" Jake laughs.

"Yes. Why?" she asks as she carries Sydney into the kitchen.

"It doesn't freak you out?" Kendall asks.

Tessa rolls her eyes as she sets Sydney on the counter. "If I did believe in ghosts, I would still have slept in there. Aunt Ann would never hurt anyone. I wish you could have met her, Sydney. She would've loved you."

"You had nightmares forever," Kendall says, confirming what I already deduced.

Jake nudges her. "Well, Kendall, she was here when she died."

"Hey, I wonder about her Joe." Phoebe giggles.

"Collin, who did you buy your place from?" Jake asks.

"The church. It was a mess. I have fixed it up over the years." I look at Tessa, who finally looks at me.

"You're Joe." Her voice is barely a whisper.

This confuses me.

"My aunt liked you." Tessa smiles, softer than she has yet. "Very much."

"This is Ann's Joe?" Molly gasps. "I thought he was, like, our parents' age."

"Hey, Collin"—Tessa nods—"I'm not sure I ever said it before … back then, but thank you."

"No problem. Your aunt was very nice." I clear my throat and nod. "I'm going to head home. It was great meeting you all."

This is all too much, and I can't get out of there fast enough.

I watch as they all say their goodbyes. I watch as she waves to them, all smiles, and then hugs herself as she turns and looks at the house, a soft smile on her face.

I watch as she walks through the house, straightening things up and tidying, as she disappears into the room where she held her aunt as a teen—for twenty-seven minutes exactly.

I watch as she walks out to their patio. I watch her sit there, knees curled into her body, hugging them as she looks out at the ocean with Leia beside her.

Then I decide fuck it.

———

"I'm going for a run; can I take Leia with me?"
"Uh-huh."

I wait for her to look at me, but she doesn't. It messes with me.

I open the gate, grab Leia's leash, walk in front of Tessa, and squat down. I take her face, and she leans into my touch, looking at me with tears in those beautiful eyes.

Wiping them away, I tell her what I feel. "If I did this to you, I'm sorry. I told you I didn't do this kind of thing, and I'm so angry right now that it's messing with my head."

She inhales slowly then lets it out even slower. "You didn't. I've never been like this. I'm broken and damaged, and none of this has anything to do with you. If anything … you've been a beautiful distraction. Please don't think for a minute that this is your fault. I'm sorry if I've confused you. I'm sorry I've made you angry. And Collin, I'm so thankful that you've been such a gentleman."

I nod, even more confused now, as I hook Leia up and head out.

Anne's Joe

Chapter Nine

Tessa

The phone rings, and its Phoebe. It has only been an hour since they've left.

"Hey, Tessa, how are you? Don't answer that, I wanted you to know that all us girls are coming to see you on Thursday night!" she yells, hoots, and howls. "Are you excited?"

"I am. It'll be great. I'm just super hungover right now." I laugh. "But now I'm focused and will find some great things to do. In the meantime, I will let my liver rest knowing we have a DD."

We talk for a few minutes more, and then say goodbye.

I tidy up a bit, do the dishes, and try to think of how I can fix this—make amends with Collin, Ann's Joe, the voice that was recognizable but not, the touch that brings me comfort even when I'm being ... not so ladylike

"I'm so sorry, Aunt Ann," I say sincerely then laugh at how ridiculous she must think I am.

After the dishes are done and there is no more tidying up to do, I grab a glass of water and head to the patio. Perfect timing, too, as Collin and Leia come running up, her dragging ass behind him.

I open the gate, hand him the glass, and he drinks it down. Then we stand there, looking at each other, while he catches his breath.

"Your spirits look lifted," Collin observes.

"They are. You look a lot less stressed." I take the empty glass.

"Can I come back later? I, uh ... I told your family I'd see that you're okay."

"You don't have to, Collin. I'm a big girl, but if you want to, I'll be here."

And that's where I sit for most of the afternoon.

I am dosing off when the phone rings, and I answer it.

"Hey, Tess, how's it going?"

"I've missed your face, Ben!" I laugh, and so does he.

"You doing all right, Tess?" Ben asks.

"I am, actually. I'm ready to start over, and it feels great."

And this is when Collin appears. I wave for him to come in as I stand and walk into the house.

"I'm glad. You're going to be all right. If you need me, Tess, I'm here. You know that, right?"

"I need you and your fiancée to be happy, Ben. I love you, and your friendship means more than I can even tell you. I'm so happy I've had you in my life for all of this. I am, however, sad that ... well, it doesn't matter. I just wish I didn't drag you through all this."

"Tess, I'm glad I was there." He laughs. "We've had some very good times."

"We did. You've always been amazing." I sigh as I grab a glass from the cupboard. "I miss your face, Ben Sawyer."

"You know I could come home now."

"I hope you can come home in November. Doe Camp isn't the same without you."

We both laugh.

"My family just left, and I got super loaded last night, and the girls are coming up Thursday night. I really just want you to be happy, Ben." The last comes out way more emotional than I expected.

"Tess, you crying?"

"Nope, not anymore." I wipe away the lone tear. "Everything is great."

"I have to tell you that your ex-friend drunk dialed me a week ago. Didn't know who it was and didn't answer."

"Glad you didn't." I laugh.

"Called him last night."

"Why would you do that?"

"Because he's a douchebag, and I wanted to make sure he remembered that."

"Would you just be nice?" I laugh.

"Nah." He chuckles. "Why the hell are you?"

"Because … I don't know. I have to be nice to him, so he doesn't fall apart. I was with him for a very long time, and I can't just shut down *all* of my feelings. I'm perfectly fine knowing I'm not going back to him ever again, but I can't be mean."

I pull out some leftovers and make up two plates, popping them in the microwave.

"Wow … For once, I believe that you actually believe that," Ben says sweetly. "All right, I have a hot date with a blonde, and I don't want to keep her waiting. I love you, girl. Hopefully, we'll see you at camp."

"I love you and miss your face, Ben." After he says goodbye, I hang up and make Leia her dinner.

When the microwave time ends, I grab the plates then walk them over to the island and set one in front of Collin, who looks confused, which makes me confused.

He shakes his head. "I told your family I'd look after you. Who's Ben?" He runs his hand through his just show-ered hair.

"My friend … Are you spying on me?" I laugh.

"No, I … You knew I was here and …" He shakes his head again. "I'm sorry, I just—"

"I'm joking. Lucas is my ex. Ben's my friend. Has been since before you and I met."

"And you love him …? Ben?"

"He's helped me through so much. Yes, I love him. Like you do family. He's been a friend for a long time."

"And before that?" he asks.

I attempt to lighten the heavy. "I thought the emotional stuff wasn't fun for you, my creepy hot neighbor?"

Collin looks at me as he runs his fingers through his hair again. He is clearly agitated. It should be noted that Collin is scary as hell when he's agitated.

When he grabs my shoulders and guides me to a chair at the table, I sit. Then he pulls one up in front of me and sits so we're knee to knee. No, fuck that, I move mine inside his and scoot forward.

He watches every tiny gesture I make and does so like he's memorizing my movements to later analyze. I regret letting my shit with Lucas in immediately.

Finally, he looks in my eyes and starts. "I'm going to talk, and I don't like to talk. I'm stepping way out of my comfort zone here. Please just listen to me." He looks almost pained.

I nod.

"I'm the youngest of three children from a very broken family. None of my siblings share the same father, none of our fathers stuck around to get to know us. I watched my mother become emotionally attached to every man she brought through the door. She was drunk all the time and used every drug she could get her hands on. She was only caring when it was an act to try to impress whichever man stumbled out of her bedroom on any given morning. We went hungry while we watched as she chose to buy a steak for whoever it was she expected to come through the door after she fed us cereal and shoved us in our bedroom so that we didn't screw it up for her."

"I'm sorry."

"Appreciated but unnecessary." Then he pushes back and stands up as he continues, "I went through a very rough spell for a few years, but then I threw myself into my education and graduated when I was seventeen. I would have graduated at the top of my class but decided not to go back. I went to a community college that summer and finished the core courses that I hadn't taken in high school. I graduated college at twenty, joined the military, and earned my Doctorate at twenty-three. I was honorably discharged a year ago. I've never had an emotional attachment to anything, and I mean anything, except for my work. I fuck women who are as cold as I am and am very honest with every one of them about that. I see my mother only when she needs something from me, and that is out of a need to know where she is, logistically."

"I'm—"

He cuts me off with a laugh. "Then you and that furry little thing walk in here the first time in three years that I take a break from work. I travel a lot. In fact, I'm leaving in four weeks for a month. I wanted to spend time on the boat and the beach and bring different women over to have emotionless sex with. My point is that I never learned to love. I'm not even sure I ever knew what it really meant. I saw how you care for this dog, and then your family, and I didn't just see it … I felt it. I want you, I need you, and after talking to your brothers, I know that you aren't emotionally available. I know that sex feels good and fills a void. I also see how a kiss affects you, and how yours affects me. I don't kiss, or hug, or talk, and in the past three days, I've done more of that with you than I have in my entire life. Christ, even your brothers and sisters hugged me before they left."

He continues pacing. "I fell asleep with you upstairs, and that has never happened. I am a fucking mess here, Tessa. You are, without a doubt, the most beautiful person inside and out that I have ever met in my life. And you sit here and listen with what I think is care in your eyes … and I feel guilty. You've been through some sort of hell, and here I am, pouring my heart out to you, and for that, I'm sorry, Tessa. *Beautiful Tessa*. I know I have very strong feelings for you. I can't name what it is, because I've never felt it before. It's frustrating as hell."

He clears the distance between us and sits, capturing my legs between his. Then he grabs my face, and I imme- diately tense.

"And now I've scared you. Never be afraid of me. I'll never hurt you." He lets go, pushes back, and stands. "I'm done. I didn't mean to unleash on you, and I certainly regret having done so. I just wanted—no, needed—you to know where I'm coming from."

We stare at each other for a long time, and I feel tears begin to fall.

He looks horrified, angry, and confused all at once, and he looks stunning even then. I didn't mean to make him feel this way.

I stand, walk to him, take his hand, lead him to the couch, and sit. I nod to the spot next to me, and he sits. I then wrap my arms around him and hug him tightly, so tightly, and everything hard in me softens.

I try to stay awake, but the heat of him, the comfort, is like a sleeping pill, and I only wake when he puts me in my bed.

When he steps back, I sit up. "Don't go. Please don't leave. I want you to stay."

He sits on the edge of the bed, and I move to him, crawl on his lap and wrap my arms around his neck. I press my forehead to his, and we stay just like that, looking into each other's eyes. I kiss his cheek, slide off his lap, push against his chest, which is the best I have ever seen, and he lies back. I climb up next to him, cover us up, and lie facing him, my arms around him, his around me.

He falls asleep first, and that brings me an odd amount of joy. His grip never loosens, the heat he emits never lessens, and eventually, I fall asleep, too.

We wake to the sound of Leia whining. He sits up quickly, bringing me up with him, because his arms are like a vice grip around me, and then he looks down at me. I smile.

His confusion lessens, and he says, "Thank you."

"Best sleep I've had in ages." I smile as I crawl out of bed.

"That's saying something—you sleep a lot," he says, getting up.

I look back at him.

"No offense."

"None taken." I turn and step to him, hugging him, not wanting this cuddle fest to end.

He looks down at me, somewhat suspicious, somewhat amused, and hugs me back.

Leia then barks, reminding us of why we woke.

"I'll take her out. Need the fresh air," Collin says.

"No offense taken at that, either." I laugh as I follow him.

"None meant by it." He grabs my hand. "Anyone ever tell you that you smell like a lilac tree? Swear to God, that's all I smell when I'm around you. And I know it's not your hair products." He quickly looks at me to see my reaction.

"Not weird at all," I say, trying to hide my amusement.

"I'm observant."

"I'm becoming aware of that."

He stops at the door and faces me, holding back something. Then he brushes his hand through his hair again.

"Go ahead. Kiss me."

He cocks his head to the side.

"It's a thing, and if we're exploring emotions, that's what you're fighting." I shrug.

He kisses my lips quickly then looks as if he's trying to figure out if it worked or not. Then he smiles as he does it again.

I grin against his lips.

While he's out, I dump the plates that I heated for us earlier into the trash then dig through the fridge that Mom fully stocked. I get the container of marinating steaks, some corn, and then open the pantry and find the salt potatoes.

Filling two pots, I set them on the stove then turn on the burners, rinse the potatoes, and then the corn.

Dumping them in their prospective pots, I grab the steaks and head out.

I see them in the distance as I fire up the grill, which is not my specialty, but I can manage. Then I head in to grab some water and a big blanket.

When he walks through the gate, I am lighting a candle —citronella but still.

He looks at me, then the candle, then back at me.

"I'm making dinner, and you're going to sit and relax."

"And the candle?"

"Dual purpose," I explain as I set the lighter down then head back to the grill.

"What can I do to help?"

"You can sit and relax."

"Then you can't."

"Cooking is oddly relaxing to me."

"Are you—"

I point the tongs at the double chaise. "Sit and relax so I can cook and relax."

"But—"

"I'm on vacation, Collin … whatever your last name is, and so are you. So, sit and relax."

"She's bossy," he says, and I turn to see him talking to Leia.

"And clearly he's never been bossed."

"Not in many years," he says, sitting down.

I walk past him and into the house to check on the corn and potatoes. Then I get everything ready.

Thirty minutes later, I am sitting between his legs, feeding him steak and potatoes. No words are spoken, and it only takes a few bites for him to stop looking at me like I'm insane.

We eat, face to face, looking into each other's eyes. I'm not sure he knows it, but my choice of food was not a coincidence; it was purposeful. My beautiful vacation distraction, the man who held me while I fell apart years ago, would not be eating cereal tonight. He would eat steak.

It's still warm when we finish eating, and after getting rid of the dishes and feeding Leia, I walk back out and reach out for his hand. "Take a walk?"

I lead him to the beach, and we walk to the water's edge. I sit, hoping he does the same.

He does.

As Leia plays in the water, I sit behind him and lift his shirt over his head, tossing it to the sand. Then I cup water and let it pour over his head. I do the same thing to his upper body, bathing him in the only way I can here, and then I kneel in front of him and kiss his face, one side, then the next, softly and gently. As I get ready to move, he pulls me to sit between his legs, knees bent, one arm around my waist, holding me closely, the other holding my hand, and we stay there as the sun begins to set.

As we walk back to the house, I grab a pair of his shorts hanging to dry on his lower fence, and we walk inside.

I dry him off, and then he walks into the bathroom and changes.

"Toothbrushes are in the drawer."

I change quickly, and when he comes out, I take his hand, and we lock up together before we ascend the stairs and lay face to face, fingers entangled, both fighting to stay awake, to stay in the moment.

He wins.

House Rules

Chapter Ten

Collin

I wake alone to the smell of lilac mixed with something else. Bread maybe? Two out of the three, I like a lot. The other, not so much, and that is unsettling.

I get up, use the bathroom, brush my teeth, and head down to find her. She's sitting in the study, feet on the chair, blowing across a hot cup of tea, deep in thought.

It's not lost on me that the chair is in the spot Ann's bed used to be.

Leia's tail begins to thump on the wooden floor.

"Good morning," I whisper as to not startle her.

She turns and looks at me, untucks herself, and smiles

as she stands. "Good morning. Sleep well?" Then she walks past me and into the kitchen

"Coffee or tea?" she asks, seeming nervous.

I follow her out and stand beside her. "Whatever you're having would be fine."

She pours a cup of water from a kettle then drops a tea bag in it. "You take sugar or—"

I take the cup from her and set it down. She looks up at me, wide-eyed.

"I want to take you somewhere today."

She smiles and nods. "I made breakfast."

Leia walks in and sits beside me.

I turn fully toward her. "I woke smelling lilacs and bread."

"Did you need fresh air?" she asks.

I shake my head. "Give me twenty minutes to—"

"No. House rule: you eat before you set your mind to working."

"House rule, huh?"

She nods once, brushes past me, and opens the oven.

I watch her pull out a casserole then biscuits.

"You made enough for an army."

"Yeah, old habits."

"Your ex?" I ask, and she turns and looks at me, blue eyes wide. "Part of your life, Tessa. If it's off limits, then—"

"Did you miss the caravan of people in and out over the past couple days?" She smiles. "Growing up with a big family, you cook big meals."

We eat, and I love that she eats, not just picks.

I help her cleanup, which she allows, and then we stand looking at each other, and I know she likes doing that— looking at me—almost as much as I like looking at her.

"I'm gonna go. You have thirty minutes."

"What if I need thirty-five?" she asks with a playful smile.

"Tessa, you don't need but a minute."

She pouts her bottom lip out, and that does something to me.

I don't move, although I want to. I want to kiss those lips, let her wrap her arms around me, make me burn again.

She giggles.

"What's so amusing?"

"I think we're both obviously uncomfortable and, well, I, uh, I laugh when I'm nervous … sometimes."

I nod and step forward. "I'm going to hug you before I leave."

She meets me in the middle. "Yes, please."

That burn still hits, but that changes to warmth surging throughout my body. It comes faster, and it stays longer.

"Better."

"Much." She smiles, thinking I was asking her a question when I was honestly making an observation.

"Okay … See you in half an hour, Tessa?" I step back, turn, and remind myself, even though something has changed in the world, it's still one foot in front of the other.

"Hey, give me an idea of what we're doing today. What I should wear? Are we sticking around here or leaving? How long do I need to prepare Leia—"

"It's a surprise," I call back.

After making a few calls, I head back to whisk Tessa away for a bit more of this relaxing, and I do so bringing over some things that I had delivered for Leia.

I walk onto the porch, and she prances out.

"Hey, Leia, here's a big bed to lounge on while we're gone." I pull one of the toys out of the bag and squeak it. "And some toys."

When I look up, Tessa is standing there in khaki shorts, and I have to bite back a laugh because I'm wearing the same damn kind of shorts. She has on a light blue tee that complements her eyes, and a denim jacket on over it. Her hair is blown out straight, and she has a little bit of makeup on, just mascara and lip gloss, but … damn.

"So, you went into town, found a pet store, did some shopping, showered, and changed all in thirty minutes?"

I shake my head. "Sydney asked why she didn't have a bed or toys like she does at home. I ordered them. Just came in."

"Sydney and you had a conversation about Leia?" she jokes.

"We did, while she was at the helm, under the impression that she was driving the boat."

She bends down and pets Leia, a smile on her face at learning I had a conversation with her niece. "See you later."

I take her hand, pat Leia with the other, and open the door.

Getting to the car, I open the car door for her, and she slides in. Then I hurry around to jump in and start it up.

"So, where are we going?"

I take her hand and kiss the back of it. "You'll see in a minute." I hold her hand against my chest and want to keep it there, but I can't.

"I have to shift, I have to let go of your hand, and I don't want to let go of your hand."

Tessa reaches over and sets hers on my knee. "Good?"

I nod and shift into gear.

I watch her more than I do the road as she takes in the town.

"Different than when you drove in?" I joke.

"Hard to take it all in when you're in the driver's seat."

I look over at her, and she glances at me.

"What?"

"Very true statement."

"Then I'll drive back so you can—"

"I drive."

"Don't let that Jeep fool you. She's old but taken care of."

"The man should drive."

"Oh yeah?" She laughs, and I nod. "So, you're *that* guy?"

"What's *that guy*?" I ask as I throw on the turn signal.

"That one, the one who doesn't"—she throws her hands in the air—"let the girl drive."

I turn down the dirt road then take her hand and hold it against my chest. "Hard to take it all in when you're in the driver's seat."

"Oh my God." She laughs.

"What?" I ask, pulling into the empty parking lot.

"That was seriously a really good answer."

I kill the engine and turn to her. "The truth usually is."

I yank up the emergency brake, hop out, walk around the car, pop the trunk, grab the basket because, apparently, I'm now *that guy*, too, and then walk around to open her door. I hold out my free hand, and she takes it.

We cross the parking lot and head to the docks. Her eyes catch the sign that says, "*whale watching*."

I give her hand a squeeze. "You good with this?"

She nods, and a grin spreads across her face. "I've never done this before."

As we approach the boat, Stone steps out to greet us. "Welcome aboard, Mr. Abraham. Everything is as you have requested."

"Thank you. This is Tessa, and this is her first time whale watching, so I'd like to get at it right away so she can have the full experience," I instruct, handing him the basket.

"Of course, sir."

I lead her up front and open one of the compartments to grab two life vests.

As I help her with hers, she asks, "Do we really have to wear these?"

"Captain Stone likes his license, so yes, at least until we get out far enough so no one sees us."

I grab her hair, twist it around into a ponytail, and then lay it over her shoulder. I love that hair, but I like to see her face, those eyes … Then I grab her hand and kiss it before leading her to the front of the boat as the engine comes to life.

I sit on the long-cushioned bench, while she drops my hand to step to the front, holding onto the railing and looking out over the water.

She looks like a picture on a postcard, with the breeze blowing her hair. As much as I want to be next to her, I'm also aware she dropped my hand. If she wanted me there, she wouldn't have. She wants this moment, and I want to give her all of them.

When my mind catches up to that thought, as fleeting as it may have been, there it is— there … it is.

The horn blows, and then Stone eases the boat forward.

She looks over her shoulder at me, gives me a smile, albeit a whisper of one, and then turns to face the sea again.

I get up, walk behind her, and place my hands on the railings surrounding her. She leans back a bit, her back to my chest, and looks up.

"Beautiful."

"Yes, you are."

She gives me a look, as if she thinks I'm joking. I'm not.

"Those eyes, those lips, you … just you. Beautiful."

"You're not hard on the eyes, either, Collin Abraham?"

I nod.

"Hmm … Collin Abraham. That's a good name."

"Glad you like it, beautiful."

Blush colors her cheek as she turns her attention back to the ocean.

Within an hour, we are up close and personal with humpback, orcas, pilot, and finback whales. Seeing her light up, and really take in the experience, I feel like I am doing it for the first time, too.

After a bit, I walk us back to the long-cushioned bench, sit, and stretch one leg out, keeping the other on the deck. Then I pull her down to sit between them. Arms wrapped around her, I twist her hair in a ponytail and lay it to the side. Then I rest my chin on her shoulder. Her hand is resting on my leg as she runs her finger up and down it mindlessly.

"It's beautiful out here. They're beautiful creatures. Thanks so much for bringing me."

"Take this kind of thing for granted living here. Was nice experiencing it with you."

"You do this a lot?" she asks.

"Every time I come back for more than a week, I try to fit it in a couple hours out here clears your mind."

"And the captain, he seems to know you. You must, um … make an impression. Typical date for you?"

The unasked question is as clear as the sky, but I answer it, anyway. "I've never been on a date. I don't have time for what that entails. Captain Stone knows me because I sign his paycheck."

"You're his boss?" she asks, more confused. Then she looks away, contemplating something.

Normally, I like silence when I can find it, but oddly, not with her. Therefore, I explain, which is something I never do.

"Captain Stone is a good man. He's retired military, and this was his dream second career. A friend told me about him, and since I enjoy being out here once in a while, I figured: why not?"

"You know, there really isn't a lot that I know about you. I actually just learned your last name when the captain used it. What do you do again?"

I would like to tell her that she's known me longer than any other woman who's ever been in my life, but we're not there yet ... *yet.*

"I earn a paycheck by writing papers based on my medical research," I explain. "And when I'm not doing that, I travel to teach people around the world how to"—I pause, trying to figure out how to explain, but not go into detail—again, not yet—"thrive. I own a house here, a few"—*dozen*—"other properties, and this boat."

"Other properties here? Like house flipping? Real estate?"

"Not here, no."

She turns back and looks at me, eyes damn near insisting an answer.

So, I give her one. "Around the world."

She smiles, but it doesn't touch her eyes. "You must be very proud of yourself."

"Hard work pays off. But since being back, I am real-izing travel is tiring."

Boots on the ground get heavy.

She looks back at the water and is quiet for several

minutes. Then she moves to stand. "Could you tell me where the bathroom is?"

"Sure, follow me." I start to get up.

She holds out her hand. "I can find it; just tell me where it is."

Not Again

Chapter Eleven

_I_ head down the stairs, walk down a corridor, pass through a galley kitchen, grab the bottle of wine out of the ice bucket that is sitting there with clear intention of being part of this sitting on the counter, and make my way to the bathroom at the end of the hall.

After shutting myself in, I pull the cork out of the open bottle and take a much-needed drink, then another, and another, attempting to drown out the events leading up to this moment.

I wish I could turn back the clock to the night that I woke at Ann's house, the moment I saw him with that woman on his deck. Turn it back far enough that I remembered that moment that should have been a beacon of light shining on his *character*. Maybe he's no Lucas, but he's still a man who doesn't have "relationships." That lighthouse literally giving me that too-close-to-the-rocks siren visually.

The real issue is that I came here to fall back in love with me, find my strength again, and here I am, finding myself so drawn to him that, when my family came here, came here to make sure I was okay, took time from their lives because they're worried about me, the focus was on him. And, in a way, that is upsetting the Tessa moon plan.

I should have never come here. I shouldn't have let the lure of the water bring me here. A nunnery would have been better place to heal and grow. Yet, that need to take care of him superseded in such a way that I took him to the water. *Who the hell do I think I am, John the Baptist?*

I take another … several drinks and drink more than half the bottle when I hear a knock, followed by, "Tessa, do you need anything?"

"Nope, I'm coming." I stand and immediately feel tipsy. I assure myself that it's the fact I'm on a boat, but when I open the door, six-foot-four of perfection is filling it, and then I feel woozy.

He smiles. "You found the wine."

"I did. Pretty good stuff." I hold up the … more than half-empty bottle.

He takes my free hand, gives one firm yank, and I am in his arms. "Why didn't you tell me you were thirsty?"

His hugs are so, so different than Lucas's. They're soft and all-encompassing. They're the kind of hug that makes you feel like no other will compare, and that nothing, not one thing, could ever cause you pain.

Nope … no.

I step back, creating distance as best I can in the small space.

"Tessa, what's wrong?" he asks, taking my face in his hands.

"This, all this, you … What am I doing here?" That one little string that's held me together, the one that's strength I've tested for months now, it snaps. "Four months ago, I called off my wedding and graduated from college. Up until four days ago, I did my best to work twelve- hour shifts, and when one wasn't available, I seriously considered slashing tires of coworkers so I wouldn't have time to think about all that."

He cocks his head to the side in question.

"I didn't actually, but God, I was *this* close to reaching that level of crazy." I hold my thumb and pointer finger two inches apart for a visual. "I saved every penny so that I could just get away, figure out who I am for the next month without all the noise." Tears begin to sting my eyes, and I get angry. I am so *over* crying.

"I know where I've gone wrong, starting with promises I made myself as a child when I wasn't full of this poison I let—no, not let; I invited … begged for—inside of me, all broken. And here I stand, drunk in front of a man who is" —I search for a word to describe what it is he looks like. When I shake my head, all of those jumbled-up, and astoundingly accurate, word choices of who Collin Abraham is come out—"intense, incredibly successful, emotionally unavailable, and scary hot. A man who likes to '*fuck women as cold as he is*,' says all the right things. Things a normal girl on vacation would lose her ever-loving mind over. But, Collin, I am so far from normal. I'm toxic."

I hate that his eyes are guarded. *Hate it.*

"And, right now, I'm fighting this internal battle to be that girl—me, the real me—or get drunk, screw you until neither of us have even an ounce of curiosity left in us, then go home knowing that'll be the end of this … this … whatever it is. But looking at you, and knowing what your touch—hell, even just your proximity—does to me, I know I will not recover quickly. So, I, uh …" With nothing left to say, I simply shrug and lift the bottle to my lips.

He takes the bottle from my hand, sets it down, and steps toward me. Hands on my cheeks, he swipes his thumb across my lower lip, and like a match head striking a box, *I burn.*

Leaning down, he kisses the corner of my mouth, down my jawline, all the way down to the base of my neck, and then up the other side of my cheek until his lips rest on the top of my head. Then he pulls me in tight, all-encompassing, and God … how it feels so … right. And God, how I know … it just isn't. But I can't think about that, not now when all I can think about is his warmth—no, *heat*—his lips, his kisses, soft and gentle, lingering at just the spot at just the right time.

I want more.

I tilt my head back, forcing his lips from the top of my head. His eyes now unguarded … unveiled windows to a view so deep that I'm terrified to dive in, so I close my eyes.

When his lips surround mine, he unzips my life vest and pushes it off my shoulders, along with my jacket, and I shrug it off as his lips move, a sexy cascade of kisses down my neck then stops just above my rapidly beating heart.

Oh God, I think as my nipples pucker, anticipating him to continue moving lower, taking my offering of moments ago, *taking me.*

He pushes his hand up through my hair, gripping the back of my head, pulling back gently, taking my lips softly, parting them with his tongue, as he wraps his free arm tightly around me, lifting me off my feet. I hold on to his shoulders, strong, thick, and bulging, as he begins to walk.

Everything inside my head tells me to stop him, but my body, my heart and, dear God, my soul is screaming at me to turn off my mind.

So, I do.

Within seconds, my head hits a bed—a bed—and again, my mind is kicking and flailing, but when he's kissing me, it's like I'm high, but not on drugs, on … *something else.*

Lips against my neck, chest pressing against mine, he asks, "Tessa, is this what you want?"

"Yes."

"Are you sure?" he asks as he rubs his nose behind my ear then inhales deeply. "Tell me what you want, Tessa." He wraps his lips around the lobe of my ear and tugs slightly.

Without hesitation, I answer, "I want you, Collin."

"You're sure?"

"Yes, please, now."

His lips taking mine, lightning strikes. My back arches, trying to connect with his as he hovers over me. "Please, I beg—"

He sits up abruptly, bringing me with him.

Eyes dark, feral, he takes my face in his hands. "That's one."

When I realize he's referring to my use of *beg*, which was totally under duress, I get pissed.

He narrows his eyes, but they begin to soften as he says, "I want nothing more than to rip these clothes off you and go at it with you until dawn, but it's not going to happen. I don't want you like this, not when you're intoxicated, or wanting to fuck me out of your system. I don't want you when you're questioning me or my intentions. I don't want you until you're ready."

I shake my head. "I'm—"

He somehow manages to get me on my back again, with no struggle on my behalf, and then he stands off the bed, adjusts himself, and then squats down beside the bed and takes several frustrated deep breaths, nostrils flaring, jaw tight. He then snaps his eyes shut and lets out what sounds like a growl, and then he does it again. Definitely a growl.

As he starts to stand, he does so abruptly, shoving his arms under me and lifting me up so that I am cradled in his arms, *cradled* … one hand moving up my back, folding me up. Then, taking my lips again, all I can do is hold on for dear life, and I do the holding, fingers tangled in silky, thick, wavy hair.

As deep and complete as this searing kiss is, I am not ready for it to end when it does. Nevertheless, it does, and he deposits me back on the bed before he again squats beside the bed. This time, though, he punches at the foot of the mattress, not near me, and not hard, but three quick jabs, before standing, turning, and walking right out the door and closing it—yes, closing it—behind him.

Frustrated, angry, feeling rejected, and so, so stupid, I roll onto my stomach and scream into the pillow. I scream all those feelings into the cotton, and then … I get pissed.

That man had the nerve to tell me *that's one*! Seriously?

Body still trembling, and he walks out!

Hell no, I think as I shove off the bed, walk to the door, and throw it open. Then I decide I really should use the bathroom before going to tell him, Collin Abraham, what I think about him.

Once finished in the bathroom, I head to the stairs and look up to see him, phone to his ear and pacing. Then I hear, "No, not here, I'll fly up in the morning." A pause and then, "I miss you, too."

Numb, I turn and walk down the hall, grab the bottle of wine that he took from me, and walk back to the bedroom … on a whale-watching boat.

Yeah right.

After closing the door behind me.

I drink several sips, set the empty bottle on the floor, climb back in the bed, shove under the covers, and will myself to fall asleep, or pass out.

I wake to him holding me and me holding him, as if I'm trying to keep him here with me. Head pounding and feeling sick to my stomach, I lie still, eyes closed, wanting to drift off and sleep this off.

"We're docked." He runs his hands softly through my hair.

I pull my arms from him as I open my eyes and see his soft ones. "Sorry."

I roll to my side, slide off the bed, and walk to the stairs. I hear him behind me as I climb the stairs, exit the boat, and see Captain Stone walking toward us.

As I near, I thank him, and he gives me a warm smile as I feel Collin's hand on the small of my back as he extends his other hand and takes a set of keys from him. The keys are to his car, and when we get to it, he opens the door for me, shuts it behind me, walks around the vehicle, slides in, and then we drive back toward the house in agonizing but much needed silence.

He walks me to the door, opens it, and Leia runs to him.

Softly, he asks her, "You want to go out?"

She tap dances around him before sitting pretty at his feet.

Flirt.

"I'll take her," he says as he grabs a tennis ball from her basket of toys and heads out.

Realizing I'm being sort of a bitch, I call to his back, "Thank you."

Knowing that he will take his time with her, I take the opportunity to take a quick shower.

When I walk out, thankful I left freshly laundered pajamas in the bathroom, Leia is eating and Collin is standing, arms crossed, back to me, looking out the back windows toward the ocean.

I want to tell him that I'm fine and he can leave, but it would be rude, so I walk to the couch, sit down, pull my feet up, and rest my chin on my knees.

When Leia walks over, announcing she needs to do her business after eating, he opens the door and lets her out. Then he heads to the kitchen, opens the fridge, and pulls out a charcuterie board that was left uneaten, due to the fact that we cook way too much when we're all together. Then he grabs a couple bottles of water and the Tylenol from the windowsill and heads toward me. He sets it all down on the coffee table, loads a cracker with hard salami and a slice of cheese, and starts to hand it to me.

"I'm really not hungry."

With his free hand, he reaches up and pushes my fallen hair behind my ear as he says in a soft and sweet way, "If we'd have eaten today, you may have fared better with that bottle of wine. I won't take no for an answer."

So, I take his offering, not wanting to end this … whatever it has been … on a sour note because I've learned bad goodbyes sit so heavy on my chest that it oftentimes feel like it's crushing me.

When I finish, he hands me another, and then another until I finally old my hand up in gentle protest.

He pops it into his mouth then cracks open the bottle of water, hands it to me, and then does the same with the Tylenol.

"Are you okay?" he asks with genuine concern in his voice as he hands me two Tylenol.

"I feel like an idiot," I say as I grip my feet and rest the side of my head on my knees. "I took a wonderful day and made it ugly. I'm sorry, I really am. Other than that, yeah, I'm fine and very ready to go to sleep."

"I don't know what happened today. I wish it went differently, but I'm not sorry that I'm here with you." He stands, kisses my cheek, and then goes to let Leia in.

Unable to forget the conversation I overheard and having zero reason or explanation for the unsettling feelings caused by it, I avoid responding and give Leia some love.

When she walks away, he holds out his hand to me, and I again have zero reason or explanation as to why I take it, yet I do, and I follow him up the stairs.

I climb in bed, and he tucks me in before lying next to me, taking my hand, and entangling his fingers with mine. He holds that position for mere seconds then pushes his hand under me, grips the side of my head, and pulls it to his chest.

The beat of his heart eventually settles into a gentle lullaby, and I fall asleep.

I wake to an empty bed and his voice in the distance.

"No, I need to do this, Tomás. I won't need you to travel with me." Pause. "I'd like you to stay at the beach house until I return. I will email you instructions when I get a minute. I've booked a flight for tomorrow morning, returning Saturday at six a.m."

Who the hell is Tomás? I think as I hear water running. When it stops, I roll to my side, fake sleep, and when the bed buckles, his chest hits my back, and his arm surrounds me, I decide I don't care. I don't because this feels good, and if nothing more, it is healing that part of me that thought I would loathe a man's touch for a really long time and settles me into the mindset, that yes, maybe after I love myself … anyway, I can one day love another. And that one day, I won't feel this poisoned, and maybe, just maybe, my dream of having children to love, and teach, and coach might just be something I can still do … anyway.

"Goodnight, beautiful. Sweet dreams." He kisses the back of my head, and God how I wish I was cheek to chest with him, being rocked to sleep to the sound of his heart.

———

I hear my phone ring and jolt up, blindly searching the bedside table for it before I find it.

Opening it, I slide out of bed and whisper, "Hello."

"Baby, what are you doing?" he slurs.

I look at the red lines on the clock telling me it's seriously too early for this.

"It's three o'clock in the morning, Lucas."

"We need to fix this shit." He says *fix* as if it tastes bitter.

Instead of telling him to choke on it, I do the right thing. "Are you okay? Safe?"

"Fuck no, I'm drunk and gutted, having to make this call."

I say nothing, because what more is there to say?

"Heard Doe Camp is moving next weekend to Cape Cod."

I hate that he knows where I am, but I refuse to let him know it affects me.

"Yes, they're coming up Thursday. But I'm a little confused as to what you needed to call me for at three in the morning?"

"I want to come up. We need to talk face to face," he slurs.

"No, we do not need to talk face to face. The last time we did, we covered everything."

"Not even close, Tessa Ross," he says angrily.

"There really isn't much else to talk about. I want you to be happy, but my happiness, Lucas, it matters more now."

"Fine, not how I saw this going down, but whatever. I am dating someone. Seriously, too. I'd want to know if you were, so I'm giving you that curtesy."

I wait to feel the stitches that are holding my heart together rip apart and to bleed out.

They don't. Hell, I don't even feel them pull.

"Well, I hope she makes you happy."

"You wanted this. Don't get all sarcastic—"

"I'm not being sarcastic," I cut him off. "All I ever wanted was for you to be happy."

"You hate me then, right?" he asks in a way that hurts, but it doesn't break this foundation I am building.

A foundation, I think at the oddest of times, *I chose to start building on sand.*

"No, I don't hate you."

"Come on, TT—"

And, I am done.

"Thanks for letting me know. Although, I don't feel it's any of my business—"

"Because you love me—"

"It's been five months, Lucas. That love has changed. I want my friend back someday. I want you to be happy, healthy, safe, and to—"

"But you do still—"

"Love doesn't just stop." I sigh. "I'm exhausted and still a little unsure why this call had to happen at this time a day, or at all. But, I wish you happiness and hope things work out for you."

"Want the same for you," he whispers.

"Me, too. Goodbye, Lucas." And I end the call by closing my phone.

I turn on the water and fill up the empty bottle before taking a drink while looking in the mirror. I'm not sure if I'm expecting to see a physical change, or to wait to fall apart, but neither of these things happen.

Okay, time to breathe.

And I do. I take several deep breaths, and emotions, thick and suffocating, do not come.

In my reflection, I catch a smile on my face. Although slight, it's there and, more importantly, it's the kind that comes from deep inside, seeking the sun, knowing it will grow because the clouds are parting and the shadows are lifting, and I know this to my soul, because Lucas Links is healing. And me? *I want that more than I want him.*

A New Dawn

Chapter Twelve

Collin

hen I hear the outside door open on the ground floor, I quickly sit up.

I know she needs a few minutes after the conversation I heard. I also know that, on the other end of that call, was the dumbest fuck on the planet, and I only briefly allow myself to feel sorry for whoever this Lucas character is. But that moment was lost because he hurt the wrong girl, and that girl warranted a three in the morning phone call because the dipshit knows that he knows …

After what seems like too long, but is only moments, she still hasn't come back in, so I get up, use the bathroom, and head down.

I walk outside with a glass of water as she throws a tennis ball for Leia inside the fenced-in area.

When I shut the door, she looks back and gives me a small smile, a gift. I walk to her and hand her one of the glasses of water, and she thanks me then takes a drink. Then she sets the glass down, takes the ball from Leia, and tosses it again.

I finish my water, set the glass down, stand behind her close but not too close, and ask, "Do you need anything?"

"My girls to talk to, but it's only four in the morning." She obviously knows I overhead the conversation.

"You should just tell me what you'd tell them; unburden yourself. Then maybe you could come back in, head upstairs, and get a couple hours more sleep."

"Thank you, but I'm going to pass." She again takes the ball and throws it. After a few seconds, she looks over her shoulder, searches my eyes, and then lets out a held breath. "I knew his bed wouldn't be cold. Hell, it wasn't when we were together and I wasn't in it." She stops and rolls her eyes. "I truly hope and pray that he finds happiness. I don't hate him. I can't say it's his fault entirely—we were toxic together. Never going back. Ever."

She looks back again, and I search her eyes in the dark. Even in it, I see truth.

"That being said, thank you for listening, even when I said I wasn't going to talk." She turns and looks up at me. "I'm sorry for today. I feel honored that you felt you could trust me enough to open up to me last night, and I'm blessed that you have been a gentleman enough to fight off my drunken sexual advances. I hope that, if anything, you know I respect you and am very happy you have made me feel desirable and interesting enough to spend time with." She finishes on a yawn.

I take her hands and kiss the backs of them. "You look tired; let me take you to bed, hold you."

She nods.

"Which, in case you can't tell, I enjoy a great deal, and thank you for letting me experience that."

She searches my eyes, seeking my truth, and softens. Then she squeezes my hand.

We walk up the stairs, hand in hand, Leia following behind us.

She climbs in bed, and I follow. She rests her head on my chest without prompt, and I run my hand up the back of her neck, palm the back of her head, and take her other hand. I inhale her scent and stroke my thumb across the back of her hand until she falls asleep, forcing myself not to think about having to leave this place, a place I normally have to force myself to come to, hoping to find the bit of peace I found so many years ago.

W hen I walk in the room, breakfast tray in hand, she's stretching as she looks out the window.

I move quietly, as to not disturb her, and place the tray on the nightstand as she looks over at me, small smile on her face.

I slide back into the bed, forcing myself not to lie down yet. Then, still wanting her pressed against me, I move so that I am behind her, legs stretched out, framing her as I pull her back to my chest. The branding burn is gone now, but the heat, the closeness, the contentment is growing in spite of that.

"Good morning, beautiful." I kiss the back of her neck.

She leans into me, giving me her weight. "Good morning. This is unexpected, thank you."

"Necessary because I would prefer you don't forget me."

She looks back at me and waits for an explanation.

"I have to go away for a couple days."

She nods.

"I really don't want to leave you here alone, not emotionally and not physically. I have some things to take care of. My assistant, Tomás, is going to be staying next door. If you need anything at all, you are to ask him. I'll be back on Saturday morning before you're even out of bed."

"Is everything all right?" she asks.

"Yes, just a couple things to deal with then back here."

"Okay." She starts to scoot forward, but I wrap an arm around her.

"Where are you going?"

"Thought I'd get in a run before——"

"House rules: breakfast first." I pull her back, grab the tray, and we eat in silence, and it's only mildly different. Her body molds to mine, but there is no small talk.

After eating, she kisses my cheek, thanks me again, and slides off the bed. "I'm going to run."

"Would you like company?" I ask, pushing off the bed and grabbing the tray.

"Nope. I need to take care of my head right now. I hope you understand."

"Of course," I answer, because I do understand, but it doesn't mean I have to like it. "I'll leave you to get ready."

I head downstairs where I start cleaning up the mess I made when I fried egg whites and made toast.

When she comes down, I tell her, "Don't push that ankle too hard, okay?"

"Pretty sure it was the immediate swelling that caused so much pain," she says then laughs. "Or maybe it's the fact I've become a giant baby."

I shake my head in disagreement. "Physical pain always seems worse when there are uncertainties and worries here." I tap the side of my head. "But you know this; it's why you're here."

"Still …" She shrugs as she ties her sneakers.

"Removing yourself from that situation to heal makes you anything but a baby, Tessa. Allow yourself to believe what I know is true. You're exactly where you should be."

She looks up from tying her sneakers and cocks her head to the side.

I nod once then tear my eyes from hers, and it's not without more difficulty than I'm comfortable with.

I walk to where her phone sits and open it. "I'm adding my number here. Should you need me, just call."

She stands and says, "Collin, I—"

"Anytime," I cut her off.

"Okay, but I will be fine." She gives me a forced laugh.

"I'm certain you will be."

As she starts to leave, words I never knew were in me fall out. "In this house, you don't leave without at the very least a hug."

She steps to me, with zero hesitation, and gives it to me.

Leia seems more hesitant about leaving me behind than her mom. Tessa makes jokes about her liking me more, but the reality is dogs sense more than humans, and she knows Tessa is going through changes, but she knows how she reacts to change. She senses the rush inside me, the adrenaline pumping through my veins at an alarming speed where Tessa is concerned, and my unease, yet no uncertainty, about the changes I'm experiencing. She senses my world is about to change and knows that her own will be doing it in tandem.

When she leaves, I send Tomás a message then busy

myself with finishing cleaning up the small mess that I made in the kitchen while making breakfast for the cause of the changes forthcoming.

I am not a man who lives with the delusion of going back in time, yet she makes me wish that. I wish that I did not have to leave her like I did after Ann's death, because I knew, even in the chaos, that she was something to behold. Of course, the age difference wouldn't have allowed me, at that time, to pursue her, but having kept in touch with her would have readied her for the freight train that is me coming at her now.

Had that happened, there is a possibility that she wouldn't have endured whatever heartbreak she experienced. Regardless, this desire, as it was back then, to care for her, it hasn't lessened over the years; it has only intensified. I shouldn't allow it, yet here I am, throwing more wood in its fire to keep it alive when there is an ocean of reasons that I should be doing the opposite.

When I hear the lock open, I am finishing throwing the clothes I will need for this unexpected yet necessary trip into my suitcase. Then I toss my toiletry bag in and zip it up.

When I walk out, Tomás is standing in the foyer, looking around.

"I think you should meet Miss Ross before I leave."

He nods.

"She has friends and family coming in. Those I've met are good people. I'm sure the others are, as well. I'd like to make sure they have everything they need until I return."

"Of course."

I've known Tomás for years and, because of that, I know he's studying me in this situation.

"She's special."

Again, he nods. "I've surmised."

At her return, I watch out the window and give her time, time that is needed, yet I feel it's wasting away.

After I see that she's showered, dressed, and heading to the back patio, where she spends a lot of time, I head over, stopping at the gate with Tomás behind me.

She looks up from a book as Leia grumbles a bit and heads toward me.

"Tessa, I have to leave for a few days, and I wanted to introduce you to my"—I pause, realizing I've never introduced Tomás to anyone and am not quite sure how to do so—"associate, Tomás," I quickly settle on.

She sets her book down—a textbook—stands, and walks over, hand extended as she smiles. "Nice to meet you."

"While I'm gone, he'll be staying next door, so if you need anything at all, he's to see to it."

She blushes a bit before saying, "Collin here takes a promise seriously, doesn't he?"

"Yes, ma'am," Tomás states.

"I'll let you in on a little secret." She smiles. "That promise was made to my family, who worries too much. I'm perfectly able to take care of myself, Tomás, and my name is Tessa, not ma'am."

"Understood, ma'am."

She looks at me as she moves her hand to her hip and quips, "Really?"

I can't help but smile, and then I look to Tomás. "That will be all for now."

He nods, turns, and leaves us.

She pushes up her sunglasses, crosses her arms, and taps her foot as she looks up at me. "I'm fine."

"You're better than fine, beautiful." I open the gate and walk through, giving Leia some attention as I ask, "So, what are your plans this week?"

As she walks to her chair and ignores my question, she asks, "When do you have to leave, and is there any way I can get you to change your mind?" She grins as she begins to sit, but I take her hand and pull her to the double chaise.

"That run did you well." I sit and drag her down with me. "I don't want to go. Trust me, I want to stay like this." I wrap my arm around her and tuck her into my side. "But, to answer your question, my flight leaves at six tonight. I'll be home at six on Saturday morning."

Alerts from her phone begin to go off, and she pulls it from her hoodie pocket but doesn't pull away from me.

"Go. Have fun. I'm on a mission to chill. And besides, in two days—"

"You'll have your friends here and probably will have long forgotten me?"

"Not likely." She sighs then looks up. "My aunt thought you were a lot of fun to watch."

"We should talk about that, huh?"

"My aunt? Why? Did the two of you hook up?" Tessa laughs.

I give her a squeeze. "No, she fed me *a lot*. But on a serious note, I wonder if that's why I feel so …" I stop before saying *drawn to you* and instead admit, "Holding you is comfortable to me. It just feels—"

"It feels comfortable, not awkward, like it's happened before. And it has." Tessa giggles.

"Very comfortable," I admit.

"I wonder if …" She stops.

"What is it, Tessa?"

"Nothing. This is nice." She smiles up at me then rests her head on my chest.

Nice is far less than what this is, and I don't enjoy this… *feeling*.

I'm only aware that I've grown tense when she looks up at me in question.

"As I mentioned, Tomás will be staying at the house until I return. He has instructions to look after you in my absence."

"And what, Mr. Abraham, is he to do? Fill in here, too?" She pushes up and kisses me.

This question brings forth yet another emotion that instantly cause yet another feeling I'm not used to. "Not if he values his job or life."

"Jealous, Mr. Abraham?" she teases. "I would love for you to remember that feeling while you're away on *business*."

"Why would you want that?" I ask, pulling away.

She cocks her head to one side "I was joking. You know, ha, ha funny?"

"No, not funny at all," I say, attempting to stand, needing a bit of space, but she holds on tighter.

I look down and softly warn, "Tessa, I am—"

"What's your favorite color?"

"Not green," I say tightly.

She pouts out her bottom lip, frowns, and then says with an apologetic smile, "Mine's blue."

I settle back in. "Mine, as well."

We spend the next few hours talking, touching in a way that seems more intimate than sex, and of course she feeds me, dotes on me, and it seems to be something she truly enjoys. I have to put aside the need to do the same.

I know her favorite place to think is behind her parents' farm, next to the falls in the woods. She knows I like all kinds of music but appreciates instrumental pieces. I know this kind of music drives her crazy, and she has the need to make up words to any Kenny G song she has ever heard.

We take a long walk with Leia along the beach, which I now find even more beautiful than before. Many times, throughout the day, I would catch her looking off in the distance, almost dejected, and this is bothersome. Those moments were fleeting, and the fact that I felt at peace here, a depth I've never discovered previously, and I felt it because of her.

Until her, I never wanted to wake up next to someone and share my day, and the fact I am interested in sharing many with her isn't something I want to push aside.

Knowing she's hurting yet not stuck in that shows her strength and character, which is something I admire. *Something I fought to maintain within myself most of my life.*

As the time nears three, quiet contemplation settles as we sit on the couch. When the doorbell chimes, she stands and makes her way to it.

When she opens it, she greets Tomás kindly, and then turns and looks at me with that same dejected look.

I nod to Tomás. "I'll be out in a moment."

"I don't want to hold you up," she tells me when he leaves.

I wrap my arms around her, and she leans into me. "Then let me just hold you."

She looks up, and I press a kiss to her lips, her cheek, her forehead, and then I finally press my lips to the top of her head and inhale. I rest my chin on her head, still enjoying her warmth, her scent.

"I'll be back on Saturday. Please don't put yourself in any danger. I want to spend more time with you."

When she looks at me oddly, I realize my blunder and right it.

"Watch out for the driftwood."

She smirks.

I step back, open the door, and step out. When I turn back to say goodbye, I see her sliding on her flip flops.

"You going somewhere?" I ask as she reaches out, takes my hand, entwines our fingers, and brushes past me, saying nothing as she walks toward the SUV.

Standing at the passenger door, she inhales a deep breath, turns to me, and dives headfirst into my chest as she wraps her arms around me, holding me tightly.

I wrap an arm around her running my hand up her back, under her hair, and grip the back of her head so that I can pull her head back and look down at her. She pushes up on her toes, takes my face between her hands, and kisses me, and she doesn't kiss me like she has previously. She kisses me way deeper.

She pushes her tongue between my lips and gives mine a nudge, and I feel it in places I've ordered to stand the hell down.

I rub mine against hers, and then she wraps her lips around it and pulls back slowly. Then she steps back completely.

"Fly safe, Collin. Let me know when you've arrived, please." Then she turns and walks away.

Regroup

Chapter Thirteen

*H*eart beating against my chest, back splayed against the closed door, I wait until I hear the huge black SUV pull away before shoving off the wall and stomping through the house, needing to get outside so I can freaking breathe.

Pissed, annoyed, frustrated, I push the door open, grab Leia's leash, inhale the salt air as I hook her up, kick off my flip flops, and stomp through the sand to the shoreline.

Inhale, exhale. Breathe. Do not freaking cry, I think as I sit my ass in the sand and let Leia's ... *new?* retractable leash stretch out enough that she can play in the sand or water as I try to swat away the memory now etched in my damn brain that's flooding me when I almost tackle-hugged then kissed him *like he was mine*. Collin way-too-perfect-to-be-real hottie neighbor, Ann's Joe, the man who held me together long ago when I fell apart. The memories of Mom lining us all up before Dad left on the truck for a delivery. We all kissed him goodbye and told him to drive safe, and that we loved him. The last almost slipped from my mouth ... almost.

I drop my ass in the sand, flop back, and groan. I hate the feeling that there is *something* about him, and then over-hearing the call and the fact that a-freaking-gain I want to dismiss a warning sign.

"What the hell is wrong with me?" I ask the sky, and of course it doesn't answer, but Leia bounds up to me and shakes off before deciding to lick the hell out of my face.

Laughing, I tell her, "We need an island vacation. A deserted one. One where warning signs aren't needed because it's obvious that they draw me in like one of those fly zappers, and we all know how that ends."

She licks me again, and I laugh.

I push myself up and hug my knees. Leia drops her ass beside me, and we both look at the water.

After a long time has passed, time needed to remind me why I came here, time to allow the heat of the sun and the sound of the waves to be the only noise I allow in my head, I feel it. It's the comfort I felt when deciding to come here, that comfort always gained by Aunt Ann's wisdom and Toby's kind of love.

I look down and smile at my girl. "We have company coming in a few days." I scratch behind her ear. "Dresses to mess and goodbyes to be said in a way with my girls." I lean in and whisper, "Mostly Jade." Then I speak normally as I continue. "Know this is the final chapter in this toxic trudge through my hell. And that all is, and it will remain well in the world."

I push up, smack off as much sand as I can, and then we head back with a mission.

Looking down at Leia, I smile. "And then, after that, we continue the quiet process of getting stronger."

Inside, I grab a pen and paper from the drawer and sit at the island, setting out to plan the perfect destination Doe Camp retreat. I do this by making a list of things I will need to turn the patio and yard into the oasis it should be. Therefore, I will be doing some landscaping, amongst other things. I also draw a layout.

Wallet and list in hand, I head to the door as I throw my hair in a ponytail. When I reach for my keys, I see Collin's white hat, with the Sox logo on it, sitting next to them and decide to put it on and drag my ponytail through the back.

"No disrespect to the Yanks, but when in New England, do as New Englanders do." I look down at Leia. "Am I right, or am I right?"

If anyone ever saw me in this thing, they would die, or kick my butt. I laugh to myself as I walk out the door and lock it behind me.

When I return from the hardware store, I see Tomás sitting on the back steps of Collin's home. I lift my hand and wave to him as I round the Jeep and open the back to begin carrying bags of topsoil and mulch down to the backyard.

Tomás appears behind me, and I jump at the shock of seeing him there. He says nothing; simply reaches in, grabs two bags, and throws them over his shoulder.

"Thanks, Tomás, but you don't have to do this."

"Yes, ma'am, I do," he responds matter-of-factly.

I reply just the same. "Well, then if I am to allow it, you better call me Tessa."

He nods and follows me down the slight inclined pathway between the houses, from the parking area to the yard.

We make several more trips until the back of the Jeep is empty and I am ready to begin.

"Thank you, Tomás," I say as I walk inside to fill up my water bottle.

When I come back out, he is still standing in the same spot. "Is that all, ma'am, or should I stay and help?"

"No, *sir*," I joke. "That's all. This is all mine." I look at all the dirt and plants splayed out. "And I'm going to enjoy it."

With a nod, he exits the area, and when I look up, he has seemingly vanished.

So odd, I think and wonder if this should concern me, but I dismiss it because … Doe Camp.

I get busy laying out the beds, making sure there is plenty of room for kids and dogs to roam, as well as the visual stimulation that I have planned out. Then I set to digging out the beds, pouring out bags of topsoil, planting copious amounts of lilac, butterfly bushes, pots of magnolias, and several flats of blue and green ornamental grass.

With plenty of plants left over, I head to the back porch and grab the carefully hung window boxes and fill them, too. Once they're back where they belong, I wash up then fill Leia's dishes and take them outside. Then I come in to grab a drink and some leftover chicken and salad for me.

As soon as my butt hits the chair, my phone rings.

I lift it up, look at the screen, and see his name, remembering he had put his number in my phone. The grin that spreads across my face would be embarrassing if seen by anyone else as I answer, "Hey, Collin."

"How did you know it was me?' he asks, a smile in his voice.

"I am pretty sure you know the answer to that." I sigh contently then ask, "How was your flight?"

"It was good. Short."

"Collin, where are you?"

"New Jersey," he answers.

My body stiffens. "I hope you're all right." *Stupid. Of course he is.* "I mean, well, have a good time, I guess."

"I'll be back shortly, I promise," he promises with a whisper.

As soon as I hang up, I begin analyzing the whisper. Why? I mean, seriously, why do I care? Why do I wonder? Why does he think I need to know he's coming back? Why fucking Jersey! But the one that hits hardest: why do I want him so freaking badly?

New plan, after Doe Camp, the Cape edition, I am packing up the Jeep and heading to the nearest nunnery.

Almost in tears when I realize how deep my feelings, my stupid need for him, is, and so soon, I close my eyes, forcing myself to remember it will all be okay. I need to figure out what I need before worrying about bringing someone else into this. My sweet distraction is no doubt a gift from above. How long it is mine to enjoy, only God knows.

No. Nope. Not happening. I shake away the thoughts.

I force myself to eat then take Leia for a short walk as the sun sets. It is stunning, and I am grateful and blessed to see it, and I am also finally exhausted.

I call Mom and chat as my bathwater runs, promising her that I'm good, better than good, and before we hang up, she makes me promise if I need anything to call and assures me that she'd come.

I know she would, and it saddens me that I felt she

wouldn't, and then I am too ashamed to admit I needed her when everything in slow motion, the slowest slow motion ever, an almost five years long episode, fell apart.

I wish she knew, although things had gone awry, the foundation that she helped build, never crumbled, *and it sure as hell won't in the sand*.

Stepping out of the bath, my eyes feel heavy, my muscles tense from a hard day's work, now relaxed as I wrap my towel around me, I take comfort in that. Upstairs, I grab a tee-shirt, throw it on, and slide into bed.

I could easily fall asleep; except I can smell him on my pillow—his for two nights. I shove the thoughts away and pray, and only when I've given my worries to God, do I fall asleep.

The next morning, I wake and immediately become angry because he starred in my dreams, freaking *fairy tales*, and I shove out of bed, put on a sports bra, socks, panties, and shorts, and I set out to run.

My body still sore from the previous day's work, and my ankle still tender, screaming for me to head back at the halfway mark, yet I push. I push hard, and it feels … amazing.

Halfway back, I remind myself that I have big plans for the day and slow it down. As we approach the gate, I see Tomás standing up high, peering down at us.

I fight the urge to flip him off, because he doesn't deserve it, and I'm just being TT, so I wave to him instead as Leia and I pass through the gate.

I stand and look around at the oasis that I have created and take greater pleasure in it knowing that what I've started here will remain for those who rent and those of us who return to rest our weary minds and take in the serenity.

Inside, I grab a glass of water, drink it down, and then set about making breakfast for Leia and I.

After we eat, I head upstairs to shower and notice I have messages on my phone.

I pick it up, open it, and hit the digits to retrieve them. And when I hear Collin's voice saying, "*I just wanted to say good morning,*" warmth surrounds me, and when I hear the next, I become irrationally annoyed.

"*How was your run? Am I safe to assume you won't be limping when I return in two days? I didn't sleep well last night—my arms were empty. Yours better have been, as well.*"

I shoot him a text.

- Run was great, my night sucked, busy day ahead. My girls will be in tonight.

Collin immediately responds.

- Will you be staying in tonight? If not, Tomás could take you wherever you need to go. In fact, I would feel much better if he did.

I huff as I tap out my reply.

- Well, I'm not sure, but I do know I'm an adult and will be just fine.

Then I throw my phone on the bed, head down the stairs and outside, where I take in all the plants still left to find their place to root.

I plant some climbing rose bushes on the side of the house then look around, trying to figure out where the now homeless flowers in greens should go. When a shadow casts over me, I look up to see Tomás and notice his lips are turned down. I wonder why that is. This thought is sarcastic, as I'm sure that the man who is causing me irrational irritation, the man behind the distant sound of my phone ringing, has already informed him that I am annoyed.

What's good for the gander is good for the goose, I think as I head next door to get a closer look at Collin Abraham's landscaping situation.

"I'm not gonna talk to you since you don't seem to be much on conversation, but I am gonna tell you these empty deck boxes need to be filled. I would appreciate you allowing it to be a surprise for His Royal Highness." To that, I notice his lips twitch up, but it comes and goes so quickly that I am unsure if I really did see it or am just imagining.

Regardless, when I began carrying over topsoil and plants. Tomás lends a helping hand as I set about filling the planters, moving an empty flower urn to the corner, the one in which he stood in the night he silently howled at the moon, the night one of his no-strings ladies was obviously on her knees, and I feel that space, too.

Standing back to take in my work, I decide, "Needs more."

By around noon, everything is done in the planting world and I have come up with even more ideas for destination Doe Camp.

I take Leia with me as I set to town to hit the hardware store, where I grab boards and paint to make some signs. I also grab some galvanized buckets, like the ones I potted on Collin's deck, to ensure no plant is left behind. Then I head to the grocery store to grab enough food, wine, and munchies needed for the all-girls retreat. A little more comfortable with the area and wanting to explore it further, I drive down a side street and stop in front of a familiar building.

Memories of my summer here with Ann flood my mind and, before I know it, I'm pulling into the driveway, throwing the Jeep in park, and stepping out to look up at the church that Aunt Ann was a member of. A church in which I attended vacation Bible school for the first time.

"Hello, miss, can I help you?"

I turn and look behind me to see a man in a suit. "I am sorry. I was just kind of drawn here. And now I know why. I've sat in the pews many times when I was younger. And there was a summer I remember coming here for VBS. My aunt's name is Ann."

"Ann Munn?" He smiles. "Tessa, is that you? It's Pastor Lou. I was the youth pastor that summer. Now this is my church."

Smiling, I nod. "Yes, it's me."

"Also spent some time with you on that day when Annie went to meet her Lord and Savior."

"I'm so sorry that day—parts of it, anyway—feel like they happened to someone else. But I thank you, Pastor Lou. Your words carried me through until my family arrived."

"Swear I remember you as a kid at VBS. You know, Saturday night, we're kicking off a very late summer VBS. Would love to have you come."

"I'd love to help. I'm here for a few more weeks."

"Absolutely. How about you assist in the kitchen?" I nod, and he smiles. "I remember you loving the music and oh how your aunt loved to watch you sing. We have someone already doing the musical segments, but she may need someone to assist. God willing, there will be a lot of children in attendance."

"Great. What time should I be here?"

"Starts at six, so how about five thirty?"

"Excellent. That's great ... I truly look forward to it. I'll see you then."

After possibly one of the warmest hugs I've ever been

given, I jump in the Jeep with renewed faith in whatever feeling brought me here.

Driving back, I am truly happy and ready for the next few days of relaxing while saying goodbye, laughing with friends to help assure them, as well as myself, that I am fine. But, for some reason, I am more excited about spending the week ahead, surrounded by blind faith, love, and a little bit of Jesus.

After finishing up the buckets, I carry two next door and set them on each side of the door, and the other I place on the deck. The entire time I work, I do it knowing that Ann would be happy to see that I am being kind to her Joe.

After that, I run next door, grab an old toolbox, take them out back, and nail the pieces of wood together, painting the front white, then leave it in the sun to dry. After, I head inside and crank up the music, a very odd mixed tape, the majority is Casting Crowns tossed in with some Pearl Jam, but hey ... Then I set to marinating the steak and the chicken I will later make in two kabobs to grill with my girls.

It's now three, and the girls would be here in less than two hours, so I decide to finish the sign. I carefully draw a cabin and write the words on the sign. I let it dry as I fill the beverage coolers with wine and beer.

The sign finished and mostly dry, I hammer it into the landscape then rush back to the Jeep to grab and place the few solar lights that I purchased on clearance.

A quick look at the clock, and I realize it is time to wash off the day and prep for the night. Thankfully, I do so in record time because, when I walk down the stairs, Leia begins to bark, and when I look out the window, I see two minivans pull in. *Yes, minivans.*

Phoebe hops out, belly first, and gives me a side hug.

Laughing, I plant my hands on her belly and give it a rub. "It's been less than a week and you're all baby."

"Well, look at you, all skin, bones, and boobs!" Phoebe laughs. "The weight you've lost, I found."

"You look gorgeous and happy. I'm so excited! Seven more weeks, right?"

"Hey, Tessa." Jessie —*Jessie?*— hugs me. "I rode in a minivan for seven hours, listening to these two talk about vaginas and breastfeeding the entire way—you owe me! We're going out this weekend, got it!"

Okay, yes, she was part of the wedding party, but um … again, *Jessie?*

I hug her back and decide to go with it. "You'll get no vagina talk from me."

"Thank God." She steps back and looks over the house. "This is insane."

I point from Collin's house to Ann's and laugh. "This way."

"Super cute!"

I'm not sure if she drank the whole way, but the Jessie I know is not bubbly, at all, but again, we'll roll with it.

Seriously, I swear she is one of the most beautiful women alive. Shorter than me, now bobbed, brown, thick as hell, wavy hair and deep brown eyes, her mouth full and pouty, and she was sassy, not bubbly, but …whatever.

Jade opens the sliding door and looks amazing. Her flowing black hair and big blue eyes are as bright as the sun. Jade is also gorgeous, in the drop-dead kind of way.

"I'm ready to have a great time, are you?" She hugs me.

"Of course!"

Molly, Kendall, Sarah, Cassidy, and Becca all pile out of Molly's black minivan, and Molly looks … anxious.

"You okay?" I ask, hugging her first.

"I'm just a little nervous about leaving Sydney with Mom and Dad, but this will be fun," she says in the way she's trying to convince herself.

"They didn't break us. I'm sure Sydney will be fine. Better than fine. She's going to have a blast."

"Uncle Jake will make sure of it," Sarah says as she hugs me, and I watch Molly begin to gnaw at her lower lip.

Laughing at Molly and Sarah, I ask her, "So, are you and Jake officially dating yet?"

Sarah rolls her eyes. "Every time I tell him yes, I'm his *girlfriend*, things are great, perfect, actually better than perfect, but—"

"Then what's the problem?" I laugh.

"He'll eventually get around to just screwing everything up by asking me to marry him. Always does."

Remembering when we first met, Jessie mentioned she always turned down her man's many proposals. I laugh. "Sarah, you've met Jessie, correct? I believe you two have something in common."

"Not anymore." Jessie shakes her head. "I finally said yes, and he decided he wanted to be a free agent."

"I'm sorry, Jessie, truly."

"Better to know that now." Jessie shrugs.

My foot is not tasting all that great right now.

We unload the vehicles and get everything settled inside.

"Water still warm?" Phoebe asks.

"Doesn't matter. We're at the beach." Kendall wraps an arm around her. "We're going in."

After everyone chooses their rooms, we throw on our suits, run to the water, being total girls, and jump in. Then we spend an hour soaking in the sun.

Sarah, Jade, and Kendall set the table as Molly and

Cassidy help me get the food off the grill and set out the salads.

Once everything is set, we all sit down and begin planning out Friday night. After dinner, over my third glass of wine, the realization that I drink way more around men makes me … uneasy, or is it, easier, I ask, "So, where are the dresses, ladies?"

"Are you sure this is what you want to do, Tessa?" Kendall asks.

Without hesitation, I state, "Absolutely."

"Let's fucking do it," Jade says right before tossing back her glass of wine like it's a shot.

We all head to our prospective rooms—Kendall and Molly are sharing with me—and I help them get dressed. Then, without me even asking, they leave me to it.

I unzip the white bag containing the ivory dress, a simple ball gown style, with cap sleeves and very little embroidery. Mom thought it was understated yet elegant, and that's exactly what I wanted. I didn't want tons of beading, or poufy sleeves, nor did I care if the train was long enough to reach down the aisle. And the more I look at it, the more detached I feel from all of it.

He gave no input, none, and I excused it away that he was busy with ball, which he was, but if I could change my whole world for him, he could have acted a little bit interested in the day he pushed so hard for. One day, I'm sure I'll reflect on this moment as one that was a lesson, but right now, it pisses me off.

How stupid was I?

I dress quickly, not wanting to wallow in it for too long, and also because the longer I take, the longer Jade and Phoebe will have to orchestrate how they should all act, as to not upset me. I'm not upset. I'm pissed.

After dressing and managing the zipper by myself,

which an overthinker like me should have also easily read that as a sign, I pull out the veil, and this, this I have a problem with messing up, because Mom picked it out. I let her win that battle, and it was very much a crown and princess-like.

When I get to the bottom of the stairs, they all stand looking at me, and I them.

"You all look amazing." And they do. The dresses I picked are black and elegant and could easily be cut off at the knee and worn for another occasion.

Molly sniffs and says, "You look stunning."

Kendall laughs. "She knows it, too."

To that, I laugh. "This isn't a funeral, ladies. It's a do-over! Once these are gone, there will be nothing physically left to remember my near-fatal mistake." I look to Phoebe, who is snapping pictures, and laugh. "Phoebe, where is the tripod? I want group shots."

After inside shots, we move outside and do various poses, drinking the whole time. We do cleavage pics, several *Charlie's Angel* poses, recreating our prom shots. Another, we lay in the sand on the ground, heads in a circle, and Jessie offers to take the pic standing on a chair that one of them had dragged out. Then we get stupid and have a blast doing so.

The sun having set a while ago, I look toward Collins's house and see Tomás looking at us.

Irritated a bit, but also wanting to amuse myself, I yell, "Hey, Tomás, I could use your help over here."

He doesn't hesitate, walking to the stairs, down them, stopping at the sand to kick off his shoes, peel off his socks, and cuff his pants, he finally walks toward me. And that's when I realize that all of them are lined up on either side of me, gawking.

Tomás, out from the shadow that Collin casts, is seriously hot, and I didn't even notice.

"Well, hell."

Holding back a laugh, I introduce him, "Ladies, this is Tomás. He's going to help us out."

"Tomás, what big feet you have," Jade purrs.

"Wait. Who is Tomás?" Phoebe asks as I take the camera from her and hand it to him.

"Hell if I know." I laugh as I grab hers and Jade's hands and run to the water.

"Hold on!" Cassie yells, stopping us, and when I look back, she and Kendall are hell-bent on something.

They all rush me and, before I can react, I am above all their heads, laughing as they walk me into the water.

"Lens off my ass, Tomás. Aim it up here!" Jade snort-laughs.

"And ten, nine …" Molly begins, and they all join in on the countdown to one before tossing me … sort of, and sort of dropping me into the water.

When I come up, they all jump in, splashing, laughing, and swimming.

Gowns once soiled by a broken promise and toxic love are, in a sense, baptized … but they still need to burn.

"Hey, Tomás, how about firing up that hot tub? We could all use some warming up," Kendall eventually yells, and then we all swim in.

Dresses hanging over the deck railing to dry for tomorrow's burn party, we sit in the hot tub, dressed in our bras and panties, as Kendall sets about figuring out the sound system.

"Radio, please," I request. "The owner has, um … eclectic taste in music. Who knows what will come out of his speakers?"

"Let's blow them," Jade says, smiling up at Tomás, who

is setting the cooler beside the hot tub, and this is why Jade is one of the best methods of entertainment in the world. She so said this to purposely attempt to make him squirm.

When he looks down at her, eyes narrowing slightly, she laughs.

"You do not intimidate me. I've fed teething babies from my boobs and pushed kids out of my vag—"

Thankfully, Kendall covers her mouth, and they all laugh.

"Sorry, Tomás," I say, trying to keep a straight face.

He looks away and reaches into his pocket, pulling out his phone and quickly walking away.

I don't give a flying fig that he is more than likely tattling on me, but I do *not* like that that thought was in my head.

"Check this out. You've been busy doing landscaping over there and he has here," Sarah says.

"Wow, did you *do it* together?" Kendall asks then snort-laughs.

"No, Kendall." I scowl when I see them all laughing.

I look at Jade and see the wheels just a-turning. Then she looks away from me and at the three of them. "Do tell, sister. Come on; we would love to know what our little Tessa has been up to for the past week with Tomás, who does *anything* she needs."

They all burst out laughing.

"It's not Tomás." Phoebe laughs then she shakes her head and looks at me. "By the way, who the hell is Tomás?" Phoebe asks, dangling her feet in the water.

"As far as I can tell, Tomás works for Collin and is house sitting while he's away." I really hope they catch the warning glare I'm tossing.

"House sitting or Tessa sitting?" Kendall asks.

They so did not.

I decide, *screw it*. What better way to let them see I'm fine, good, over it, and moving on than to lay it on thick. "I don't know what you think is going on, but nothing has happened."

Phoebe arches a brow, and Jade says, "Nope. I know you. Spill it."

"Fine, he's an amazing kisser and next level hot, but that's it. Swear it."

"Hold up and reverse. Tomás?" Jade asks.

"Collin," Molly, Sarah, Kendall, and Phoebe all say in unison, and they say it all dreamy-like.

I wave them off and continue, "He's not getting any. His little 'business trip,' so not a business trip," I explain. "I heard him on the phone with some woman and he said, 'Not here. I'll meet you. I miss you, too.'" And I say it in a sexy Collin voice.

"I don't know. He was pretty into you, holding your hair out of the toilet as you blew chunks last week and the whole shower thing." Sarah giggles.

"Well, he has taken care of my drunk ass again since that too," I confess. "But that doesn't mean—"

"Tessa!" Becca says. "How much are you drinking nowadays?"

"A lot." I shrug, and they all laugh. "No, seriously, Becca, I just can't stand to be around him sober. I don't feel like I'm even on the same playing fields as he is. He is major league hottie. No joke."

"Major league, huh?" Jade laughs. "As opposed to National Football League hottie? You're a sports whore, Tessa!"

Again, we all laugh.

"Seriously, he can't be that good-looking. I mean, you're used to Lucas," Jade adds.

"No, I don't think Collin plays sports. But I bet he would kick ass at naked Twister."

Becca looks at Molly and Kendall, and they sigh out, "Great view."

Then we all laugh hysterically… again.

"Holy shit!" Jade gasps. "This must be why all our men are drunks … They just feel inferior when they are around us sober."

Then we sing, and laugh, and drink, then decide it's time for midnight snacks.

Tomás stealthily laid towels out for us but was somehow inside.

I lag behind with purpose, and once they're gone, he steps out.

"Tomás, good night and thank you. We'll be back tomorrow morning for our dresses; can we please leave them here to dry?"

"Yes, ma'am." He steps back inside and closes the door.

"Come out, come out wherever you are, Tomás! Don't be afraid. We don't bite," Jade calls to him from the stairs.

Becca grabs Jade's hand. "Behave!"

"Loosen up, girl." Jade throws an arm around Becca.

We all head next door and, after we clean up from dinner, get showered off, and throw on pajamas, Kendall drags out some snacks and Phoebe sits at the head of the table, producing a Kodak picture envelope and dumps them all on the table.

"You took all these?" I gasp.

Jade snatches one of Collin. "You have *got* to be fucking kidding me? Holy shit, Tessa. He isn't just hot; he's … beautiful." Jade grabs one and holds it up. It's of us on the chaise lounge then the group picture that Phoebe made him sit in on. "And he is looking at you like he is ready to take you right there."

"Well, Jade, he didn't."

"Yeah, that would have been a bit uncomfortable for all involved," Kendall chimes in.

"You think those are hot. Check out these ones." Phoebe pulls a couple out of another envelope and lays them out, one by one.

They are all closeups of … me.

"Collin took those."

My phone messenger alert goes off, and Jade grabs it. "Who might that be?" she teases, looking at the screen. "Collin … Oh, Collin, he says—"

"Jade." I grab the phone away from her.

"If nothing's going on, I dare you to read it," she teases.

So, I do.

"Tessa, hope you're having a great time with your friends. Behave!"

"Behave?" is said by the entire group.

I type out my response. "Having a great time. Don't tell me what to do." Then I add, but don't read:

- Goodbye … Stay safe.

"Behave? Seriously, he told me to behave? He is out of his mind," I huff then turn the phone off.

They all stare quietly at me, and I laugh.

"Ladies, we are going out tomorrow night then coming back here and throwing a big old dress burning party … Behave? *Seriously!*"

Going Out

Chapter Fourteen

e sleep until noon and wake to pounding headaches. Jade grabs the OJ from the fridge and pops the cork on a bottle of champagne, and we all moan.

"Seriously have you learned nothing from the boys? This shit actually works," she says as she pours mimosas.

I decide if we're, in fact, doing this, we will be doing it with food in our bellies. So, we make toast and cut up fruit, and then we carry everything out to the patio where we sit, eat, and chat about family and work, and then about their men.

"Damn, girl." Phoebe points. "That is one sweet sign."

They all look at the sign I made and laugh.

DOE CAMP.

"Lucas and I may not be together, but *we* are. No

matter where we go, or what we do, I hope we can all remember that."

"You mean, who we do," Jade adds, and we all laugh.

"Are we ready to have a good time tonight?" Kendall yells.

We all yell back, "Hell yes!"

"Phoebe and I will be driving," Becca says as she pops a Tylenol and washes it down then adds, "I don't much care for feeling this way again tomorrow."

After we clean up and start staggering showers, I sit down on the couch next to Jessie, who hasn't said much, and I don't want her to feel excluded. "How are you feeling?"

Before she has a chance to answer, I hear, "Hello, this is Jade, Tessa's assistant and stunt double for the weekend."

"Oh, hell no." I jump up and have to chase her around the island as she continues.

"May I ask who's calling? Oh, Collin, she's right here, but if she gets all weird on you, just tell her to give the phone back to me." She winks at me. "I've been told I'm always a good time."

"You're insane," I laugh out as I grab the phone and practically run out of the house as they all laugh at Jade.

Closing the door behind me, I say, "Hello."

"Tessa, you don't sound good. Are you okay?" He seems rather bothered.

I shock myself by saying, "I'm actually very good. We're going out in a few hours. Do you know any good singles' bars in the area? With music? We want to dance tonight."

"How long have you been drinking? Tomás said you all put on quite a show last night. I think you should stay in," he all but sneers.

I bark out a laugh. "You know what? I really don't

think it's any of Tomás's business. I didn't realize he was my father. I will not be staying in. I'm going to be taking *a business trip* tonight. You know, blow off some steam." I continue, "So, you enjoy yourself, as I'm sure you have the last few nights. I'm going to be shaking my ass with my girls all over town."

I hit *end* and hear laughter coming from inside.

I turn and see them all basically pressed against the window.

Phoebe throws open the door. "Well, if you're going to be shaking your ass, Miss Tessa, we'd better get started on dolling you up. I will be in charge of hair and makeup this evening. Not sure you're in much shape to do that."

"Tomás!" Jade yells across the yard. "You've been a very bad boy. When I get home, I'm going to huff and puff and blow that door in, and then I'm going to have my way with you!"

Becca grabs her arm and pulls her inside. "For the love of God, girl—behave yourself!"

Cassidy walks over and throws an arm around me. "You're such a dick magnet."

Short dresses, tall heels, and looking good, we all pile into the minivans, and Jade and Phoebe walk around, handing out floppy cowgirl hats that they had bought for the bachelorette party.

I can't contain my laughter at the way Jessie looks at it. Then she just shrugs and puts it on her head.

By eight p.m., we pull into the first place on their list— a small seaside bar, with a DJ on the deck. We drink fruity frozen cocktails with umbrellas in them, dance like we don't care, *because we don't*. Then we were out the door and on to the next.

The next place is much the same, minus the DJ, but we don't care. We load up the Juke Box and dance, anyway.

Stepping out of the minivan, I hear Metallica, and as much as I like a good rock band, this cover trio was slaughtering the music, so we decide to hit another bar.

When we walk in and see they have karaoke, Phoebe throws her arms in the air and says, "Nailed it!"

It doesn't take half a drink before I am at the mic with Kendall and Molly, singing ABBA.

One song leads to another, and the drinks seem neverending, so we keep at it and have a blast doing so.

When nature calls, I step off stage mid-song and head to the ladies' room. When I come out, Jade grabs me and nods to the back of the bar as she says, "Hey, is that Tomás?"

I lean in to get a better look, and she laughs out, "He wants me."

When the man who looks a hell of a lot like Tomás leaves, I decide, "Next!"

And we leave.

The next place is a bit shady, *but whatever*, not like anyone knows us.

I point to a table that a woman is dancing on and say, "I call next."

Phoebe cracks up like I'm joking, and Cassidy, ever the good friend, hands me a shot.

"I'm going to be up there tonight, and you, baby belly or not, Phoebe, are coming with me." I toss back the shot and drag her to dance.

In less than thirty minutes, five of us are on the tables, which I realize, at closer inspection, are not tables at all. It's a stage, and we're dancing our foolish heads off.

A group of young men—*probably not even legal*—are gathered around us, drinking and gawking, as Jade puts on one hell of a show and all, and totally for our amusement, not theirs.

Becca scolds her, and we lose it, but we eventually climb down to give the other females waiting for a chance to be properly objectified.

When we move to dance, our admirers follow. We dance with each other and the guys. One of the cute ones gets a bit handsy, and I step back and wag a finger at him, telling him no. He is persistent but finally gives up and walks to the bar to get more drinks.

Without him in the way, I get a good look at a man, and not just any man, sitting at a table, glaring at me, arms crossed over a broad chest.

There is no way, I think as I pull Sarah closer and point to him.

"Okay, doesn't that guy look like Collin?" I snort. "I must be *so* wasted!"

"No, Tessa, that is Collin." Sarah giggles.

Our whole group turns to look and sees him staring at me.

An arm splays across my middle from behind, shocking me, and begins to grind on my ass. I turn to see No-No punk, and he grabs my hips, turns me and jacks me against him. I grab his wrists and back his ass up to the wall as I go off.

"Did I ask you to touch me?"

"Dancing up there, dressed like that, teasing me the way you did, yeah, doll, you did."

"I'm gonna share some truths with you. Feel free to spread this wisdom to your pals. I dress like this to feel good about myself. I was dancing like that because it's fun. And lastly, it was not for you, so don't you think for one—"

My words catch when another arm wraps around me, lifts me, and I am turned around, set on my feet, and hear a growl.

Sweet, sweet baby Jesus, I sigh when I am met with intense, blue, angry eyes.

"Feet fucking planted," comes through his teeth as he turns his … *white hat* around while turning toward No-No.

"No. Fuck that, man. Control that ass," No-No stupidly says.

One hand around his throat, Collin pins him to the wall, and he shoots his other arm back, fist clenched.

I react by jumping on his back, grabbing his fist, and yelling, "Collin, don't. Please don't. I already took care of it."

"Beg me," he sneers, not lowering his fist that I have palmed.

"Please don't!"

"What?" he snaps.

"I said, please don't!"

Glaring over his shoulder at me, he asks, "Are you begging?"

I nod.

"That's twice."

That's twic—

Before I have a chance to get pissed about the whole begging thing, he whips his head back around and hisses, "It's your lucky day, punk." He releases him. "Now walk and keep on walking."

Then he shrugs me off his back, turns and bends so I see angry, um nope…beyond angry, like his eyes are wide and borderline crazed. Then he picks me up and tosses me over his shoulder as I struggle stupidly because he is freaking strong. Then he turns toward the girls, who stand watching, jaws dusting the floor.

"Ladies." He nods then asks, "Who's driving?"

They point to Becca and Phoebe.

"Good. Tessa has had a long night. She'll be leaving with me."

"Am not!" I snap.

"Tomás, is the car out front?"

Tomás nods.

"Please see that these ladies get home … soon." And then we're heading to the door.

I watch their faces. Jade wags her brows. Phoebe? She may as well have pulsing cartoon hearts in place of her eyeballs. Kendall and Molly are laughing. Becca, poor Becca, looks fit to be tied, and Jessie, she's texting. And all that is well and good, but I'm pissed.

"You better let me down!"

"Not happening," he snaps back as he stomps across the gravel.

"I walk off the fucking field!" I yell, and they all bust up in hysterical laughter.

"That was a bar, so clearly, you've had enough."

He throws open the car door and tucks me inside with stealth-like quickness … or *maybe I am* that drunk. Then he shuts the door, and I attempt to open it.

"Do not," he warns, shutting it and walking around to the driver's side.

I hit the lock button.

"Tessa, open the door," he demands, and I shake my head.

Now the girls are rolling, and yes, that totally feeds my need to be a badass, *as well as entertain my girls*.

"Tessa, open the fucking door now!"

I flip him off as I yell, "Are you begging, *Collin*?"

Every emotion drains from his face, and a wall near visibly climbs. "I am going to ask you one more time to unlock the door, and then I'm going to smash the window in."

The look in his eyes tells me he's not beyond doing so, and *for the love of this car*, I hit the unlock button then turn to look out the window and blow them a kiss as he peels out.

He's not talking to me, so I'm ignoring him, too. Otherwise, I would flip the fuck out.

Music, I think and turn on his radio. It's Kenny G playing through the speakers.

"Not this shit," I huff, reaching to turn the channel.

He pushes my hand away. Control has clearly crumbled.

"You need to calm the fuck down. This may help you out a bit," he growls. "So, while I'm away, you get loaded and strip in front of my assistant? Do you think I want him looking at what I have been resisting for the past week now, Tessa?"

Ignoring him, I begin to add lyrics to the song, begin to sing along in tune with the wordless music. "*Collin's mad, and I'm drunk. That's kind of weird. I am going to throw up, if you don't pull over, dear.*"

I continue singing as he downshifts while pulling over.

As soon as he throws it into park, I jet.

Throwing open the door to Phoebe's minivan, I dive across laps and yell, "Go, go, go!"

Phoebe laughs as she hits the gas. "First time squealing the tires on our family wagon! Mark the date!" Not to miss a beat, Becca passes her, and we all laugh.

"He's behind us!" Phoebe yells. "Right on our ass!"

I look up and see the moon roof. "Open the roof!"

She does, and I stand, lifting my arms in the air, and even though his lights are nearly blinding me, it doesn't diminish my ability to see his angry eyes. And the closer he gets, the more anger I see.

I'll blame it on the booze, but he looks seriously sexy angry.

Sexy angry, or just plain angry, he has no right to be scolding me like I'm his or, more accurately, his child, so I show him that I'm not, either.

Reaching inside my dress, I unclasp my bra and pull it out through the top.

"Oh shit!" Jade cracks up, and I let it go.

It hits his windshield, and he turns on the wipers, pushing it away like it's nothing. And it is something. That's a forty-dollar freaking bra!

"Don't stop there, girl. Show him what Grandma gave you!" Kendall snorts.

"Where's Tomás?" I call down to them.

"With Becca, Molly, Sarah, and that other ho. What's her name again?" Phoebe snorts.

"Jessie." I laugh. Then, knowing they're ahead of us, I lift my dress and flash him.

"Are you crazy!" Kendall pulls me down, laughing.

"You told me, too!" I laugh back.

"Do not listen to drunk Kendall, not ever!" she barks out, laughing her fool head off.

"You better get us back to the house." Jade snort-laughs. "Or i'm going to piss the minivan!"

As soon as we pull in, Jade and Phoebe both bolt to the house, fighting over who gets the downstairs bathroom.

Kendall and I are bent over, holding our stomachs.

Kendall stops laughing and nods to the house. "Meet you, um, inside?"

I call to her, since I find myself again lifted up and being carried. "If I'm not back in five, send Jade!"

Once inside, my ass hits granite. He steps back,

creating distance, and crosses his arms over his chest … *his chest …*

I shake my head to gather my thoughts. Once gathered, I light into him.

"I had my bra on last night. I was with my girlfriends! I did not strip for anyone! And Tomás is someone who you trust enough to let stay in your home, *alone.* He didn't see my tits. I am not a whore!" I attempt to push myself off the counter, because I need to leave, because stupid emotions are rising inside of me, but he steps closer so I can't, so I continue. "You managed to make me feel like one with this shit tonight." I shove him to get him away, yet he doesn't budge. "You went away. I heard you on the phone that night on the boat. *Don't come here. I will come to you.* Let's see … *I miss you.* A business trip? Doesn't sound like business to me!"

The door swings open and, without looking to see who it is, he snaps, "We're busy."

"Sure, we'll see. Hey, Tessa, you okay?" Jade asks in a silly, cutesy voice.

"I am, Jade." I look at her then nod my head to him. "Collin, Jade. Jade, Collin."

Eyes still locked on me, he reaches his hand in her direction, and she shakes it. "Hello, Jade. Tessa and I need to finish our conversation; could you please give us the time to do so?"

I glare at him.

"Maybe, maybe not." Jade shrugs, and I look back at her. "Tessa, is this man scaring you?" she asks in a little girl voice.

"No, Jade, he isn't," I say, holding back my amusement.

"Are you afraid of him?" she asks in the same cutesy tone.

I shake my head, smiling. "No, I am not."

"Do you trust him enough for me to leave you alone with him?"

"Yes, Jade."

"Do you trust yourself not to take advantage of him." Jade giggles.

I laugh and lean over to hug her. "Yep. I have this covered. I won't hurt him, either."

"Now you two kids play nice. If either of you need me, I will be right next door, trying to seduce Tomás, who tried to keep me out of here." Jade laughs. "Nice to meet you, Collin."

I look down as she leaves and silence fills the air. Finally, I break it.

"Here's the deal. I have no reason to be getting angry at you. You owe me nothing. So, I truly just want you to stop playing games with me. I can't lie next to a man and wake up with him when there is obviously sexual tension between the two of us. I told you I'm a mess. I'm jealous as all get out at the thought of you with another woman and that's probably due to residual pain. I hate being lied to and made a fool out of, so please, I beg you, please just leave it alone. I am going to go back home next Friday. I'd be leaving sooner, but I made a commitment to an old friend. I will be out of sight, out of mind, and you can go on with your no-strings-attached way of life." Happy with what I've said, I finally look up.

"Tessa, that's three," he says abruptly. Then, before I have a chance to react to that, he says, "I was with my mother." He pulls up a stool and sits down, tossing the hat off his head and onto the counter. Then he runs a hand through his hair and looks up at me as the blood drains from my face. "I'm not lying to you." He pulls his phone out of his pocket, sets it next to me on the counter, then grabs my hips, pulling me down onto his lap.

"Collin, I think—"

"Don't think. Be informed." He grabs his phone, presses some numbers, and then holds it out as he speaks into it.

"Tomás, could you please confirm my whereabouts over the past few days?"

Tomás asks, "Sir, I'm confused as to what—"

"Just answer the question, Tomás."

"In New Jersey, assisting your mother," he states.

"Why?" Collin asks.

"Sir, is there something wrong?"

"No. Answer the question."

"You were assisting her in getting settled after a fire caused her to move."

"Thank you, Tomás. That's all for tonight. How are things going over there?"

He pulls the phone to his ear, and I feel the tears building.

"Yes, she's tenacious. Remain professional."

He then flips the phone closed and looks at me. "I've not given you reason to question me."

"I just—"

"You've been hurt. I understand that. But I will not hurt you. I know this may be hard to comprehend and may take some sort of trust building exercises or just time, but I'm here for either, or both, or—"

"I've known you for—"

"A week and two days, Tessa." He closes his eyes and sighs. "But longer, and we both know that, as well." He opens them and gives them to me. "There's something here. I'm not walking away from the discovery, regardless of if your past slows it or makes it even more difficult than tonight. I'm here. I need to know."

I look down and admit, "In one week, you've made me

almost completely forget about the hurt of the past five years of my life. It scares me. My heart says yes; my head says no. You don't owe me anything. Do you understand that? Not one thing."

Collin grabs his phone and dials it. Again, he holds it out so that I am privy to the conversation.

A woman answers. "Sea Brook House Rehabilitation Center, how may I help you?"

"This is Mr. Abraham. How is my mother doing?"

"One moment please, Mr. Abraham."

"You do not have to—"

He puts his finger over my lips.

"Collin, this is Jim. Is everything all right? You left today and seemed very tense?" the man asks.

"Everything is fine now, Jim. How is my mother?"

"She's good. Sleeping now. I think it was a good step for both of you—you being here to see her and help her through the first few days of detox, a good move. Will you be back next week?" he asks.

"I will call back in a couple days with my decision. Thanks, Jim." Collin hangs up and sets the phone down then looks at me. "Do you believe me now?"

Tears fall as I nod.

"Then maybe it's your heart you need to listen to and keep your head out of it." He grips the back of my head and pulls it to his shoulder.

I lift it up, take his face in my hands, and kiss him. With his tongue, he asks for my mouth, and I give it to him willingly.

When I deepen it, he pulls back, breaks our kiss, and takes my face in his hands. "Tessa, you have a feisty group next door who need to know you're okay. I've acted like a Neanderthal in front of them and think we should go over there and let them see that you're okay."

He lifts me up, moves the chair back and stands, while I stand on my own two feet, knees shaky, trying desperately to listen to a heart that's beating too fast to understand.

He adjusts himself. "Go ahead. I'll meet you there in a moment."

"Well, look, there's our little Tessa." Jade smiles as I walk in and close the door behind me. "Should we call an ambulance or is he going to be all right?"

"He's fine. He'll be over in a few minutes. I'm going to go change."

As I'm leaving the room, I hear Jade say, "Wow, Tomás, what did your boss do to her?"

"I am not sure, ma'am, but I see she is fine," Tomás says as I ascend the stairs, giggling.

I change into pajama pants, a tank, and throw on an old, tan, wool cardigan that I found in one of the bins the day I was busy looking for tools to get some work done, a bin I knew I didn't have the mental capacity to look through but didn't have the willpower to leave that sweater behind. It's an Ann classic. I then brush out my hair and put it up in a messy bun, then wash the makeup from my face.

When I get downstairs, I see him standing, hip to counter, arms crossed, one hand loosely holding a beer. He's in dark jeans and a long-sleeved, heather gray tee-shirt.

"So, Collin, how long have you known Tessa?" Jessie asks.

"Just met last week," he answers and flashes a killer smile, one that makes him hot as hell and not in the intense way that weakens my knees due mostly because of his intensity. This smile, a laidback, panty-soaking, frat boy smile.

What in the actual hell?

"Sort of," I say, making my presence known, because I am not losing his attention to Jessie, not like I did Lucas's. And yes, that is juvenile, *but whatever*. I stand beside him and tell them—well, mostly Jade since the others already know, "This is Ann's Joe."

Her eyes widen and gone is the flirty, I-never-get-out-of-the-house minx that Jade came here as.

He turns and smiles at me as he pulls himself up to sit on the counter, spreads his legs wide, and pats the spot between them.

It may be way too much way too soon—okay, it definitely is way too much way too soon—but again, *whatever*.

"So, Collin, are you married, divorced, have any children?" Jade begins the questioning.

"No, none of the above." He lifts his beer to his lips.

"Do you go to church?" Becca continues the Collin interrogation.

"No, not recently. I did as a child," he answers. "Just been really busy the past few years."

"What do you do for a living?" Sarah chimes in.

"I'm a doctor, licensed MD, but recently, I have been working in the research and development field."

MD … that's kind of, sort of … Well, it is news.

Molly's jaw drops. "How old are you?"

"I'm twenty-eight," Collin answers, setting the beer down and wrapping his arm across my shoulders, pulling me closer.

"No shit?" All of them—well, except Becca—ask in quiet shock … maybe in awe.

I turn my head and look back at him. "Anytime you want this to stop, let me know."

"I think I'll be all right." He pulls me back even closer so my back is snug against his chest.

"So, when was the first time you wanted to tear Tessa's clothes off and do her?" Jade asks.

"When she opened the door and smiled at me last week," Collin answers without hesitation.

"So, when did you two first *do it?*" Jade pushes.

"Hasn't happened. Sorry to disappoint ... Jade, right?"

She nods.

"But when we, as two consenting, *sober* adults, make that decision, I'm sure you'll know." He winks at her.

There he is ... the haughty Collin has now shown up to play.

"Will you videotape it for me?" she asks.

"Not my thing," he retorts then picks his beer up and finishes it.

Kendall quickly hands him another. "What is your thing?"

"Tessa is my thing, but not until she's ready," he answers.

And I'm sure my jaw just hit the floor.

After I have regained the wind that was knocked out of me, I look at Jade. "Okay, let's change the subject. Have you all introduced yourself to Collin?"

My sisters chime in with, "We have."

He smiles at them. "Molly, Cory's wife and mother to the beautiful Sydney. Kendall, future world traveler, José is your guy, right?"

She nods.

"Sarah, Jake's girlfriend? Or not this week?"

We all laugh.

He turns and smiles at Phoebe. "And Phoebe, Alex's wife. How am I doing so far?"

They all smile.

"I'm Becca, wife of our youth minister, Joshua," she introduces herself.

"I'm Jessie, friend," Jessie says.

"I'm Jade, cousin, and married to Ryan. I'm a therapist and a mother of three." Jade bows.

"Nice to meet you all," he says. "I should apologize about earlier."

"No need," Phoebe gushes.

Dear God, I laugh to myself.

I push away from the counter and announce, "Time for that bonfire, ladies."

He puts the wood in the fire-pit then starts the fire before walking up to me, grabbing my shoulder like a bro as he walks past me but pauses long enough to kiss the top of my head, and then he walks next door, and Leia follows.

Then we do it. We throw the dresses into the fire, and it's a moment I was sure would be emotional, painful, and I was sure I would cry.

None of those things are felt. I don't cry.

Phoebe takes my hand and squeezes it as I stare at the fire feeling ... peace. I squeeze hers back then turn from the flames and look at her.

"*Peace*. I feel peace."

"Good, because Collin," she smiles so big as she says. "He gives me Alex vibes."

"Oh God." I laugh.

"Not a visual she wants when they get busy," Jade scolds her.

Everyone laughs, and then Kendall begins handing out champagne flutes, ones I ordered for the big day.

Once everyone has theirs, I lift my glass. "To friendships that last through each chapter."

After that, things get quiet, and when Leia comes bounding through the gate, Collin following her, goodnights are said and everyone heads inside, except Jade and Jessie, who pour out pictures that they had developed from last night.

When our eyes meet, his begin searching mine. He doesn't have to do it for long. He nods once and visibly relaxes as he walks to me, sitting beside me at the table where the pictures are splayed out.

Jade holds one of me in my dress up. "What do you think?"

"She looked beautiful in her dress." He strokes my hair.

They keep looking through the pictures as I gave Leia some love.

"Collin, these are the ones you took," Jade teases.

"Oh, I don't think those were mine, but whoever took them seems to have a real *thing* for Tessa." He kisses the top of my head like it's natural to do so.

"Move by the fire?" Jade asks. "It's getting cold."

So, we head that way. Collin sits on the double chaise, spreads his legs wide, and pats the spot between them.

I sit and he grips the side of my head, pulling it against him. I curl up into his warmth, wrap my arms around his thick middle, and settle in to let his heart lull me to further peace.

When I wake, I do with rain falling down on us and realize it is just us—him and I.

We hurry inside where I rush to the bathroom to grab a couple of towels and toss him one. He throws it over his shoulders then opens the Tylenol, dumps two in his hand, and hands them to me. Then he dumps two in his hand while I grab two cups from the cupboard and fill them with water.

Before tossing the pills in my mouth, I hold my glass out. "I'm sorry, Collin."

He taps mine. "Don't be. I get it. The fact that you have been hurt, I get it. But I need you to do something for you."

I toss back the Tylenol, drink it down, and nod.

"First, listen to your heart. Second, know I will never intentionally hurt you. Third, don't try to make me jealous. Fourth, never lie to me. And last, never try to make me jealous."

"You said that twice."

He narrows his eyes. "And I mean that. I never knew what that was until you." He throws back the pills in his hand, drinks it down, and then sets the cup on the counter. Then he takes my face, kisses my cheek, then the top of my head, and steps back. "I'm going home now. I need to sleep, and so do you."

"I don't want you to leave. I want you to stay." Tears form in my eyes, and I want to kick myself. "I need you to stay."

"Tessa, don't do that. You have friends here, family. I interrupted your night. I shared you tonight, but not again." He presses his lips to mine quickly then turns and walks out the door.

As I am seriously staring at his butt, and it is incredible, he turns and says, "Lock this behind me."

T he next morning, I wake feeling better than I should and decide to start my day with a run.

When I get downstairs, they are all in the kitchen, talking, and when they see me, they all stop. Knowing I'm about get a million questions that I am not ready to answer, I hurriedly walk to the door and shove my feet in my sneakers, saying, "Good morning, ladies. Anyone want to go for a run?"

They all just smile.

"So, is that a no?" I laugh. "Okay, I'll be back soon."

After my five miles, I return.

When I walk in, the counter is covered with breakfast foods.

"You hungry?" Phoebe smiles sweetly.

"Yes, I'm starving. This looks great. I'll do dishes." I grab a plate and pile it up then head out to the patio. They all follow suit.

And then, *quiet*.

"Is everyone hungover? Why are you all so freakishly quiet?" I laugh.

"Just wondering how last night went," Phoebe asks.

"We got drunk, had a blast, Collin showed up a little upset," I joke, and no one laughs. *Tough crowd.* "He and I talked, everything is fine, you all questioned him, and I think he passed. We fell asleep, got poured on, came inside to dry, he left, and I went to bed. The end." I down my glass of orange juice.

"That's all?" Jade asks.

"Yes, that's all. Sorry." I nod. "What do you guys want to do today?"

"The hottie neighbor came over this morning and asked us if we wanted to go whale watching. We said we would have to ask you. Can we please go? Please, please, please?" Jade begs.

Molly adds, "Oh, and Phoebe is really tired, I miss Sydney, and Jessie has some stuff to do, so we're thinking about leaving after breakfast. Will you be okay with that?"

"Yeah. I had a great weekend. Today should be pretty relaxing. I don't want you to feel like you have to stay. Go, really. It's no big deal. Are you rested enough to drive?"

"We'll be fine, Tessa, as long as you're okay." Molly begins to tear up.

I laugh. "Molly, I'm great! Sitting here in our families' beach house with friends and family, and the view is great."

She smiles.

"I truly am better than I have been in years."

We finish breakfast, and then they start to pack.

When I walk out to wave them off, Collin is outside, helping load the van. He hugs Molly and Phoebe and nods to Jessie as she gets in the car then waves as they drive away.

He turns to me. "How was your run?"

"Quite boring. You should have come with. I would love to actually run with you one of these days before I head back."

He frowns, and I playfully shove him.

"You've run with my dog, so you owe me."

"I need to talk to you about something. Would you come over for a few minutes?"

"Sure. Just let me tell the girls."

He takes my hand. "Already did."

I look over my shoulder and see them all lined up, waving for me to go.

Chapter Fifteen

e walk into the house, and he leads me to the couch. I sit, and he squats in front of me, taking my hands.

"I'm going to tell you something that may upset you. I myself am upset by it. And I'm pissed off that—"

"Please just tell me. Whatever it is, I know I have done to myself," I interrupt him.

Collin rolls his eyes. "It's nothing to do with me and you, Tessa, all right? Just listen."

I nod.

"Last night, when I left your place, I opened my bedroom window—it's ten feet from your back porch— and Jessie was arguing with someone. She said the name Lucas several times, so I walked to the window. I only heard one part of the conversation, so I wasn't sure what was going on. When things got *mushy*, I walked out my back deck, and she saw me. She got off the phone pretty quickly." My stomach twists as he continues, "I called her over, and she came without hesitation. I asked her to tell me what was going on. She started crying—it was forced—and said she and your ex were together and have been since you two split."

Numb.

"Said she didn't mean for it to happen. She was looking for sympathy that she would not be receiving from me. I asked her why she bothered coming, and she said she didn't know and cried more."

Pissed.

"I told her I think it best if she left in the morning. So, this morning, I heard them all in the kitchen. Saw her on the back deck, went over, and asked her if she planned to tell them, and she did. Your sisters decided that it would be best if she left, partly because they wanted to kill her and partly because Jade attempted to go after her. Are you with me?" he asks, and I nod.

"So, your sister got on a page called Six Degrees and checked out his page? I don't know much about it, but his page stated he was in a relationship with her. There were graduation pictures—of your graduation, I'm assuming—and he was kissing her neck? Tessa, again … this is way out of my league—this whole relationship thing—but I need you to tell me if this is too much or at the very least what I can do to make this better for you, because what I really wanted to do is let Jade loose on her, and that is not me."

I sit there silently for a few minutes, and he stands and waits for my response. Once I process it, I realize I have, again, not listened to my gut, *God's voice*, when I knew something was off.

I will not make that mistake again.

I finally take a deep breath and smile. "Do you know I was supposed to marry him today?"

He nods firmly once, and I laugh.

"Wow, I'm so glad I called it off."

He asks if I need a few minutes alone, and I assure him that I've wasted enough energy on Lucas and this subject. Then I stand, and so does he. I hug him, step back, take his hand, and we walk back to Ann's place.

When we walk into the kitchen, they all stand somberly, and I can't help but laugh. They look at me, then Jade, and then back at me.

It isn't lost on either Jade or I that this is happening.

"Oh, fuck him!" Jade snaps then starts laughing and hugs me. "And a little fuck you, too."

"Me?" I laugh harder now.

"You don't have to continue dancing around my stupid sense of loyalty because he was Tommy's best friend, or his father is Ryan's boss, or—"

"We are Luke's godparents and will act accordingly."

"You will. He'll still be Lucas," she huffs.

"He and I will be friends always, even with all that. And we'll all love him, anyway." I step back and look at her. "I didn't stay with him because of that, Jade. It just happens to be part of my life." I laugh and add, "My journey."

I slide my gaze at Collin, who looks completely bewildered, and start to laugh again.

"And the laughing bit … also somewhat normal." Kendall chuckles.

Jade literally pushes me toward Collin, and I attempt to explain, "I'm not sad. I'm disgusted that she came here. I don't get it, but honestly, I don't care, and that's a good thing."

Jade reboards the angry train. "I told you a year ago I

didn't trust her. Dirty-ass, used-up bitch." She pushes out a laugh. "I wonder what that car ride home must be like. Thank God for Becca, or she would be screwed. Never seen Molly so pissed."

I clap my hands. "Let's not waste this beautiful day. Don't we have a boat to catch?"

I hop in the shower to wash off the run, dress quickly, and then meet them outside.

Watching Collin load the cooler in the back of a minivan, it does something to me. Instead of overthinking it, wondering what that little wave—that heart-gasm—means, I just decide to roll with the tide.

As I approach, he looks back, and Kendall whistles to gain his attention then throws him the keys. "You're driving a minivan today, and I call shotgun."

As soon as we load up, Kendall pops a CD into the player and hits *play*.

"*Dearly beloved, we are gathered here today to get this thing called life*," rolls through the speakers. And the five of us—Kendall, Jade, Cassidy, Sarah, and I—join in.

"*Electric world life. It means forever, and that's a mighty long time, but I'm here to tell you there's something else—the afterworld*."

As we sing and car dance, I see his lips turn up just a bit, and God how I love that smirk.

Walking down the dock, toward the boat, my phone rings in my bag. I dig it out and answer.

"Tessa, how are you?" Molly asks.

"Honestly, I'm fine. Are you okay?"

"Aside from being stuck in the minivan for the next five hours with someone whose sanity is questionable, yeah great. But are you truly?"

"We laid it all to rest." I laugh.

She laughs, too. "Oh my God, did Kendall find her perfect opportunity to play—"

"Prince? Yeah, she did." I laugh, and then, because Molly is the more serious heart, I give her a bit of serious. "It's a sad, kind of funny … for them, not me. I want him to be happy. Good Lord, I even want her to be happy. I just wish it wasn't so … dirty, you know? I want to know why she came here."

"I can ask her," Molly snaps.

"No, don't. But please let her know I forgive her. He wasn't my husband. He was a live-in. Not the way it's supposed to be, and that's probably why it didn't work out. I love you, Molly. Thanks for taking her home. Jade may have done unspeakable things to her had you not." I laugh. "You and Phoebe drive safe and kiss my niece for me."

"Love you, Tessa Ann. Speak soon."

"Love you back, Molly. Call when you get home, okay?"

"Of course."

When I shove the phone back in my bag, someone takes my hand. That someone is Collin.

"You good?"

"I'm more than good. I'm back to perfect."

"She will be fine. One of her BFFs is a shrink. If that doesn't work, there's always this." Jade holds up a bottle of wine. "And if both of those fail, I have a sneaking suspicion that …" She stops and takes my hand, pulling it behind him and setting it on his ass. She then laughs and falls back with the others.

Collin chuckles. "She is a treat."

"We've been through a lot together." Understatement of the millennium.

We walk onto the boat, and Captain Stone greets us. I smile apologetically, and he chuckles as we walk by.

After getting us situated, and again vesting me up, Collin leaves us to it and joins Captain Stone.

"What's with him?" Sarah asks, sitting beside me.

"Emotional overload," Jade replies. "Not all men are like our guys."

"That's because they weren't raised with us," Kendall says as she begins filling the plastic cups with wine.

I look back at him and smile, and he dips his chin once.

"He's different." And he is.

I sit quietly as they all overthink my statement, but I don't. I take it at face value, recalling the night on the patio when he revealed his family life and opened his heart to me. Unlike most people, including me at the present time, he doesn't wallow in his misgivings; he made a decision to not become a victim of the cycle that people tend to fall into. He studied his ass off and made a good life for himself.

"He's kind of amazing," I say as I stand, leaving them to overanalyze that. I walk back to him, throw my arms around his thick center, and snuggle into him.

He runs his hand up my back, under my hair, splays it across the back of my head, and moves it to rest over his heart—*my favorite lullaby*—and I have to remind myself not to overthink the thought that just popped into my head.

Lips to the top of my head, he asks, "How are you doing? You girls having fun?"

"We are. Thank you so much for doing this for us."

"For you, Tessa. I'm doing it for you." He kisses the top of my head again.

"You know they come with me, right?" I ask stupidly and regret it, but hey, there it is.

"Get that."

He hugs me and nods for me to look. When I turn, I see them all with the same heart eyes that Phoebe had, and then Jade giggles and makes an inappropriate hand gesture with one finger, pointing, and the other hand in the shape of an *O*.

"Not yet," he says loud enough that only I hear it, and I look back up to him.

A challenge …

I take his face in my hands, push up on my toes, and plant one on him. After it gets a little deep, he pulls back.

"How much have you had to drink today?" he asks with sincere concern in his voice.

"Two. Why?"

"You are a little more *free*. I'll admit, it's been a struggle to keep this the way you wanted it based on a conversation we had a few days ago, and others I've observed. I'm not sure how long I can keep that up when you kiss me like that."

"Are you trying to protect my virtue, Collin, or trying to win a bet?"

"What do you think?" he asks. He then turns me around, puts his arms around my center, and whispers, "Answer with your heart and not your head."

I look up at him, push his shades up, and gaze into his eyes. Everything he's done and said screams from them in truth, and behind that truth, their beauty, lies a question: *What has she done to me?*

He kisses my cheek. "Go. Have this day with them."

"Thank you for everything."

"It's been my pleasure."

Chapter Sixteen

Collin

"*H*ey." Kendall, Tessa's younger sister, stands beside me. "I know Tessa is an adult and can make all her own decisions, but please don't play with her heart. She deserves happy."

"Me, too, Kendall, me, too."

"Besides, if you hurt her, I will not be able to control what Alex and Jake may do to you."

I give her my word. "I won't, I promise you. The ball is completely in her court."

She looks at me and nods, but before she heads back to the whale watching/dance party, she says, "I have a good feeling about you, Collin."

For the next few hours, I watch her interact with

those she loves, and my feelings intensify. The depth of care they have for one another, I've had little experience with, but once I pulled myself from the depths of despair, I was focused on making and obtaining goals. I have avoided this feeling, this ... deeper desire and want, as not to be distracted from those goal. To not be hurt again.

Until her.

When a song by Rick Springfield begins and Kendall stands, holding a wine bottle like a microphone, the captive audience watches as she begins the whole song, changing the words thing that they all seem to enjoy.

"*Jessie is a pig. Yes, she's always been a little unkind. Lately, something's changed, and it's hard to define, why that little skanky pig wants to eat the poo I've left behind.*"

They all fall into a fit of laughter, and Kendall quickly hands the makeshift mic to Tessa.

"Yeah, she was squeezing him with those thighs, and she's lovin' him with that snotty, I just know it, and he's holding his bowl every stinkin' night, yeah. I'm glad that I'm not Lucas's girl. I'm glad that I'm not Lucas's girl. Now can I get a hell yeah right now!"

They all start dancing and playing 'air' instruments. It's ridiculous yet funny and kind of interesting to see them laugh at a situation many would sit crying over.

When the song ends, she sees me watching and raises her glass. I raise my bottle of water, shake it side to side, and she giggles.

"Should we anchor here?" Stone asks as he points to the pod of whales ahead.

I nod. "Perfect."

They stand and watch, gushing over the gentle giants as they swim, dive, and surface long enough that the birds land on their massive bodies and heads to rest. Then they clap in excitement when a pod of dolphins—highly social creatures—show off and play in front of them

I am more entranced with watching her eyes dancing before she bends over the side of the boat, Kendall gripping her to keep her from toppling over the side, and she's able to pat the top of ones head. She seems so happy, unbroken, off guarded right now, and I swear she looks more and more beautiful each day.

When I think of leaving her, it's always accompanied with a pain in my chest. Three weeks from now, I will be leaving for a month, something I have done time and again, and right now, I can't bear the thought of it.

I shake away the thought and live in the moment, like the creatures in the ocean swimming before me are.

When the sun starts to set, I head down into the galley and carry up the steamer, and Stone grabs the coolers that he had prepared, at my request. When they all go to change into warmer attire to protect them from the night air that chills them after being in the sun all day, I start the steamer in preparation to feed them king crab, shrimp, and clams. Fresh seafood, my favorite.

Stone pulls up the anchor, and we edge toward shore.

When the food is done, I pull up the basket of food, dumping it into a large, stainless pale, and beside it, I set plates and cups of melted butter. Then I sit for the first time all day and watch them fill their plates.

Tessa walks over with a heaping plate, crab legs damn near falling off the sides. She sits on her knees beside me, and we feed one another.

When the girls finish, they set to cleaning up, even though I've offered, and Tessa takes that opportunity to feed me more. But it's different now that we are alone.

She smiles as she dips crab meat into the butter then places it in my mouth, her fingers caressing my lips with every bite I take. She leans into me and licks the butter off my bottom lip, and I close my eyes, attempting to stay rooted and not take what she's truly offering me. *Not yet.*

When I've had enough, I grab my bottle of water and drink some to cleanse my mouth as she straddles me.

I toss the empty bottle aside, take her face, and kiss her the way she's begging to be kissed—deep and hard. Cock stiffening, she begins moving her hips just enough to tell me she's feeling me, and when I groan, she takes it as encouragement to sway a bit more. I tear my lips from hers and still her hips. However, she just tangles her fingers with mine and kisses down my cheek then my neck.

"Tessa, you're slaughtering me." I lift her up and deposit her beside me. Then I stand, reach down my shorts, and adjust myself. Knees slightly bent, I rest my hands on them and take several deep, calming breaths and hear the others coming up the stairs, so I head to the back of the boat.

Once calmed down, I grab a bottle of water, walk back to where they are gathered, remove the wine glass from her hand, and replace it with the water. "Drink this." Then I turn and walk away.

"What was that all about, Tessa?" Jade teases her. "Is he playing daddy?"

Tessa says nothing, but Jade seems to know her pretty damn well.

"Oh, I see … When the girls were away, my little drunken Tessa wanted to play."

A rriving back home, it's more than clear that everyone else is half past tipsy. Everyone except myself and Tessa, who finally lost her buzz.

Once the minivan is unpacked, I take Leia for a short walk before heading back to the house, where Tessa has her food ready.

The girls disappear to get ready for bed and begin to pack for their trip home tomorrow. And finally, we're alone.

She tries hard to avoid eye contact, and I assume it's because she's embarrassed about earlier. I need to clear the air about a few things before heading back to my place and again jerking off in a cold shower.

As she walks past me again, I take her hand and turn her to face me. "What's wrong?"

"Nothing," she says softly and walks by.

I release her hand, grip her waist, and carry her out to the patio, her back to me, hands on my wrists.

I walk to the table, set her down on her feet, and press my hand between her shoulders, pushing her forward slightly. "I want you like this." Then I wrap my arm around her, pull her up, lift her, and toss her gently on the lounge before grabbing her ankles and lifting them to my shoulders. "I want you like this."

Dazed, but certainly no longer confused, her eyes get even bigger than before.

I drop her legs and lay between them, pressing against her as I take her sweet, hot mouth with mine then abruptly pull away. "I want you like this." Pushing myself up, I then take her hands as I step back and sit on one of the other chairs. Giving her hand a firm yank, I pull her to sit on my lap. "I want you like this." Then I quickly turn her so her back is to my chest, hand splayed on her trim waist, pulling her against me, back to my chest. "I want you like this."

"Collin," she whispers, and ... *fuck, fuck, fuck.*

I pick her up, stalk to the table, deposit her ass on it, take her neck gently with my hand, and guide her back until she rests on her elbows, looking at me, heat in her eyes that I am sure mirrors mine. I grip her thighs, spread her legs, and stand between them. "And like this."

I pull her up, and then I bow down as I grip her hips, kiss her belly, and run my tongue across the skin that's exposed, and under her waistband. "I'm going out of my mind thinking about how good this is going to be." I kiss down her hip, her thigh, and trace the path with my tongue and lips.

She grips my hair and moans, back arching, knees tightening.

I take her hands from my hair and stand, leaning in and kissing her hard again before saying, "Goodnight, Tessa." I turn and see them descending the stairs and call in, "Goodnight, ladies."

I take my time climbing my deck stairs and eavesdrop on their conversation.

"Wow, Tessa, what the hell is going on?" Jade asks, holding back a laugh. "Have you been Tessa the tease?"

Yes, she has, but she now understands more fully what teasing does to me.

"Looks like he is wound pretty tight, girl. And look at your eyes. Tessa, did you O yourself fully cloth—?"

"Shut up, Jade," she answers breathlessly.

"Wow, he really is the shit, huh?" Jade laughs.

Tessa stands and walks inside with a quipped, "Goodnight."

Sweet dreams, beautiful, I laugh to myself.

Lord Help Me

Chapter Seventeen

$\mathcal{I}$ wake feeling like a million bucks, and I undeniably have no right to that. I sit, stretch, and then roll to my side and nearly jump out of my skin when I see five sets of eyes looking at me.

"Shit," I grumble and flop back. "I'm still asleep."

"*Riiiight*, then start sleep talking. And start at the part about the O-face you had last night," Jade insists. "I couldn't sleep just thinking about it."

Yep, busted, I think as I shove out of bed and head down-stairs to get a glass of water, telling her, "You have got two questions, make them count."

She fires off question one as she, followed by Kendall,

Cassidy, Sarah, and Becca, follow me down the stairs. "Did you have sex?"

"Nope," I answer honestly.

"Did you orgasm?" Jade asks in disbelief.

I bypass the kitchen, head to the bathroom, and decide to pee first while answering, completely confused myself yet also honest. "For about twenty minutes after he left and that was two."

As I'm peeing, the door flies open, and Jade walks in. I hold a handful of toilet paper up and stop her. "That was two."

"No way, girl. Not fair. Did he touch your bits? Your clothes were on! I'm so confused?" Jade is in utter shock, followed by Kendall, and Cass. *I imagine Becca is completely mortified.*

"All right, this is going to be quick, and then we will promise not to talk about it again, right?"

They all nod their heads yes.

"Every time I drink, I come on to him. A crutch? Bad habit? *Really bad habit.* Totally never drinking again. Well, probably." I shake my head, motion for them to turn so I can wipe with a little privacy, and when they do, I continue, "He told me one of the first nights we met that I would be begging for him before he had sex with me. It's a little foggy, but I think he said five times, and we're at about a three. Pissed me off." I wipe, flush, and then walk to the sink to wash my hands. "I told him that he would be on his knees before God and my family before he would ever get what I had to offer. Well, I don't know if he is trying to win a bet, or wants me sober, or is trying to be respectful, or something. Anyway, last night, I was drunk and … well, you know nothing has happened *yet again.* When we got back here, long story short, he showed me where and how he wanted me, and then he licked my belly, just beneath my waistband, and just the thought of him gave me"—I pause and look up at them from the towel I am drying my hands with—"tingles, pulses … everywhere."

They look at me disbelievingly.

I explain, "I swear to you, no hands, no heavy petting, no grinding; just the thought of him is all it took." I sigh, and they all follow suit. Then I nod and state, "End of discussion," walking past them, prepared to face Becca.

"Holy shit," I mutter under my breath when I see Collin standing there, holding a huge tray with breakfast foods on it for all of us, biting the inside of his cheek and trying not to smile.

He clears his throat then heads to the island to set it down. "Good morning, Tessa. Good morning, ladies."

"Good morning, Collin," they all croon.

Jade looks around. "Doesn't that damn dog bark anymore? Where is Becca?"

"Not sure where Becca is, but Leia clearly likes him more than she likes me." I glare at Leia, who is at his heels.

"Not gonna lie"—Jade sighs exaggeratedly—"I think I might, too."

Everyone, including Collin and I, laugh.

I look at him. "How much did you hear?"

"Probably more than you wanted me to." He kisses my cheek then answers a question not intended for them to even hear, "I was protecting her virtue."

They all laugh as he walks away, grabs Leia's leash, and heads out.

As we sit to eat pastries, I notice Jade looking at me happily. I smile, and she gets misty-eyed.

"Yesterday was supposed to be *the happiest day of your life*, and I think it was. You look happier than I've seen you in years. He is amazing, so amazing that you lose yourself in just the thought of him. That's pretty special, Tessa. Like Ryan special." A tear falls from her eye, and she bats it away with an annoyed huff. "And besides, if you had married that Lucas, there's no way you would have had an orgasm like that on your wedding night."

Definitely not like that.

I hug her. "Touchless O or not, I am happy, Jade, but Collin isn't the cause. I choose to be."

After eating, I help them pack up, hugs are given, and see you soons are said.

I stand at the back porch and wave until they are out of sight. When I walk in, Leia is back. I sit on the couch to process all of it, *except the spontaneous O.*

I knew that Lucas and I would have never worked, and I feel an unexplainable peace with the whole Jessie situation. If I stepped aside from the hurt he caused me, and himself, I could easily look at Lucas and see a good man, a loyal friend, good-looking—okay, great-looking—hard-working, and driven, but his ability to be emotionally unattached to the person he professes to have loved for five years, unacceptable.

When the glass door behind me opens, I look back as Collin walks in.

One look at me, and he asks, "Are you all right?"

"I am." I look away and continue, "I don't think I can ever make eye contact with you after you heard me tell them … *all that.* But I will be fine." I smile and look down.

He walks over, squats in front of me, lifts my chin, and says. "Just so you know, it was not news to me. I knew exactly what happened last night. I could see it in those beautiful eyes and felt it in that hot, sexy body of yours." He kisses directly left of my cheek then stands and walks to the kitchen. Without thinking, I follow him.

Looking out the window, he drags his hand through his

hair before turning, lifting me up, and depositing me on the counter. Then, with narrowed and serious eyes, he tells me, "This is what's going to happen. We are going for a run, a long, hard run together, which is going to kick both of our asses. Then we will get showered and dressed for lunch. We will go to a very public place to eat. When we get home, it should be about two. We are going to take an afternoon nap. When we wake, it'll be between three and four. I'm leaving at five to fly down and see my mother; her doctor called and suggested it. You will hang out and rest, and I'll be home tomorrow night by seven. Then I will take you out to dinner. The next day, we are going to run hard again. I may have my trainer come over, and you can learn how to box—one of my favorite releases. And that is how we are going to suppress this attraction or, at very least, slow the burn, understood?"

"Only one problem. I'm volunteering at the church in town. I'm going to help at their evening Bible school program this week."

While he looks confused and a bit dazed, I hop off the counter, skate past him, walk back into the living room, and sit back on the couch.

He's not dazed for long, because before my ass is fully seated, he is next to me, pulling me closer. Then he takes a couple minutes to ask, "All right, when is it?"

"Sunday through Thursday from six to eight p.m. I will be there from five thirty until eight thirty, and at their Thursday service, they present a little skit for the congregation."

He nods, face unreadable, and asks, "Okay, why? What brought this on?"

Pulling my knees to my chest, I answer, "Meant a lot to me when I was young. I've done this at my church at home, and I enjoy it a great deal." I shrug. "It makes me happy."

"Did your ex go with you?" he asks.

"Sometimes he went to church, but in the end, he said that was my thing, and I left it at that," I answer honestly. "I hoped it would be his thing someday, but it wasn't."

He studies my face a bit then nods. "It's important to you, isn't it?"

"I was raised believing. I never stopped. I turned my back, manipulated my beliefs so I didn't feel like it was wrong." He says nothing, so I continue, "You know, you go through life thinking you know what's best and working to get what you want or think you want, but if it's not God's plan, it's not going to work. I spent five years working for something that started all wrong. Pleasing him and giving myself to him, every part of myself, it didn't work. I'm grateful that I returned to church. Had I not, I wouldn't have had the strength to walk away. I would have married him, maybe had a child, and it would have eventually ended, and been ugly. No child deserves ugly." I think of Lucas, of Collin, but I don't say anything. "If I had listened …" I shake my head.

"To instincts? To God?" he asks.

"I think your gut instinct is God's voice. To me, they're one in the same. Sorry, that's kind of a heavy conversation, isn't it?"

"Yes, it is," he agrees.

"And I feel like such a hypocrite acting the way I have been—drinking and allowing myself to basically go after you. I haven't been true to what I believe or want."

He sits quietly for a long time, looking at the floor, and I feel he needs that, so I sit quietly myself.

When he finally looks at me, I do not like the—for the lack of better word—blankness in his eyes, or the stiffness in his body.

When he stands, he does so abruptly that something inside changes.

"I feel like I'm hindering your desire to be who you want to be. I don't want that to be the case."

My stomach has felt good and bad butterflies, uncountable amounts of times, but it has never dropped so quickly, so suddenly, so … shockingly.

What have I done?

"Are you all right?" he asks, and instead of reaching for me, like I know he wants to, he shoves his hands into his pockets. *Ouch.* "You're shaking."

"No, I'm not all right. I feel sick to my stomach, and my head is spinning." I stand and head out the door, and I whisper my admittance, "I'm terrified that I have just pushed you away."

I walk the beach, secretly hoping he'll come after me and hating I am being that girl, but what I hate more is the fact that I know he won't. Couple that with my wanting to do exactly what I said—get back to me—I continue walking for a really long time, long enough that, when I return, he's gone, and I do it knowing he would be.

Immediately, I head up the stairs and crawl into bed. Leia lies at the foot of it, and she does not lick away the tears like Chewy did. I swear on everything that she scowls at me.

When I hear her bark, I wake up and walk down the stairs. Collin is standing on the patio, sunglasses covering his eyes.

He wastes no time in speaking when I open the door, and he does so in a detached, clipped manner.

"I'm leaving. Tomás will be looking after my house. If you need anything, let him know." His tone is cold, words clipped, and demeanor all business-like, and it continues just like that when he says, "And thank you for the work you did on my deck." Then he turns to walk away.

Without thought, I call after him, "Wait, Collin, fly safe."

Collin stops, turns back, looks at me as I hug myself tightly, and he lifts he chin. Then he turns back around, and he … walks away.

No way will I let myself fall victim of my own self-inflicted sickness. My heart was tricked, and no, it wasn't all Lucas Links doing. It was mine, too. I allowed my weakness to be misconstrued as sickness, and that will not happen, *not again.*

I pull myself up by the figurative bootstraps and march myself inside. I dig through the fridge, make myself a meal of leftovers, set them on the counter, crank up some music, and make a plate.

I am going to fuel up, head to church, and give help for those kids.

Walking into the church, I notice a lot has changed over the past few years. It seems bigger, which is odd because, as children, things always appear bigger, not the opposite. I immediately spot Pastor Lou as he walks toward me with a warm and loving smile on his face.

"Hello, Tessa. I need a favor. Could I ask you to do something different tonight than we planned?"

I nod.

"Our musical director has the flu; could you do the singalong with the kids?"

"As long as you don't expect miracles, I'd be happy to do that."

We both laugh.

I not only lead the singalongs, but I have been entrusted with the group of older kids. Kids who are attending, and not all of them are happy to be doing so. They are all a bit hesitant to let go and sing, which I understand, but a few of them must see my struggle and graciously step up, helping the others follow suit.

The memory song for tonight is one I know from my own childhood. With the younger kids, we simply sing in memorization whereas, with the older group, it felt right to actually dissect the song, discuss the lyrics, and put them into perspective. This goes over much better when everyone finds a connection, because every person has faced a struggle.

By the end of the night, I feel a little high on Jesus, as do some of the other women tasked with teaching. A few of us even make plans to go out to dinner tomorrow night when we finish.

Pulling into the driveway, Jesus in the rearview, I park in his spot.

Ha.

It's not hurting anything, and it's not like he would know, anyway. Still …

Leia and I head out to toss the stick, running off some of her energy, and then I go inside to take a long, hot bath before heading to bed, feeling that sense of calm that I had while driving here return. Even though I can still smell him on my pillow, and even with the heavy cloud of angst, I still fall asleep feeling content.

The next day, I decide to check my emails and return some calls. The first call is to Mom. We talk about church, and then she asks about Collin. *Apparently, my sisters spilled the beans.* I explain to her that things have slowed down, and I am getting my head back where it should be, which pleases her.

I go for a long run and, upon my return, I see Tomás standing on the deck. I give him a wave as Leia and I make our way back into the house.

I check my phone and see that I have three missed calls, all from Lucas, that I decide to ignore. I go into the laundry room and find an old clothesline in one of the cabinets, take it outside, and hang it. Then I hang a load of towels out to dry.

I continue tinkering all day, attempting to make the house feel a little more like home. Then I shower and dress.

Downstairs, I make a sandwich and pop on the computer to check and see what assignments I have coming up. I feel good about the fact that I have done so much of my reading before coming here that I have nothing to do for another five days.

I then check my phone again, still seeing Lucas's name. My curiosity gets the best of me, and I pop onto the Six Degrees site, laughing when I see Jade has uploaded a few photos.

All of the photos are from our day on Collin's boat, a few has him standing in the background, looking directly, unmistakably, and intensely in my direction. Several people commented on them, and several asked about the hottie in the photo. I laugh when I see Jade's, Molly's, and Kendall's replies to the inquisitions. They vary from "*The First Mate*," "*Her cousin ... lol*," "*Someone they picked out of the ocean*," and then I see Lucas's response. "*My replacement*." Jade followed with, "*You're a dumbass, Links.*"

I can't help myself. I click on his profile.

There is a commonly used phrase, "curiosity killed the cat," and it is commonly used because there is irrevocable truth to that statement.

I probably shouldn't be shocked at what I see.

However, I am. Posted on his profile are pictures, several pictures, of him with his arm around Jessie. The most shocking is from our graduation party. Standing between us, Lucas has a sloppy, drunken grin in place, and there is a giant X over my face. Clicking through the photos, it's shocking to see just how many there are of Lucas and Jessie. But nothing is as shocking as seeing a caption under one photo of him and her that reads, "*It's complicated.*" The date is the same as our wedding date.

I click back, not wanting to fall down that rabbit hole, and look at Jade's page again to see a picture she has uploaded of me in the ocean, in my dress. Beneath it is a comment from Lucas saying, "*Seriously answer your phone!*"

This not only annoys me, but is utterly embarrassing.

Jade's next photo is of all of us smiling, having fun, and I leave the comment, "*Missing my girls.*"

I then log off, turn off my computer, and go out to play with Leia before heading back to grab some more much-needed Jesus time.

B efore starting the evening, I spoke with Pastor Lou and gained his permission to do a little something different with the high school group.

I had a blast with the younger kids, singing and rocking out to some gospel, but the time I spent introducing the older kids to some amazing Christian rock bands was my favorite.

This is truly the time in my life that I need guidance, guidance that I won't take from my family, or friends.

I do the same thing tonight with music; just a different song. When I play "Honestly" by Stryper and tell them it's not a big hair love ballad, but a Christian Rock song, they are all shocked. I am then so psyched that they introduce me to of their favorites—Jars of Clay, Third Day, and Newsboys, to name a few. They seriously get into it, and they aren't alone.

Afterward, as planned, a few of us have dinner at a lovely restaurant and sit on the dock overlooking the water where we talk about their families and the sports their children are playing. Lily, a mother of two teenagers, asks what brought me here. I give the edited version.

They all seem concerned, but I assure them that I am fine. "It was a leap of faith. I know it'll all be okay."

Then Loral, another mom, who is younger than me, has the waitress take a Polaroid of us, and we decide we'll do this again on Wednesday night, too.

It's ten thirty when we say goodnight, and I leave with the picture—a memory—in hand.

Lullaby

Chapter Eighteen

$\mathcal{I}$ take a drive to a twenty-four-hour chain store to waste some time, knowing he's due home and wanting to avoid confrontation. I grab some clothespins, some treats, and some dog food for Leia.

It's about midnight when I finally roll in. Even knowing he's more than likely back, my heart still drops at the sight of his vehicle.

I make it safely inside and decide that I'll hang the laundry that was in the washer to avoid a funky smell that may be caused by leaving it overnight.

Leia does her business as I hang the clothes then clean up her business and deposit it in the outdoor trash can. It's not until I'm walking in that I hear a loud clearing of a throat that causes me to nearly jump out of my skin.

"Someone going to pop up from behind that fence again?" I say loud enough for him to hear.

"Not tonight. You want to come over and try it out?" His voice is un-Collin-like—he slurred.

Uh-oh, he's drunk.

"March that fine ass on over here and beg, Tessa."

"Pig," I huff as I walk inside and slam the door.

After washing my hands, I realize I left Leia out and head to the door to right that wrong.

When I open the door, she's standing at the gate, waiting for him.

I march over, take her collar, and mumble, "Come on, traitor." When she makes no move to do as she's told, I have to give her a tug.

"You coming over here, or am I coming over there?" He laughs haughtily and stands. In the light, I see him glare at me. "Oh … I forgot you're in church until almost midnight." He brushes a hand through his hair then shakes his head. "Tessa Ross, you make my head spin!"

"And Collin, you break my heart," I say as I all but drag Leia to the house.

Emotion boiling up in my throat, I get inside and shut and lock the door before tears start to spill. I quickly head to the bathroom.

Looking in the mirror, I scold myself and will the tears to stay away when I hear a loud knock on my door.

"Tessa, open the door."

"Go away!"

"Dammit, really? I know the code. I can get in if I want to!" he yells the last part.

"If that's what you need to do, then go ahead, Collin.

But I would prefer …" I stop when I hear Leia tap dancing on the floor outside the door.

"Where are you, Tessa?" he taunts.

"In the bathroom. Please don't come in." I start the bathwater and hear nothing from him.

Unsure if I should be glad that he left or sad, I undress and step in, set to soak the day away, when I hear the door handle jiggle.

I turn off the water. "Collin, please don't!"

"We need to talk, Tessa."

"Then talk, Collin."

"Where the hell have you been all night?" he demands.

"Out with friends," I snap my answer, because it's seriously not his business.

"What friends?" He sounds angry.

"What does it matter?"

He bites out, "I want to know who the hell were you with?"

"I went to dinner with friends, and then I went to the store."

"Friends? You have friends here? Bullshit, Tessa!"

His tone freaks me out, so I tell him just that. "Collin, you're scaring me." Instead of him leaving, as to not freak me out, I hear the door handle jiggle again, and it pisses me off. "It's locked!"

"Not for long," he mumbles.

I hear a pop and grab a towel as he walks in.

"Seriously, Collin!" I wrap myself in a soaked towel as I stand.

He's … livid.

Eyes red, jaw clenched, the veins popping out of his neck, he insists, "Who, Tessa? Who were you with?"

I step forward to get to the door, and his body fills it.

I stand toe to toe with him and look up, way up, and snap, "Move, Collin. I'm wet and cold!"

He reaches beyond me and grabs a dry towel. Then he looks up to—I assume—give me what he deems as privacy, so I make the best of it by wrapping the towel around me and letting the other drop.

"I want you to move, Collin," I say as calmly as I can.

He dips his eyes down to meet mine and crosses his arms over his chest. "I want—no, *need*—you to tell me who you were with tonight."

In order to distract myself from being seriously dazzled by his depth of pure sex appeal when he's angry, I cross my own arms and scowl. "I already told you."

Still unmoving, I devise a plan. I step toward him, grab his hands, uncross his arms, raise them, and step closer, as if I'm going to hug him. His body relaxes, his eyes soften, and I take the opportunity to duck under them and run.

As I take the stairs three at a time, I yell back to him, "You suck, Abraham!"

I slam the door behind me, jet to the closet, throw a tee over my head, step into some panties and sleep shorts, and then step out as he storms in.

I brush past him, head down the stairs, grab my purse off the counter, dig into it, and grab the Polaroid. Then I stomp back to him and slap it against his chest. "Satisfied!"

Eyes narrowed, nostrils flaring, jaw tight, and through clenched teeth, he answers, "Not even close."

"Look at the picture. I was out with the Mom squad!"

He looks at it then sets it aside and steps to me.

I step back. "I'm asking you to stop playing games."

He grips my chin and lifts it while closing the distance between us, and then he ... takes my lips, crashing his against mine like a storm, but with the calming effect of ... water.

I grip his shirt, mind saying *push him away*, but hands driven by the need to pull him closer. Our tongues glide over one another's, exciting and calming at the same time. Words, feelings ... so many in this kiss that it's unreservedly confusing but clarifying in the same breath.

Logic lost but for a moment, returning when the need to breathe breaks us apart, and I whisper a plea. "Collin, please stop, please."

"Beg," he says, lips to my neck, slowly moving closer to my lips.

"Please stop," I whimper. "Please."

A growly sound escapes him, and he steps back, lips, hands, and body moving away from mine. Then he turns and walks toward the door, tossing back, "That's four."

Pissed—more at myself for being so easily played than him—I grab the closest thing to me and throw it at his retreating body. It hits him in the ass, and yes, that was the target.

A loud squeak fills the silence.

He looks over his shoulder and toward the ground where one of the many squeaky toys that he bought Leia freaking mocks me as it squeaks with each bounce.

When his eyes hit mine, there is no humor. He's annoyed. "Did you just throw that at me?"

"Well, who the hell else would, you ass? I'm so pissed at you that you're lucky I didn't crack you in the head." I throw my hands in the air. "You're an asshole. You walk into my house, break into my bathroom while I am taking a bath, treat me like I'm some whore, demand the truth yet don't accept it, and try to intimidate me!"

His eyes travel down my face, and I realize I'm freaking crying ... in anger, frustration.

God, seriously, why does that happen?

"I am not weak!" I bat away tears and point to the door. "You need to leave *now!*"

His face changes, guilt lies in his eyes, confusion replacing it as he holds his hand just below where his heart lies, and we stand there, both either crazy or something else completely, until he finally turns and leaves. And when he leaves, it feels like a thousand swords have fallen from the heavens piercing me … *It hurts.*

I hurry to the couch, grab a pillow that's embroidered with, "*Home is where the love is,*" and I scream into it as I fall to the couch, curl into a ball, pull the Afghan from the back of the couch, and I cry myself to sleep.

I roll off the couch when I hear my phone ringing from somewhere and realize it's morning. I nearly trip over Leia as I make my way to my purse, seriously shocked the phone's battery is not dead. By the time I get to it, it ends.

After pulling it from my purse and seeing missed calls from Lucas, and then see a voice message has been left, I toss it on the counter and head to the bathroom.

After peeing, I look at my face. A tear-stained, raccoon-looking reflection stares back at me. I quickly make work of washing my face, because I'm seriously over this crying bit. Then I brush my teeth and march to my phone as if I'm going to freaking war—*war against anything with a penis!*

I grab it, hit a few buttons, and then listen to the angry, cocky, fuck-you voice of dick number one saying, "We need to talk. Call me."

That's when I decide he deserves some TT right now, and as I am hitting his information … it dies.

I try to lift my spirits by muttering, "That's God giving you grace." Then I stomp up the stairs to change into running clothes, so that maybe, just maybe, I can drive my spiteful demons out and have a good freaking day.

When I walk outside, I want to cry again when I see Collin asleep on the chaise outside the door, but no, he doesn't get that, either.

As I try to sneak past him, Leia decides to jump on the chaise and lick him awake.

He groans and sits up, one hand petting her, the other holding his head.

"Hungover?"

"Yeah," he whispers.

"Good," I huff, grab the leash, and call Leia, "Let's go. Now."

After an hour, I return, and he is still sitting there. *He must be freezing.*

I walk in, decide to give him the same treatment he gave me, walk out, and hand him two Tylenol and a bottle of water.

"Thank you, Tessa," he says in an almost pout.

I fight the urge to tell him that I didn't know he was out here all night, that I'm sorry I left him, and should have helped him to his house. Then my phone rings, and when I see *his* name, I decide he gets that bitterness from me, because he freaking created it.

"Hello, Lucas," I answer, not hiding my annoyance one bit.

"Baby, the shit stops now. We need to talk."

I throw my hand in the air, even though he can't see me, and say, "I have nothing to say, but clearly, you do, so talk."

"I had every intention of telling you about Jessie before you found out that way. So—"

"I do not care who you fuck, Lucas. I do not even care who you date."

"Bullshit," he huffs. "Baby, I can hear the anger in your voice. Bet your stomping those little size sixes now."

"I wear a freaking eight, jackass!" I snap, and he chuckles, which pisses me off even more, so I let it go. "Fine, I am pissed. The giant red *X* over my face was seriously immature, but so was our relationship, so there's that."

He sighs exaggeratedly, further pissing me off.

"I also loved the pictures of you kissing her neck at the graduation party *I* planned for *us*, setting my feelings aside so *you* could celebrate *your* accomplishment, because regardless of all the other promises you broke to me, you kept that one. Baby steps, right?"

"You're bitter—I get it—and jealous of Jess—"

"I am absolutely not jealous. I do, however, feel the need to warn you that she's just as crazy as the others."

"See? Jealous," he says smugly.

"*Jealous?* No, jackass, I'm trying to yet again warn you to proceed with caution. Her level of crazy was revealed by her showing up here!"

"She was invited and—"

"She was a bridesmaid because Miguel was in the wedding. She was not my friend. And God, Lucas, you did that to Miguel? Do you not see how wrong that is?"

He says nothing, and it hits hard.

"Is that why they were so hard on you in Jersey? Is that why you came home?"

He doesn't answer, because Lucas has some screwed sense of his word being truth, and there's confirmation. Pissed reaches a new level at this revelation.

"I stayed and helped you until Audrianna and your sisters came!"

"Didn't ask—"

"You are so fucked up!" I cut him off.

"And you're not?" he says in a tone that slices through me and cuts deeply. "You're playing grab ass with Captain fucking Ahab—"

"You don't get to judge me, and you certainly know nothing about him, so you shut your mouth."

"Yeah, well, you gave unsolicited advice, so you're getting it back at you, baby. Jessie said he was borderline obsessed with you, and—"

"Oh, so Jessie is a character witness to my life? And you're allowed to give input on who I have in it? Wrong, Lucas. Freaking wrong."

"You're not so perfect. You know that, Tessa Ross?"

"Oh my God, I never said I was! But I will not let you have a say in who I am, or who I spend time with, or—"

"You fucking him?" he snaps, and I realize that this conversation is counterproductive to me getting back to … me.

"I'm not doing this again. We ended our relationship. If I can get over what you did while we were together and still want you to be happy, you should have no hard feelings toward me. I want you to be happy. I ask that you figure out how to want that for me so the crazy stops."

"He laying beside you now?" he asks in a demanding-the-answer kind of way.

"No, he's not laying next to me. And don't ask those kinds of questions again, because that's none of your business."

"You finding Jesus up there, Tessa?" he sneers.

"Do not mock my beliefs, Lucas. They are the only reason I have chosen to forgive you. Goodbye." I close the phone, toss it on the counter, and then head to the bathroom to shower.

W rapped in the warmth of my robe, I walk into the kitchen and find Collin, hip to the counter, picking up a cup of tea.

"The kettle whistled," he says as I take it.

"Thanks."

"I'm sorry I behaved so badly."

"I accept your apology."

"But you won't give me your eyes," he states. "What can I say or do, Tessa, to make you look at me again?"

Silly man, I enjoy looking at you, I think as I look up at him, seeing his eyes full of question, his hand again resting below his heart, and without thought, I say, "Collin, it's not up to me. It will be what it is, right?"

"I suppose?"

"I just think, if we are going to keep hanging out, we should make a pact. Honesty, trust, and"—I laugh— "sobriety."

"I feel horrible about last night, and Sunday night," he says with a raw sincerity that I don't think I've heard from him before.

I nod to the cup that he clearly poured for himself yet hasn't picked up, and then I walk to the couch and sit down.

"Well, Sunday, I was being honest, and I think I freaked you out. I certainly wasn't acting on the outside the way I feel inside."

He sits beside me.

"However, last night, you were an insatiable ass."

"I'm sorry, Tessa." He hangs his head in shame.

That … that hurts to see.

I set my tea cup on the coffee table, take his and do the same, and then I wrap my arms around him. We stay like that for some time.

When I look up, his eyes are squinted.

"Head hurts, huh?"

He nods once. "Just a little. I don't drink that much, normally."

"Cold?"

"Not as much now, no," he says, rubbing a hand up my back.

I lean over, grab his cup, and hand it to him. "This will help."

He takes it as he looks at me in such a way that it makes me feel like he's waiting for me to kick him out, *again*.

It hurts to see that, too.

"Sit, drink. I'm going to make some breakfast."

"You don't have to feed—"

"It's what I do, Collin. Just let it happen."

I cook eggs, toast, bacon, add some kiwi to the plate, and refill his tea when it's empty, and as he sits at the table, I run a bath *for him*, and then we eat in silence.

"You're very difficult to read," he admits as we carry our plates to the sink.

"I'm not surprised."

"Meaning?"

"A story about the past is easy to read—the story is already written. Easy to guess how a person's story will continue based on that, unless they're hell-bent on changing their path. In that case, you have to sit back and watch as it unfolds."

He looks maybe more confused now.

"I'm altering my direction, my story. This is the

chapter that my life changes. Even I don't know where it's going, but I do know I've learned what hasn't work previously and am moving forward with the wisdom and lessons gained."

He says nothing, and I laugh.

"You have a bath waiting. Go, get warm."

"I need to get clothes—"

"Still have the ones you gave me the night you tossed me around in a cold shower." I walk around behind him and gently push him toward the bathroom. "I promise the water's warm. You seriously still need to thaw out. Your lips are still sort of matching your eyes."

"Maybe lighter, like yours," he says as he steps in.

I totally ignore that and close the door behind

While he takes a bath, I shower upstairs. When I come down, he is walking out, toweling off his hair, and God, he's seriously something … otherworldly.

Walking toward him, I ask, "Tired?"

He lifts a shoulder. "Shouldn't be."

"We're both on vacation; naps are good." I take his hand and start toward the stairs.

He pulls back the blanket, and I climb in and lie down. He slides in beside me, pulls the blanket over us, pushes his hand under me, cups the side of my head, and pulls my head to his chest. I wrap my arm around his middle, and he presses his lips to the top of my head.

His heart is racing, not calming in the least.

My lullaby no longer.

I want it back.

I take a chance in moving my hand and placing it where he placed his own on two separate occasions, and when I do, he inhales a sharp breath. When I chance a glance up, his eyes are shut tightly, and he looks … pained.

I start to move my hand, not wanting that for him, for

me, but he immediately grabs my hand and puts it back before pulling my head back to his chest.

Eventually, his heartbeat slows and, with it, mine.

I feel it—*him, me, us*—and it's terrifying to think that he and I could have something, and that something would no doubt be beautiful. But God, how do people do it? The rebound, the moving on without all the pain that accompanies it.

I do not ponder that thought long because it's back —*my lullaby.*

Church

Chapter Nineteen

Collin

wake in an empty bed, and although it's been that way most of my life, *by choice*, it has happened a couple times now, and no longer enjoy it at all. I also made the choice not to sleep, *actually sleep*, with anyone, knowing it crossed a line. But, with her, *with Tessa*, I want to cross every damn line I've ever drawn. Smash every fail-proof plan ever made and crush self-preserving promises I've made myself.

I heft my lazy ass out of bed, piss, wash my hands, and then I head down the stairs to find her sitting cross-legged on the couch with her computer on her lap.

"Hey, did you sleep well?" she asks with a smile like a beacon as she pats the spot beside her.

I take her hand as I sit, brush my thumb over her soft skin, kiss the back of it, and hold it to my chest. "Mmhmm …"

She lifts my hand and wraps my arm around her. Then she smiles at me and leans into my chest.

"What are you looking at?" I ask.

"Organizing pictures into folders from a disk that Phoebe gave me." She pulls her computer over and sets it on her knees, and I watch and learn more about the people in her life, events of from the past, and realize even more than before that the people who she is closest to are her family, and that is beautiful and utterly terrifying at the same time.

While looking at a picture of her parents, she asks, "How's your mom?"

I push myself to step out of my comfort zone and answer as honestly as I can at the moment. "A mess. She's angry. Drying up and not doing it gracefully. She tried to sign herself out, and I had to promise to come back on Wednesday in order to get her to stay."

She sets her computer to the side and snuggles up to me. "I'm sorry, Collin. That must be incredibly hard."

I've never felt it was my responsibility to help my mother get well. She never felt it her responsibility to be a mother, which is a gross understatement. She put me through a living hell for the first sixteen years of my life. A mother, she was not. A vestal into the world, at best. Until right this moment, I never considered the possibility of being a father, but if that happened, I would protect my children with my life.

I look down at her, the cause for this change, and wonder, *what are you doing to me?*

We eat dinner, and I laugh that she won't throw out food that is still good, but she must be sick of eating, and we both laugh when I mention I was sure Ann's love of cooking kept me from skipping many meals. We hug a lot, and I watch as she primps to get ready to go to church.

Our interaction is fluid, unforced, and the amount of non-sexual touches exchanged … insurmountable and supersede any orgasm I've ever experienced.

Her hesitation thus far, albeit warranted—and she doesn't even know the half of why yet—is something of an internal challenge. No, a battle, because I can't walk away, and I can't continue living the life of a fucking frat boy, either.

"What are you going to do while I'm gone?" she asks.

"I have some colleagues coming over for a work dinner. We have a big trip coming up in two weeks and need to get all the wrinkles ironed out."

"Sounds like a lot of fun." She smiles.

"It's one of the few things I know I'm good at, Tessa. I love my work."

"I wish I could watch you in action."

"I wish I could go with you tonight and see what it is that makes you so happy." This statement is true, but also somewhat of a reiteration that I was a complete ass last night. "And meet your new friends."

She gives me an *aw* face, and it's the first time in my life that I have felt that type of consideration from another human being. It shocks me.

She points to her beautiful face, and then defends, "It wasn't pity. I don't—"

"Tessa"—I take her hands—"it was kindness, and I graciously accept it."

She buries her face in my chest. "Good." She then looks up at me and beams as she repeats, "Good."

I want to kiss her, but she beats me to it. It's quick, it's effective, and it's sweet as hell. Then she steps back, holding my hand.

"When are you going to return from your visit with your mom?"

I look at our hands as I answer, "Thursday, about three in the afternoon. That way, I can attend three of her counseling sessions."

Giving my hand a squeeze, she whispers, "Do you think, Thursday night, I can take you on a date?"

"Are you asking me out?"

"Depends. Are you accepting my request?" She blushes, and that hits me in a place that hasn't shit to do with these feelings, but it's not unwelcomed. It is just untimely.

"Will you beg me?"

Her perfect and naturally arched brow raises. "I wouldn't push it."

"Tessa, I'd love for you to take me on a date." I pull her in for a hug.

"You're going to love it." She laughs and looks up at me, still laughing as she asks, "How do you feel about hanging out with one hundred and fifty little people?"

"I'm going to regret accepting, aren't I?"

"If you do, I will buy you dinner afterward. Maybe you can meet my new friends." She pushes me away yet grips my shirt and pulls me back toward her. "And just so you know, we are going to have dinner and conversation Wednesday night again. You all right with that?"

"I know I shouldn't feel like I have a right. Logically, it doesn't make sense." I pause.

"I wasn't trying to upset you."

I cup the side of her face, and she closes her eyes and presses into my touch. "You don't have to come. I shouldn't expect you—"

My thought escapes me, "God, you're beautiful."

She opens her eyes and looks into mine.

"I want to come with you on Thursday. More than I can even begin to wrap my head around." I kiss her forehead. "You need to get ready for church."

I receive a text from Tessa as the meeting ends and the dinner part is concluding. She informs me that she's going to the store to grab some groceries, which makes me laugh, which causes everyone to look at me oddly.

I don't laugh.

Then she follows up with a sweet:

- You need anything? … T

- This damn meeting to end, and you to be home … C

I heard her pull in, as does everyone at the table, which is why they work for me.

I try not to notice her throwing the ball to Leia as the conversation continues, yet there she is.

It dawns on me then she is, in fact, *my* distraction. The only one I've encountered since the age of sixteen, and that situation was nothing like this.

When at nearly ten p.m., she starts weeding one of the flowerbeds that she created, I shoot her a text.

- You are very distracting out there in that dress and bent over those flowers … C

- Probably would distract you more if I told you I was wearing nothing under it … T

- Would you please go inside so I can pay attention? … C

- Hmm, nope … T

I lift my eyes from my screen and see her smiling at me. I simply nod to the house, and she ⸻ simply ignores me.

"Dr. Abraham," Douglas calls my attention, and I look at him as I push back my chair and stand.

"We are all in agreement as to what our roles are for this one?"

They all nod.

"I'll email you the notes from the meeting tomorrow to confirm."

I shake Douglas's, Ingrid's, and Klaus's hands, and nod to Tomás. "You'll see them out?"

I don't wait for a response; I immediately head down the stars, cross the boardwalk, and stand at the gate.

"Good evening, Tessa."

She looks over her shoulder and smiles.

"You look beautiful."

"How was your meeting?"

"It was very productive until about fifteen minutes ago." I open the gate and walk to her. "You confuse the hell out of me."

"Why?"

"Here I am, busting my balls to make sure we're keeping this PG, based on what you said, and then you drop the no-panties text."

She walks over and sits on the edge of the chaise. "Sorry. I know I shouldn't have. I think—"

"Your heart is beautiful. You said it was one and the same with God?"

She blushes. "Well, yeah, but I'm pretty sure God didn't make pant—"

"I shouldn't have said anything. Please forget I did." I walk over and sit beside her, petting Leia as I apologize and lean over to kiss her neck. "Stop overthinking this. The constant fight within makes me pull away, too, and I don't want it to anymore."

She looks at me thoughtfully then gives me a hug before standing and walking over to light the fire in the fire pit.

When I start to stand, she tells me, "Stay." Then she walks into the house.

When she returns in a pair of shorts and a hoodie, my sweatshirt from yesterday hung over her arms and two bottles of water in her hand, she tosses me the sweatshirt. Even though I'm not cold, I put the thing on.

She sits between my legs, back to my chest, and hands me a bottle of water. Then we sit under a clear, moonlit, starry night, her pressed against me, me wrapped around her, and everything about this feels … right, regardless.

When she looks back at me every few minutes, her blue eyes sparkle, and I can safely assume mine do the same.

I trace my fingers up and down her bare leg, and I watch the goosebumps follow in the wake of my touch, and that is more beautiful to me than the stars. *She is more beautiful than the moon.*

When she shivers, I kiss the side of her cheek. "You're shivering, Tessa. Let's go inside."

"I want to stay like this forever," she says in barely a whisper.

If I could, I would, I think as I do the only thing I can to prolong this moment. I pull a blanket off the back of the chaise and cover her as she presses her head to my chest, and I watch her fall asleep.

I wake to rain falling, and by the time it registers that we're outside, it begins to pour.

She jumps up, startled, and I stand. Both of us begin to laugh as we hurry to the house. But as she steps in, something comes over me. Need and want collide as I pull her back outside and into the rain, take her smiling yet startled face in my hands, and kiss her.

She shoots her arms up as she laughs against my lips, the sound beautiful, and I break the kiss to step back and take it in. That sound, that smile, her happiness.

She looks up at the sky, arms raised, Leia barking at us both from the open door, probably telling us we're fools for standing in the rain, as Tessa laughs and spins in a slow circle, arms raised, laughing harder.

"Tessa!" I call to her, and when her eyes meet mine, words that I've never said to a woman fall from my lips. "I'm in love with you!"

She stops spinning and looks at me, hurt etching her face, and she begins to cry.

I close the distance between us and lift her chin so I have her eyes and see what I've done.

"I'm sorry. Don't cry." I use my thumb to wipe away her tears and wish I could take back the cause of them. "I didn't mean to—"

She wraps her arms so tightly around my neck and hugs me as she wraps her legs around my waist. Fingers tangle in my hair as she pulls my head back, her sweet, full lips covering mine.

Thunder, lightning, and rain surround us as we kiss while I walk us to the door, step inside, and kick it shut behind me.

I lay her down on the rug and watch her chest rise and fall rapidly, mine doing the same, both of us wanting each other so badly that the words are etched in the thickness of the air. I don't make a move, because she has told me, as I have told her, what comes before that.

When she grows impatient, she sits up and begins lifting my shirt, kissing my chest, nipping my nipple, pulling the shirt higher then tossing it over my head. Then she takes my lips.

"Tessa, as much as I want you, please stop. I don't know how much more I can take."

"I don't want to stop." She maneuvers to her knees, takes my face, and kisses me as I run my hands up her sides, lifting her shirt, ready to give in to this … *this love*.

A loud bark and frantic scratching at the door has us both scrambling to our feet. Tessa opens the door, and Leia barks at me, then at her, then at me again, and I can't help but laugh.

When Tessa laughs, Leia looks at her and begins to shake off, water flying everywhere. I grab my sweatshirt and cover Leia as Tessa runs to the bathroom then returns with towels.

When we collectively finish doing the best we can to dry her, she plops on her ass and lifts her chin, poised as ever, and we both laugh again.

"I guess we are just not meant to do this." Tessa grins at me, and her words hit hard, disappointment follows, and regret in the admittance of my feelings comes raining down.

Unable to look in her eyes, I look over her head at the door, wanting to leave, to recollect the dignity I left out on the patio and—

"What's going on? Are you regretting what you—"

"I'm just sorry if it made you uncomfortable."

"Uncomfortable?" she asks, voice squeaking. "No,

Collin, not uncomfortable. Happy, ecstatic, elated. Far from uncomfortable."

Confused further, I look at her.

"I'm sorry I've upset you. If it was just at the moment, I get it. If you want me to forget you said it, I can try … I guess." She places her hand over her belly as her face turns crimson.

"You don't have to act like you're happy that I said I love you." A flip switches and fleeing is the farthest thing from my mind. "I understand if you don't feel that way about me, but I promise you will, in time."

She starts to laugh, and if I'm being honest, it pisses me off.

"Collin, no, that's not it." She unexpectedly slaps her hands against my chest, and my ass hits the couch. She immediately straddles me, places her hands on my face, and holds it steady as she kisses me sweetly. "I love your lips, even when they are not touching mine," she begins. "I love your eyes that seem to be able to pierce right through my heart. I love your perfect nose." She kisses it. "I love your shoulders that I'm quite sure were made to hold me up." She moves down and kisses my chest. "I love your heart; it's beat a lullaby and seems is mine for now." She takes my face again and continues, "I love you, Collin Abraham, and I think I have since the night we sat out there with my family, and that scares me to death."

"Never gonna hurt you intentionally," I whisper against her lips. "I'm not a stupid man. I know what I have. Do you understand me? Couldn't do that to you."

A tear slides down her face, and I brush it away as I pull her into my arms, and we stay like that until she starts to dose, startles, and sits up.

She looks around then smiles as she looks back at me.

"It's three in the morning, and it's been a long but perfect day. Can we go upstairs to sleep?"

"Of course. Anything you want."

Upstairs, I watch as she stands in the small closet, stripping off her wet shirt, exposing herself with unabashed confidence, and she has every reason to be. She's stunning, every inch exposed to me, and I can't wait to explore her inch by inch.

She then drops her shorts, and the love I feel for her body turns to something altogether different when I see pale blue, lace panties kissing the milky white skin of her tight, round ass.

She then unhooks her bra and lets it slide down one arm then the next, and blood rushes to my balls.

When she slides on a tee-shirt, covering her body, I smile knowing I will give it all to her, everything she wants, as long as she is accepting.

Regretfully, I stand and remind her, "My flight leaves at eight. I'm going to run over and grab my bags. I'll be back in a few minutes, all right?"

"Uh-huh, hurry back." She yawns as she slides into bed then smiles up at me. "Hey, Collin Abraham, I love you."

Hand to chest, I hold my heart steady and nod.

When I turn to walk away, she says, "If you still mean it, house rules dictate that you say it back."

I turn back, lean down, and kiss the top of her head. "I'll say it a million times if you need that. But when I said it, I knew it would never go away."

Men like me do not act like *that guy*. We don't walk around with our heads in the clouds, with hearts like blinders covering our eyes, but damn if I don't like the thought of allowing that feeling to overtake logic, reason, and realism.

I should kick myself for falling into this state. But, how could I not?

To rationalize this, I will admit that there is nothing more real than love that doesn't end, and it's not always accompanied by hearts and flowers. Sometimes love of the truest form cuts so deeply that it leaves scars that people cannot see, but it doesn't make them lose scars any less real.

So, as I walk out the back door, feeling drunk on love, and see Tessa's Jeep, the normal height of seventy inches—give or take, depending on tire size—sitting a little lower than normal, love, although ever present, takes a backseat to necessary action, action to preserve that love, protect it if necessary.

I hurry to her vehicle and sputter, "Fuck," as I round it to see the damage. Four slashed tires.

Pissed that I left my phone at my place and priorities being her and not the phone, I run toward her house, head back in, lock the door behind me, and rush up the stairs to find her asleep and think, *Thank God*, when I see her unscathed by the ugliness that *that guy* could shield her from.

I quietly grab her phone then exit the room while sending Tomás a message—three letters, three numbers, a code, in which he will not confuse for anything other than eminent danger, and then I call 911.

"This is Collin Abraham. I need someone down to my place now."

They know who I am; therefore, they bypass the BS. No questions asked. A simple, "Right away, Mr. Abraham."

Within minutes, they arrive and begin their process.

The place crawling with cops, I know she's covered, so I run over and grab clothes, my toothbrush, iPad, and phone, noticing immediately that I have several missed calls, which is why I left the phone behind in the first place. Anyone who needs me knows that I am off duty, and their first call would be Tomás if they needed to contact me. A boundary I've just placed before signing off days ago that now seem like a different lifetime.

Standing on the back porch, I wait for them to conclude and for Officer Wesley's brief.

"We dusted for prints on the Jeep. Not much was gathered, but we will run what we have. Something of concern is the footprints around both yours and this home, which were distorted from the rain. I wish we had more, Mr. Abraham. We'll let you know what we get back on the prints."

"What's going on, Collin?" Tessa freaks out, understandingly so. "Are you okay?"

"Yes, Tessa, I'm fine," I tell her then turn to the officers.

"Thank you, Officers. Please let me know when you find something out. That will be all for now," I dismiss them then head to her.

"Collin—"

Pulling her to the couch to sit, I explain, "Someone slashed your tires, Tessa. I called the police, they checked everything out, and will be getting back to me when they have more information."

She says nothing but is justifiably shocked.

I give her a moment, and then she stands. "I want to see."

I follow her through the house and out the door, holding her hand as she stares at her Jeep.

"Who would do this?"

"I don't know, but I intend to find out. Let's get back inside."

As soon as we walk in, she heads to the fridge. "Hungry?"

I know this is what she does—she stress cooks then feeds people to make them feel better, which in turn makes her feel better—so I nod. "A bit. Yes."

Trying to help but realizing this is something that is more a hindrance to her process, I step back.

She looks at me and rolls her eyes. "Sorry. It's a thing."

"It's what you do. Nothing to be apologetic about."

I decide to check my messages. I listen to them once, twice, and then a third time, allowing the gravity of the situation to sink in before slamming my phone on the counter as she places a plate in front of me. "Shit."

"Collin, what is it?"

"My mother checked herself out yesterday." And she did it in a way she will be held accountable. *Thank God.* "They don't know where she is."

"You should go and find her."

"No, I have a feeling she's here." Realizing the words were uttered, and not just a thought, I look at her.

"Do you think your mother did that to my Jeep?"

"You're safe and under my protection, but yes, I do." I open my phone and hit the sheriff's department. "Yes, this is Collin Abraham. I need to speak to Detective Spokes, please." I wait for him to answer, which seems to take forever, but I know it's only a minute.

"Spokes here."

"Wesley has prints. I want you to run Catherine Abraham's prints against the ones you found today. She left the center yesterday."

"You've got to be shitting me with this bitch," He grumbles then says, "Will do. Be in contact."

"Thank you. I'll be waiting for your call."

I then call the tow service. "This is Collin Abraham. Could you please send a tow truck to my house. There is a Jeep in the parking lot that needs four new tires."

She pushed her food around on her plate. She's shocked, and I can tell she feels bad for me.

Sensing me watching her, she looks up. "Are you all right, Collin?"

"No." I shake my head as I look over all that is beautiful sitting across from me. "What was I thinking bringing someone into this hell?" The hurt in her eyes causes me to look away, and when my eyes land on my plate, rage dances with fury, and I reach across, swiping my arm across the table and causing her plate to soar across it and onto the floor. "Don't eat that!"

She jumps up, causing her chair to fall back, and she nearly topples over it as I reach for her to stop her fall.

"I should have never gotten emotionally attached to anyone, least of all you."

After ensuring she's stable, I make quick work of cleaning up the mess I made, the only part of the mess within my control to clean up.

I see her moving toward the door and quickly grab her arm, stopping her. "You will stay with me until we have some answers. It won't take long, but you're going to have to deal with it. Nod your affirmative."

"Aye aye, Captain." She salutes me with a deep crease marring her beauty.

"I deserve that—your anger—but you, Tessa, will be fine You're safe with me."

"I get things are a bit fucked right now, but you told me you loved me last night, and today you say you wished you never got attached." Tears begin to fall, and she bats them away. I hate that I made her feel that, so I grab her hands as she continues. "I wake up to cops in the house, and you think it's your mother? Leia killing the mood last night … it's all too much." She pulls her hands away. "Maybe we aren't supposed to be together. I seem to cause you pain and confusion, and that's not what it is supposed to be like. That's not love."

Two steps, and she's in my arms, caging her with that exact purpose. "Do not question my words or confuse them. I love you. I left the baggage behind a long time ago. She has resurfaced. I'll fix it; trust me."

She looks up at me, finally giving me those eyes.

"And, beautiful, hell doesn't send warning signs, and love, this kind, *our kind*, doesn't come from a place other than heaven, and heaven doesn't give a man like me a taste of that by mistake."

"I'm not weak. So, you love me, you tell me what's going on. I need you to be honest with me, and I'll help you through it. We're in this together."

"Sir," Tomás speaks from behind me. "I'm here. Your place is secure."

I kiss her quickly then nod, agreeing to all she has asked for. "I need you and Leia to come to my place while Tomás and I do some work."

Chapter Twenty

S tomach nervous more, so over the admittance of being in love than the crazy mother, I sit on the couch, listening in on as Collin give instructions to Tomás. But just like when he said he loved me, when he said he would keep me safe, I feel it to my core.

"Detective Spokes is in charge of the case, so he is our local contact. You should call our guy in New Jersey and anybody else you have down there and get them on this. I need about five people around here, and any approved PIs on the list need to be brought in. I want this over ASAP." He looks over at me. "I have a date tomorrow night."

He loves me.

Then he takes a call.

I watch as he stands, broad chest puffed out, shoulders squared, eyes intense, and seriously hot as he answers, "Abraham. What do you have?"

Butterflies and seriously ill-timed heat pooling, I think as he listens intently.

"Thank you. Please keep me posted. Be advised that I'm adding people to this."

He closes his phone and looks at Tomás. "Call Newark, New Jersey's main station. Detective Thort. Have him fax you her latest stunt."

Tomás nods.

"All right, let's get this ball rolling."

Tomás lifts a case onto the table, opens it, and hands Collin a Glock 22 caliber semi- automatic handgun.

What the hell?

Collin checks it over then stuffs it in the back of his pants. Tomás then hands him a compact handgun, a Beretta, and Collin puts that one in his pocket.

He glances at me and apparently thinks I am in shock, and yeah … a little, but when he says, "Tomás, take these away," I realize he thinks it's the guns. No, it's not the guns; it's the fact that he needs them for things other than target practice or hunting that has me a bit freaked.

"This is a lot to deal with, I know, but I promise you'll be okay." He turns to Tomás. "Everyone you can find. I want that bitch caught." Then he turns back to me and says, "You need to know a few things." He then walks to me, takes my hand, and leads me down the hall to a closed door. When he opens it, I realize it's his office.

After closing it, he takes my face. "Talk to me."

"So, medical research is a pretty dangerous occupation here at the Cape?"

He narrows his eyes as he searches mine. "I know guns are intimidating."

"Not if you know how to use them properly."

"I will teach you how to handle a gun someday, but today—"

"I've shot both a Glock and a Beretta." His brows shoot up, and I explain, "Not a badass medical researcher like you. Dad hunts and loves his guns. I know how to handle them—we all do. But I'm better with a bow. When this is done, I'll teach *you* how to handle them."

"If this situation wasn't serious, I'd tell you that was seriously sexy and completely unnecessary when this guy" —he points to himself—"says he loves you, it means he's your shield, too."

"If this situation wasn't serious, I'd tell you how hot and completely unnecessary that is when this girl, who knows how to take care of herself, and—"

"Not how you and I are going to work, and failure is not an option." He pulls out a chair. "Sit, be informed, and then we can debate after the suspect is apprehended."

I don't back down from a good debate *ever*, but when terms like suspect is apprehended pop out of his mouth in regards to his mother, I decide to listen to the man with two guns strapped to him.

He opens a way nicer laptop than I have ever seen and types, faster than I can type, the name Catherine Abraham in the search engine.

WOMAN SUSPECTED OF ARSON
WOMAN SENTENCED IN SHOOTING DEATH OF HER DAUGHTER
WOMAN SUSPECTED IN DEATH OF HER SON
WOMAN SUSPECTED IN CHILD PROSTITUTION RING
WOMAN SUSPECTED IN SALE OF DRUGS

And the badass in me shoves its tail between her legs as

I whisper in a shaky voice, "Collin, this is your mother, the one you think slashed my tires?"

Eyes guarded, jaw set, he nods.

"Really?"

"Do you remember what I told you about her?"

I nod.

"This is the rest of it."

"Collin, you don't have to do this," I tell him.

"Tessa, full disclosure, open and honest. I love you, and you say you love me, but if this gets to be too much, I will understand, and you are free to go, but not until she's apprehended." He pauses, leans down, and kisses the top of my head swiftly before stepping back just as fast. "If you need to take a break, let me know."

He clicks the first link, and I read. Article after article, I read of the monster who gave birth to this man, the man I know I am in love with, and I know it because I've been there before. This time, even with this, I am unafraid and have no doubt that he feels the same. This in itself would be huge for me and should be celebrated, but instead, I am reading what seems like a script from a horror show, but there are no ghosts, zombies, goblins, or ghouls. It isn't the product of someone's imagination; it is his life, his upbringing.

I look at him, and he doesn't wilt or seem self-conscious about it. He doesn't see concern or care as pity. He does the opposite—he sits taller and squares his shoulders, he grows visibly stronger, but as he strokes his thumb over the back of my hand, I know—God, I just know—he is more than I could have every wished, or dreamed, or begged God for Lucas to become.

Then he begins to speak.

"The woman who gave birth to me is a monster. She was heavily involved in drugs and sold them to feed her habit. She brought men in and out of her life, mostly deal-ers. Some of those dealers fathered her children. I'm unsure who my father is, nor do I wish to find out. She used them, and *us*, to lure men in. I was the youngest of three. All of us are three years apart in age. However, she was pregnant a great deal more than that.

"My sister was beautiful but had health issues, mental as well as physical, and when I was old enough to under-stand what they were trying to do to her, I stepped in."

"Collin," I quietly gasp.

He shakes his head. "Let me do this, Tessa. Full disclosure."

"You don't have to."

"I do."

I close my mouth and fight with all I have to hold back tears as he continues.

"When the older two came of age to leave and finally escaped her clutches, they ended up dead. My brother's death was deemed an accidental heroin overdose. I knew this was a lie, but until my sister's death, on the heels of her contacting DSS when she informed them what was happening in the house, I couldn't prove that. And after she was convicted, they chose not to reopen the case. She spent eleven years in Bedford Hills women's prison in Downstate NY. She was released due to good behavior and because she had been deemed fit for society."

I say nothing, nothing at all.

"Can we take a break from this?" he asks, voice finally showing signs of pain.

"Of course we can. Whatever you need." I stand, pull him into a hug, and kiss the top of his head.

After a good minute, his body still doesn't relax, and I lean back to look down as he looks up and asks, "Are you good?"

"Of course."

"Would love nothing more than to stay right here, but I need to deal with this."

I step back. "Of course."

We walk out to the kitchen and head straight to the fridge. "May I—"

"Yes, of course. It's likely you won't find much in there. The freezer is well stocked."

And it is, *unfortunately for me*, since I am now standing here without him to care for, or comfort, or freaking cook for, but fortunate for him, there are dozens of prepared dishes.

I pull out a pan marked *Chicken Parm* and set it on his counter. Then I preheat the oven and glance at Collin and Tomás huddled over yet another laptop, whispering, and realize I am wearing a tee-shirt and undies.

Walking toward the door, I tell him, "I'm going to run next door and grab a few things. I'll be right back."

"Tessa, no. If you need something, Tomás will go grab it," he insists.

I shrug. "Wouldn't want to be a bother."

He walks toward me, slows to open a drawer and grab a notebook and pen, and then walks toward me. "It's not a bother. Make a list."

"I really don't need anything, but my phone." Then I whisper, "Pants and clothes for tonight."

"Tonight?" he asks, looking down, eyes narrowing as he realizes I have no pants on.

"Church," I remind him.

He reaches up and pushes my hair behind my ear. "You can't go tonight."

My stomach twists in a knot. "What do you mean? Do you think she'd show up at a church?"

He says nothing.

"Collin, answer me."

"Yes," he states, completely void of emotion.

The oven timer goes off, and I walk past him and toward it. I unwrap and place the parm in then turn to walk to the couch, but the wall of Abraham blocks me, holding a pair of … leggings?

I look up at him, shocked.

"They'll be big on you, but serve a purpose."

It is not the time to argue with him, but seriously, what the hell?

I snatch them from his hand and mumble, "Humiliating," under my breath, not wanting him to hear me because of everything going on, but also wanting him to so he knows this is not okay.

I attempt to close the door, and he fills it.

"I'm trying to show some dignity and—"

"You will meet Joan at some point. She's my housekeeper. She occasionally does her laundry here. As I told you, no woman has stayed the night with me. You will be the first and the last, Tessa."

"Also humiliating," I whisper as I step into Joan the housekeeper's pants.

"I'm sorry you feel that way, but I am not surprised. I expected it would be a difficult path to trusting again."

Shocked, I look up at him.

"And, beautiful, when this is over, when she is found, I will love you in a way that nothing he has done to your heart won't be healed."

"Oh my God, please just go and let me find my freaking dignity," I groan.

"Make that list when you're done?"

I look up and nod and try to avoid eye contact.

"I love you, Tessa, and part of that is gonna be times like this right here. Other times, we're gonna have to step away, and that's not easy but necessary to keep you, us, and in the future, our kids, safe."

"Fuck me," flops out of my mouth.

"Never gonna fuck you, Tessa. I'm here to love you."

To this, I place my hands on his chest and push him out the door.

When I finally walk out, I do so having stolen a little bit of Collin's confidence, and his scent.

I used his deodorant.

"Your things, ma—"

"Tessa. My name is Tessa. I am Tessa." I kind of crack, and Collin stands from his spot at the table.

"Tomás, please call her Tessa."

"Tessa, your belongings." He points toward the table.

"Thank you, Tomás." I grab my phone and computer. Then I reach down and give my lazy princess a pat before heading to the couch.

I open my computer, needing some normal, and hit up Six Degrees to see if the girls have posted more pictures, crossing my fingers that I get the chance to see Queen Jade's little loves. But what pops up is an album cover with a nurse on it. Blink 182, and his caption of, "*No more perfect cover. What's My Age Again, TT?*"

The next picture is the cover of Limp BizKit with, "*You asked for it, M. She'll bring you that cookie. LL out.*

The next is the Goo Goo Dolls cover and, "*I wasn't the only one who fucked up. Takes two. Pick Up Your Phone!*"

Ben commented with, "*Seriously, leave her alone, ass clown! She literally ran the fuck away from home to get away from your diseased ass.*"

I laugh out loud then quickly cover my mouth, because seriously, not the right time. Thankfully, my phone rings, giving me the opportunity to leave the room.

I grab my laptop, look at Collin, and point to his office. He nods, answering the question I didn't ask, yet he knows.

I close the door behind me and fumble with my phone to answer.

"Hello."

"Tessa," he says my name in a rush that freaks me out.

"Is everything all right?"

"No!" Lucas snaps.

I wait for him to explain, but he doesn't, so as I set my laptop down and ask, "Please just say whatever it is you need to."

I hear him breathing, yet he doesn't say anything as I sit down, pull my feet up, and wait.

"We need to fix this." Then his voice breaks when he says, "I love you, Tessa. No one else. No one ever."

"Please don't do this," I whisper.

"You need to come home. I'll do whatever it takes," Lucas nearly begs.

In the background, I hear a noise and a knock, then a whisper, and I know damn well it's Jessie.

"Lucas, you're asking me to do something I can't do ever again. Things have changed."

"Then you're asking me to live without love. Could have done that. Was doing it fine until you fucked up my life," he accuses.

Pissed, I hiss, "You're seriously doing this with her there? You're doing that to her? That's why you're living without love, Lucas. And you know what? You have to love you before—"

"I loved me when I was with you!" he snaps. "I loved that guy. This version of me fucking sucks."

I fist my hair. "I don't have it in me anymore to make this all right or easy for you. I know it's not my responsibility, and you know it's wrong for you to ask it of me. You have a woman there who walked away from a very long relationship to be with you. She is who you chose to get you through this."

"You left!"

"Come on; you know better than that. I was living with you, and I wasn't enough. You have to figure this out for you. Figure *you* out. That's the only way you're going to be better."

"You're killing me, Tessa Ross," he says in a broken tone that cuts deep.

"Why don't you go visit your sisters? You're happier when you're with them. Take a break from whatever is going on in your dirty little mind and listen to your heart, Lucas," I whisper.

"You're my goddamned heart!"

"No, nope, I'm not, and as soon as you figure that out, you'll see what I saw for all those years. You're a great man. I know it. I felt it. The only thing standing between your hurt and happiness is you. So, fix you." I feel like I am going to cry for him ... again, and it pisses me off when I am sitting just one wall away from Collin. "We're done, but it will never mean I don't care. It'll never mean I don't want you to find happiness. Please, Lucas, want that for me, too." And a tear falls.

"Don't cry, baby," Lucas says softly.

"I'm sad for you. You don't want me to cry. I don't want that for you, either." I force a laugh. "And seriously, stop calling me baby! It pisses me off."

"Sorry." He sighs, and then silence, and I feel like this is finally enough for him. Then he fucks it all up by asking, "Are you sleeping with Ahab?"

"Lucas," I snap.

"Just tell me. I need to know," he begs softly.

"I haven't had sex in months. Better now?"

"Oddly"—he chuckles—"I am."

"Well, great, I'm happy to have done that for you," I say sarcastically.

"I think I'll go to Jersey. You should come down, Tessa. We could take a drive and go to that little spot in the woods."

"I'm good."

"Best I'll ever have. I love you, Tessa Ross."

"Take care of you, Lucas."

"No love, TT?"

"Love for my friend," I whisper.

"Thanks, baby," he says sincerely.

"Call me that again, and I'll seriously kick your ass next time I see you."

"Well, then I have to say it. A guarantee to see you again."

"I'm hanging up. Go to Jersey. Hug the girls. Show them their knight."

I hang up the phone and hear something behind me. I turn and see Collin, jaw tight, eyes narrowed, arms crossed, one hand over his heart, legs spread slightly, body filling the door that I shut completely.

"Collin—"

He turns away from me as he says, "Give me a few minutes." His voice is raw and then it's gruff as he says, "I need to speak to Tomás."

My phone rings again, and even though it's Jade and I need her, I need to fix this with Collin, because as much as it hurts to hear Lucas in pain, the way Collin just reacted to a conversation he heard half of, it's seriously killing me.

I shoot Jade a text.

– Can't talk right now, but guess what? I heard the three sweetest words from the most beautiful man I have ever met, inside and out. He

amazes me every day. Been busy. I'll call you soon.

When I feel a breath against my neck, I jump out of the chair and turn. "Stop sneaking up on me. It's freaking me out!"

He moves with scary stealthy speed and invades my space. "You sure that's how you feel?"

"Are you spying on me?" I accuse.

"I guess I am."

"I'm not hiding anything from you. I never will. He called. I'm used to talking him down, helping him get through his shit. I want him to be all right, Collin. I'll never go back. I don't love him that way."

"But you said—"

"As a friend, someone I grew up with, loved, and went through so much with. I am not in love with him. If I'm being honest, the minute I saw him, I knew he would hurt me and—"

"I need you to know I'm never going to be the kind of man who wants to know how many people or who you've slept with. And I can tell you in all honestly that it's best I don't know for their safety and my freedom."

I laugh at his joke. Then I stop laughing when I realize it's not one.

He continues, "Did you need to talk to him because you doubt who I am? Because of what you just learned and are currently knee-deep in the situation that is me?"

"No!" I exclaim. "Not at all. I'm upset about the fact that I have to sit here and not do anything to help find the bitch." I stop and shake my head. Then I say what I truly mean. "I hate her for what you've had to live through. She deserves to rot. She will rot. And because I met some kids last night that really need me to be there. I can call Pastor Lou and—"

"I already did," he tells me, looking at the ground. "They've canceled tonight."

"Why?" A chill runs up my spine, and I step closer. "Collin, why?"

"There was a note left in the sanctuary."

"Collin, what did it say?"

He looks up hesitantly.

"Truth, full disclosure."

"The authorities have it to build their case, Tessa, but it was bad. We're going to catch her. Things will be okay."

"Collin, tell me, please."

"A note was left on top of a piece of the tire, and the knife. It said, '*The whore with the voice is next.*' So ... no"

Eyes wide, hands shaking, I nod. "Okay."

"I'm so sorry I got you involved in this. It will be taken care of."

"I'm fine," I lie, and I do what I do—say something to try to lighten the situation. "So, does that mean she likes my voice?"

"Tessa ..." He takes my hands and gives them a firm squeeze. "It's all right to be upset."

"It's easier this way." I try yet fail to stop my lips from their downward drop as I pull my hands away and move to the leather couch and sit.

He immediately moves so he's behind me and wraps his long, strong arms around me, kissing the top of my head and assuring me with, "When this is over, I can promise you that you'll never have to worry about her again."

"I believe you." *And I do, in a scary kind of way.*

"Wish I could wipe this away, shield you from the ugliness that was once my life, but will not be again. Not gonna promise there won't be difficult times with me. Can promise there will be. But the times in-between will be good, *really* good."

I look over my shoulder at him. "The times that are difficult can still be good, Collin."

The look he gives me is unbelieving, and it hurts because I know he hasn't had that, but I swear to myself that I will make sure he does.

I turn, knees between his legs, and take his face. "I promise."

He shifts his eyes, from one of mine to the next, and then again, before he looks at my lips, and I see the unspoken request, one in which I also give him.

What begins as a light brush of my lips to his starts an inferno. He grips my hips, pulling me closer to straddle him, as he takes my face, deepening the kiss. He tastes hot, wet, sweet as he sweeps his tongue over mine. I open wider to him, allowing him to taste me deeply, so much deeper than before. I tangle my hands in his hair as I push up, rising above him.

Panting, we pull apart only to go at it just like that again until breath is needed, and not just because it is necessary to breathe, but so we can continue lavishing one another with touch, taste, with … love.

Pulling me back to sit, he trails his lips down my neck, my jaw, as he moves forward, lowering me to my back. Body on top of mine, only clothes between us, he presses his full weight onto me and covers me like a shield. And for the first time since I awoke, I feel as if nothing can go wrong. Kissing, tasting, loving each other causes the heat in my body to blister, and this time, I know there is more to come, and I will make damn sure it does.

I press my hands to his chest, pushing him so he is again sitting. Then I straddle him, feeling him hard beneath me, heat spreading at the connection, wanting him, needing him, but his eyes hold a conviction, a resounding restraint.

No. Not today, I think as I take his hand and bring it to my mouth. I arch my back to feel him between my thighs as I gently kiss his palm, and then each finger from left to right. I stop on his third, his middle, and lightly flick my tongue across the tip, tasting his skin, and then I continue taking it in my mouth, slowly flattening my tongue and circling it to surround him. I watch his reserve crumbling, and his chest rising and falling more rapidly, until he closes his eyes and holds his breath.

I make my way back to the tip and nip at it. He opens his eyes, and I tell him, "Don't close your eyes."

Then … a tap on the door and Tomás saying, "Excuse me, sir. When you're free, we need to talk."

The sense of urgency in his voice has me hopping off Collin's lap and him standing.

"Give me a minute, Tomás."

Standing, he reaches inside his pants, adjusts himself, and mutters, "Fuck." Then he bends down and presses his palms to his knees.

Peering up at me, blue eyes nearly black, he warns, "One of these days, Tessa, you'll be finishing what you just started." Then, as he moves past me, he kisses the side of my head before he stalks to the door.

As I sit in his office and look at the empty walls, all I can think about is wanting to fill them with pictures like the ones on Jade and Ryan's walls. And I know this isn't the thing I should be concerned with at this moment, but whatever. I want to make beautiful moments worthy of being captured in photos to hang on his walls so he has something to look at while he's being a … whatever it is he does. I should be concerned, yet I am not, not even a little, which should also be disconcerting, but again … whatever.

And then *whatever* leaves when I hear him bark out, "And how the fuck did that happen, Tomás? Who the fuck are the guys you brought in? A bunch of fucking idiots! You'd better get some more people on this! I want this to end tonight. If you can't make it happen, I will! Updates every fifteen minutes!"

"Yes, sir," Tomás says, and then I hear a door shut right before I hear a loud crack.

I jump up and rush to the door, heading toward the kitchen where I see a … hole in the wall as Collin paces. I look to his hand and see blood.

What the hell is wrong with guys? Hit a pillow, for God's sake.

I don't ask this question. Although, I will at some point. Instead, I head to him.

"You all right?"

He takes my face firmly but gently, blue eyes full of pain as he tells me, "One of my men took Leia to the emergency veterinarians. Tomás thinks she was poisoned."

Bile rises in my throat, and I try to pull away, but he holds me more firmly.

"Let me go."

Regret mars his perfect features. "Can't do that." His grip tightens as I wrap my hands around his wrists.

"Collin—"

"She's where she needs to be. Best vet in the area. If you think I'm letting you out of my sight after this, you're wrong and, for that, I'm so sorry, but—"

"Are my tires fixed?" I ask, trying not to start flipping out.

"You're not going anywhere."

I whirl around, and he lets go of my face to wrap his arms around my waist, lifting me off the ground.

"She'll be scared, Collin! She'll be so scared! She hates new people!" I try to push his arm away as I tell him, "I'm going, and there isn't a thing you're going to do about it. You can't keep me here against my will! I need to be with her." The tears fall. "Don't you understand? She needs me. She needs me!"

He holds me tighter as he sits on the ground, holding me as I lose my shit.

"I love you, Tessa. I'm sorry."

Lower Level

Chapter Twenty-One

Collin

I told them—*the experts*—that she outsmarted them, which bruised their egos. The parole board sided with the mental health *experts*. I'm unsure if the parole board even read the letters that I wrote on behalf of her victims—*my two dead siblings*, and one survivor —*me*. I will now be forced to have my team of lawyers open an inquisition to obtain that information, although the findings will no doubt be tainted.

Like leopards, psychopaths don't change their spots. Once she was released by *experts* who felt she was rehabilitated enough to reenter society, she manipulated them, and I was asked to sit at counseling meetings at the requests of *experts* who believed she changed.

I declined until Tessa.

Tessa, who has managed to cry herself to sleep in my

arms while reading the messages that I was receiving every fifteen minutes from the vet, until I realized the sound alert was what was keeping her up and turned it to vibrate. Tessa, who may possibly wake up having decided this was too much. Tessa, who when she wakes up may decide to call the cops and tell them I am holding her against her will, is absolutely within her rights. Tessa, who could leave when this is over and head back to her hometown and never come back.

I'm not sure if it's this—*love*—convincing me otherwise, but I believe against logic and reason that she will do none of those things.

Once I have successfully laid her on the couch, I go to work to give her what she is giving me—a little bit of good in a difficult time. And now I'm waiting for her to wake so that she can see some good with her own eyes.

When I see her stir, I squat down near her head. When her eyes open, she looks around, confused, then sits up and asks, "Any news?"

"She's stable and resting."

She moves to the side and pats the spot beside her.

Thank God.

I don't sit. I hold out my hand. "We believe it's antifreeze poisoning. Found a few drops that appear to be antifreeze next to her dish. The vet has that information and is pumping fluids to flush her system." I pull her up and walk her to my office, where I pull out the chair for her, and she sits. "Would you like to see her?"

When she nods, I turn on the monitor. When she sees her, she reaches out her hand, touches the screen, and whispers, "I'm right here."

The amount of love inside of her, astonishing.

"You'll be able to see her whenever you want. Forty-two-inch monitor set up right in front of the cage, the camera right here is being fed through a satellite signal." I point to it. "Just press the red button, and when it turns green, she can see you."

"I still want to be there."

"I understand, but along with the fluids, she is receiving a sedative to keep her calm, so I assure you, she's none the wiser." I kiss the top of her head. "I'll leave you two alone while I go check on the Catherine situation."

As I'm walking out, she calls to me, and I look back.

She gives me the most sincere blue eyes and even attempts a smile. "Thank you."

"Unnecessary."

She clears her throat. "I'm sorry that your um … Catherine—"

"Appreciated. It will be done soon, and she'll be dealt with by whatever means necessary."

I text Tomás to come in and give me an update as I head to the door.

Opening the door, I ask quietly, "How is she?"

"Still touch and go, sir. They have her sedated so that she doesn't get agitated. She's comfortable and still alive. They say that's a good sign."

"Nothing better happen to her, Tomás, or heads will roll. She's a good dog, and she's Tessa's."

He nods as we walk over to the counter.

"Food's still warming in the oven. Eat if you'd like and tell me what else is going on."

"My contacts have talked to the local drug dealers. The subject's picture has circulated. They know there is a reward." He hates that it was offered to dealers just as much as I do, but I can't be out there looking myself, so it is by whatever means necessary. "We'll hear something soon, I'm sure."

"How many have already been in contact with Catherine?"

"Apparently, two. She came in last night, looking for a drug, specifically bath salts, and traded for them."

Meaning she fucked some low-life for a high.

"Rehabilitated, my ass."

"The second confirmed sighting was at noon today, and same exchange was made between the two. She should be trying to get more within the hour," Tomás concludes.

"Has a report been filed for each law broken and violation since she has been in town?"

"Yes, sir."

"Thank you, Tomás." I lower my voice. "Tessa has already said she was going to leave once. Please make the men aware that she is to go nowhere, understand?"

Tomás looks past me, and I know without looking that she overheard the conversation.

"Yes, sir," Tomás says then leaves.

I turn and see her scowling.

"Please let me explain."

"I know this isn't your fault, but you need to get that that wasn't cool with me."

I do know that, but it will not change.

"I'm sorry you feel that way."

She looks at me as if she's waiting for more, but that is truly all I have.

I open the oven and pull out the now *very* warmed-up meal. "Eat with me."

She shakes her head.

"It's not up for debate."

"I'm not hungry."

Grabbing two plates, I tell her, "Neither am I, but we've haven't eaten today."

She walks over, and I know she's going to attempt to plate the meal, but I would like to feed her as she does me.

"Would you grab the milk from the refrigerator?"

She rubs her hands up and down her arms. "Are you sure it's, um, okay?"

"No alarm was triggered. The house has twenty-four-hour surveillance. Tomás has gone through the tapes."

I grab two glasses, and she fills them.

"Would you mind taking them to the table?"

At the table, I feed her, and when she holds her hand up and says, "Full," I hand her the half-full glass of milk, and she finishes it. "Thank you."

"Of course." I push the plate aside then turn her chair toward me. "Would you like to watch a movie?"

She lifts a shoulder.

"Or we could go watch Leia?"

She nods and looks over my shoulder as the door opens.

"Sir, can I speak with you?"

Tessa pushes back in her seat and stands. "I'll be in there."

Once she's in the office, I walk to Tomás.

"One of our men just radioed in. She has been in contact with one of the dealers down by the wharf. She had a man with her, and a gun. They took everything the dealer had. She was last spotted on foot, coming into an area just a mile north of here."

"Good. This ends tonight."

"Sir, I think you should take Miss Tessa downstairs."

I removed myself from this entire operation in order to ensure Tessa's safety, but that doesn't mean I don't want to be the one to take Catherine down.

Tomás is my right hand for a reason, his instincts never

fail, and he knows what I am thinking at this moment. Confirmation comes when he speaks.

"Now."

I run my hand through my hair and nod. "Okay. Good job, Tomás. Please make sure the room is set up and the live feed to and from the vet's office is available downstairs as—"

"Already done, sir," Tomás confirms, eyes looking beyond me again.

Without turning, I ask, "Did you catch all that, Tessa?"

"Good."

I grab her hand and lead her to the bedroom, through the closet, push aside my suits that I rarely wear, and open a door. "This was created for this purpose. It may seem over the top, but I can assure you that I take safety very seriously."

"I couldn't tell," she says dryly.

She follows me down the stairs to the bottom where I use my fingerprint to unlock the door, and then we walk in.

I immediately attempt to explain. "This isn't a room that is often used. Its intent is not intimidation, although I'm aware that any situation that drives us here is, in fact, intimidating."

I watch her take it in, eyes wide and shadowed with fear.

The large room is all concrete, with no windows. It's a cell to some, but freeing to me. It's safe. She's safe. The floor is stamped concrete, making it feel less cell-like. In one corner is a king-sized bed with a wooden canopy. It looks like something you would find in an old English castle, which is why I had it custom made. *Irony, freedom in a cell, living like a king.*

A large armoire stands in the corner. There are red velvet curtains that can be pulled to separate the area, making it private from the rest of the space, if necessary for changing A desk sits on the opposite side of the room. It houses computer equipment and monitors, twenty of them, all with views of every inch of the property.

There is a wall with storage housing staples, such as water, some MREs, paper products, and canned goods stocked from floor to ceiling. Beside it is a door that leads to a bathroom, which is also concrete and locks only from the inside.

I head to the monitors and switch on the live feed from the vet first. "There's our girl. Stable and recovering, Miss Ross." I look back and see she's looking at me and not the monitor.

"I'm truly sorry about this." *More than I can express.*

Walking over, now looking at the monitor, she says, "This is all a lot."

"It is, but once explained, it won't be. And I assure you that I will explain everything when there is time." I pull over a chair, one that Tomás must have brought down, as well, since this space only has ever had one. "Sit with me."

I switch on the monitors then hit one of the buttons on the console.

The door locks, and the sound startles her. I take her hand.

"The door is locked. There is no way for anyone to get in here. You are completely safe."

She blinks a few times, shaking her head, and then she nods.

"Tomás is the only other person who has access, and he would lay down his life for me, if necessary, as I would him."

She inhales a deep breath then exhales slowly.

"Every entry into the house is secure, and if, after this, you decide not to run, I'll go into further detail as to why this is necessary, which will make things less overwhelming." *I hope.*

I watch her, waiting for a reaction.

She simply takes it all in then finally says, "Okay."

With that one word, hope returns.

As she sits, now curled up into a ball, watching Leia, I put in my earpiece.

"Update."

"Last visual of both suspects was five minutes ago. Ten minutes out."

"All entrances covered?"

"Yes, sir."

"Including bird?"

"Affirmative."

"Second check on safety. Night vision and vests."

"Done."

"I don't want anyone hurt."

"No one will be."

"Both are to be apprehended by any means possible."

He replies, "Understood."

"Authorities?" I ask.

"We have contacted them. Hopefully, they won't get here in time to fuck this up."

"They better not," I growl.

After silencing my audio, I turn to Tessa. "She's close. She and her partner are armed and high, which makes them extremely dangerous, but you are safe, I promise."

She nods.

"Do you have any questions?"

"What is this room for?"

"It's for situations like this. And it will be over soon."

"I'm sorry I have been so awful today."

I shake my head. "You've been reacting to a situation that you should have never been in. You woke to officers in a house you love, a place you love. Your tires have been slashed, a threatening note left at a place that is a sanctuary to you, and someone tried to kill your dog, yet you're sitting here, holding it together, so no, Tessa, you haven't been awful at all." I push a lock of hair that has fallen from the knot she places her hair in on top of her hair. "I'm actually in awe of the fact you haven't called the authorities to press charges for me holding you against your will."

She shrugs. "My phone died. I couldn't."

Shit.

She shrugs. "Not good with my comedic timing."

She was joking.

"Love your sense of humor, just not used to it yet. I sincerely hope that, after all this, you'll still give me the chance to—"

"Love doesn't stop because bad times are had, Collin."

Christ, she is perfect.

"I'm just sorry you have to have rooms like this, and that the vagina that spit you out may have been poison, but God surely wrapped you in His protection as you made that journey."

To that, I chuckle.

She sighs and looks away. "See? Poor comedic timing. I was being serious."

"She's here," comes through my earpiece, and I look at the screen as I hit the audio.

"Location?"

"Unknown at this time," he huffs out, and I know he's running.

"What do you mean, *unknown*?" I snap.

"I'm on the man."

"Do you have backup? Location, Tomás!"

Tessa points to a screen. "Here!"

"Got eyes on you and don't see her. Watch your six."

I grab Tessa's hand. "Thank you."

I see her nod in my peripheral but keep my eyes on the screen.

"He's going for his—" I stop as I watch Tomás dive on him and, within seconds, he's cuffed.

"Suspect two, apprehended," he announces. "Find her now!"

"Excellent job, Tomás. Are you okay?"

"Will be when that bitch is found," he says as I watch him stand, grab the cuffs, and jack him up, thankful Tessa can't hear the audio when the sound of what I assume is now a dislocated shoulder, followed by a painful cry, fills the air. "Police have arrived."

"Good. Let them have him. Find her."

"Is that her?" Tessa points to the monitor.

I hit the audio central so that all the men can hear me. "Suspect one going under the deck, moving toward the boat launch. She is armed, weapon drawn and in hand. I repeat, she is armed. Take all necessary precautions."

We watch as she looks up, gun raised, and it discharges. Then a dark figure shadows the camera lens, and she is down.

Tomás.

"Suspect apprehended," Tomás states calmly as he kicks her gun.

"Did he just jump from the upper deck? Did he get shot? Is he okay?" Tessa asks, voice and body trembling.

I take her hand. "Tomás, have you been shot?"

"I'm fine, sir, but I need bracelets for this bitch *now*!"

When I see the police swarm the area and cuff her, I turn to Tessa. "He's fine, and she's in custody." I stand. "We can head up now."

And she falls apart.

"No! Collin, don't you open that door. I want to stay

here! Please don't leave. Please don't make me go out there."

I grab her and pull her up, holding her together. "We can stay here as long as you'd like."

Then I ask, "Tomás, you good to handle—"

"It's all under control."

A New Day

Chapter Twenty-Two

Tessa

*I*t's dark when I wake, and he's not here, in this … control center? Dungeon? Hideaway?

I lost my shit, and he held me together. I'm embarrassed, because I should have been able to stay strong. I'm not the one who needs a damn cell to lock myself in to stay safe because I have a crazy mother.

I walk to the monitors and see Leia resting. I hate that I can't be there, and it dawns on me that I can. Catherine Abraham is in custody, and the world is now a safer place.

I head to the bathroom and see that it is all set up for me. A new toothbrush and paste, some of my clothes freshly laundered and hanging on a hook. On the shelf next to the shower are two towels and a washcloth. Next to them, a razor, body wash, shampoo, and conditioner.

I look in the mirror and see that I am as much of a freaking mess on the outside as I was—well, still am—on the inside. At least I know I can remedy that situation.

Standing under the hot water in—whatever this room is—the most peculiar of places, I ponder and process all that is Collin Abraham. And even with yesterday's nightmarish happenings, there is no feeling inside of me that screams *run!*

Aside from the fact that that bitch tried to kill my dog, which tears me apart, here I am. Leia is doing well, and the vet did say she expects her to recover, and Collin has been super sweet about it, and sincerely so, but I am definitely holding back my anger and trying to hide the emotions. And I'm doing that because she actually killed her own children—Collin's siblings—amongst other horrible things that monster of a woman has done, things he lived, things that he's still living in the aftermath.

He made me feel safe, so safe that I didn't want to leave this seriously intimidating place. And even though I clearly haven't a clue as to the depth of who Collin is, he has worn his heart on his sleeve the entire time I've known him, and yes—God, yes—how I know it's been such a short time, but he's Ann's Joe. He's held me together more than once, and neither time did I fight it, and I cannot say the same for the last person I loved.

On the surface, he is not *my type*. But, after yesterday's revelation, I know that he's definitely the alpha male I usually find myself attracted to, but he's… *more*.

Unlike Lucas, he's not cocky or arrogant —and doesn't cheat of me. He commits to love like Ben. But unlike Ben, he fights for what he wants. He is confident like Toby, but it's with an aged, polished, and cultivated confidence, he's... refined.

He's also stunning, with deep brown, thick waves of hair, dark blue eyes with specks of ... light? His bronze skin, full lips, and his body, more manly than athlete, a different kind of strong. He's an Adonis, an enigma, a freaking god. He's all those things. But, more than that, I feel his words to my core, and every time he looks at me when he says them, the earth moves.

The love he has shown me, I have felt so much deeper, at a cellular level, than I have ever felt from anyone in my life.

There is no rush with him to touch me. I don't get annoyed when he slows things down, because there's a reason; I know there is. He's not done making sure I'm with him, totally with him, and I love that about him.

Collin brings out my desire in a different way. The sex appeal, need, and want I feel for him is different than I ever felt with Lucas. The pain Collin has endured in his life, although not easy to divulge, he did, and when I hurt for him, he didn't try to hide it; he used it to explain who he is unhidden, and he did not take my reaction as me thinking I'm better than him, or see my reaction as pity. He saw it for what it was.

The comfort I found refuge in with Toby's love and Ben's smile, spunk, and heart, also different with Collin. He is not a means to getting over someone, he's not a rebound, or me trying to better myself by being with someone deserving. Not that it was Toby or Ben's fault. I did feel for them, but it was my confusion. If this were an equation where all the things I've ever felt were multiplied by a hundred, the correct answer would be a resounding, Collin Abraham.

I am head over heels for him, and logically, that's terri-

fying, because of last night and not my past. At this point, I
don't care what it is he's keeping from me, because I know
he's a good man, and I know I love him to a depth I have
never felt, not ever.

This realization is like a punch to the gut of me *B.C.*—
Before Collin—because that girl, she didn't believe she
would ever truly get over Lucas Links.

After dressing, and making myself halfway presentable,
I walk back out and find Tomás is at the desk. He turns
and asks, "How are you feeling, ma'am?"

I look behind me then back at him, and this is when I
know for sure that Tomás, with stealth-like ninja skills,
has a sense of humor. He reacted to my sarcasm. *Well,
almost.*

"Rephrase."

"How are you feeling …" he pauses then forces out,
"Miss Ross?"

"Annoyed."

He arches his brows to that.

"It's Tessa."

"Mmhmm …"

"Ninja or not, I will break you."

He purses his lips to hide amusement.

"Where is Collin?" I ask.

"I messaged him when you woke up. He was leaving
the justice building and should be here any minute." He
then pulls his phone out, hits a few numbers, and says,
"Miss Ross, for you." Then hands me the phone. "Dr.
Mackey."

"Hello?"

"Your girl's a fighter. I don't know how she made it this
far." I wince as she goes on, "She needs to stay calm, and
we're going to keep her sedated for a couple days. I really
think it best if you don't visit. I get the sense that is going

to be very hard for you. Dr. Abraham has gone to extremes to ensure you are able to see her."

"Do you think she is going to make it?"

"I didn't think she would make it this far. Dr. Abraham told me differently."

I can't help but smile.

"So, her being stable is a very good sign. If I were a betting man, I would bet on her. Her vitals are strong. Once stable, she has remained that way. You have full access through video, and if things change, I now have your number, and I promise I'll call."

After thanking him, I hand Tomás the phone.

"He's a good man. I hope you know that," Tomás states, and I know he's speaking of Collin.

"I do, Tomás. I know."

This is the first time I've seen Tomás with his sunglasses off. He has deep brown eyes and long, dark lashes, a really attractive, really military-looking man.

"How long have you known him, Tomás?"

"Twelve years, ma'am."

I glare at him, and he rolls his eyes.

"Miss Ross."

"Fine, I'll give you that, but you have to tell me your last name."

"I don't have one," he says as he pulls his shades back down over his eyes.

The door opens, and Collin steps in, looking all GQ, on the outside, but I know he's GI Joe under his black suit pants, gray shirt, with a black and gray woven tie.

He walks to me, stops, and looks down into my eyes. Well, I think, because he, too, is wearing shades again.

"How are you this morning, Tessa?"

"I'm good. I'm sorry I was so awful yesterday." When I wrap my arms around his middle, he relaxes and presses his lips to the top of my head, and I press my forehead into his chest. "I hope you can forgive me."

"No apology necessary. You were a trooper." He pulls my hair back gently so that I have to look up at him, pushes his shades back, and shows me his eyes as he presses his forehead to mine. We stay that way for a good minute, searching for answers from one another, giving acceptance, and silently saying we're okay.

"Excuse me, sir. The lawyers will be here soon," Tomás announces then leaves us.

I step back but don't let go. "How are you doing, Collin? Are you all right?"

"If you're okay, I am."

I shake my head, not accepting that answer. "How are you really?"

"This is going to sound harsh, but it is the reality. I'm great. She's where she belongs. She has done so much damage to everyone in her path, and now you. She's locked up and will be for life, God willing. I'll make sure of it."

I take his face in my hands, pull him closer, and kiss him.

When his phone buzzes, we break the kiss, and he reads the message.

"The DA's here. You ready to get out of here?"

"I would follow you anywhere."

Collin grabs me, lifts me up, and swings me around to his back. I hold on tight as he heads out with me riding piggy-back.

Outside the door, he looks back and asks, "Ready?"

"Absolutely."

"Good to hear, beautiful," he says as he opens the door. "You feel okay out here or—"

"I'm good," I assure him.

He does not go the same way we came in, not that I truly remember the way we rushed down to safety last night, but I do remember it was through his closet and not under the boat launch and down the stairs that we are heading up, leading to his back deck.

Once my feet are planted on the deck floor, he informs me, "There are donuts and coffee in the kitchen. You need me, you simply think my name, and I'll be here."

Good God, I think as I look up at him in the sun.

"Just gonna get some fresh air."

It is not lost on me that he looks lighter, like a weight has lifted off his seriously amazing and strong shoulders, and I'm so happy the bitch is behind bars, too, because I realize how much it has weighed on him from the day I met him ... *again*.

When I look next door and see the grounds filled with uniformed officers, amongst a handful of others who look like ... civilian badasses, he tells me, "They should be done soon. Then it's going to be cleaned, all food taken out and tested. If she messed with it, more charges can be placed on her. When they're done, Tomás and my people will be over there for a while." He watches my eyes, and I do my best to not freak out.

He lifts my chin, searches my eyes, and then he kisses me gently. "It's going to be okay. I won't let anything happen to you. As a matter of fact, you and I will get that fresh air later. I want you to sit in on the meeting. I think it'll help you feel safe again."

We walk into the office, and it is filled with a handful of people in suits and uniforms. He pulls a chair out for me, and I sit. He stands behind me.

"Good morning, gentlemen. This is Tessa Ross, and she'll be sitting in on our meeting today." He moves to sit beside me. "I want to go through the events step by step.

Tomás will be heading this if anyone has questions. Please write them down, and we will have a Q and A at the end. Tomás, the floor is yours."

Collin takes my hand and gently brushes his thumb over the top of mine.

"I'm sure you have all had a chance to go through Catherine's rap sheet, so we will begin with her release from Bedford Hills on August 20th, when the suspect was released and reported to her parole officer that afternoon. She was allowed to move to New Jersey, where she stayed in approved housing. Dr. Abraham secured a place for her as part of the agreement for providing her a home. She agreed to attend NA meetings, as well as bi-weekly meetings with a psychiatrist, also paid for by Dr. Abraham.

"On August 22nd, she was reportedly at a bar, drinking and trying to score drugs. She paid her bar tab with a check from an account that Dr. Abraham started for her upon her release, which was our first break. We have access to her account and have copies of the check, which is in the packet in front of you. We also have her on camera at the bar, talking to James Rico, a known drug dealer in Trenton. A copy of his rap sheet is also in the packets before you.

"While cooking meth, they burnt down the house that the suspect was residing in. Again, we have evidence proving that she bought the ingredients needed to make it. On September 1st, the house burnt to the ground, and both suspects were hospitalized and signed out against medical advice.

"Catherine had drained the bank account set up by Dr. Abraham the day before—she purchased a car. Dr. Abraham was in contact with the authorities in New Jersey. Because Catherine served her sentence in full, they would not extradite her to New York. The judge's decision was to send her to a rehab facility, believing that, with counseling and the fact that she had served her sentence with good behavior, she was not a high risk. Dr. Abraham contacted a facility and worked with them to set up a recovery plan for Catherine. He traveled to New Jersey and took part in a few very intensive therapy sessions with his mother. Catherine's counselor believed this could help to make it personal and less the institutional garbage that doesn't work." He looks at Collin with anger in his eyes and shakes his head.

"James was to spend a week in jail, and then be released. Thanks to surveillance cameras at local retail locations, we can place James at a pier downtown. He was looking through binoculars in the distance, watching Collin, Tessa Ross, and some guests. Another tape revealed he was also seen taking pictures of Miss Ross and her friends. Two days later, he went to the rehab facility, and he and Catherine walked out the door, got into a car, and drove here. The rest is in the report filed this morning by Dr. Abraham." Tomás sits down.

Collin stands and loosens his tie. "The ball is in our court now. The most serious offenses were committed here in Massachusetts—stalking, prostitution, felony assault, animal abuse, attempted murder, and trespassing," he states. "Who was in charge of searching Miss Ross's home next door?"

An officer stands. "Sir, we suspect that some of the food was tampered with. One of your men found a hidden camera in the main bedroom upstairs. It was connected to the Wi- Fi in the house and had a live feed to a site online. We have people checking into it now."

Collin grips the edge of the table, knuckles turning white. "Who searched the car owned by the suspect, and what was found?"

Tomás spoke, "The preliminary report was faxed a while ago. There were detailed logs of when you or Miss Ross left the property. Details about the places you went, photos from the whale-watching trip with guests from next door, specifics about the dog, including where her food and water dishes were placed, and dates and times of the volunteer work Tessa was doing at the church."

I watch Collin's eyes narrow as my stomach turns, and then a new level of fear shoots through me as Tomás continues.

"There was duct tape and rope, along with a sleep-inducing drug. There were notes on how they were going to execute their plan. I have made copies of our surveillance tapes and have given them to the detective."

Collin steps behind me, hands on the arms of the chair that I'm sitting in, bending over me, caging me in his safety. "Please tell me you now have enough evidence to convict and put these people away for life?"

"Yes, sir, without a doubt. Airtight case, Dr. Abraham," the woman in a navy suit says, sounding sure of herself.

"I want a detailed list of the items confiscated from the house next door. Tomás, you and your men get a few hours' sleep, and then you go through her house again. Then this one," Collin instructs.

"Yes, sir. And there's a team at the church doing the same thing now," Tomás replies.

"Okay, when that's done, I want the boat done, as well," Collin instructs then steps back. "All right, any questions?"

No one speaks.

"Good. Thank you, ladies and gentlemen. If anyone needs me, you all have my cell number. I'm taking Tessa away from this mess for the day."

I blurt out my fear, "Do they have names of my family and friends? Will they be safe?"

"No names, ma'am; just photos, and we have them, and the electronic media they used. They won't get them back ever. And *Tessa*," Tomás actually says my name, "they don't even know your last name."

Collin gives my shoulders a squeeze as he dismisses them. "That's a wrap. Great job, everyone. Tomás, show them out, please." He turns my seat and holds out his hand for mine "I have a date to get ready for."

I take his hand, and he pulls me up.

"It's been a long day. We're going to go and rest before you take me out on our date and sweep me off my feet again."

I nod, and he pulls me behind him to the door.

Chapter Twenty-Three

hen he pushes the remote to his keys, I hear a *beep*, see the flash of lights, and look up at him. "Did she slash your tires, too?"

"No, I traded in the car; got an SUV." He reaches out and opens the door, and I climb into the Range Rover.

"When did you go car shopping?" I ask as he slides into the driver's seat.

"Do you like it?"

"Yes, it's nice, but ..." I stop when he lifts the console separating us.

"Now you can sit next to me."

"You bought a car so I could sit next to you?"

His face turns a bit pink, a complete transformation from the powerhouse, in control man in a suit. "Yes, I did. Does that offend you?"

"No, Collin, it's kind of cute. But a little, um …
impulsive?"

"The other vehicles needed to be checked out,
anyway," he mumbles as he starts the vehicle.

This makes me laugh. "You're so adorable."

Then Collin Abraham looks at me, narrows his eyes,
takes my hand, and yanks me to his side.

A beautiful distraction.

C ollin pulls the vehicle in front of a hotel and slides
out, opens the back, grabs a suitcase, one that he
obviously already packed, walks around, and opens my
door.

Inside, I stand behind him, looking around at the
swanky hotel, and watch as the blonde behind the counter
unmistakably flirts with him while I stand right here,
looking like hell.

When he turns to me, he obviously sees my annoyance,
and the dazzling smile he shows me falls. "You okay?"

I glance back at blonde and see her eyes glued to his
ass. I wrap my arms around his waist, give him my own
version of a dazzling smile, and say, loud enough for her to
hear, "Take me to our room now, please."

He looks between my eyes, and amusement lights the
grim caused by that woman.

I toss him an it's-not-funny look.

He turns and looks at her. "Are we done here?"

She hands him the room key as he wraps his arm
around me and tucks me into his side. Then he bends and
kisses the top of my head. "Let's go upstairs, beautiful."

In the elevator, he turns, facing me, the amused glint
returning, and it's clear he thinks this is funny.

I stand, saying not one thing, hoping he gets the hint.

When the elevator door opens on the fifth floor, and a couple women, who have clearly been drinking, step in, he moves to the side, and they giggle.

My jaw tenses, and he chuckles. I give him a warning glare and know—God, how I know—he finds it amusing.

Each floor we ascend, I wait for the gigglers to exit so I can explain to him that this isn't funny and because a man as smart as him obviously isn't catching that. So, by the time we get to the tenth, and he steps off, I decide to show him by stepping right back in as the doors close. When he turns, I give him a little wave.

Eyes wide, mouth gaping, he shoves his foot and grabs the door, stopping it from closing. He then reaches in, grabs my hand, nods to the women, who are now laughing, and pulls me out into the hallway.

He looks down at me, confused, and forces a laugh.

"It's not funny." I pull my hand back. He still looks confused, like seriously. "Do you like all the ogling?"

His eyebrows shoot up, and he crosses his arms. "I guess it depends on where it's coming from."

"Are you—"

"I have a good understanding on your past relationship, Tessa, and I accept the challenges it may cause now, and in the future. I hope you, too, understand that I haven't had one and that I haven't because none of those in my past were you. From the minute I saw you, I haven't noticed anyone."

"Really, because the girl on her knees—"

"And trust me when I tell you, she may have worked at it, but even my dick knew it was yours." He picks up the suitcase that he dropped and takes my hand.

"The desk clerk—"

"Didn't notice," he cuts me off.

"The girls in the elevator you—"

"Thought your annoyance that we weren't alone was cute. I didn't know it was unwarranted jealousy."

Feeling seriously stupid, I look around and realize I don't want to be here. "I want to see Leia."

He pulls out his phone and shows me a message from the vet. "She's doing great." He then bends down and kisses me before pressing his forehead to mine as he says, "We've had a very stressful twenty-four hours. We're going to reset, relax, and reclaim what is ours."

Seriously sweet.

In the room, he sets the suitcase on the table as I ask, "Do you have my phone?"

"I'm sorry, the authorities confiscated all the electronics. A new phone will be here within the hour." He turns and ruffles through the bag. "As well as a computer."

I inwardly cringe at the thought of someone buying me extravagant gifts … again. "That wasn't necessary."

"I don't know how or when yours will be returned to you, so it was very necessary. You have school and family that will be concerned when this gets out."

"Oh God."

"It should be contained to local airing, and because we were involved, the media. It should take a couple days before they catch wind of it."

When he pulls out some shopping bags, I shake my head and step back when he tries to hand it to me.

"It's clothes, Tessa. I want everything cleaned that was in the house because who the hell knows what she did when she was there. I picked them out myself. See for yourself."

I look in the bag. Inside are two pair of Capris—one khaki, the other black—two crew tees—one blue, the other a light green—as well as two pair of jeans, a black strapless dress with a black shawl, running shorts, with a matching shirt, and a blue dress. All of it is in my size.

He hands me another bag that is made of satin. I peek inside and see three lace bras; one black, one red, and one powder blue, each with a pair of matching boy short style underwear.

Clearly, he likes lace.

Then he hands me a box.

"Collin, this is way too—"

"I ordered these while I was away after the image of you wouldn't leave my head."

How can you not want to see that?

Inside the box, tissue paper surrounds a white silk and extremely short nightie.

He hands me another box, exactly the same. Inside it is the same nightie in a pale powder blue.

I look up into dark eyes searching mine and ask, "You really do like blue, huh?"

"I love blue on you."

"Thank you, Collin. They are all wonderful and mysteriously all the right size. That was very thoughtful of you." I set the box down and am in his arms when his phone rings.

"A minute of peace," he grumbles as he kisses me quickly, steps back, and pulls out his phone.

"This better be important," he snarls. Pause. "Seriously?" Pause. "Unbelievable!" Pause. "It has to be now. Do these idiots know that we have made their case?" Pause. "Are you available to be here, Tomás?" Pause. "Fine. This is ludicrous! See you then."

He turns and looks at me as he tosses his phone onto the table, and then I watch as he runs his hand through his hair in frustration. "I am needed at the justice center at four."

"Okay." *So … no date.*

He steps forward when there is a knock at the door. Sighing his annoyance, he takes my hand. "I will not let this screw up our night."

When he opens the door, he steps back as a bellboy brings in several packages. He reaches in his pocket, pulls out a wad of cash, peels off a few bills, and hands them to him with a, "Thank you."

After he leaves, he turns to me and answers the question that was interrupted, "No more than a couple hours. The DA needs some more information, and I have to sign a statement. Otherwise, Tomás could handle this. If this wasn't necessary for the case against Catherine, I'd blow it off."

"I understand."

"I'll be a little late, but I will be here, I promise." He kisses me, sealing the promise, and then steps away. "I need to change."

"Of course."

As he changes, I look at the packages and boxes, feeling a little like Vivian in *Pretty Woman*, being showered with gifts and the wealthy hot guy in the next room. He bought me under clothes, for crying out loud! Couple those feels with the 007 shit, and the villain—his mother—tried to kill my dog, wanted to poison me, kidnap me, bugged Ann's place, and slashed my tires … my head's a damn mess, and I seriously need a nap, and some Jesus time.

When he walks out, he's on his phone, ordering room service, as I grab some hangers to hang the clothes. Then I set about trying to figure out my new phone. The brand Kyocera? I know it's just like his, but it's seriously above my comprehension, so I decide to charge it.

As soon as he hangs up, his phone goes off again. He

mutters something under his breath as he walks away and takes the call

Once I'm done, and the phone is charging, I lie down.

This is not how I expected this to go, but I will be damned if this case gets fucked up because of oversights or pure laziness.

I glance around and find her asleep on the bed, looking beautiful and *safe*.

I see her phone charging and realize she isn't "connected," and knowing how important her family and the ability to see her sweet Leia are, that's priority.

I'm learning about her needs and what's important to her, but I obviously misread her today in the lobby and the elevator. *I'll fix it. I'll get us back on track.*

I also now realize she doesn't like gifts, that they make her uncomfortable, but that's something she will have to adjust to, because basics, such as clothing, shouldn't make her cringe, outdated electronics are unnecessary when I am able to give her that convenience, and the evening attire wasn't a gift for her; it was for me.

I finish with her phone then connect it to her new computer. I download the necessary software and plug it into one of my hard drives. Then I begin uploading my music to hers and make a mental note to grab late 80s and early 90s discs in the genres she enjoys.

I use the information I had Tomás get for her email

account and set that up for her, too. If she wonders how I attained the information, I'll tell her the truth. My hope is to share everything with her, and soon.

This phone is going to blow her mind. She takes a lot of pictures, and this is the first mobile phone to have a camera, made in Japan. I'm sure a million others will copy the technology, and then the world will have the same luxury at their fingertips. *Yet big pharm hides cures for disease to enhance profit, and women and children are unprotected and used as commodity.* I shake away those thoughts, the ugly, and focus on making my beauty smile.

I take a picture of myself, not giving a damn how ridiculous it is, and set it as her screensaver so every time that idiot, *Lucas*, who I refuse to gain information on because, frankly, I would make a sport out of ruining his life for hurting her, calls or sends her a message, she'll see me. Although, I already know down deep that he's no competition for fate, something I never believed in until her. She's my gift, my prize. She is where happiness lies for me. I felt the world shift back then, and it's only shifted a handful of times in my life.

I know it. I feel it. I accept it. I will cherish it.

And … I need a cold shower.

Once I'm done, I walk out of the bathroom in a towel, drying my hair, and I smile at the gorgeous woman in bed.

"Did you have a nice nap?"

As I walk toward her, her face immediately turns red, and I can't help but chuckle. I give her a quick kiss then step back.

"I'll get dressed. Give me a minute."

*D*amn, *damn, damn.*

Waking up to all that is Collin Abraham has been a truly amazing experience every time it has happened. Dr. Double O, in a towel that left almost nothing to the imagination.

I watch him walk across the suite. Large feet, leading to strong, muscular calves and thick thighs. His ass, a perfect bubble that leads to his thick, strong waist and seriously broad shoulders. His body is naturally defined lean muscle and not shredded. I love it.

Watching his back muscles work as he towels off his hair … seriously sexy. His steps, a masculine kind of graceful.

I hug my knees, bury my face in my knees, and grin. Then I peek up as he walks by in jeans, *just jeans.*

He walks out of the bedroom and into the suite's living room area, and then walks back in with a covered silver platter in hand.

Collin sits at the top of the bed, back against the cushioned headboard, positions his legs—as I suspect—spread wide for me to sit between. He confirms that suspicion by patting the spot, and I move up, sitting as I always do—my back to his chest.

No words are exchanged as he places the platter beside us and we feed each other artichoke hearts, grilled chicken stripes, and then we finish with strawberries and grapes.

When we finish, he places the lid back on the empty platter, sets it on the bedside table, wraps his arms around me, pulls me in tight, and asks, "How are you really?"

I quietly answer, "Right now, rested, nourished, and safe in your arms."

"You say right now. What does that mean?" The way he asks is with all the sincerity in the world.

"It's been a crazy couple of days," I admit, "My emotions have certainly been all over the place. One minute, I feel like this; the next, I feel guilty that I do when Leia is sick. And when I say that, I feel like a complete bitch, because it's nothing compared to what you've endured, are still enduring. And then seriously safe and hopeful that Leia will be okay, that you'll be okay. In the same heartbeat, knowing that, in two weeks, I say goodbye to someone who makes my heart and head do flips."

He presses a kiss to the top of my head and replies, "I'm truly sorry things have been so complicated, Tessa. I love you. I assure you things will be okay. I hope that settles some of your concerns. And …" He stops when there is a knock on the door.

We both push out a laugh.

Moving out from behind me, he sighs. "I think it's time we get you ready to go to church." Then he leaves the room, and I hear the door open, and then, "Come on in, Tomás. We will be ready in a bit."

He returns to me. "I have to leave in a few minutes. I need to show you a few things." He grabs my hand and pulls me up. Then we walk into the living area. "Everything you need is here. I set up the phone. Tomás has the same one, so he'll show you some features you may not be familiar with." He points to the computer. "Same goes for this. It's more user-friendly than your old one. And before you get cross, or stomp your foot, you needed a new one, anyway. I saw that you hung up the clothes. There are bags and shoes in the same closet. I have to go. Call if you need anything."

He walks to the closet, opens it, and pulls a long-sleeved, black Henley shirt off the hanger and puts it on as he walks back to me. *Damn, damn, damn.* Then he grabs me and pulls me against him.

"I'm very excited for our date, even if it includes one hundred and fifty kids." He takes my face, tips it up, and kisses me. Then he whispers against my lips, "I love you, Tessa. I'll see you soon. Let Tomás know if you need anything."

In less time than I have to catch my breath, he's gone.

I shower, wrap myself in a plush white robe, set the new laptop on the counter, click on the live feed, and watch my girl ... heal as I brush my teeth, blow out my hair, use the complimentary moisturizer, and decide that moisturizer is seriously going to be part of my skin care regimen *that I am starting right now.*

After kissing my fingers and touching the screen, I close the computer then set to getting dressed.

I open the closet and see the bag that he picked out for me, and when I see the brands, I want to throw up. The first is a Coach messenger-style bag in brown leather; the next a Vera Bradley quilted mail bag, blues and whites; and the last, a black vintage Louie clutch. *Unbelievable* and seriously too much.

The shoes he handpicked for me are not my definition of extravagant, which are comfy Berks, my loafers from Aurora Shoe Factory, Nike tennis shoes, or old navy flip flops. There are a pair of black, strappy heals with red bottoms, a pair of metallic silver sandals, a pair of brown sandals, a pair of linen wedges, and a pair of running shoes that are Nike, and to that, I smile.

I dress in the khaki capris and blue shirt, throw on the brown sandals because it matches, and I bring my computer to sneak away and check on Leia if the mood strikes in the brown Coach messenger.

When my new phone begins playing an instrumental piece, I walk over and grab it. When I see the picture of him, with his name on the screen, I get stupid giddy and answer, "Hello, Collin."

"Hey, beautiful. You have some time to spare, so I've arranged for you to hit the hotel spa. Get a massage or manicure—whatever you want."

"Collin, I—"

"They're expecting you in five minutes. Got to go. I love you, Tessa."

"Collin, I love you, as well. However, this is all over-whelming."

"All the more reason to head downstairs, relax, and destress. See you soon." He then hangs up.

When I walk out into the living area, Tomás is opening the door to the hallway. "Ma'am."

"Rephrase," I remind him.

"Miss Ross."

"Tomás, this is too much."

His lips twitch, and he shakes his head. "I'm breaching professionalism here by telling you this, Tessa, but this is bringing him joy, so allow it."

"And, how do you properly give back the kindness to—"

"See who he is, accept it, and mean it when you tell him you love him. He's never allowed anyone in, and he chose you. Don't take that for granted, or with a grain of salt."

"Tomás, how—"

He pulls his shades down, ending the personal part of

this conversation and returning to badass. "You have an appointment. Let's get you there."

I've never in my life received a mani and pedi at the same time in a private room in a spa, and as amazing as it is, I miss my girls.

They work fast, and then, without asking, I am whisked into the next room where I am given a thirty-minute massage, and then I decide to have my eyebrows cleaned up. When I remember that Collin will more than likely get an itemized bill, I add a Brazilian wax, because I want him so close there is nothing between us, and looming over us is the black cloud, which is two weeks.

I know, without a doubt, the love I feel for him, and that he feels for me, is real, and if two weeks is all that love has in store for us, I am simply glad I get to experience it, but I need to experience it naked, too.

When I walk out of the spa and into the lobby, Tomás is waiting. He sweeps me away to the waiting Lexus and to the church.

When I walk in, Pastor Lou meets me at the door with a hug. "How are you, Tessa? I'm so glad to see you're okay. What an awful experience for you."

"I'm ..." I shrug and look around at the beautiful chaos. "Just sorry the kids had to miss out on a day here."

"Better safe than sorry." He nods to the mass of adults and the kids as they come in. "Let's wrap them in the truest love there is and give them a great time tonight."

Better Late Than Never

Chapter Twenty-Four

Collin

J sit in the balcony, *unnoticed*, as I watch her interact with the kids, smiling, laughing, singing and, yes, dancing. She loves this—the music, the fellowship —and the kids truly seem to love her.

Each group that comes to her is of a different age, and she quickly adapts to them. When the older group comes in, she sits on the floor and plays music from a boom box, and they discuss its meaning as it pertains to their lives. She is certainly intuitive and gives advice in a way that is friendly, sisterly, more than adult to child.

"How long are you going to hide out up here and watch her?" Pastor Lou asks, sitting beside me.

"As long as I can." I smile and offer my hand.

Shaking it, he asks, "Could use your help on the grill, if you don't mind? I have two hundred boiled hot dogs to put grill marks on."

S tanding at the grill, I pull my phone out and read the two messages that I've sent so that she knows I am here.

- Hey, beautiful, I will be there at seven.

- You look stunning, dancing and singing with those children.

- When you get a minute, come to the window. I'm the man in the apron.

Still no reply, and that's perfectly fine with me. There is no doubt the kids in there are here for a respite from home.

"What are you doing?"

When I hear her voice coming from the church's kitchen window, I look up. "Lou here thought I would be just the man to grill two hundred hot dogs."

"I'm done in here. Can I come out and help?"

"We would love that," Lou answers.

She comes out with a blinding smile and dives right into helping set up the tables where the food for after the end of the week ceremony will be served, picnic-style.

We load the warmers with dogs and buns, place the bags of chips in swallow buckets, and place the drink coolers full of lemonade and tea on the end of the table.

"Thank you both for the help. Now, go wash your hands and get into the sanctuary. The kids are ready to show us what they have learned. Maybe we'll all learn something today." Lou winks.

We head in, hands brushing against one another's. I

link our pinkies, and she smiles up at me, before we split ways and do as we're told—wash our hands.

I wait for her outside the ladies' room, but as soon as she steps out, she's surrounded and whisked away by some of the kids who she warned me would be accompanying me on our first date. She glances back, looking at me, mouthing, "*Sorry*," as they pull her into the sanctuary, and I find a spot in the last row to sit.

The program starts with some of the younger kids reciting memory verses. Next up is the mission story—a school in Haiti will reap the benefits of all offerings collected this week. Then the musical part of the program begins, and the little guys and girls watch the big screen as they dance and sing along, and they are not alone—they pull Tessa up to join them. They sing three songs then sit; three on her lap and several others hanging off her arms.

She is so much more than beautiful. *So much more.*

When the music stops, Pastor Lou takes the stage like I've seen him do many times.

"I'd love to thank our amazing group of volunteers for donating their time this week to help you each take a step on your walk closer to God. Let's give them a hand."

When the applause dies down, he continues, "I want to also thank the parents for bringing all these beautiful children here. You have given them a gift by doing this.

"I have some wonderful news to share with you. We have a donor here tonight who wishes to remain anonymous. He would love you all to have the opportunity to attend an overnight week of winter camp in February, or a week of your choosing next summer, at one of our camp locations. All you need to do is fill out an application for whichever week you choose. Your registration here this week at VBS is proof that you are eligible. It's a life-changing and fun-filled gift, so please accept it."

Tessa looks back to me before ducking around the kids and making her way back, sliding in the spot beside me and whispering, "You're some kind of amazing, Dr. Anonymous."

I take her hand, keeping my eyes focused forward.

"I wanted to share a slide show from the past fifteen years of VBS. Kids, we have some pretty fantastic pictures of you all toward the end, so pay close attention—you may see yourself."

As the slideshow begins, Pastor Lou walks to the back of the church.

The pictures start passing slowly, and I sit and watch them. When I see one of me and Ann, I get teary-eyed. Then I hold my hand over my heart when I see one of the older boys who I can't stop thinking about. He is so beautiful yet never smiles. He looks sad. I want to see him smile.

A few pictures pass, and I can't help but laugh, because that day was when I decided I'd make him smile, and I kissed the cheek of the little boy with brown, wavy hair.

The church sighs a collective *aw* ... and I look at Collin, and Collin looks at me, and we both speak, and when we do, we say the exact same thing.

"That was me."

Tears immediately pour down my cheeks as Collin holds one hand below his heart, his other gripping the back of my head, pulling it to his chest, as a hand grips my shoulder and Pastor Lou says, "He works in mysterious ways. If He intends for it to be, it will be. Sometimes, the things worth having are worth waiting for."

We sit there like that, my head to his chest, neither saying a word, because what could be said that wasn't already?

We stay until the sanctuary is empty, and then we stare into each other's eyes, lost yet never more found. It's that calm, content feeling that I felt leaving Blue Valley, but so much deeper.

He takes my hand and brushes his lips across the back. "Shall we?"

I nod. "Yeah."

When we walk out, Pastor Lou walks to us and hands me a photo album. "This is a thank you gift for all your help this week. Collin, thank you for your very generous donation today. What a blessing it will be to all these children."

"Thank you." I smile and hug him, not letting go of Collin's hand.

We each grab a hotdog then head over and sit under a tree in the distance.

"First act of kindness from anyone in my life, aside from those who worked here, was you."

Smiling, I tell him, "My first crush. First kiss." I laugh. "No joke. I told Jade I was naming my first son Collin. Well, I didn't remember it was Collin, but I did remember it started with a C."

He looks back and forth between my eyes and states, "You're serious."

"Totally obsessed with the boy who I wanted to see smile."

Then silence as we eat.

Once finished, I open the book, and we look at it together. The first page is a picture of me smiling so big, hands in the air. The next is him sitting next to Pastor Lou, both playing the guitar in front of the group as I sit with my hands under my chin, grinning. He is looking in my direction with a half-smile on his face. The next is a picture of us swinging on the swing set next to one another. The next page is me handing him my snack. Then a picture of him staring up at me, smiling, as I sing my solo at the weekend program. The last is the picture that was on the screen, of me kissing his cheek.

"Tessa," he finally speaks, "I'm pretty sure this is the best, and only date—damn … the best *day* I have ever had."

I kiss his cheek, unironically. "I think for me, as well."

Several of my little people come over to hug me and say their goodbyes. I stand as a few introduce me to their parents, and I can feel Collin's eyes on me the whole time, even after he excuses himself and heads over to help break down the buffet.

Once finished, I stand and take him in as he shakes hands with Pastor Lou, and then I watch as the past comes back to me in a way that is otherworldly.

Hair blowing in the breeze, he runs a hand through it and continues toward me. Never in a million years would I have imagined that little boy who I met all those years ago, the first boy I kissed, would be standing in the same churchyard, walking toward me all these years later.

Taking my hand, he flashes me a gorgeous smile. "Let's get out of here."

He leads me to the Rover, opens the door, and I get in.

As I buckle, I watch him jog in such a casual and relaxed manner that it makes me seriously hot, and in a church—*our church*—parking lot, around the front.

He opens the door, slides in the driver's seat, takes my hand, kisses it, and then he winks. "All right, let's get back to the hotel."

My stomach flips, and all of a sudden, I feel like I'm eighteen again.

To break the silence, *the seriousness of what we just experienced*, I ask something also serious and hope it's behind us. "How did things go at the Justice—"

"Everything's good. We'll talk about it, but not tonight. Tonight's special, Tessa. Tonight's for us, a reunion of sorts."

My head floating, my heart dancing, I flip the console up and get as close to him as I can while wearing my seat belt.

When we pull up in front of the hotel, Tomás is waiting, and it worries me. But when Collin tosses him the keys and walks around to my door, eyes smiling as he opens it for me, I realize everything is as he said—good.

We walk to the elevator, and I see heads turn. I glance up at him, and he's laser focused on the elevator, and me. I can't be jealous. I get why they look as shockingly stunned by how Collin is shockingly stunning. I'm sure they all notice the light surrounding this confident man.

When we step onto the elevator, we're joined by three women, and when he positions us, my back to the rear wall, his body turned into mine, his eyes connected to mine, I swallow hard and remind myself to breathe.

We exit the elevator on our floor then enter our room. He takes my bag and sets it on the table, eyes never leaving mine. He holds the side of my head in one hand and lifts my chin with his thumb. "Tonight, nothing but you and me. Everything and everyone else can wait."

He searches my eyes briefly and finds his answer, and then he kisses me. He kisses me in a way he's yet to kiss me

—harder, deeper, claiming, giving, and taking. As he pulls me closer, I move my hands up his chest, his shoulders, his neck, and into his soft, thick, wavy hair, and I pull him even tighter against me.

One hand still gripping the back of my neck, he reaches down with the other, behind me, lifting me off my feet as he kisses the hollow of my neck.

No longer afraid, nervous, or second-guessing anything about this, I am ready to give him everything.

Heat intensifies inside of me as he lightly scrapes his teeth down my neck while carrying me to the bedroom.

And then … my phone rings.

We look at each other, and I say not a thing, because maybe, just maybe, I'm expecting an interruption, but when it continues, he says, "You need to take that."

I nod, and he sets me on my feet.

Taking a deep breath, I grab my phone from my bag. "Hello."

"Tessa, you, uh … busy?" It's Jade.

"Hey, Jade, is everything, *uh* … okay?" I joke as I watch Collin bend and push on his knees and can't help but laugh. He looks up, narrowing his eyes at me. "Nope, I am not busy. What's up?"

"It's Phoebe. She's in lab—"

"What!" I gasp and nearly drop my phone. "It's too early, Jade! How many centimeters?"

"Three, and she's freaking out and says she's not having a baby until you get here."

"Tell her to try to relax and cross her damn legs. It'll take me seven hours to get there, but I *will* be there."

"You want me to tell her to cross her legs?" Jade asks, sarcastic humor in her voice.

"If she's only three centimeters, I will be there on time. It's Ithaca, not the moon."

"Her water broke," Jade says, and I can tell she's about ready to freak. And she's had babies for God's sake!

"They will let her go twenty-four hours after her water has broken. Jade, you're going to have to suck it up, pull on your big girl panties, and get in there."

And then she freaks.

"I'm not you! That's your thing."

I calmly tell her, "Love you, Jade, but you're seriously capable. You're a counselor, for God's sake. I'll get there before any vag is flashed and deal with all that."

To that, she laughs. "Fine."

After I hang up, I look at Collin, who is on his phone.

When he hangs up, he shakes his head. "I can't believe you're leaving me now."

And ... I break.

"Shit." He hurries to me and wraps me in a hug. "I'm just teasing you. It seems appropriate, given the current situation."

I look up.

"I know you need to be there. I've called and booked you on a flight, the earliest direct flight leaves in two hours. It is only an hour flight. A car will be at the airport to pick you up and take you wherever you need to go. The closest I could get you would have been Ithaca, but it would have gotten you there two hours after the flight into Syracuse, and it had a connecting flight. I hope that's all right."

Then it hits me.

"I can't, Collin. I need to get my dog."

"The vet says he thinks she will be ready to travel soon, but not today. She needs to be weaned off the drugs. We'll figure it out. You just worry about getting there for Phoebe." He uses his authoritative and sexy voice. "I've ordered a light meal. It should be here soon."

"You're absolutely amazing, Collin Abraham." I throw

my arms around him and hug him. Then I decide how to make the best of the hour I have between now and when I leave for the airport.

"I need to take a shower. It's going to be a long night,"

He groans and steps back. "I'm going to take my time with you. Go."

W rapped in a robe, I step out and see yet another bag.

"I got you some clothes. These should be more comfortable for traveling. Also paid the spa tab. Did you have fun before church?"

I feel my face get hot, knowing his mentioning the tab he's aware of the *services* I received. "Yes, thank you."

Collin winks. "I'm glad."

When I open the bag, I see a pair of black linen pants, a white tee, and a black jacket. In a smaller bag, there's a cotton white bra, a cotton nude bra, a cotton pink bra, and four pairs of thigh-high cotton briefs. I look at him, confused, until I see the smug look on his face.

"They're okay, right?" he asks.

"Yes, Collin, they are fine. Thank you again."

"Just making sure."

A knock at the door has him leaving me to answer it. I dress in the ... maternal clothes and can't help but laugh.

When he wheels the food service cart in, he stops and looks me over. "How is it you can even make that outfit look sexy?"

"I know I have to go, but I really feel like ... well ..." I pause then decide to just say what I feel. "I don't want to leave you, and I don't want you to look at someone else the way you look at me. I don't want to go to bed tonight without my head on your chest. I'm afraid, when I leave, you'll find someone—you know, the without strings kind of girl—and release all that pent-up frustration."

He walks to me and cups my cheek in his hand as I finish.

"I don't want to be without you."

"I'm not going anywhere. I told you I love you, and I mean it. I cannot, however, lie to you and say that I won't find another girl to help relieve—"

I push his hand away. "Oh, I see."

For some reason, he laughs.

"I'm so angry with you that I want to leave. I want to leave now." I walk out of the room, mumbling under my breath, "Just like him. How did I let myself feel like this? So fucking stupid."

He grabs me from behind and pulls me tightly to him. "I am nothing like him. The girl I plan to spend time with is Leia. I'm hoping she will be one hundred percent so that she and I can chill at home while waiting for your return."

I turn on him. "Do you like to make me crazy, Collin? Because I'm not okay with that."

He grabs my face firmly and kisses my lips, and then my neck. "No, I wasn't trying to make you crazy, Tessa. You didn't let me finish. Let's get one thing straight here; I am *not* your ex. I am a man who knew immediately that you would change his world. A man who knew what love was when he allowed himself to see you *again*.

"The vet is weaning her off the meds as we speak. I'm going to take you to the airport then go straight there to be with her. She's doing great. No trace of toxins in her system. I will hang out with her until you're done at home."

I push him. "*You* make me crazy, Collin." And then I pull him close.

His face becomes serious for a moment, and his eyebrows crease as he takes a deep breath and stands up. "I am not your ex, Tessa, but you do need to know who I am. I have packed this carry-on with some things. I want you to take your computer, and I'll email you a file I want you to read. It's all about me, the things you don't know, and the things I need you to know. You can read it on your flight. Some of it is information from me; others are from outside sources. I would prefer you not share it with anyone else— it's very personal information. I want you to really read it and ask whatever questions you need to ask. After that, if you want to run, I wouldn't blame you, and I won't stop you."

I shake my head. "If this is going to cause you pain or upset you, I don't need to read it, Collin."

"I need you to." His voice is barely a whisper.

I nod. "If that's what you want."

We eat on the couch and watch the clock the entire time, and when it's time, he helps me up.

"It's time to leave. You've got a flight to catch and a baby to help deliver, Miss Ross."

S itting in first class, I pull out the computer and check my email. I open the one that's subject is labeled: *confidential*. Then I save the file and delete the email. After it downloads, I turn off the Wi-Fi as the plane begins to taxi down the runway.

Tessa,

This is organized in order from my early years until now. Please take notes of any questions you may have, and I will reply as promptly as I can.

All my love,

Collin

The first thing I read is what looked like a scanned school record; lots of documentation about fights starting in grade two through five. He was suspended for breaking a peer's nose in grade five. Grades six through seven have no documented incidents. Grades eight to eleven, he did amazing—all grades were ninety-seven and up—and it looks like he doubled up in grade ten. Grade twelve was all AP classes.

He attended school at Cape Cod since he was in second grade, and no one could see what he was dealing with at home?

Okay, I think he was a scrappy little guy until he was, like, twelve. After that, he did great, except the blank in grades six and seven.

The next scanned document is from the police. I read a four-page report, through the tears.

Collin was arrested at twelve years old for murdering his mother's boyfriend. In a statement received from his mother, she indicated that it was because her son was jealous of her boyfriend. Collin had come home after being out with friends, and her boyfriend told him it was time for bed. He grabbed a knife and stabbed him four times in the chest. The man was taken to the hospital and died two days later in Provincetown Medical Center. He was taken into custody that night and sent to a juvenile detention center near Boston.

Another statement taken from Pastor Lou stated that Collin had attended a youth service that same night, that he had stayed after and had dinner with his siblings and Lou's family. He reports that he left at nine p.m., and that Pastor Lou had walked them to their home.

Neighbors stated that they heard arguing at about the same time the kids returned home, and that the mother walked out on the porch with a bottle of vodka in one hand and a small pipe in the other. While she was outside, they heard the boy telling someone inside to keep his hands off his sister, and then they heard glass breaking and kids screaming.

Collin refused to make a statement. He went to trial and was convicted of manslaughter. He spent a year in the youth facility and was released on good behavior.

Collin's note reads:

Tessa,

We can talk about this, but I can assure you it was self-defense. I chose not to testify after making a deal with my mother. She ensured me that she would not let anyone harm my brother and sister, in exchange for me not telling the authorities that she was allowing men to harm us for her own personal gain.

Pastor Lou and his wife watched out for them and for me. Lou brought my siblings to visit me once a month, and they assured me that she was keeping up on her end of the agreement. I ask that you call Pastor Lou; he will confirm what I have told you.

I also want you to know I understand if you have reservations. I would if I were you. This is some pretty dark stuff.

Collin

Of course I believe him. How could I not? What he went through as a child was horrific. Catherine is a monster.

The next document is another police report. Collin was arrested again at seventeen for aggravated assault. Again, it was another boyfriend of his mother's. This was after the death of his sister. He was pulled off this man by the police. The man was taken to the hospital and Collin to jail. The man recovered after being in ICU for over a month.

Tessa,

After this incident, I was told that, although my prior arrest was sealed, I was going to jail. Again, our friend, Pastor Lou, intervened and begged the court for mercy. I was given the choice to either join the military or go to jail. I chose the military.

This is a lot to process, and I have put it all behind me until now. I need you to know I am sorry if this changes how you feel about me, Tessa, but I promised you full disclosure, and I am a man of my word.

All my love,

Collin

His military record was spotless. He received his medical degree while enlisted, and he became a highly decorated officer. He did two tours in Iraq and received an honorable discharge.

While reading, I have to take several breaks as I process all of it. He had no childhood, and the person who was supposed to teach him right from wrong and show him love is a monster. Looking at him now, I know it's a miracle that he is even alive, sane, and sober. What he has accomplished in life is a miracle.

I love him now more than ever before. He is a gift from God.

The stewardess announces that we are approaching our destination and asks that we please fasten our seat belts and place our seats in an upright position.

I take a deep breath and look out the window to see the city lights. I can't wait to call him.

And then it hits me.

I just flew, and I did so without freaking out.

When the plane lands safely, I grab my bags. And, as I walk out of the airport, I see a black car waiting for me and pull my phone from my bag.

"Tessa," he answers quietly. "How was your flight?"

"It was very emotional," I say as I get into the back of the car.

There is silence for a few moments as I try to hold back tears.

"Are you still there?" he asks.

"Yes, of course I am. Nothing has changed, Collin, nothing at all. If possible, I love you even more now than an hour ago."

"Thank God," he sighs out, "Thank you, Tessa. There is more I need to tell you, but that's the absolute worst, I promise. Unless you have anything pressing right now, I'd love to hold the questions for when we're face to face."

"I can wait till I see you. Nothing has changed, do you understand?"

"Yes, I do now."

Again, there is silence.

"Switching subjects. Guess who is here at my place with me, acting like she's a puppy."

"Leia?" I laugh. "Is she okay, Collin? You can tell me the truth, please."

"She's great. We are actually getting ready for bed."

"Lucky girl," I grumble. "I miss you already."

"The feeling is mutual, Tessa. If you need anything, just say the word."

"I need you."

He replies, "I need you, too. How far are you from the hospital?"

"About ten minutes. They actually brought her to Syracuse. Thank God you didn't fly me to Ithaca. By the way, was first class really necessary?"

"For you, Tessa, it's not nearly enough. Why don't you give me a call when you get there? I have a few things to do before bed."

"All right, I will. I love you, Collin." *So, so much.*

"I love you."

Labor and Special Delivery

Chapter Twenty-Five

Tessa

*W*alking through the double doors leading into the labor and delivery wing, I hear the sweetest voice bark out a demand.

"I can't wait anymore. I want it out!"

Phoebe.

As I hurry down the hall, I pass the extremely full waiting room and stop, turn around, and head in.

"Hey, everyone. How is she doing?"

Becca, Joshua, and Ryan all laugh, get up, and hurry to me. I see Lucas sitting in a chair, arms crossed, looking at me completely devoid of emotions.

"When did you get in? We weren't expecting you for four more hours," Becca says as she hugs me tightly.

"I flew into Hancock; came straight here. I couldn't miss this."

"No drugs. Drugs are evil," comes from down the hall.

"She's not wrong." I laugh as I step back and glance at Lucas, who now has his hat pulled down over his eyes.

Just as I'm about to say hello to him, Jessie walks past me, beelines it to him, and plops down on his lap.

"I'm sorry I'm so late. I had an awful day. This city is a mess."

I simply smile at him, which seriously pisses him off, and he pulls her head to his neck and, while looking at me, says, "It'll be okay, *baby*. You're tried."

"Well"—I clap my hands together loudly, and Jessie jumps and gives out a shocked gasp at seeing me. I smile at her politely then look at Becca, Josh, and Ryan—"our girl needs me in there. See you all soon."

I stop at the nurses' station where some of my old coworkers are working.

"Hey, ladies. Can anyone get me a pair of scrubs? I'm here to help make your night a little bit easier."

Excited to see me, they whisk me into the break-room and, within minutes, I'm getting changed.

When my phone rings, I see Collin's picture pop up and answer it.

"Hey, I'm here."

"Know that, beautiful. Just wanted to wish you luck."

So sweet. So, so sweet.

"Gonna need it." I laugh. "She's having a time."

"Is there anything I can do to help?" he offers.

"I haven't been in yet. Heading in there as soon as I get dressed. But I'm guessing one of those hugs of yours would be perfect after she delivers a healthy baby."

"Anything you need, Tessa, it's yours."

Stepping into the blue pants, I whisper, "Love you."

"I love you. See you soon."

"Not soon enough," I admit.

He chuckles softly. "Get in there. We'll talk soon."

When I hang up and drop my phone in my bag, I look up and see Jade grinning.

"You totally got laid."

"Nope. What I got was a phone call interrupting that from happening and a flight here."

"I'd say sorry, but I'm not." She hugs me then steps back. "Lucas brought Ryan, and then Alex thanked him for coming. That's why he's here and—"

"Seriously, it's okay," I cut her off. "He's part of this—us. We all need to adjust."

"I hate her," she hisses.

I laugh. "Get over it, Jade. I have."

She gives me a firm nod. "Okay, now get dressed and come on. I've almost seen her vag three times now."

"Phoebe, just four more hours, and she'll be here," Alex says soothingly.

"Or how about now?" I ask as I walk into her room.

Alex smiles, and Phoebe cries, "You're here!"

"No place I'd rather be," I tell her and mean it I as I hug her. "Now, give me some updates."

"It's too early." She sniffs back tears.

I take her face and tell her the reality. "Your child seems to think it's exactly the right time. Everything is going to be fine." *And I mean that, too.*

Hours later, I've talked her into pain meds, and she is seven centimeters dilated and one hundred percent effaced, but she's still refusing the epidural. But, for now, she's resting

I head to the waiting room to give them an update, knowing that none of them will leave, yet expecting Lucas and Jessie would have. I was wrong.

"She's resting and, honestly, it may be hours or minutes, so you can all leave. I'll text everyone, I promise."

No one moves.

"Or, at the very least, go get something to eat."

Jessie and Lucas are the first to do so.

A t eight in the morning, I walk into the labor and delivery unit, and as I pass the waiting room to ask for information, I notice Jessie standing with a man who truly spends a hell of a lot of time at the gym, and it is not lost on me who he is—Tessa's ex.

I can't help but laugh to myself, because her hands are always in my hair, something I find sensual, and something else he missed out on. I laugh because it truly ranks at the bottom of all the things this Lucas has missed and will always … miss.

As I get closer, I see Tessa sitting against the wall outside, face buried in the knees that she is hugging. I walk over and squat down in front of her, finding she's asleep. And I stay there, just like that, watching her sleep until she finally gives me my favorite color—blue.

"Good morning, beautiful."

Her face breaks into a stunning smile as reaches for me. "Collin, you came?"

"You said you needed me."

She wraps her arms around my neck and, as we stand, I hug her tightly.

"This what you needed?"

Head to my chest, and hand to my heart, she nods as she looks up, eyes full of tears but still smiling.

"Everything's going to be all right," I assure her.

"God help me!" comes from the room, and she steps back.

"Go. I'll be here when you get back."

"Quick question?" she asks.

"If you're going to ask where Leia is, she's at your home. I contacted Jake."

She gives me a smile. "Not going to ask how you ascertained my address; just going to say thank you."

"But, just so you know, she is fond of Tomás, so that's always an option."

She shrugs. "She's got badass fever."

Laughing, I kiss the top of her head.

When we step apart, she glances down the hall, and I follow her eye to *him*.

"I hate to leave you right now."

I take her face and kiss her. Then I tell her, "I'm a big boy; I'll be fine. Go help Phoebe and your brother."

"Just don't ..." She shakes her head. "Just ignore ... Just ... *just* ignore—"

"Go." I laugh, amused she thinks the likes of some dumb gym rat is going to intimidate me.

"Love you," she whispers.

"Love you," I *don't* whisper.

I lean against the wall and listen to her inside the room.

"You ready to meet that baby?" Then, "If you want to leave, you can. Collin's here. He might enjoy seeing a friendly face."

A few seconds later, Jade walks out. "Hey there, neighbor. How are you doing?"

"Hello, Jade. How is everything going in there?"

"Let's go to the waiting room, and I'll fill you, and all of them, in."

I follow her.

We walk into the waiting room together, and Jade wastes no time making introduction.

"Becca, you remember Collin, Tessa's *neighbor* at the Cape?"

"Hello, Collin." Becca smiles warmly. "Nice to see you again. This is my husband, Joshua."

"Nice to see you, as well." I reach my hand out to her husband. "Pleasure to meet you, Joshua."

"Collin"—Jade smiles—"this is *my* husband, Ryan."

"Hello, Ryan." I reach my hand out and don't miss his glance at Lucas before shaking my hand.

When she doesn't continue, I nod to Jessie. "Hello."

She lifts a hand, and then I look at Lucas, finding it amusing that he's looking me up and down.

"And this is Lucas," Jade announces.

He lifts his chin as he glares at me.

I simply look away.

When Jade sits on her husband's lap, I decide to sit and attempt to be cordial.

"How are you doing, Jade? You tired?" her husband, Ryan, asks.

"I'm scarred for life," she says with dramatic flair, and the whole room erupts in laughter. "Glad Tessa is in there and I don't have to be."

"Bet Phoebe is, too," the ex chuckles.

Jade agrees, "Phoebe's a trooper. No epidural for her. She's ready to have that baby now. It shouldn't be long."

"Would anyone like some coffee or tea?" I stand.

"Would love some coffee," Jade and Becca say at the same time.

"I'll be back."

As I walk out, I hear a grumbled, "Can't wait, *Ahab*."

"Don't start," Jade scolds him.

"Douchebag's not even in the room; chill," he retorts.

Upon my return and approaching the waiting room, I hear, "So, is she banging him now?"

I walk in and look at him as I set eight cups on the table and take the two teas out of the holder. "I don't *bang*." And then I make my exit, staying in the hallway, waiting for her to walk out to give her a cup of tea.

The way he spoke of her struck a nerve. I don't trust that, if I go back out there, I won't punch the asshole in the face, so it's best I stay put.

Feelings of jealousy aside, it's infuriating to think he has ever put his hands on her when she is so clearly mine.

It doesn't take long before I'm offered a chair, and I accept it. Not much longer than that is when I hear Phoebe crying in pain and Tessa telling her, "You're crowning, Phoebe. Soon, really soon, you can rest."

"I can't!" she cries.

"You're doing great," Tessa soothes.

"Let's check you and see where we're at," an unfamiliar voice states, and I assume it's her doctor.

"I feel useless. There isn't a damn thing I can do," Alex

whispers loud enough that I hear it out here, but not loud enough for his wife.

"You did what you could, and she did exactly what she needed, Alex. Now she's tired. It's time for you to step in. She needs to bare down and is too exhausted to hold herself up. So, right now, you are going to help her sit up. She isn't going to like it," she warns hurriedly. "Then you're going to climb into bed behind her, put her between your legs, and act like a chair holding her up," Tessa instructs. "Then you're going to kiss her head and rub her back, and when she calls you an asshole, Alex, you're going to calmly say, *I know*."

I can't help but chuckle.

I hear a commotion, and then Phoebe sputtering, "What the hell are you doing, Alex? Isn't this what got us here in the first place!"

"Phoebe, doggy-style?" Tessa asks.

Phoebe cries out, "Yesssssss!"

Tessa laughs. "We're going to have a boy today."

"How do you know?" Phoebe yells at her.

"Hold for the answer," Tessa says, and then, "Grab behind her knees and gently pull them toward her."

"Dammit, Alex, that hurts," Phoebe yells.

I then hear the doctor laugh. "I know what I'm doing, Tessa. Concentrate on keeping her head together. I can handle this."

"Just make sure she doesn't tear," Tessa whispers, then louder says, "Phoebe, do you want to know why I think it's a boy?"

Pause.

"The sperm that causes the baby to be male are like sprinters. They run fast for a short amount of time. The female sperm takes their time. They check things out, and you know, kind of hang out with their friends and enjoy themselves. They can go much further and have endurance. So, if you were doggy-style when this little one was conceived, the chances are great for a boy. Deeper penetration, you know, especially if it was a Friday night when Alex here had been in the fields all week after classes, holding back the little Ross army for a few days."

Phoebe laughs through her pain.

Tessa continues, "Could you do me a favor and push really hard now, like you're going number two. I need to see if I'm right. Alex, when she starts pushing, you pull her legs up, got it? I love you, Phoebe Ross. Let's get this done."

I hear grunts and groans, and then Phoebe cries out, "Ouch, dammit! I can't do this!"

"Look at this mirror. Pheebs, you can see the baby's head. One more push like that, and your baby will be out and in your arms."

Phoebe's scream echoes through the hall, and then, "Did I do it?"

The doctor answers by saying, "Alex, you want to climb down here and do the honors?"

"It's a boy?" Phoebe asks. "I have a boy? We have a boy, Alex?"

"You did amazing, Phoebe. He's beautiful. You have a boy. We have a boy."

"I have a nephew!"

When it's quiet, I listen as the delivery crew takes over, does his APGAR test, and announce that, even though he's early, he is perfect. He's seven pounds, and nineteen inches long.

Tessa laughs, but within that sound, I hear tears of pure joy. "You did great, and he's healthy and perfect. Alex, you better go call the family, and then go let the crew know, but hurry back—*your family* needs you."

I sit beside Phoebe and watch her fall in love *again*. He looks like both of them—blond hair and beautiful.

When Alex walks in, he looks like he did before the accident that took his best friends away as he announces, "They all can't wait to meet little Remington."

"You want to name him after a gun?" Phoebe asks, trying to sound annoyed but fails when she laughs.

"I think it's a good name. Phoebe, please?"

"All right." She kisses his little head. "Remington it is."

"It's beautiful, Phoebe." I kiss her cheek then slide off the bed so Alex can climb right in.

As I'm walking out the door, I hear him whisper, "You and me, Remington, are so lucky to have your mother to love."

"You'll make me cry," Phoebe whispers as I close the door behind me.

I turn, tears of my own filling my eyes, and see Collin stand from a chair in the hallway.

"Hey, beautiful. How's the little guy?" he asks.

I wrap my arms around him and steal a moment with my ear pressed to his heart before answering, "Walk down here with me. I'm sure they are all anxious to hear more about him, as well."

We walk into the waiting room, hand in hand, and I ignore the fact that Lucas and Jessie are still here because, honestly, so what? All I ever wanted him to be was happy and loved, and if this is how he gets it, then good.

"Well, you all will be happy to know that she has agreed to Remington."

They all clap and howl.

"He has a lot of hair, and it's very blond. And, even though he is early, his lung functions and APGAR scores are great. He won't be moved to Upstate."

"You going to introduce your friend, Tess?" Lucas snaps.

"Well, I figured that has already been done. Sorry, how rude of me. Collin Abraham, this is Ryan and Josh. They have been friends of mine since forever. You have met Jade, Becca, and Jessie at the Cape. And this is Lucas."

"Nice to meet you all again." He wraps his arm around my shoulders and tucks me into his side.

"Why don't you two get a fucking room?" Lucas stands abruptly and puffs out his chest.

"Why don't you sit down?" Collin responds in a far less than warm tone.

"He's right," Becca interrupts, shocking me. "This is neither the time nor place for you to act like a jackass."

Joshua's mouth drops open, and we all stare at her.

"It's a stubborn animal, a donkey, not a curse word," Becca rationalizes her outburst.

As we all laugh, I remind her, "We're all human; I'm sure it'll be forgiven." When her face turns red, I reach out my hand. "She's your sister, too. You and—"

"Ryan and Jade first," Becca concedes. "We can wait."

"I'll go make sure she's ready." I look at Jade. "We wouldn't want to scar you."

Then I look up at Collin and give him a *you good?* look. He nods, and I head out. I am met in the hall by Mom and Dad, who had been out of town at some tractor convention that Alex didn't want to interrupt; Molly and Cory, who were waiting for his mother to come stay with Sydney;

and Jake and Sarah, who were waiting for Kendall to get in from Albany.

After hugs, Mom and Dad rush down the hall to meet Remington Ross, whose name I didn't share because, obviously, that's for Alex to do.

"You came back from the Cape?" Kendall asks as we head back to the waiting room.

"Wild horses wouldn't keep me away."

Molly smiles. "Was hoping the neighbor would."

When we walk into the waiting room, the tension in the air immediately dissipates when they see Collin, and then it gets even heavier than before when Lucas watches them hug him.

Collin smiles. "Good to see you again."

"Line just got longer," I announce. "The family has arrived."

"Did he already see him?" Lucas jabs a finger toward Collin.

"No, Lucas, he hasn't, but he will soon. Remington is my nephew."

Hurt flashes in his green eyes.

"This is for Alex and Phoebe, okay?"

"I'm going in first! First," Lucas directs that at Collin.

Collin's eyes flash red, jaw tightens, and he turns and looks at me.

"Might wanna chill the hell out, man," Jake warns.

"Jake, don't," I whisper then look at Collin. "Can you and I take a walk until they've all met Remington? Because today is about him, not the order people go in."

Hand in hand, we walk toward the nurses' station, and I bring him back to the break-room.

"I'm sorry about that. He has … issues." I give him a weak smile as I begin sitting down in an old, orange tweed chair.

He scoops me up, sits down, and buries his face in my neck as he pulls the elastic band from my hair and runs his fingers through it. I rest my head on his and sigh.

When the door opens and Rosie, one of the older and sweeter nurses I worked with, walks in, face ablaze, she holds her hand to her heart. "Oh, please, excuse me."

"Rosie, come in. We're just going to wait in here until everyone else has gone in to meet the newest member of the family."

"Oh, no problem at all," she says as she heads to one of the cabinets and grabs some supplies. "You've had a long night. Can I get you anything?"

"We're good. But if you happen to see Jade, would you let her know I'm here?"

"Certainly." She smiles. "Was that your mother I saw?"

I nod. "Sure was."

We sit in silence, holding each other; me reminding him this is where I want to be, him showing up here because I simply mentioned I needed a hug and doing it without words.

"What's going on in here?" Jade calls as she and Ryan walk through the door. "You hiding from big bad Lucas?"

When Collin speaks, it shocks me. What he says, blows my freaking mind.

"Not hiding. Just putting a hold on teaching him when it's appropriate and when it's not to push buttons. He is not to ever speak to her like that again."

"He's just figuring out that he's actually lost something he didn't know how to hold." Ryan sits across from us in a dingy, green tweed chair and pats his lap. "Don't let him get to you, man."

I change the subject. "Did you see him?"

Ryan smiles. "Looks just like Alex."

"He's all Ross but definitely has Phoebe pouty bottom lip," Jade adds.

Once everyone has met him, Jade pops her head in. "Everyone has gone in."

Collin helps me stand before getting up. Hand in hand, we walk down the hall, and I open the door and peek in. "Hey, guys, Collin is here to meet Remington."

"Collin is here?" Phoebe asks in surprise.

"He's been here a while." I laugh as we walk in.

"Hello, Phoebe, Alex. Congratulations." I watch his eyes move to Remington as they thank him. "Happy birthday, Remington. Such a strong name." He steps closer and looks down. "Welcome to the world, little man."

I immediately fall a little deeper, knowing that was all for Alex. I mean, not that it isn't a strong name, but I love that he gave that to Alex, too.

"Why don't you take a picture?" he asks, and yes, that was all for me.

"The camera is at the house." Phoebe cringes. "See? I knew we'd forget something."

"Her phone has a camera, and I'm sure, after you get some rest, Tessa and I will be back, and we'll bring it for you."

And that, that was for Phoebe.

"A camera on her phone?" Phoebe asks, and I nod. "Well then, after you take a picture, make sure you let Alex take one of the three of you, too."

Collin smiles as he pulls his phone out. "The three of you have to have the first photo."

"How does it come out?" she asks a question I wondered, too, but didn't want to feel foolish asking. But

Phoebe has a new kind of confidence now, and I love, love, love that for her.

"I can email it to Tessa, and she can email it to you."

"Seriously crazy." She beams.

E xhausted, we walk out, and I see the Jeep and smile up at him. As we get closer, though, I see a note on the windshield. I grab it and notice Collin looking around suspiciously. So, to ease that, I read aloud.

Tessa,

You really are pissing me off! Which I'm sure is exactly why you brought that dick here.

I stop, and he shakes his head.

"Don't stop on my account."

"But—"

He opens the passenger door for me. "Unless you don't want me to—"

"Deal with his shit?" I ask.

"You're not alone in this. You have me. We'll deal with it together."

I continue reading.

You need to grow up and get over it. I've moved on. Maybe you should do the same when you're ready. I know you're not over me yet, because you're trying to rub my nose in shit, meaning that douchebag.

You may want to keep him away. I'm not fucking joking.

It's not signed, but it's obviously from Lucas.

I look up and see his eyes narrowed and jaw set. Immediately, I wish that I wasn't so smitten over the idea of dealing with it together.

"Sorry, I shouldn't have read that."

"I would have insisted," he growls as he shuts my door then stalks around the Jeep.

When he gets in, exhaustion of the physical kind, as well as mentally from all Lucas's shit today, I laugh.

Through his teeth, he says, "It's not funny, Tessa," as he starts the Jeep.

I lean over, take his face, and tell him, "You're kind of hot when you're mad, and I'm—"

We hear the honking of a horn, and then Lucas yelling, "Don't start being a whore now, Tessa!"

Collin pulls away, throws the Jeep in drive, hits the gas, and cranks the wheel in such a way that we do a one-eighty and the front of the Jeep is pointed at the back of what I assume is Lucas's new ride.

"Ignore it, Collin. He's being stupid."

He doesn't ignore it. He nails the gas and whips through the garage to catch up to him.

Fingers white knuckling the wheel, his jaw muscles pop in an uncharacteristic Collin way.

I ask as calmly as I can muster, "Please, just let it go."

"He is not going to talk to you like that. You're not his anymore," he hisses.

Two cars ahead of us, waiting to pay the parking attendant, I throw the Jeep into park and pull the keys out.

"What are you doing?"

"He is trying to push your buttons, and you're letting him. I don't care what he says or does. I've dealt with enough of him. And straight up, you're scaring me. Please, stop."

"Tessa, give me the keys," he demands as a car behind us signals for us to move forward. "Tessa," he says again as he holds out his hands. "Keys, please."

I hand them to him, and then he pulls up and we wait for the car ahead to pay.

Thank God they're taking forever.

"I fell in love with you because you're nothing like him.

I fell in love with you, Collin, because you made me feel like I mattered. Right now, I'm not seeing that, and you don't seem to even care that I am speaking. Do whatever it is you need to do." I turn on the radio and pull my feet to the edge of the seat. "But do it quietly and wake me up when we get to my parents' place."

Chapter Twenty-Six

*J*wake to my belt being unbuckled and lips to my forehead. I open my eyes and immediately notice we're about half a mile from home, and on the side of the road. He gives me a quick kiss then slides out of the driver's seat. He opens my door and holds his hand for me to take.

I get out, and he walks us to the front of the Jeep where he lifts me up and sets me on the hood. Eyes searching, confused but determined, he starts. "I need you to understand a few things. Please, don't interrupt. That ass has been in my shit all day. I've sucked it up, and the final straw was when he stressed *go first*. It makes me sick knowing he has touched what I want, that he had you for five years.

I'm disgusted that he feels he can determine when you should move on." He runs his fingers through his hair. "I'm going crazy thinking he knows you better, and that maybe he knows you're not ready, but I know damn well you are."

"I'm ready to fuck him up after having heard him call you a whore, especially remembering you tell me you liked being a whore in the bedroom. I'm ready to blow, Tessa. Then you lay that shit on me in the car. What're you trying to do to me?" He doesn't wait for me to reply.

"This is new for me. I told you I don't do relationships, and this feeling in my gut and anger in my head is exactly why. The last person I loved … she was … I fucking killed someone because a piece of shit touched her, abused her. He thought he could …" He stops, turns, and kicks a rock. "Dammit!" Then he turns back. "Do you understand what I'm saying, Tessa?"

Tears start to flow from my eyes.

"Dammit, Tessa!" he yells, causing me to jump. Then he shakes his head, throws his hands in the air as he turns his back to me, and yells, "I know my way, I'll walk!"

Freaking the fuck out, I don't think anything except I will not survive seeing him walk away a second time, so I jump down, get into the Jeep, and peel out.

A few minutes later, hands shaking, I get out of the car and walk into the house, fire burning inside my chest. The frame built where the ruins of my heart once laid are being decimated again as Leia runs toward me, tail wagging. I drop to my knees and hug her as she licks my freshly falling tears.

"Well, hello, girl. You look great." She all but hops back and heads to the door, sits, and waits expectantly. I grab her leash and decide to let her lead me to wherever it is she wants to go. My girl.

As soon as the door slams, she starts to run.

Five, I start the countdown as I pound my feet against the sidewalk that is no longer cracked, but fresh and new, just out the back door of the old farmhouse.

Four. I inhale deeply as I run between the fields of sweet yet dusty-smelling hay, feet pounding against the hard, uneven, rutted dirt driveway.

Three. Body exhausted, mind blown, I push myself harder as I approach the corn. Rows and rows of it. No doubt a good year ... for most, just not me.

Two, I pant as my feet hit the freshly cut grass with colorful blue and white flowering weeds outlining the spot where the five of us became twelve, an even number because Kendall and I are unmarried, and yes, Jake, too, but he might as well be, and we have Sydney and Remington now. Sydney and Remington who will, no doubt, spend summer lunches, picnicking with Mom and Dad together again, on the grass, learning what love truly is all about.

I head into the woods, the path mowed down, no longer full of burdock bushes, ferns cut back to line a clear path to stay on, not to step over in hopes you won't get yourself stuck in the mud.

I make my way down the steep hillside, where a road is now tied expertly to help you steady yourself as you head down to the place I go to be alone, to think, to scream, to shout, to cry, and to wash away all my worries.

"One!" I yell up to the sky to hear my echo through the woods as I stand on the edge of the creek, toeing off my sneakers then pulling off my socks while watching the birds fly from their resting places.

Carefully, I step into the cool water and look upstream, trying to control my breathing as I take in the sight before me.

The falls …

"Okay, girl, go wash it all away," I say as I unhook her leash and watch as she plays and dances in the cool fall water.

This wasn't going to end well, and I knew it. I knew it was too soon, and that he was farther from ready than even I was.

I sit against the tree and wait for the tears to dry up, and I wait so long that … I fall asleep.

I wake to Leia barking, feeling out of sorts as I stand up to see what she is barking at.

Standing next to a tree a few feet away, Collin squats down as she bounds up to him, and he gives her some love.

"Your brother told me he thought you might be down here."

"Oh."

"I was worried about you. You've been gone for two hours," he says, trying to hide his annoyance.

I grab Leia's leash and start to walk up the trail, he and Leia following behind me.

At the edge of the field, close to the driveway, he speaks. "Tessa, would you say something please?"

"I'm tired." I hook Leia back up—my lingering fear after losing Chewy—and then I keep on walking.

We walk into the house silently. No one is home.

"Make yourself at home. I need a shower."

After I'm done, I walk out of the bathroom in a robe, and he stands, eyes wide and waiting for me to react, but I don't have it in me.

"There are towels in the bathroom if you want to shower. I'm going upstairs to take a nap."

After changing into shorts and a tee, I climb into my childhood bed and fall asleep.

Collin

After a shower and changing my clothes, I head upstairs and find her asleep, *peaceful* yet unsettled. I climb in beside her and cautiously move her so that her head is where it should always be—on my chest.

A few hours later, I wake, shocked that it's dark, that I fell asleep, but I shouldn't be. I fell asleep with her, and though she's not next to me, she is everywhere.

I make my way down the stairs of a house that is old, well-kempt, with walls that ooze love, and then I make my way to the kitchen.

Maggie looks up from the cutting board. "Well, hello, Collin. If you're looking for Tessa, she's out helping her father dry beans. If you walk out and hang a right in the driveway, you won't be able to miss them."

"Thank you, Maggie."

"We drink coffee around the clock here. If you'd like a cup, it's fresh."

"I appreciate that but think I should go out and speak to Tessa first."

She smiles. "I think so, too."

Maggie was right; I couldn't miss her. Standing on a ladder, high up, a good twenty feet in the air, I see her.

She's dressed in cut-off jean shorts, a tight thermal shirt, wearing a baseball cap and black rubber boots that hit just below her knees. That look hits me below the belt in a way that has me reminding myself that she's pissed ... and standing with her father.

I walk up and shake his hand—no sense in saying anything, since the dryer is too loud for conversation—as we watch her come down the ladder. I move to it and steady it, stepping back when she's down four feet.

On the ground, she smacks her dusty leather gloves and turns, startled when she sees me.

Eyes locked with hers, I have to shove my hands in my pockets to stop myself from reaching out and dragging her to me.

She kicks at the dirt a bit before stepping to me and looking up.

I mouth, "*I'm sorry.*"

She steps up to me, takes my wrists, pulls my hands from my pockets, and wraps them around her. Then she hugs me tight.

When the dryer turns off, she looks to her dad as he says, "Supper should be ready in a few minutes."

When he's far enough away that our conversation will remain private, I look down. "I'm sorry I was an ass. I'm not angry at you. You did nothing wrong. It was me."

She says not one thing.

"Tessa, will you please say something?"

"Do you love me, Collin?"

"Yes, Tessa, I do. Why?"

"I accept your apology. Now let's go eat supper."

Confused that that's the extent of our conversation, but happy she forgave me, we walk to the house.

Supper is wonderful, I'm sure, but I simply go through the motions to get through this so she and I can dissect this … this … relationship. Set parameters, tell her it is never going to be okay for anyone to talk about her, make her understand and find out just how the hell he's still involved so much that he's at such a private family moment.

We eat salad, corn, potatoes, and steak, the majority

grown here on the Ross farm, including the beef. But the best part is watching her interact with her family, and them with her.

After dinner, she offers to clear the table, so I help her. Her parents head out on the back deck and wait for her siblings to arrive. She washes and I dry, neither saying a word. She seems well, relaxed, and happy.

When we finish, I look at her. "Tessa, can we take a walk?"

"The rest of my family will be here soon. I'd like to see them." She smiles up at me. "And I need a shower."

"I promise it won't take long, Tessa. Please?"

She grips my forearm. "After I shower. I'm dusty." Then she walks past me toward the bathroom.

I walk outside and sit with her parents.

"It's beautiful here. So peaceful."

John laughs. "It is when you're not staring at it all, thinking of what has to be done."

I look around. "I'm sure."

"But, when you think deeper and realize what your hard work does, you get a feeling that can't be replicated and a smile in your heart. We feed more people with these crops than there are people in our community. There's a lot of satisfaction in that," Maggie adds.

I understand this on a level deeper than they know. Someday, I hope to get the chance to share. However, right now, I'm in purgatory.

"Something to be proud of, for sure."

John and Maggie talk about how important the farm has been in raising their kids, and how they feel it fostered the closeness they all share.

Tessa pops her head out the door. "You ready, Collin?"

I stand and look at John and Maggie. "I won't keep her long."

F lashlight in one hand, mine in her other, we walk across the main road and toward a field across the way.

"You must have a lot to say to me, so please say something—anything."

"You scared me today. I didn't understand, if you love me, why you just didn't let it go like I asked. I'm sure of my feelings for you. I just got in my head and decided that, if you were this freaked out already and not trusting me …" She stops and shakes her head. "I talked to my dad today, and he mentioned Lucas was basically attempting to mark a territory that he's long since lost. And that, because of that, you felt angry and … well, anyway."

She stops and looks up at me. "I'm sorry you were not my first *physical* love, Collin, but you came here for me, so I know you actually care. And here"—she places her hand over her heart—"has never been touched by anyone as deeply. Even though, at the time, I thought that Lucas and I loved each other, it wasn't love like this. We were kids. We were toxic.

"You have me here, Collin, and if you think about it and let go a bit, you may realize you had me way before Lucas. I hope, for right now, that's enough to put you at ease." She shrugs. "Now, if for some reason that doesn't work and you'd like to piss on my leg to mark your territory, I guess I could allow that. Definitely won't be the first, though."

She laughs, and I abso-fucking-lutely don't laugh, but I do close the distance and pull her into my arms.

"Please don't be mad at me for talking to my dad. But I didn't listen to them before. Had I listened, the last five years would have been different. You also need to know he's going to be around forever. We have friends, family, and a past that isn't going away. You have to trust me, and I know that's a lot to ask. That being said, I love you, Collin, I do."

"Then you'll have to trust me to have a talk with him. Maybe not today, or not tomorrow, but he's not allowed to talk to you the way he thinks he can. I love you."

"If he starts a fight—"

"I'm capable of deescalating a situation, and once you get to know me better, you'll understand that, too."

"Okay." She nods.

"Okay." I kiss her cheek, and then we head back, hand in hand.

W hen we return, her whole family is there, along with Jade and Ryan.

"Where have you two been?" Jade wags her eyebrows suggestively as we walk up onto the deck.

"Just went for a walk. I have to go inside for a minute; I'll be right back," Tessa excuses herself, and I sit down with her family.

Maggie speaks first. "So, Collin, we know so little about you. Tell us about your family."

Jade hands me a beer and I nod my appreciation. I take a long pull off of it, then a deep breath. *Well, this will save her from going through it.*

As I start to speak, Tessa walks out. "Collin, you don't have to do this."

"Eventually, they should be privy to the information. And this way, you won't have to." I sit back and pat the spot between my legs.

Arm around her waist, I start with father unknown, to

Mother's addiction, neglect, and abuse, *without too much detail*. I explain how that life's issues spilled into school and a wakeup call, with my focus being on my education.

"Okay, Collin"—she looks over her shoulder at me, tears flowing down her cheeks—"you don't have to. I love you, they will, too. No need to go on."

I gently wipe her tears. "I'm fine, Tessa. Are *you* okay with this?"

"I just don't want you to have to keep going through this."

So, I switch gears with Pastor Lou, and church, and tease with my first kiss and the kind, beautiful little girl with the blue ribbon. I then tell them about the life I took, dusting over why it was necessary.

Her sisters, mother, and Jade's eyes leak tears. I tell them about the deal I made with my mother, and Pastor Lou looking out for my siblings while I was locked up.

I tell them about the death of my brother that I believe to be at my mother's hand and not a drug overdose, and the same with my sister.

Then I immediately tell them about my education and military time.

And, in detail, I tell them what happened just a few days ago. They look horrified, *as they should be*. They love her. And, with perfect timing, Leia comes and sits beside me, basically asking me to tell them her part in that story, as well.

I finish by telling them about our last night of VBS and the realization that the little girl in the blue ribbon was Tessa. After that, I thank God that's what their focus is on —*the aw moment*.

I head inside and grab the album that Pastor Lou gave her then watch as they pass it around. A perfect distraction from the horror story they just heard.

John brings it back around. "You've overcome the impossible, son. I'm honored to know you."

Later, as we sit around the fire, I hear Jade whisper in Tessa's ear, "You sure you're okay, Tessa? That's a lot to deal with."

"I'm fine. We'll analyze him in great detail later. But, Jade, no need, really." Tessa yawns.

Jade and Ryan are the first to leave. The rest of them start to trickle out soon after.

"I'm ready for bed," she announces to her parents.

"Collin can have your brother's room tonight. I already put fresh sheets and a blanket on it," Maggie says as she stands.

Surely, she's joking.

"Do you want to show him where it is, or can I?" Tessa asks sarcastically.

"Go ahead, dear. I'll be up to tuck *you* in soon," Maggie replies just as sarcastically.

I guess she's not.

Tessa snatches my hand, pulls me up, and stomps—*yes, stomps*—up the stairs.

"Sorry it's not what you're used to."

"It's perfect, truly." I hug her and kiss the top of her head.

"I don't know how I'm going to sleep tonight without you in my arms," she says. "But I don't think the warden would go for it."

We both laugh.

"I'll be up in a minute, Tessa. Goodnight, Collin," Maggie yells up.

"Where is she?" I whisper.

She looks around, mocking horror, before leaning in and whispering, "Everywhere."

Again, we laugh, and damn, that feels good.

Sleepover

Chapter Twenty-Seven

Tessa

"Do you need anything before bed? She'll probably deadbolt us in here tonight."

His eyes soften and lips twitch. Body tension completely gone, he's finally relaxed and chill. Collin is … stunning. He also looks so caught up in this … this love, and I know—*God how I know*—he probably completely bypassed the school-age crush thing because he was too busy trying to survive.

I want to give him that—the flirting, teasing, the sneaking because you're worried you'll get caught, if only for a night.

I push up on my toes, brush my lips against the corner

of his mouth, and whisper, "Goodnight, Collin Abraham. I will see you in the morning."

When I turn and head into my room, I hear Mom walking up the stairs, and then she walks in my room.

"Tessa Ann, I'm not kidding about this. Not under my roof, not while I am living in this house. You will not have sex with anyone, do you understand me?"

I cringe. "Mom, seriously, could you keep your voice down? He's in the room five feet from here. He can hear everything you're saying."

"Well, good." She kisses me on the forehead then steps back. Then, loudly and with purpose, she says, "That way, I won't have to repeat myself."

I hear Dad laughing from downstairs.

"Even Dad can hear you," I whisper-hiss at her.

Voice still loud, she states, "That's right, and he is downstairs. You'll do well to remember that, young lady. And you, too, Collin."

I pull the blanket over my head when Collin chuckles as he says, "Yes, ma'am."

I throw the blanket off me and sit straight up. "Honest to God, Mom—"

Hands to hips, she says, "I couldn't keep you from making mistakes back then, but I will now. Both of you, got it?"

"Yes, ma'am," we say in unison, and then I hear him chuckle, which makes me laugh.

Mom winks at me, kisses my head again, and then walks across the hall. "Collin, I'm asking you—"

"Good Lord! Dad," I yell out, "will you stop her?"

"She's not wrong. Had we not screwed up back then, you wouldn't have made the mistakes you did and gone through the heartache. Sorry, I'm with my Maggie."

I'd be pissed at him had he not ended with such a sweet *my Maggie*.

Mom pipes back in. "As I was saying, I don't know what happened at the Cape house, but I don't want any nonsense in here, understand me?"

"Ma'am, I can promise you that. I can also tell you that your daughter and I have not had sex."

"Oh my God, Collin! Really! She doesn't need to know about my sex life or, in this case, lack thereof."

I hear Mom whisper, "Really?"

Collin whispers back, "I swear, ma'am."

Me? I want to open the window and toss myself out of it.

"Well, all right then. Goodnight, you two." I hear her shut the door, and it's followed by the three loud beeps.

"Mom! For real!"

"Yes, dear, for real. Sweet dreams."

Well, I think, *she's not wrong*. Had they not been a mess and stayed a strong family, I probably would not have pushed so hard to be with Lucas. *And we wouldn't have screwed each other up as badly as we did.*

I grab my phone and send a text.

- FYI, there are seriously alarms on the door, the kind that chime like store doors when you open them ... XOXO Tessa

I hear Collin laugh.

- Thanks for the heads-up. She is a treat, Tessa. Put your phone on vibrate; she might hear it ... XOXOXOXO Collin

- Is there a white board still above the beds? XXXXXOOOOO Tessa

- Yes. Why? XOXOXOXOXOX ... CURIOUS Collin

- We used to hold the magnets opposite against

the door, and it would disarm the alarm, so we had enough time to reach out and turn it off. XOXOXOX ... VERY NAUGHTY Tessa

- I think I would like to meet very naughty Tessa ... XOXOXXX Still CURIOUS Collin

- Then you shall. When they're asleep, I will message you ... XOXOXOXXX Naughty Tessa Out (For Now)

As I wait, I devise a plan, and when I hear the TV turn off, and my parents walk across the floor, I send him another text.

- Naughty Tessa calling CURIOUS Collin.

- I'm here. XOXOXO ... Collin

- You okay, or is being locked in there annoying? Please tell me the truth. We can leave anytime you want. I love you ... Tessa

- I am great, honestly. Today was highly emotional but freeing, all because of you. I love you, beautiful ... Collin

- Very sweet. Now let's do a U-turn and back this up. My parents' room is honestly at the very bottom of the stairs. This house is over a hundred years old (as if I have to point that out). And I want to see you!!!!! I NEED TO SEE YOU!!!! I am going to try the magnet trick ... Wish me luck ... Tessa

- Oh, Tessa, you're going to get us in trouble ... but I won't stop you ... XOXOXOXXXXX Collin

I grab the magnet then expertly disarm the ten-dollar system and shoot him a text.

- OK, I DID IT, NOW TRY YOURS!!!! WAITING ... Tessa

He does it even more expertly, *of course.*

I blow him a kiss then run to my bed, grab a pillow,

and flop down just inside my doorway. I place my hands under my chin, and he grins.

I send him a text.

- Aren't you going to get in your PJs? Tessa

- Are you? Collin

- Sure … Tessa

I hop up and shoot him another text.

- I want your shirt. Toss it to me? As far as I know, she hasn't installed motion sensors … Tessa

I lean against the doorjamb and watch as he slowly unbuttons his shirt, smiling when he tosses it to me. I snuggle it, holding it close enough to my nose to smell his scent and ogle his superior upper body unabashedly.

And he dares interrupt me with a text. A very… naughty text.

- Now I want yours … Collin

I feign offended.

Smirking, he shoots me another text.

- Now … Collin

I plant my hand on my hip, step back, close my door, and then send a quick text.

- What kind of girl do you think I am?!?!?! Goodnight … See you tomorrow … Tessa

- I can't wait. Sleep well, Tessa … Collin

I wake, jump out of bed, open the door, hit the chime to trick Mom, and turn his on. I hurry downstairs to the shower, dress fast, and then head out to start breakfast for Collin and my parents.

I'm too late.

"You just missed him, Tessa. He went to help your dad

with hay in the barn next door," Mom says as she rinses a cup.

"Good morning, Mom." I kiss her cheek. "I'm going to—"

"I'd love to talk for a minute." Mom sits and pulls out the chair next to her, so I sit. "Honey, are you okay? I didn't want to say too much in front of Collin, the poor dear, but I really am disturbed about the whole Cape situation. Why didn't you call, honey?"

"It was really crazy, Mom. I planned to tell you, but the police had my phone. Collin got a replacement, and then Jade called about Phoebe, and, well … I'm home now, and I have to say, honest to God, there's no place like it." I hug her.

She squeezes me tight. "Are you sure you don't want to talk to someone about this, to process it?"

Sitting back, I smile. "Thank you, but Jade was here last night. I think it will be well processed after she gets a hold of me."

"Okay, Tessa, but I want you to talk to me if you need anything," she presses.

"I will, Mom. We'll chat, but right now—"

"Go." She smiles.

I grab a ball cap, twist my wet hair under it, and then shove on my boots. "I'll be back."

I pull up behind the old hay barn and hop out. Looking up, I see Collin and stop when I see him throwing bales. Sweat drenched tee clinging to his body, arm muscles bulging, jeans hanging low on his hips, and a white hat turned backward. Seriously impossible which version of

Collin Abraham is the hottest, but this one is a farm-girl's fantasy, for sure.

I hurry over to the wagon and look up at Dad. "Where do you want me, Dad?"

"You're seriously going to do hay?" Jake laughs from the mow.

"I was pushing hay bales when you were still in diapers, Jake."

"You and he unload." Dad hops on the bale that he just loaded and rides it up.

"Think you can keep up?" I ask Collin, who is looking at me a lot like I was looking at him seconds ago.

He smirks. "I sure would like to try."

I climb to the top of the wagon and kick a bale down. "Better pay attention."

"That I will. You can count on it." He grabs the bale and loads it.

"Did my daddy teach you how to do that right, Abraham?"

"No, ma'am, but I think I can catch on." And he does. He loads them as fast as I can get them to him.

When the elevator stops, I hop down the bales, jump off the wagon, unplug the elevator, climb up on the tire, and scale the bales to get to the one that's jamming things up, throw it on the ground, and then shield my eyes as I look up. "Sorry, Daddy." I climb back down, plug it back in, and take Collin's offered hand as he helps me back up.

"Feisty little thing."

Nose in the air, I smack him on the ass as I walk past him. "You better pace yourself, boy. Wouldn't want you petering out on us."

I toss bales, and he loads them one after another until we're finished. Upon completion, Collin unplugs the elevator, and the guys in the mow start coming down.

When Dad gets down to the bottom, he calls Mom. "Hey, hold on breakfast. Tessa seems to have a point to prove to the new guy. We have five more wagons if we keep this up. We may not have to do hay tomorrow."

"Tessa, when did you get home?" Frank, one of our long time hay helpers, smiles.

"Yesterday. How are you doing, Frankie?"

"Much better now." He winks.

"Hey, Tessa." Mark hugs me. "How's it going since the breakup? You know I'm still single, right?"

"Shocking, Mark." I roll my eyes. "I'll keep that in mind."

Jimmy scoops me up and swings me around. "Tessa, look at you. Damn, you look fine."

"Thanks?" I laugh. "When have I ever not?"

I glance to Collin, and he's looking less than impressed.

I walk over and grab his hand. "Hey, guys, this is Collin."

I glance back up and see he's not only unimpressed, but he's not even looking at me. He hops off the wagon, nose to nose with them, steps past the crew, and grabs a bottle of water.

"Hey, Tessa," Jimmy says, "the fall festival starts tonight. How about we make a little wager?"

"What did you have in mind?" I ask, shaking the hay chaff from my shirt.

"Holy shit." Frankie coughs.

I glance up and see them all looking at me. "Seriously?" I slap him on the back of his head. "It itches, you adolescent jackass!"

They all laugh.

"There is the girl we grew up with, not the lap dog she was with Links," Mark goads.

I kick hay at him. "Shut up, you little weenie."

"About that wager?"

"Let's hear it."

"You and your friend take the mow. You can have your dad, too. If we can unload all five wagons, and you don't fall behind or say uncle, you win," he says, smiling.

"What's at stake?"

"You got to dance all night with us at the fall festival and do a shot an hour." He winks.

"When Collin and I win, you help my dad every weekend until hay is done, free of charge."

"Sure." He sticks out his hand.

"Deal." I shake it.

"You been in a mow yet, Collin?" I ask.

"No, but if those punks can keep up, so can I."

"We better"—I laugh—"we are going out tonight. Let's get this done." I push up on my toes and kiss his sweaty neck.

"Hey, Ken," Frankie calls after him, "get your hands off my girl's ass."

"Keep walking, hot stuff." I pull Collin behind me. "Keep walking."

After the wagon is changed, Dad climbs up and locks eyes with me. "Tessa, what the hell is going on? What bet did you make? There are five of them on the wagon, and three of us up here. Have you lost your mind?"

"Nope, we are working on free help for the rest of hay season. I'm going to start the unloading, you two stack."

And it begins. I start on unload, throwing them back as fast as I can, and I do not get behind. Collin stacks three to one of Dad's, while the guys take turns sitting down and taunting me.

After the third load, I call Mom. "Hey, call Dad's cell and pretend a pipe broke or something. He looks tired, and

I want him out of the mow. It's my fault I made a stupid bet."

When Dad answers his call and tells me Mom has an issue that needs attention, I tell him to go ahead. As soon as he leaves the mow, I flop down and rest.

"Tessa, you going to be able to keep up?" Collin asks, handing me a bottle of water that he just returned from getting.

I laugh. "Are you?"

"Absolutely. You just throw as far as you can. I can handle it." I take his hand, and he pulls me up.

"Do we get a third up here till Dad gets back?" I yell down.

"You givin' up, baby?" Frankie yells up.

"I can come up there and give you a hand or two," Mark says, and I roll my eyes.

"Shut up, assholes," I hear Jake yell from the tractor.

"What's going on?" Ryan yells as he jumps out of his truck.

"Nothing, bud." Jimmy chuckles.

The elevator starts up, and we get to work.

"One down, two to go!" I throw the bale.

"Tessa, just say the word, and I'll go down and finish this now," Collin sneers.

I grab my phone and send a text message. Then I smile at Collin as I shove it back in my bra and grab the next bale.

On the next load, I start to slow down, and he notices. He steps up his pace, and we manage to finish.

Jake comes up with water and looks at us then at me. "Tessa, are you out of your mind?"

"Let it go, Jake. We got this."

I take the bottle of water and down it. Then I look at

Collin and smile apologetically as the elevator starts back up.

Midway through, Dad reappears and takes over unloading, and I help stack.

Collin is a complete animal and doesn't slow down at all. Impressive and intimidating.

The bales start coming slower and slower, and I laugh out loud. "Backup's here."

Collin looks at me, clearly confused, and then Dad laughs. Collin catches up, comes over, and looks down, where Jade, in tight pants with a halter top and pigtails in her hair stands, talking to the boys. When she bends to pick up bottles and cups, it starts to really slow down.

I look back at Collin, who rolls his eyes, and I push him. "Sit and relax. We've got this."

"I am not—"

"Let me do this for bragging rights. There's only a couple dozen bales left, anyway."

"Goes against—"

"She sets her mind to something," Dad cuts him off, "may as well let her at it. This isn't her first rodeo with these clowns."

I look down and yell, "Skirts off girls; let's get this done. Collin and I have plans."

Once finished, Dad heads down, and I take this moment to peel Collin's shirt off him.

"I missed you last night, especially here." I kiss the place his hand lays to rest, near his heart. "I missed you here." I kiss lower. "And here." And even lower.

"Tessa," he hisses as I kiss right above his belly button. He closes his eyes, and I blow on his abs and laugh as I stand and step back. "Let's roll, Abraham. We have babies to see, and then a night to plan."

Once at the bottom, I point to Collin. "Not bad for a new guy."

They all grumble, and I give Jade a wave as she and Ryan pull out.

"So, Dad, these *girls* are yours for the rest of the fall; don't take it easy on them."

Chapter Twenty-Eight

S he throws the old Jeep into park, jumps out, and runs into the farmhouse. "Let's go!"

While I'm still attempting to process what all just went down, near the back door to the mudroom, I hear her laugh.

"Mom can you pack a lunch? We are going to the pond."

As I open the door, she drops her pants and runs through the house.

When Maggie sees my face, she laughs. "Sorry about that. I'll grab you a towel. No chaff in the house. You're going to have to drop yours, too."

Well, that explains a little, I think.

I untie the boots I am wearing—a pair of Alex's old ones—and toe them off as Maggie returns with a towel.

"Leave them there; I will take care of them."

Wrapped in a towel, I make my way up the stairs and look in Tessa's room. She's standing in a bra and underwear, ones I bought her, and although I've seen her in less, there's something about it that hits me hard below the waist, yet I am still a bit confused by many happenings.

When she looks over her shoulder and grins at me, eyes smiling *all for me*, she kicks the door shut, and I can't help but laugh.

"Get dressed, and I'll meet you down there," she calls.

I decide a shower is necessary and grab my clothes before heading down.

Once finished, I dress and walk out as Tessa hurries past me in a robe to get her shower. I stand outside the door and wait, because I'm not sure what she has planned next, and I am not used to that, either.

Dressed and toothbrush in her mouth, she opens the door and nods for me to come in.

I grab her up, sit her on the long counter, one I assume was necessary having five children and one bathroom for them to share, and she opens the drawer below her, grabs a toothbrush, peels open the package, squirts paste on it, and hands it to me.

As she's making silly faces at me while brushing her teeth, Maggie walks in with a basket of laundry, laughing, and Tessa openly grins at her, mouth full of toothpaste. Maggie sets the basket beside the washing machine and heads out.

Here, there is zero privacy, flimsy lines that are often crossed, and confusion by the "wagon load." It will take some getting used to, but that part of my confusion isn't any of their fault. I know this is what family is *supposed* to be. Maggie is what a mother is *supposed* to be. However, when you spent your childhood and adolescence shielding yourself, needing privacy and locked doors in order to feel safe, it's not without difficulty.

She slides off the counter, spits and rinses, cleans off our brushes, and then sets them in one cup, takes my hand, and says, "Let's go."

When we walk out, Maggie looks at her daughter. "I'm not sure if you're fond of Collin here or trying to kill him. That was an awful lot of work you two did today, but you're going to drink a couple glasses of water before you go anywhere, understand me?"

"As long as you packed us lunch, we'll drink," Tessa teases.

Sitting at the table, drinking a large mason jar full of water, Tessa sets her phone down, and I see her type out a text to Jade.

*- Thanks for the backup sister. I owe you one ... **Tessa***

She pushes *send*.

One comes back immediately, and she reads it out loud as I read along.

*- You do! Meet us at the festival tonight. Sing ... just one song for me PLEASE! ... **Jade***

"If that's what you want to do, we will. All part of getting to know you."

R iding shotgun, Leia between us, we drive down a long driveway that runs along a corn field. On the opposite side of the corn grows what I believe are black-berry bushes.

When I look ahead, I see a massive pond.

She parks in front of it, throws open the door, and hops

out, Leia following her. "Grab the basket from the back, and Ill grab the blanket?"

"Sounds like a plan." I step out and grab the basket as she pushes the seat forward and grabs an old, flannel, red and black checked blanket, fans it out beside the truck, and we watch as Leia sprints around the property.

"She's doing great," I say as I sit down across from her as she kneels next to the basket and rummages through it.

"She is, thanks to you and Dr. Mackey. Does she have my address to send me the bill?"

I take the sandwich wrapped in butter paper she's handing me and explain, "The bill is my responsibility. What happened to her was because of my mother."

She stops unwrapping hers and shakes her head. "You're a smart man, Collin Abraham, so you know her actions do not in any way—"

"This is non-negotiable."

She shakes her head. "Then you will take payment for today. And before you refuse, that's ten bucks a wagon. Do you know how much Old Milwaukee, PBR, or Red Cat that can buy for a field party?" she jokes. "Well not much, but pooled together, it's one hell of a Saturday night."

I roll my eyes. "Put it toward the cost of last night's accommodations."

"I'm serious. I want her bill," she sasses.

"Can we share a meal without discussing money?"

"Sure, we'll revisit."

I take her hand and kiss it. Then I pull her toward me as I lean against the truck tire, and she nestles between my legs, and we eat.

"Beautiful here, too."

"This is one of my favorite places."

"I can see why. It's peaceful and private. A great place to go and think."

Leia saunters over and lays beside us.

After we finish eating, I decide to ask the question. "You want to tell me about those boys at the hay barn?"

"Oh, they are just my brother's friends. They're harmless."

"Tessa, that wasn't harmless. They looked at you and talked to you like you were a part of their adolescent wet dreams. I didn't like it at all."

She looks over her shoulder at me and laughs. "Gross."

"Indeed. I'm not sure you caught it, but I was a bit irritated that you were carrying on with them."

She laughs again, like I'm joking. "It's harmless, Collin."

"If I wasn't exhausted, you'd be in deep shit." She knew I meant it, too.

"I love you." Three words meant to erase my irritation, and it does a good job, but this is something we will revisit.

"I love you, Tessa."

Head to my heart, she drifts off, and the fact I could fall asleep right along with her, outside in an unknown place, nearly erases that unease about today altogether.

I lay lips to the top of her still damp hair and close my eyes when I hear a distant rumbling. A few seconds later, Leia's ears perk up, too.

As the truck nears, a horn starts blaring, and Tessa jumps.

They pull up next to us and start piling out, all in shorts, shirts flying in her direction, and it seriously pisses me off.

She turns and climbs on my lap, straddling me as she takes my face and turns it toward her. "I'm not sure what to do to make this better, so I'm going to start by asking: does it bother you that I'm sitting on you like this in front of the boys? Does it make you feel better because they see that I'm into you? Or"—she brings my attention back to hers and presses her lips to mine—"does it make you angry?"

"I'm at the crossroads of *feelings*," I say, pissed. "Not sure I want to smash their heads together or try to figure out why you have relationships with men who think they have the right to act and speak to you in the manner in which they do."

"What do you mean?" Then she stiffens and follows it with. "What does *that* mean?"

"Ask yourself why it's all right for them to talk to you the way they do. Do you enjoy that kind of—"

"It's just joking around. It's funny." She hops up, irritated. "And I'm ready to go home." She picks up the basket and sets it in the truck. "Let's roll, girl."

I grab the blanket, hustle Leia into the truck, and hop in just in time.

She's pissed, and *so am I*.

"I don't know what's going on with you right now, and I certainly don't enjoy the emotional overload, but maybe you should search and find the answer to that question. While you're at it, maybe you should ask yourself why you called your friend to come put on a little show for them."

"Just shut up and stop talking to me," she snaps.

Seriously shocked, I ask, "Shut up?"

She turns up the radio. I turn it down.

"So, a conversation about this is what? Done because I asked that you think about why?"

She doesn't respond as she tears ass onto the main road.

"Is it wrong that I need to understand? That I love you and want to understand? This should be easy, Tessa."

She says nothing until she parks in front of the barn at the farm then turns, eyes angry, maybe even hurt, and says,

"Love isn't easy, Collin. It sucks, it's a job, and when you're the only person putting forth any effort, love is lonely at times. Right now, I need a few minutes, so you can march into the house and experience that lonely part of love." When I don't move, she yells, "Go!"

As I'm standing in the middle of the driveway, realizing I'm literally stuck here, I hear her speaking. "Jade, I'll take a ride to the festival. Apparently, I need a minute to think."

I watch as she gets ready to go with Jade to the festival and consider messaging Tomás and have him on standby with a car, but something stops me from doing so.

Her.

But she's not the only one who's pissed, or needs space, so I head to the deck, where Jake is sitting.

"Trouble in the Valley?" he asks as he hands me a beer.

"I'm not sure." I take the beer and sit.

"You wanna head down to the festival with us?" he asks. I look at him, and he shrugs. "Was in the barn when she called Jade."

I nod.

"She has a hot temper at times, mostly because she reacts to whatever needs attention. This causes the need for her to take a minute to wrap her brain around shit. I know this because we're a lot alike. I also know she'll think things through and all will be good, if you're good."

Jake looks to the door, which I'm sitting beside.

"Hey, how are you?" she asks Jake, having no idea I'm right here, or maybe she does and her head isn't *wrapped around* 'shit' yet. "Are you going to the harvest festival tonight?"

"Yep, Collin is going to chill with us, and we'll bring him to meet you. Is that cool?" Jake asks

"Actually, that's pretty perfect. Tell him I'll see him there."

He glances at me. "Will do."

"I'm just texting Jade now that I'm ready." She texts as I stand.

"Tessa, can we talk for a minute?"

"Sure, Collin," she states coolly as she drops her phone in her bag. "But Jade is on her way."

We walk toward the back field quietly, and when we're far enough so not to be overheard, I start.

"Not one of our better days, beautiful."

Looking at the ground, she mumbles, "You don't say?"

"But that doesn't matter because love is supposed to be patient and kind, right?"

She nods her head once.

"Then we figure it out because I do love you. I love you very much."

I'm a bit surprised when she hugs me, and glad for it. I know what I said is still upsetting to her. My hope is that, if I'm wrong, she can explain it to me, and if she is, we put an end to it, or I'll likely end up locked up … again.

She finally says, "You, too, Collin."

And we stay like that until a minivan pulls in.

I walk her to the driveway, and we part ways, but I hear her when she tells Jade, "Get me out of here."

Walking up the deck stairs, Jake shakes his head and hands me another beer. I sit and open it as John walks out and asks, "Where did Tessa go?"

"With Jade to the festival. We are going to meet them there," Jake answers.

"What's going on with you, Collin? You all right?" he asks.

Without reserve, I nod. "Yes, and I have something to ask you."

"Oh shit," Jake sighs out, but I ignore it.

"I'm in love with your daughter, and although she's upset right now, she feels exactly the same. We'll struggle a bit, like now, due to our pasts, but that doesn't change the fact that I'm going to marry her, and I would like your permission to ask her to be my wife."

John looks shocked but pulls it together. "You sure you're ready for that? Only been a couple of weeks."

"It's been much longer than that."

He scrubs a hand over his face. "Tessa has been through some hard times. You sure she's ready for that?"

"Dad, damn. This man just asked if he can marry Tessa, and you're trying to change his mind?" Jake jokes. "You have my permission, Collin."

"I watched a boy bring your sister to her knees, made her question who the hell she was for years. I watched her hurt and suffering as she pulled away from this family, hiding that pain. I am not saying it was all Lucas's fault. Your mother and I were going through our own struggles and not paying close enough attention. But I see Tessa again, and it makes me happy. Settles my heart." He looks at me. "Always her choice, but I'm asking you to make one, too. If you can't be the man she needs, walk away. If you can, and don't pull her away, or try to change her, you have my permission."

"I've no doubt I am and thank you." I shake his hand.

"When are you thinking this proposal is going to happen?" John asks.

"Soon," I answer.

"Gonna give Mags a heads-up, but I promise we won't ruin the surprise."

"Appreciate that, too."

"Her birthday's not far away," he says as he walks toward the door. "Two days."

I smile, and Jake laughs. "Guessing you knew that?"

"The information was not given to me, but yes, I knew."

"Are we going to the festival or ring shopping?" Jake laughs.

"The ring is already secured."

Jake laughs. "When did you decide you wanted to pop the question to my sister?"

"About a week ago. There was something about her. Then, at the church, I knew. I love your sister. I don't like how today went down with the hay help, but—"

"Bro, they're harmless. We told you about them at the Cape." He laughs. "We lit into them when you guys left. They're just worried about her, that's all. They grew up watching a strong, brave girl turn into a girl in need of a man, or a boy I should say, who made her his bitch, for lack of better words. She would have done anything for him. Made sure we didn't give him the farm boy fuck up when he deserved it. Told us to be his friend still. Asshole's been through it all, but that's no reason to fuck up her head."

The way he says that holds a warning, and I nod, acknowledging it.

"She had been so strong, independent, and confident. He rocked all that, and now, well, as Dad said, she's back. We all missed her. And if you aren't going to share her with us, you'll get the farm boy fuck up."

I assure him by saying, "She's happy when she is around her family. She has so much love inside her, and I would never want to take her away from that." I don't mention that the farm boy fuck up doesn't intimidate me one bit.

"Then be patient, man," Jake says. "You do what you feel is right for you and her, we'll give you all the support in the world. Just don't fuck her up, Collin."

I look up at the sky and nod. "I won't."

"You do know that she is going to be a pile when you see her, don't you? That look in her eyes … she was ready to teach someone something." Jake laughs.

Festival

Chapter Twenty-Nine

Tessa

*a*s soon as we pull out, Jade hands me a beer. "What's up, girly?"

"I'm so pissed at him, I could spit. He was so mad at me for the way the boys at the hay barn acted, how I acted, and said I basically pimped you out," I snap. "He wants me to think about why I need *that kind of attention*."

"Well, you did kind of pimp me out." Jade laughs, and I roll my eyes. After a couple seconds, she asks, "Do you know, Tessa? Why we act like that? It's positive attention. It feels good to have people want you. Good Lord, look what you lived—what we all lived—our senior year without guidance when we needed it the most. Not that it would have stopped us. We were at a crucial developmental stage."

I really don't want to think about it, but she's not

wrong.

"I look at Lukie and think, as much as he needed me when he was little, it's going to be that times ten when he gets into high school. Just because he will look grown, think like we did that he *is* grown, doesn't mean he will be. Add social expectations. You and I were freaks because we hadn't had sex as sophomores in high school. We let hormone-raging boys take over that roll of teachers, believed them because they were more experienced. We needed a little less high school and a lot more Jesus." Jade laughs. "You know better now. You got out of it, but right now, you want this man, and you've been in a sexual slumber."

"A sexual slumber?" I laugh.

"Hush and listen; I have a piece of paper saying I can give advice."

"Have at it." I lean back in the seat and take a really big drink of my Coors Light.

"I'm not saying sex is bad, Tessa, because it's not. And I am sure it's much deeper than that with the two of you than it was with Lucas. I loved Tommy so much, in a fiery, I-wanna-jump-that-boy's-bones kind of way. Then it was not so much his smoking hot body, but his heart and the way he treated me. But, with Ryan, my God, Tessa, he has been in my life forever, before any of that happened. I'm not going to step up on a pedestal and pretend we waited for each other; it just happened that way. It's kind of cool to think maybe you and Collin are like Ryan and I— always there, you know?"

"Ryan told me once that he could handle taking second to Tommy because he was gone. I believed it, needed him to do that for me, but he's not. Ryan and my love has a history that deepens it. Collin sees Lucas as a threat. Who wouldn't? He came into enemy territory, and now he feels like he's fighting the masses. Make him understand he isn't. Once he knows that, *really* knows that he may not have been your first but is now your only, he won't bat an eye. Swear, I think Ryan likes it when other guys check me out, because he knows I choose him and will every time. May take Collin longer. He's been through a lot, and he may not get off on it like Ryan does, but he'll chill."

"I just don't want to lose him, Jade, but I can't be Tessa at the Cape when I'm here. I can't be with him if he tries to change me, either. Look how that turned out. And I can't not be here. It's all confusing."

"Then do it right, Tessa, with your heart. Be honest about how you are feeling and avoid making him jealous. You learned that early." She laughs. "Dancing at the Cape?"

"Ugh." I palm my face.

"Yeah, your guy wigged."

"His reaction today leads me to believe he's going to run for the hills, yet his words …" I shake my head. "I don't freaking know."

"I don't think he's cutting and running. If it were that easy, we wouldn't be having this conversation. You are in love and, for once, you have one who wants to love you the right way, too. Don't push him away."

"Is that what you think happened with Lucas? That I pushed him away?"

"No. He fucked up. He fucked up huge and, from what I am learning, he did it a lot. We won't talk about how pissed I am that you hid it all from me. I know why, but you need to realize I'm stronger than I was, so no more of that shit."

"I didn't want you to feel like you had to choose sides."

"You and I, we love the same—it's forever. I love what he's done for us, that he loves the kids, and I know he'll

334

make sure Luke knows all about his father in a way Ryan and I can't. But I hate—no … *despise*—and want to cut his nuts off for what he's done to you and, in doing so, has done this to his damn self."

"He needs you." I shrug. "He loves you."

"I love my kids, but when Luke pissed in the only house plant I can manage to keep alive, he had consequences. You get me?"

I leaned against the window. "Thanks, Jade."

We drive into town through the winding tree-lined gully, and I try to figure out what I should do to make things better between Collin and me. I love him and know that he is going to be better than me at this relationship, which is totally ironic since he hasn't been in one, ever. But maybe that's why. He's not had his heart pummeled by someone who professes to love them in that way.

I sit up, freaked at the revelation, the thought I could do that to him, and send him a text.

***- I LOVE YOU. I AM SORRY. I hope you can forgive me. I want to be the woman you deserve …
Tessa***

———

e drive around a bit, chat, and I drink … maybe a little too much. At eight o'clock, we pull into parking lot of the fairgrounds where the Fall Festival is held.

"They didn't do this when we were in school," I say, looking around at all the teenage girls, who are no doubt ready to make bad choices.

"Not all about sports anymore." Jade shuts the door to the minivan. "Mostly because they all suck."

"Lukie will bring The Blue Valley Saints back around

one day," I say, linking my arm through hers.

"He can't do it alone, so you better pop out a few."

I nudge her, and we walk through a group of girls, two arguing over one boy.

"Don't you want to slap them and say he's not worth it right now? Hell, you don't even know who you are yet. There's time for that later."

"Exactly why I do what I do. And even that seems sketchy since, scientifically speaking, my brain isn't fully developed yet." She laughs.

Jade is a counselor at a girls' home about thirty minutes from Blue Valley. As a child, she went through some pretty horrible things and, despite what she was dealt, she made something of herself. She now helps others sort through the wreckage, trying to make sense of the past and set plans in motion for a brighter future. She may be flirtatious and sometimes a little too boisterous, but she's a survivor and a great woman, mother, wife, cousin, and best friend. And sometimes, she asks really stupid questions and makes questionable suggestions when I'm drinking, like now.

"You want to sing, Tessa?"

I see Adam's band and laugh. "Hell yes, I do!"

Standing in front of the stage, I throw two fingers in my mouth and give out a loud whistle. Adam looks around then smiles when he sees me.

They finish their song, and then Adam leans into the mic. "Tessa Ross, you want to come up here and sing?"

Jade gives me a shove, unnecessarily because I am totally going to sing and don't need to be pressed to do so.

Covering the mic, he asks, "'Cruel Summer,' Ace of Base?"

I nod, and he starts us off, "*Hot summer streets and the pavements are burning. I sit around. Trying to smile but the air is so heavy and dry. Strange voices are sayin'…*"

I sing to Adam and the crowd but look over it, not wanting to focus on anything but the song. When I look back to Adam and sing the chorus, he is taking in the crowd and glaring at someone, and since Adam knows only a few people and hates even less, I know it's Lucas.

I don't care, not one bit.

I want him to be happy.

I love Collin.

I avoid that area and look in the total opposite direction as I finish the song. I spot my folks and, knowing Adam doesn't have much love for country, I start singing and hope he knows the song. If not, fuck it.

"*Who doesn't know what I'm talking about. Who's never left home, who's never struck out to find a dream and a life of their own …*"

As I'm singing, I hear Adam say, "She's going rogue." Then the band immediately begins as I sing "Wide Open Spaces." In the middle, I nearly start crying, because Mom actually does shed tears. When I finish, I start to step away when another song begins. I look back.

"Get it, country girl." He laughs, and so I do.

"*I said, I wanna touch the earth. I wanna break it in my hands. I wanna grow something wild and unruly.*"

I see Ryan move behind Jade and wrap his arms around her and they sway.

"*I wanna sleep on the hard ground. In the comfort of your arms. On a pillow of blue bonnets. In a blanket made of stars. Oh, it sounds good to me.*"

Something catches my eye and forces me to turn, and as I start the chorus, my eyes lock with his. "*I said, cowboy take me away. Fly this girl as high as you can into the wild blue. Set me free, oh, I pray. Closer to heaven above and closer to you. Closer to you.*"

My eyes don't leave his as I sing the words, words

written from someone else's imagination, but I know—*God I know*—that they must have been written for us.

"*Closer to heaven above and closer to you. Closer to you. Closer to you. Cowboy, take me away. Closer to you.*"

When the song ends, Adam announces a break and walks to me.

"Adam, I want you to meet someone." I grab his hand and drag him down the stairs, beelining it for Collin.

"Adam, this is Collin. Collin, Adam was my voice and piano coach."

Adam crosses his arms. "He better not end up being a dick like that bitch over there."

"Not even close." I smile at Collin and explain, "He, uh … doesn't like Lucas."

"Well, then we have something in common. Nice to meet you, Adam." Collin extends his hand.

Adam shakes it firmly. "You, too."

After some small talk, Adam heads to get a drink.

"That was amazing," Collin whispers in my ear then kisses my cheek.

"Uh-huh." I take his face and kiss his lips.

"Collin, let's roll," Jake calls from behind us, and we both laugh.

"See you in a bit?" Collin kisses my head then my palms, one then the other, and then walks away, looking over his shoulder and smiling at me.

The boys hit the beer tent, and Jade and I stay and dance a bit then head over to get a drink ourselves.

Sippy wine slushies we sit at a table with a perfect view of the guys.

"Jade, check out that hottie. I could just sit here and watch him all night."

Collin certainly stands out from the rest of the locals. Everyone seems to notice it except for him. He's wearing loose-fitting jeans and a navy tee-shirt. Not overdressed but just the way his clothes fit his body ... perfect. No flannels, or Carharts, although he'd rock those, too. And nothing tight, showing off his killer body. His clothing simply fit him in a way that look incredible. He is so beautiful. Not that Lucas isn't, but it's like night and day.

Lucas looks like a mannequin in the window of a sporting goods store. Collin is the man who inspired the sculptor who would not sleep until his image was created so he would never forget the beauty he was blessed enough to catch sight of. Collin is confident, as opposed to Lucas, who comes off as haughty.

We watch as Jake introduces Collin to some of their friends, as well as the boys from earlier.

Jade laughs when he steps to them. "How is this going to turn out?"

"It'll be fine. Jake will make it better," I answer with confidence.

One of them extends their hand, and he shakes it. Then the others do the same.

All better.

I watch as he scans the crowd and doesn't find what he's looking for—*me*. I love that he doesn't notice the women in a circle next to him, all checking him out, and when he does, he completely dismisses their smiles and continues looking around.

His eyes stop scanning then narrow. I follow his line of vision and see Lucas, who is seriously drunk. Lucas raises his glass to Collin then flips him off. Collin's jaw clenches, and Lucas beckons him with a hand.

"There's trouble brewing, Tessa," Jade says, and we both stand.

"I see that," I say as we walk toward Collin, Jake, and the boys.

"Is it a turn-on to you?" she asks seductively.

"Nope, not at all," I say as I reach in my pocket, grab my phone, and send him a text.

- *You're looking fine, cowboy ... XOXOXO*

I watch as he grabs his phone out of his pocket and smiles as he reads the message.

- *Where are you, Tessa? ... XXX*
- *Taking in the view ... XXX*
- *How is it? ... XXXX*
- *It's a great view ... XXX*

He laughs out loud as he scans the crowd again.

Lucas catches his eye again and points down, pretending to grip something waist height and thrusting his hips forward and back as he yells over the crowd, "She's right here."

Jade and I look at each other then walk more quickly through the crowd toward Collin.

Jake gets in front of him as he stalks toward Lucas and stops him.

I run, jump up, and wrap my arms around his shoulders, and legs around his waist, as I plant a kiss to his lips. Then, against them, I ask, "Miss me?"

Collin smiles tightly but gives his eyes to me as I slide down his body. Then he pulls me into his arms and kisses my head. "Tessa, I need to deal with this."

I start to reply, but he places a finger over my lips.

"You hiding behind these little fucks?" Lucas yells over the crowd, and I know he's moved closer to us.

I look over my shoulder and see the boys all shake their heads.

"Tessa, want to come over here and show that bitch what I made you so good at!"

To Lucas's words, not only does Collin's body go hyper-stiff, but I am beyond pissed, as well as fucking embarrassed as I take in the crowd gathered around, and all eyes on us.

"Can we leave now, please?" I ask.

"No, Tessa, I want to tear his fucking head off," Collin growls.

"I'm pretty pissed right now, too, Collin, and would love to say a few words myself, but it's really not worth it." He moves forward a bit, and I push him back. "He doesn't deserve any more of my time. Can we please leave? Please, Collin?"

He looks down, holds the back of my head, and kisses me. Then, forehead to mine, he answers, "If that's what you want, then yes."

I hear a wild animal-type scream, and then my hair gets yanked back, and pretty hard, too. I whirl, fist raised, not giving a damn who it is, and when I see her, I do not hesitate. I punch the bitch right in the nose.

"Put your bitch on a leash, Links!" I scream then look at Collin, who looks shook. "Come on, everyone; let's get out of here."

"Lucas, cut the shit!" Jade yells at him, and I glance back to see him scowl and look down. And I know that, from Jade, it means something to him.

Collin opens the door for me, and I climb into the minivan. Then he buckles me in. "You okay?" I nod, and he kisses my hand then my cheek and steps back to close the door.

Jade hops in the driver's side and rolls down the window to yell to Ryan, "To the farm, lover."

"You good to drive?" He asks.

"Two slushies, I'm good," she winks.

After stopping at the store to grab snacks, I call Alex to see how everyone is and ask if we can visit tomorrow—he requested a day for just the three of them—then we head up the hill.

Pulling into the farm, I see a faint light in the living room and assume Mom and Dad are watching Saturday Night Live. We head behind the barn and drive down the bumpy road leading to the family picnic spot where a small fire has been started at the pit.

Collin is at my door before I even unbuckle. He opens it, takes my hand, and I wince.

"You okay, beautiful?" he asks, and I nod. "Did you hurt your hand on her face?"

Laughing through the pain, I admit, "Actually, I did."

Jade slides out. "So off brand for you, Miss Ross."

"Happen often?" Collin asks.

"Just when his crazy-ass exes go after her," Jade answers for me.

"Jessie's not an ex, so—"

"He's a fucking idiot, but mark my word, she will be," Jade remarks.

"Aren't we all." I sigh exaggeratedly.

"Not me," she says, opening a cooler and grabbing some ice, wrapping it in burp cloths that she nabbed from her van before handing it to me.

Chapter Thirty

Collin

Sitting around the fire, listening to Jade and Jake's stories about the little badass in her own right sitting between my legs, I learn a hell of a lot about Tessa that I wouldn't have otherwise known. There's good and bad in it. The good, she's mentally and physically stronger than I would have suspected. The bad, she actually had to go through it, defend herself against the likes of the many girls he had been with. One who apparently faked a pregnancy, then the idiot fucked her and actually got her pregnant.

When she starts getting quieter, I can tell her buzz is wearing off, and when she looks up at me, eyes heavy, she confirms, "Collin, I'm really tired. I am going to head up. You can hang out here if you want."

"I'll take you up to the house." I help her up and stand. "I'm tired, too."

"All that hay," one of them jokes. "City slickers not used to country work."

I inwardly roll my eyes but nod. "Guess not."

Walking toward the house, hand in hand, I look down at her under the starry sky. "Never loved a song with lyrics until tonight. I want you to sing that song to me, just *me* again."

"Oh yeah?" She smiles.

I nod and kiss the back of her uninjured hand.

She smirks, which I'm learning precedes her smart ass. "Sorry, cowboy, the buzz wore off."

"That good under the influence, I'm gonna need to hear it sober."

"It's country, you know. Not usually my thing."

"It should be, Tessa. Country looks good and sounds good on you." Then I take a deep breath and ask, "Busy day tomorrow?"

"Church, and then whatever."

"Love the thought of getting to sit with you at church again. Not gonna lie, looking forward to the *whatever*, too."

She looks up and wraps her arm around my waist. "Me, too."

Inside, at the bottom of the stairs, I stop her when she's two steps up and eye level to me and turn her around. "You look beautiful every day, Tessa, but today, you look especially beautiful."

When I lean in for a kiss, I hear Maggie from beyond the wall. "Church in the morning, kids."

"Seriously, Mom, I have no idea how you two made five babies, and I can't even get a damn kiss."

I have to bite my lip to stop from laughing.

"Raise 'em outside; give them lots of chores. They'll sleep through a damn tornado," John says.

"John Ross!" Maggie scolds him.

"Tell me I'm lying."

Laughing, we both run up the stairs, and at the top, I take that kiss.

"Be up to check on you soon." Maggie's words drip with sarcasm.

"No doubt you will," Tessa smarts back.

"Goodnight, beautiful. I *love* you." I turn, walk in, and shut the door.

S itting on the twin-sized bed, covered in a beautiful handmade quilt, I do exactly what I told myself I wouldn't do during my time off. I *check in*. I do this by scrolling through my emails to ensure everything is going as it should with work, and the case.

No news is good news, so they say.

Bang, bang, bang.

"If you want hot water, you'd better get up and at it, Dr. Abraham."

I drop my phone on the bed, grab my clothes for church, and head out of the room. I walk to her door and tap lightly on it, hearing the floorboards squeak as she moves across them.

Hair wrapped in a towel, she opens the door and peeks out, eyes wide, bright, and gorgeous.

I lean in and kiss her cheek. "Good morning, beautiful."

"Good morning, cowboy."

"Cowboy, huh? That about the song or—"

"I'll show you later," she cuts me off, smirking. Then

she shuts the door in my face, laughing.

After a shower, shave, brushing and flossing, and dressing in a tan suit with a white shirt and a light blue tie, I fix my belt, ensure the tie is perfect, and then walk out into the kitchen where she is sitting, sipping tea, wearing a light blue, strapless dress that just hits her knees. It's the one I bought for her and knew in my gut she'd be wearing, with a cream-colored cardigan and matching strappy sandals.

"We match." She smiles as she stands, walks to the stove, and pours me a cup.

"We go well together," I agree.

We drink our tea together, eat pastries, and do so staring at one another. When she finishes drinking her tea, we still stare at each other, smiling.

"I could sit here all day and have a staring contest with you"—she pushes back in her seat and stands— "but Mom would have a fit if we showed up late for church."

"All right, I'll meet you out there. You have to bring Leia in, right?"

"Yes, she is so happy being home."

It's a perfect Sunday, the sun shining, the temperature sixty-five degrees, a beautiful late summer day. We got to the church, and I hop out of the driver's seat, walk around the Jeep, open her door, take her hand, and we walk into church together.

"There are a lot of people here today," she whispers as we walk into the sanctuary.

She's not wrong; it's packed.

"They saved us a seat," she says as she points toward her family sitting in the third pew and laughs.

"What's so amusing?" I ask as we walk toward them.

"My whole family is here. That's unusual. Even Jake and Sarah."

After shaking John's hand and giving Maggie a hug, we sit and wait just a few seconds before the opening hymn begins.

The pastoral assistant then asks for joys and concerns. People ask for prayers for sick family and friends, and issues in the community. He then asks if anyone has anything to share, and John stands. A young girl hands him a mic, and he holds it up.

"I wanted to share that our kids Alex and Phoebe Ross, gave birth to a beautiful baby boy on Friday, a bit early, but he's healthy. I'm sure you'll all be meeting Remington soon."

He then sits, and I take a deep breath and stand, feeling nervous for the first time as the girl walks to me and hands me the mic.

I glance down and see Tessa looking at me with a look of curiosity then to her mom, who dabs her eyes.

"Hello, everyone. I'm Collin Abraham. I came today with Tessa and the rest of the Ross family." I take a deep breath and smile down at her. "A few weeks ago, I met Tessa, and I think I came on a bit too strongly, because out of her beautiful mouth came something about me being arrogant, pompous, and full of myself."

Everyone laughs, including me.

I quickly regain my composure. "Tessa told me that I would be on one knee in front of God and her family before she would ever consider"—I amend the wording— "a date." I turn and look at her. "So, here we are, in a church and in front of your family, Tessa Ross." I smile and watch her eyes widen as I step back into the aisle and kneel before handing the mic to the little girl. "On one knee." I pull the box out of my pocket. "I'm asking you to be my partner in all things in life. The only woman I would ever consider asking to become my wife. I love you, Tessa Ann Ross. Will you please make me the happiest man on earth? Will you marry me?"

Still appearing to be in shock, she stands and nods as a tear falls down her face.

I take her hand, slide the ring on her finger, and then I stand and take her hug.

As we're hugging, I hear a little voice over the mic, Sydney. "In case you didn't hear, she said yes!"

The congregation erupts in claps, some laugh, and many cry tears of joy.

We sit, holding hands and smiling at one another.

She squeezes my hand and whispers, "What do you think my parents are thinking right now?"

"They're thinking, he's one lucky man."

"I can't even look at them. I bet they're in shock."

"I asked your father for your hand last night. And I'm pretty sure, since your whole family is here, he told your mother."

"You asked my dad for my hand?"

"Of course I did," I whisper.

"You amaze me." She rests her head on my shoulder. "I can't wait to be your wife."

"Me, neither." I kiss the side of her head.

We sit quietly, listening to the rest of the sermon on forgiveness and healing, holding each other's hands, smiles never leaving either one of our faces.

"When?" she asks as we get up and start down the side aisle toward the fellowship hall.

"When?" I ask confused.

"Do I get to be your wife?"

"Name the day and time, Tessa, and it'll start then and

last for the rest of my life." My smile falls when my phone vibrates in my pocket. I pull it out and glance at the screen.

Tomás

- 911

I glance to at Tessa, who is looking at the screen.

"Is everything—"

I nod. "I need to give him a call."

"Go," she says and steps away. "I'll be with our family."

Outside I answer, "What the hell is going on?"

"Issues that needs your attention. The flight out of Ithaca leaves tonight—"

"Not gonna happen. Tessa's birthday is tomorrow. Call in whoever you need, pay off whoever's making waves. Send me updates hourly if necessary. I'll fly down Tuesday and deal. Can you make this happen, Tomás, because—"

"Yes, sir."

"Stay safe," I demand.

"Will do, sir."

I walk back into the church, fighting my need to control a situation that I built a team of trusted and capable people to do on my behalf yet have not done so in the past. Eyes to her, I'm looking at my future, one that will no doubt happen upon situations just like this. One day, she'll be introduced to that part of my life, but it cannot take precedence over her happiness, *or mine.*

I walk to her, beautiful in blue, surrounded by people who shaped a heart that I will cherish, showing them the ring.

She looks to me as if she felt my presence and smiles.

When I'm standing beside her, she whispers, "Everything all right?"

I take her hand and nod. "Something came up, but it will wait for a couple days."

"Is it your mother?"

"No, it's work. Tomás can handle it until I get there."

"We can go."

I shake my head. "Tomorrow is your birthday. I will not miss it, and neither will your family."

"Okay," she says softly. "You wanna get out of here?"

"I do."

She smiles. "I do."

"We have about fifteen minutes before they get back," Tessa says, dropping her little clutch on the counter and turning to me. "Let's make them count."

I grab the back of her neck and pull her to me, closing the distance between us, lips softly touching hers, holding back as best I can when all I want to do is ravage her, but fifteen minutes is not nearly enough, yet it will have to work.

I reach behind her, grabbing her tight, round ass and lift her, my lips to her neck, her hands in my hair as I stalk through the house to the stairs and up them.

In her room, I lay her down, determined to give her something, *just a little something*, to commemorate the day.

Kneeling between her legs, hands gripping her ankles, I remove one cute little pump, and then the other. She sits up, smashes her lips to mine, pushing my suit jacket off my shoulders. I shrug it off and take her wrists as she starts to work my buttons. I lean forward until her back is against the bed again, tasting her sweet lips and tongue as she makes a mess of my hair.

I pull back, kneeling, raising her legs, one then the over my shoulders. I skate my hands up her soft, smooth legs and stall at the hem of her dress. *Too fast. Slow down.*

Almost Paradise

Chapter Thirty-One

Tessa

oday has been a dream, every part of it ... aside from the years of drama between the time I actually met the boy I had such a crush on, a boy I wanted to name my future son after, *even though I long forgot his name*, and the moment he slid the large solitaire, diamond set on a thick, *protective* platinum band ... is like a fairytale, fate, *forever*.

I open my eyes to see him kneeling between my legs, looking hot and unhurried as I ... burn. He wraps his strong hand, *thick fingers*, around my ankle as he pulls my foot to his lips. Starting at my pinky toe, he nips and sucks the tip, causing pleasure to surge up my body, stopping at my center and causing a burn between my legs to intensify.

I moan softly as he moves to the next, and the next, and the next, before he slides his open mouth down the inside line of my foot. He presses his lips against my ankle, moving higher and higher, as I writhe beneath his scorching hot mouth.

Dress hitched up above my waist, he kisses my hip, skips my center, and moves to my bellybutton. He moves up, hands taking my face, kissing my lips, my chin, and I fist his hair, stopping him because I want him there, too.

"No," he growls and continues his trek down; therefore, making me release him for fear I'll rip out his hair.

I grip the comforter of my childhood bed that has felt like home until this moment. *My family is here, and my home is with him.*

On his knees again, he takes the other foot and does the same damn thing—kissing, nipping, sucking every inch of my body, *loving it.*

My clit throbbing, I attempt to close my legs to soothe the fire. He stops me by grabbing my thighs as he pushes his legs out behind him and pulls them apart, settling between them.

Breath hitching, I whimper, "Collin."

He growls as he runs his nose over the lace, and I fist the comforter tighter.

"You smell damn delightful, Tessa." He pushes the fabric aside then sucks on my thigh.

I cry out, eyes locked with his, and he blows a breath between my legs, chilling and enticing the burn at the same time, before his mouth covers me, sucking, nipping, licking, kissing, and then again directly to my clit.

"Oh God, oh God … Yes, yes, yes, Collin!" I cry out as I come apart.

With his mouth, he captures the rest as he kisses me while grinding against me, extending my release. He kisses softly and soothingly, leading to my ear.

I whisper, "Why are your clothes still on?"

"Same reason yours are." He pushes up, looking down at me.

"Get naked, cowboy. My turn to take you—"

Leia's bark announces the return of my folks.

"Let's get out of here. I owe you."

"Trust me, beautiful," he says, getting off the bed, "you've given me, at the very least, one a day since you arrived at the Cape."

Standing up, I fix my dress and head to the mirror to fix my hair. "Shower sex is best with two people."

I see him look up from where he is bent and pressing on his knees, smiling at me.

"I'm sure it is, but I've memorized your scent, kiss, smile, and have many, many pictures of you in my head that have made me come more times than I care to admit, to the woman who has just accepted my proposal."

I giggle.

"The first day I saw you, I wrapped my hands around my cock and jerked off to the picture of you in my head."

My brows shoot up.

He steps behind me, wrapping his arms around my waist. "How does that make you feel?"

"Oddly … turned on."

"Don't ever try to keep score, Tessa," he warns.

"You have no idea what you're getting yourself into."

"I do and …" He stops as a look I've yet to see slides across his features.

I turn to face him and look up, a thought hitting me. "When can we get married?"

"Whenever you want." He wraps his arms around me.

I bury my head in his shirt before whispering, "I want to wait until then."

"What?" He laughs.

"I know it sounds …" I shrug and look up. "I just want to wait."

Collin looks me over then nods. "Okay, so next weekend then?"

I laugh. "Sorry?"

He lifts my chin. "Don't be. But I'm serious. What kind of wedding do you want?"

I close my eyes. "Just us would be perfect."

"What's wrong?"

"I keep thinking it's all too soon, and that I need to slow down and date you, not plan a wedding after just a few weeks." I feel him tense and open my eyes. "Collin, listen to me. That's what I keep thinking. What I feel with my heart and my soul is that you were always the one. I love you. I feel safe with you. I trust you, and that's insane knowing what I have been through with Lucas, but that's my head. My heart is all yours, and I know, without a doubt, that I love you."

He releases the breath he was holding. "I'm yours and only yours, Tessa. Forever. It has to be the same for you."

I scowl because is he seriously thinking I don't feel the same? I literally just said—

"I'm not as confident as you might think when it comes to you. I do, however, read people well. If I didn't feel that you felt the same, I wouldn't have opened myself up for hurt. You could easily break me, Tessa. More easily than you could even imagine. You were an angel the first time you kissed me all those years ago. No one, not even my mother, had kissed me. I felt comforted by that kiss and the way you gave me your food … Well, for years, I dreamt of you. I thought you must not have been real, maybe just a place in my imagination or vision of an angel with the blue ribbon in her hair, giving me the comfort that I desperately needed. It was nothing sexual; it was kindness and caring. I never experienced it before … until you."

He presses his lips to the top of my head. "Regardless of the women I've had sex with, nothing ever felt like I did then. I never kissed them like I do you, or talked about anything deep, like I find myself easily doing with you. Besides my siblings, there have only been two times I've been drawn to a person in a way I couldn't step away, and allowing myself to react that way always felt like I was getting away with a sin greater than murder. You were one. The first person I actually held in my arms when Ann passed. And once at a funeral for a fellow soldier. I felt drawn to comfort a grieving girl. I'm sure that instance was because of Colleen, my sister. But this young woman was just shattered, sitting in a dress on the ground, sifting dirt through her fingers, inconsolable."

I step back and try to catch my breath.

"Sorry, Tessa, I hope that didn't upset you."

"Where was this funeral?"

"There were so many, but I am sure it was here, in Upstate. Actually, now that I think about it, Syracuse maybe? It doesn't matter. We both know—"

"Toby Green?" I cut him off as tears begin to fall.

His eyes widen. "Do you know—"

"It was me. I was the one on the ground." I feel dizzy, knees weak, and he grabs my elbows while I finish. "You gave me a tissue."

"My God, Tessa," he says, moving us to the bed, sitting and holding me. "*My God*."

Crying, shaking, feeling overwhelmed because something about that moment, the smell of him—no, his voice … *maybe both*—comforted me in a way I couldn't explain, not ever.

"Everything all right in here?" Mom asks, and I lift my head and see Dad following her in.

"Yes," I sob and look at Collin, whose eyes are brimmed red.

"What is going on?" Dad demands.

Collin uses his shirt sleeve to wipe the fallen tears and presses his lips to my cheek.

"Daddy, I'm going to marry this man, and we are going to be together for the rest of our lives." I laugh, and Collin chuckles as he pulls me tighter into his hold.

"Okay. That's good, right?" Dad asks.

"I'm going to use the bathroom. Collin, feel free to explain, because I don't think I can right now."

While washing my hands, Mom bursts in the bathroom. "Are you all right?"

I turn, and she hugs me while I laugh. "Never better, Mom."

"My God," she says, squeezing me harder.

"I met him at VBS when we were kids, he comforted me when Ann died, and he was the soldier at Toby's funeral who handed me a tissue." I start crying again.

Collin walks in, Dad behind him.

Mom then releases me and hugs Collin. "My God."

"Your daughter is my angel." He smiles down at her. "I promise to never let anyone hurt her ever. I'll take care of her and her heart until my last breath."

Mom turns and hugs me again. "My God."

"Ours, too," I joke because all this is making her act so un-mom-like.

Then I see Dad hug Collin, and when they step apart, he informs Dad, "With all due respect, we need to get married quickly because she is going to make me wait until we do."

I can't help but laugh then quickly add, "It needs to be at the Cape with Pastor Lou."

"Yes, it does." Collin walks over and takes my hands. "I have to leave the day after your birthday. The very day I get back, I want to be standing there and saying I do."

Nodding, I ask, "When do you return?"

"I'll know more when I get there, but I'm serious."

"I want that, too." I tackle-hug him.

"I know." He laughs.

I glance over at Mom, who is crying, while Dad holds her. "Mom?"

"Happy tears, Tessa," she assures me.

"Okay, Mom, don't cry, because I'll start again, and we have to cook and take meals to Phoebe and Alex."

I turn and look at Collin. "When do you fly out?"

"Two a.m. on the fourteenth."

"From?" I ask.

"Either Ithaca or Syracuse. I'll have to check the itinerary."

I tackle-hug him again. "We're getting married."

"Yes, we are."

Phoebe looks so happy as she holds Remington, and she is. The only time she doesn't seem happy is when someone asks to hold him. She tries to pretend she is, but we all see it on her face.

When Remington is sleeping, I tell her about church, and she cries like she's been holding it in for days. When I tell her about all the times we met previously, she cries like she hasn't in years.

Collin and I stay the night, and when she wakes to feed

him, I steal Remington time, offering to burp him. She is so tired that she falls asleep

"You mind if I hold him?" Collin asks, which surprises me.

When he holds his tiny little body in one hand, I shake my head.

"I'm not doing this wrong," he tells me, *not asks*.

"Not the point, cowboy. You holding a baby should be outlawed. Pretty sure my ovaries just produced a million eggs, all begging to be fertilized."

He laughs, startling Remington, who cries, which wakes Phoebe and Alex, and well, it couldn't be helped.

We don't sleep at all.

The next day, my birthday, Alex has to go to class, and Collin offers for us to stay with them. Phoebe, who I'm pretty sure is as in love with Collin Abraham as I am, in a different way, of course, accepts.

That night, we drive to Skaneateles, where we board a boat that he secured and eat dinner in the middle of the lake, in each other's arms, and he gives me a pair of diamond earrings to match my ring.

Men and jewelry.

I offer to drop him at the airport, but he refuses.

"I'd love to watch you fall asleep, kiss your cheek, and leave knowing you're not on the road at this hour. I'd also like to avoid the emotions that may—"

"If you think I'm going to cry, you're nuts. The sooner you get there, the sooner you get back and we get to share a last name."

He pulls me tighter. "Next year, your birthday celebration will be—"

"As perfect as this."

When he leaves ... I still cry.

I wake up with an attitude that needs readjusting, so I run, and I do so not counting down to happiness—I'm already happy—just miserable that I have to wait to see him again, annoyed I didn't ask where he's going, and seriously just missing him.

When I get to the falls, I don't scream out my anger; I smile up to the sky.

When I turn around and my eyes hit the tree, tears begin to build, and then rage takes place of ... everything.

What a waste. What a fucking waste!

I dig around the shale to find a sharp rock to scrap it away. When tears fall, I dig harder and harder until it's gone and my hands are numb.

Leia's bark stalls me, and I see it's long gone.

I sob and look down at my hands. I dug so hard and for so long that it caused me to bleed. However, the pain in my heart from the time with him is far harsher than that of bloodied hands. I walk over and put my hands in the water and watch as the water turns red, but only briefly.

I know this was going to hurt him, Lucas, and regardless of what has transpired between us, I did love him for a really long time. That doesn't go away, not for me, but it does change. I am no longer pissed at Lucas, because he is —in a sick and twisted way—going to be hurt and feel betrayed, and that tears me up on the inside in the same way it always has. Except now ... now I am stronger, and now I know why we were never supposed to be.

Collin.

Walking back, blood trickling off my hands, I head to the deck to sneak in and wash up before Mom sees the wreckage and starts to worry.

While rinsing my hands, the sound of the water masks Mom opening the door.

"What did you do?"

"I was digging at something I had carved in a tree away." I leave the bathroom and head to the kitchen to grab some paper towels and look back, laughing. "Pretty therapeutic until I realized I was bleeding."

When I turn back around, I see Lucas standing there.

He closes his eyes, taking away the pain I just caused because he knows, he just knows, and then he opens his eyes and locks them to mine.

"You have company. I'll be outside if you need anything." Mom kisses my cheek then walks out.

I grab some more paper towels. "Hi. I didn't know you were—"

"Our initials?" he asks, voice like broken glass.

"Would you like a drink?" I ask, folding paper towels in my palms.

"Where's your head, Tessa?" he asks sadly.

"I don't want to do this again," I almost beg.

"Then don't, Tessa. Don't walk away from us." He steps toward me, and I hold up my hand to stop him.

His eyes lock on my ring. "You're getting married?"

I look at the ground, because I can't bear to see his hurt, and answer, "Yes."

"Look at me, baby, dammit." He takes my hand, and I pull it back. "Tell me what to do. Just tell me. I will do any goddamn thing you need me to, Tessa."

"You have Jessie. I have Collin. I really don't know what else there is to say," I whisper.

"She isn't you. I can end it with her tomorrow, *now*, and we can get through this. Please, baby," he nearly begs.

Not wanting to prolong this, I look up. "I'm supposed to be with Collin. I love him."

He shakes his head and swallows hard. "You have loved others and always come back to me, to us."

"No, that's not true. Toby died, and my love for him was … different."

"And Ben? You loved him, too."

"I didn't—"

"Can't you see you're just trying to get over us? I'm telling you; you don't have to. I would never—"

"This is different. He and I are supposed to be together. We love each other. You and I, we hurt each other. You had to be with other people to feel whole or whatever, but he would never—"

"Really?" He balls his hands into fists. "And what do you know about him, Tessa? You've known him for all of five minutes."

"That's not true. We actually met at the Cape when I was much younger. Lucas, he's Ann's Joe, the man who held me when she died. He also—"

"Spare me the details, Tessa." He rolls his eyes. "That's all coincidence."

I walk over and grab the album, careful not to get blood on it, and set it on the table. "Sit, please."

He does, and I push the album toward him.

He pushes it back. "I have photo albums, too, Tessa, five years' worth of them. This means nothing!"

I say nothing.

"What would Toby think, Tessa, huh?" He grabs my hand, forgetting, or not caring, that it hurts.

I pull it back and smile. "Well, Collin met Toby."

"You believe this guy's shit, Tessa? You don't even know him!"

"He was at Toby's funeral," I whisper.

"Great, so was I," he snaps, and my phone rings.

I get up, grab it off the counter, and see Collin.

"Hi," I answer softly, walking into the other room.

"I'll return early Friday morning. Friday sound all right?" Collin asks with a smile in his voice.

"Friday sounds perfect," I whisper.

"Good. Pastor Lou is available. I have that set up, but the rest is all up to you. Unless you'll allow me to help."

"It's our wedding, Collin; whatever you want, I am sure will be perfect." I grin, even though he can't see me.

"Lilacs, lots of them," he says in a deep tone.

"And so you will have them. Lots of them."

"Forever?" he asks.

"Forever," I answer.

"I love you."

"I love you," I reply and laugh. "Oh, and by the way, where are you?"

"I'm not used to sharing this sort of information. That will change. I'll email you. Got to go. I love you, Tessa Ross."

"I love you, Collin Abraham."

Friday night, I will be his, and he will be mine, I think as I walk back into the kitchen.

I jump when I hear Lucas spew, "You love him?"

"I do." I sit across from him.

"Thanks for that. Definitely needed to hear that." His jaw clenches.

"Lucas, I forgot you were here. I didn't mean to—"

"You forgot I was here?" he gasps.

"I'm sorry. No, I'm not. Lucas, I'm going to marry him and have a family with him. He's my forever. I don't know how to explain this to you."

"Where is he, Tessa? Did he tell you where he was going? You don't even know! You're not that stupid!" he yells.

"No, I'm not!" I yell back.

"Collin Abraham, huh?" He stands and heads for the door.

I stand and point at him. "Jessie! Sadi! Jenny! Tipper, and many others. Again, Lucas, you and I were clearly not working for a reason. It certainly wasn't because *I* didn't try!" Then I laugh.

"It's funny, huh, Tessa? Real funny. I can't do this without you. You've been my strength, my reason for being! And you laugh!"

"You're fine. You'll be fine. Don't you see, you ass, that I want you to be happy! Why can't you want that for me?"

"I do. Dammit, Tessa." He stalks back to me and grabs my face. "I need to fix this for you, for us. Baby, I love you." He tries to kiss me, and I turn, so he pulls me into a hug.

"No. Not the kind of love I need."

"I can be everything you need. *Please*, let me fix this." When he begins to cry, I feel my heart start to crack.

I pull away to wipe his tears then kiss his cheek. "You need to let go of things that are broken and unfixable. I'll always need you to be okay, Lucas. I wish more than anything we could be friends. God, you have been so important to me forever. I need you to be okay."

"Need me to be okay, but you block my number?"

Well no, but I can guess who did.

I don't reply.

"Can't be friends without communication, right?" he asks more hopeful than he should be.

"Lucas—"

"Gotta get out of here, clear my head. I'll fix this. I promise."

"Friends, Lucas," I call to his back.

He leaves, and Mom comes back in. "You all right?"

"No, Mom. No, I'm not. Why does he do this?"

Mom pulls me into a hug. "Are you second-guessing things?"

"No. I love Collin. I'm going to marry him. I just need Lucas to be okay."

I wake on the couch to my phone ringing and answer, "Hello."

"Hello, beautiful."

"Collin."

He laughs. "What plans have you made today so we don't get our lines crossed?"

"Nothing yet." I sit up. "Lucas stopped by here. He's having a difficult time with me getting married."

"Is he?" He sounds angry.

"Collin, he knows I love you. It's just going to take some time for him to get through this."

"Not your responsibility, Tessa. Unless you want it to be. And, if you do—"

"Collin, I. Love. You. Only you."

"So you say," he murmurs.

"Please don't do this."

"I didn't," he snips.

"Neither did I!" I snap.

Silence.

Then he asks, "Why was he there?"

"He just showed up. He was actually here when you called. I walked in the other room and talked with you and forgot he was sitting in the kitchen. He heard our conversation, which hurt him. But I told him—"

"Why didn't you tell me he was there, Tessa? When I called, why didn't you tell me?"

"I was happy to hear your voice, happy to talk to you. Collin, you can trust me."

"I have to go." He hangs up.

I try to call him back, but he doesn't answer. I don't leave a message.

The next day, I try again, and he still doesn't answer, so I leave a message ... two times. On the third try, he answers.

"Hello."

Pissed, I ask, "Should I still be planning a wedding or is this it, Collin?"

"Excuse me?" he asks, shocked.

Embarrassed, I reply, "Forget it. Have a great life, Collin." And I hang up.

My phone immediately rings.

Before I even get *hello* out, he lights into me.

"Tessa, this is not a great time to have this chat. You told me I could trust you. I do. It's him I don't trust. The church is set. I've ordered flowers. I'm going to arrange a caterer. Our reception will follow the service at the church. Invite who you wish. Money has been transferred into your checking account. But if you—"

"Collin ..." I begin.

"Do you still want this?"

I sniff back tears, "Forever."

"Excuse me, please," Collin says, and I hear a door shut. "Don't cry. Tessa, don't cry. I am beyond pissed at the audacity of that punk. You need to tell me if he so much as breathes in your direction!"

"I ... I—"

"I love you," he whispers softly.

"You have to—"

"I trust you, Tessa," he sighs out.

I lie back down and try to calm myself. I then sit up,

clear my throat, and tell him, "Okay, I'm sorry if I hurt you."

"It's jealousy. I want to be there with you. I asked you to marry me and left. That's inexcusable. Add guilt to that. I avoid those feelings, those illogical feelings for a reason."

I sit back. "Tell me about it."

"I love you," he says sternly.

"I love you."

"I have to get this wrapped up so I can get back to you. I'll call you soon, all right?" he asks.

"Please."

"Goodbye, Tessa."

"See you soon."

Back To Good

Chapter Thirty-Two

I roll over in bed and look out the window, seeing the ocean as I reach for my phone.

"Hello, beautiful."

"Collin, it's Thursday!" I screech as I get out of bed and grab my sweats, shoving my feet in them.

"It is, and tomorrow, *hmm* … It seems like I should remember something I have to do. I can't seem to remember. Tessa, could you tell me; do you remember what I will be doing tomorrow?"

I laugh. "Me!"

"You? What will I be doing with you?" he whispers.

"I have a few things in mind," I whisper back.

"I want to hear all about them." His voice is now deeper.

"Well, I would prefer to show you, and my family will be here any minute, so you'll just have to wait."

"I can't wait for you to *show me*. I have a few things I want to show you, as well." He chuckles.

"I love you. Fly safe. See you tomorrow," I say.

"If not sooner." He laughs when he thinks I hung up.

"What?" I ask, because I thought he said maybe earlier.

"I love you." He laughs. *Wishful thinking, I suppose.*

"Then show me tomorrow, cowboy."

I throw my hair up and pull a sweatshirt over my head before I head downstairs to see Leia waiting at the door.

"Miss your runs, girl?" I ask as I shove my feet into my sneakers, and then we head out.

Leia heads right to the water, and I kick off my shoes and laugh as she splashes around. "Isn't it cold, crazy girl?"

Then, from behind me, I think I hear my name, "Tessa Ross," and I know that voice.

I look back and see Lucas jogging toward me.

"Lucas, what are you doing here?" I ask, confused, and Leia runs to my side and growls.

"We need to talk," he says as he nears. Leia growls again, and he looks down. "Hello, dog."

I shake my head. "Lucas, no, we don't."

Green eyes, cloudy, he looks out over the water, pulls his hat down, and shoves his hands in his pockets. "It's beautiful here."

"It is, but Lucas, you shouldn't have come. I know this hurts and, God, I should want you to hurt half as much as I have. But I don't, not even a little. I want you to be happy. I wanna see you laugh, and smile, and fall in love, Lucas. I wanna see you get your shit together and get back on the field so Tommy's son, our godson, can see you like his father—"

"Enough," he cuts me off as a tear falls.

"I'm not trying to hurt you, Lucas. I am so far beyond that. I just want you to be—"

"I see it, see you loving this place, him, because you think it's fate, that God sent you to him. But you forget He sent you to me, too. And think past my fuck-ups and remember just a few things in almost five years that I may have …" He stops and shakes his head. "I need to tell you a few things, and I heard he was not around until tomorrow. If what I tell you doesn't change your mind, I'll let you be, Tessa."

Just then, Leia bounds between us and shakes half an ocean of water all over us.

We both laugh as Leia plops her butt between us.

"Do you have any dry clothes?" Lucas wrings his sweatshirt covered in sand out.

"I'm sure there's something here. Come on."

When we walk into Ann's house, I take off my shoes, as he does the same while looking around.

"This is amazing. Not what I expected. No plastic covering furniture, huh?"

"Not anymore," I call back to him as I run up the stairs.

Inside the room, I dig through the closet and pull one out. Turning around, I see him standing there, pulling his shirt off.

I look down at the gray hoodie, see orange, and toss it at him. "All I have is this one."

"How much you wanna bet it fits?" He smirks.

I turn and grab clothes for me. "I guess I forgot to give that one back."

"Or you just wanted to hold onto it for old time's sake. I get it."

When I turn back around, he's still shirtless.

"You like what you see, Tessa?"

"You've always been a lot of fun to look at, Lucas. Put that shirt on." I toss him some sweats. "Your lucky day—a matching set."

"Did you forget to give these back, too?" He chuckles as I walk out the door and down the stairs.

I quickly change in the bathroom, walk out, and then turn on the stove to warm up some water to make tea as he walks in.

"Would you like some?" I ask from over my shoulder.

Looking me over, he answers, "I would love some."

That pisses me off.

"You have to understand that I feel this is completely disrespectful to Collin. And you, of all people, should know that I will fight for those I love, and I love him. This past weekend, the hospital, the festival—"

"I said I was sorry to you, but I am not going to say those words to him, not ever."

"Lucas—"

"No, this part isn't about him. So, let me talk, please." He scrubs a hand over his face and, voice shaking a bit, he begins, "I hate that I did this to us, more than you'll ever even begin to imagine. We were so good together, baby, so perfect. I know I messed it all up. So much happened ..." His voice breaks, and tears begin to fall.

I reach out and take his hand. "We're both going to be fine."

"Tessa, what we lived through that first year together, it still hurts so bad," he begins.

"I know, Lucas, it was hell. I hated seeing you hurt. I still do." I can't help but hug him. And when I do, that smell, *fucking Drakkar*, keeps me there a second.

Leia barks, and I step back. I wipe the tears from my eyes and look to the clock. "My family is coming."

"Please, give me a few minutes. Leave them a note. I really need to talk to you, and I don't want them pissed that I'm here," he pleads.

"Okay, Lucas."

After leaving a brief, went-for-a-walk note, we hurry out the door, and I leave Leia behind.

Once our feet hit the sand, Leia begins barking from inside, and we begin to run.

We reach the lighthouse and stand on the rocks, looking over the ocean.

"You're not thinking clearly with him, Tessa. I looked into your Collin Abraham. He has a very dark past, baby." Lucas turns and looks at me. "You can't marry him."

"I know everything about Collin—"

"You can't possibly, Tessa. You're not stupid." He grabs for my hand, and I step back.

"Dammit, Tessa Ross," Lucas snaps as he reaches for me a second time. "I won't let him fuck you up!"

I hear Leia barking and see her running toward us, and then I see … Collin.

Smiling, I shake my head. "I know everything I need to."

"Bullshit." Lucas grabs my hand and demands, "Tessa, you're going with me!"

"No, I'm not!" I pull my hand away and … slip.

Collin

"Tessa!" I hear him scream as I watch her fall.

And I run harder.

At the bottom of the rock wall, I see him climbing down, feet nearing the bottom, and then he falls and clocks his head on a rock. He's blocking my view of her, *my life*, screaming, "Wake up, baby!"

"Get your fucking hands off her." I grab him and pull him away from her.

"No, I don't think so, you piece of shit!" Lucas screams as blood pours from the wound on the back of his head.

Tomás jacks him out of the way as I drop to my knees and whisper, "Tessa, wake up. Come on, Tessa; open those beautiful blue eyes for me."

When she doesn't, instinct drives me to check for a pulse, and my stomach turns as I do.

I pick her up and run as fast as I can down the beach toward the house, screaming back, "Tomás! Call an ambulance!"

"Police are already on their way," he calls to me. "I'll alert them."

As we near the house, I see her entire family watching me run with her toward them, and Maggie starts to run toward me.

I get to my gate first and kick it open, take the stairs two at a time, and open the door, hurrying to the couch and laying her down. "Come on, Miss Ross; we have a big day tomorrow. Wake up, beautiful."

S itting in the emergency room, holding and caressing her hand, I wait for her eyes to open again.

"Any word?" Maggie asks as she hands me a cup of tea.

"Not yet." I kiss her hand gently.

"Why don't you take a walk? You've been sitting here for three hours, Collin. I can stay." Maggie rubs my back to comfort me.

"No, thank you." I kiss Tessa's hand again.

Behind me, I hear someone say, "She should wake up soon, Dr. Abraham."

"I know."

"I'll go alert the family," Maggie says as she walks out.

Not two seconds later, I hear *his* voice. "Is she okay?"

Lucas was brought in for stitches, and I am pissed that I didn't physically give them to him myself. And now, he'll be heading to the station.

I then hear Ryan's voice. "She's going to be. You need to let this go, Lucas. Please, man. That girl loved you forever, and it didn't work. Now look at you. Get it together, for yourself, your god children, for me, man. I'll call your father."

"H er eyes are fluttering." I hear the worry in Collin's voice. "Maggie, she's waking up. Come on, Tessa Ross; open those beautiful eyes, please."

I want to, I really do, to ease his worry and explain about Lucas. I can't lose him, hurt him, but I can't, and I fall again, into the rocks.

"Stop giving her those pain meds. Just let it go for half an hour. She almost woke up before, and then you put that shit in her IV! Tessa has a low tolerance. You should have seen her the first day I met her ... Well, met her again. Just trust me, please."

I want to laugh, but I can't even open my damn eyes.

I also want to tell them that he's not wrong.

"Hey, are you smiling at me, beautiful? Open your eyes, please. I haven't been able to see them in four days. I'm back now, Tessa, and you're making me wait even longer." I feel his lips against my hand and the warmth that brings. Then he whispers, "You seem to like to make me wait."

A couple seconds later, I hear, "No, dammit, ten more minutes. Does she look like she is in fucking pain!"

I hear another voice, but the words are not clear, but Collin's, his sure are.

"I don't give a fuck what the orders say. I'm a doctor, and I say, if she is in pain, she'll tell you."

I will myself to squeeze his hand.

"Hey, now you're playing with me, Tessa. Open your eyes before this ... nurse ... shoots you full of drugs again."

And then, "Watch her eyes, she is fighting to wake up."

Then a yell. "Are you even watching?"

Then a clearer voice. "You are not her husband yet, Dr. Abraham. We could ask you to leave. This is a courtesy."

"You can ask, but it won't happen," he sneers.

I try to clear my throat, to say something as I squeeze his hand again.

"Please, just once before I end up in jail?" He kisses my hand again. "I love you. Please, Tessa, please."

I try to open them, as well as speak. "I ... love ... you."

"You love me? Prove it. Open your eyes, Tessa. Now, dammit," he insists.

I open them, and everything is foggy. "Water."

"Get her some water!" he snaps.

I close my eyes and feel a straw between my lips. I take a sip then cough when it goes down the wrong pipe.

Collin wraps an arm around my back, lifts me, and I feel him move behind me, legs around mine, lifting my arms.

"Dr. Abraham!" the nurse scolds.

"What!" he snaps as I warn, "Careful. IV."

Mortified, I force my eyes open and look at the nurse, who is definitely old enough to be our mother, glaring at him.

"Please excuse him. He can be difficult."

The nurse winks at me. "Only on days that end in Y. Welcome back, Miss Ross."

I look back at him, and it hurts to do so. "You have a reputation."

"Nurses don't typically like me."

"Interesting," the nurse says as she begins to check my vitals. "It says on your chart that you're a nurse."

"She's anything but typical," he defends me unnecessarily.

"Man's too smart for his own good," she ribs. "Thinks because he has good hair he can act like an—"

"He really does have great hair," I interrupt.

She huffs.

"Nelly," he warns, "pay attention."

"You may intimidate the young ones around here, but you're not on the clock, and rumor has it you're resigning to go do whatever it is you do and still collect a paycheck bigger than our entire nursing staff." She looks at me. "So, he's not as smart as he'd have you believe."

Collin grumbles, "I think I can handle it from—"

"From behind your girl?" she cuts him off. "Not gonna happen." She mock gasps as she reads my pressure. "Oh dear, we may have to keep her here for a couple days observation."

He barks out, "Like hell—"

"Read the room Collin," I cut him off. "She's getting your goat. Relax, please."

She puts away the cuff then hands me the cup of water. He takes it before I have a chance.

"The *doctor* on duty will be in shortly," she says as she walks away. At the door, she then turns back. "Congratulations, Dr. Abraham."

"Thanks, Nelly," he says sincerely.

After she leaves, I turn and look back at him. "You were not nice to her."

"She did not listen." He kisses my cheek and nuzzles into my neck.

"I love you." I reach back and run my hand through his hair. "You came home early."

"I wanted to surprise you. I couldn't spend another night without you. God, I don't know what I would have done if he—"

"He didn't hurt me, Collin."

"We're not going to discuss him right now. You're alive, and I thank God for that." He kisses me again, and I close my eyes and relax against him.

"You've got to get me out of here. I have a hot date tomorrow."

When they wheel me out, I see my whole family, including Phoebe and Remington, outside waiting.

W hen Collin insists on carrying me from the SUV inside, I have to redirect him, "I'm staying at Ann's house, Dr. Abraham."

"No, you're not."

"It's the night before my wedding, Collin," I whisper. "I would prefer to stay out of my *marital* bed on the night before my fairy tale starts."

He searches my face. "You're serious, aren't you?"

"Sadly, I am. I should have waited for you back then."

"We've waited. We've done this as right as possible in today's world," he assures me.

"I don't want to take any chances of screwing this up. I want you now, but even more importantly, I want you forever."

He lays me in the bed, covers me up, and presses his lips to mine. "I'll see you tomorrow." He kisses my cheek. "I love you."

"I love you."

Going to the Chapel … But First

Chapter Thirty-Three

om woke me every four hours, checking my vitals, and I have tried to be chill about it.

Finally, I tell her, "I'm going to look like the walking dead for my wedding tomorrow if you keep this up. This is a little much."

"Well, your wedding is today but stay in bed for a couple more hours. You're right; you'll look like …" She pauses. "Well, just rest a couple more hours. Yesterday must have been very taxing."

"Did Lucas make it home? I didn't say goodbye, and I hope he's all right. He must have been upset when he left."

She looks down as she stands.

"Mom?"

"Why do you feel like you have to protect him? After

378

what he did to you yesterday ..." Her voice breaks. "He is not your responsibility."

"He didn't do anything but show up and ..." I stop when she looks at me like I'm insane.

"Tessa, he pushed you off those rocks. He could have killed you. That's twice your life has—"

"He did not! He tried to grab my hand! I pulled away and stepped back. Mom, where is he?"

Her eyes widen, and she shakes her head. "Tessa."

A chill runs up my spine. "Where is he?"

"He's in jail, Tessa," she whispers.

I kick off the blankets and get up. "Dammit."

I throw on clothes and a ball cap, shove my feet in flip flops, and head down the stairs.

"Tessa, where are you—"

"Tell Collin I'll be back!"

When I walk out, I see him playing fetch with Leia, and I'm pissed at him but refuse to start today of all days fighting.

"Good morning. Where do you think you're going?" he says on a laugh.

I get in the Jeep and start it before answering, "Apparently, to spring Lucas out of jail."

"What?" Collin roars, and I peel out.

I walk into the station and see him behind glass at a conference table, sitting next to Landon.

"What the hell?" I grumble as I make my way to the desk.

As I impatiently wait, Landon comes to my side. "Tessa, may I please speak with you?"

"Sure."

"Excuse me. Who is this?" Collin asks from behind me.

I turn and smile at my soon-to-be husband. "This is Landon Links, Lucas's father. Landon, this is Collin Abraham."

He sputters under his breath then correct me, "Tessa's husband in a few short hours."

"So I hear." Landon looks at him in disgust, which pisses me off.

Then he turns so his back is to Collin and he's facing me. "May I speak to you alone?"

"Not happening," Collin answers.

Landon continues, "And Tessa, you're going to need to talk to him, because I can't. I'm not privy to the goings on yesterday, and he thinks—"

"She owes you and your son nothing," Collin tells him as he moves to my side.

"This man you're marrying doesn't know you very well, does he?"

Before I can tell him to fuck off, he addresses Collin. "She cares about my son, so you may want to ask her if she feels the same as you'd like her to."

I stand between them, facing Collin. "I'm going to talk to both of them. I want you to understand that. The room is glass; you can stand out here and watch."

I turn back to Landon. "You know me well enough to know that when I say don't be rude to him, or I'll walk out of here and not try to make things better for your son, you know I mean it."

I take Collin's hand. "Can I speak to you first for a minute?"

We walk a few steps away before Collin, who is seriously still stunning when he's ready to lose it, says, "You're actually going to walk in there and talk to that asshole? He could have killed you yesterday."

"You're angry, and I understand we should've talked about this last night, but he didn't hurt me. I stepped away from him and slipped."

He crosses his arms and sputters, "Fuck."

"I don't want to hurt anyone here, least of all you, but I hope you understand he's not going away, so we do the right thing, and he will chill, I know he will … eventually. But he's a mess, Collin. He needs help, and I can't have that on my conscience. Please love me enough to understand that."

Collin doesn't say a word, but I can read his thoughts by the look in his eyes.

I squeeze his hands and kiss his cheek before walking to the room.

When I walk in the room, Lucas starts to stand, but he's cuffed and can't fully do so. "Are you okay?"

"Yes. Are you?"

"I'm sorry, Tessa. I didn't mean to hurt you. Jesus, I didn't even touch you and—"

"I know, Lucas."

"Are you really going to marry this guy?" he asks, nodding to Collin, who is standing at the glass.

"Yes, I am."

"He fucking killed someone, Tessa. That's what I came to tell you. I won't leave you alone with someone like that. Hate me—"

"Lucas, I love him, and if you could talk to him, you wouldn't sit here and judge his actions."

Lucas sits back. "Bring him in."

"No, that's—"

I hear the door open, and Collin walks in. I stand and look up at him.

"I know you don't owe Lucas anything, but—"

"He asked for me, he has me. This ends now, though,

Tessa. Neither of us are living in the past."

I whisper, "He somehow found out about your juvenile record."

He smiles as he looks over me then at Lucas. "I'm not hiding a damn thing."

"I'm right here, Tessa; I can speak for myself," Lucas hisses.

Collin walks over and pulls out a chair for me. I sit.

He sits beside me, eyes locked to Lucas's. "Tessa says you have some questions, Links. I have no idea why you think you deserve any answers after the shit you pulled yesterday or last weekend, but she seems to think you do, so you have my attention until I decide otherwise."

"Tessa, do you even know this clown?" Lucas sneers.

"Yes, I do."

"And you love him?"

I say it softly, as not to hurt him. "Yes, I love him, Lucas. I've told you that."

He looks at Collin. "This is a fucking joke. You fucking killed someone!"

"Yes, I did." Collin smiles. "Keep that in mind, because I don't regret it, and I would do it again if I had to."

Landon stands. "Tessa, do your parents know about him?"

"Yes, actually, they know everything, and when he asked my father if he could marry me, my dad gave his blessing."

"Is there anything else?" Collin leans forward, eyes locked on Lucas.

"Yeah, plenty."

He turns to me. "Baby, if I fucked you up bad enough for you to do this, I'm sorry, but you can't seriously stay with someone like that." He looks back at Collin. "Never drew blood before, but I will for her. So, your threats don't mean shit to me."

"Collin won't hurt me, Lucas. I trust him to keep me safe."

"Do you have nothing to say for yourself? Fucking punk-ass bitch!" Lucas snaps at Collin.

I turn and look at Collin. Who is seriously smirking at him. *What the hell?*

"Lucas, look at me. I'm not stupid, and he has told me more about himself in the past few weeks than I ever asked him to tell me. He's a good man."

"Seems like a real winner, Tessa," Landon says snidely.

"Are we done here?" Collin asks me.

"No, asshole, I'm not." Lucas attempts to stand again.

"Then, could we hurry it up? I was under the impression you had questions and, well, frankly, we have a life to start, so let's end this. We don't need to revisit it again," Collin says dismissively.

"Why did you kill that man?" Landon asks.

"Collin, you don't—"

"He was hurting my sister."

"When did this happen?" Landon continues asking things that are none of his damn business.

Collin replies, "When I was twelve."

"Collin, you don't have to."

He looks at me as he stands. "No, I want this over and done with. He needs no excuse to be in your life."

"What do you do?" Landon asks.

"I am a doctor."

Lucas laughs. "Who travels the world."

Collin rolls his eyes. "US citizens are not the only people on the planet that need help."

"Tessa, is he for real?" Lucas asks.

"Yes." I nod, a sense of pride coming over me.

"Did you work with him? Did Little Miss Perfect fuck around on me?" he asks,

"We met years ago, Lucas. I told you that at the farm. I showed you the book."

"He starts his shit—"

"This is why you're marrying him?" Lucas interrupts Collin. "A fucking book? Collin, you should see the books I have of Tessa. Way hotter than what you have. Five years with her, and your precious little book trumps that?" He looks back at me. "You are out of your mind."

"Have you had enough yet?" Collin asks, pulling out my chair.

"She never has enough of me. She comes back every time I put forth effort. I've fucked up several times, but I can promise you I never will again."

I see him begin to shake, and it hurts. It *so* hurts to see him like this.

"I won't let you waste time on him, Tessa. We love each other. That just does not stop."

Collin reaches out his hand, and I take it as I stand. "Lucas, I'm sorry if this hurts you. I love him. You have to heal and be better. I care very deeply for you, love you as a friend loves a friend. I know you know what that means, and I always will. But I love Collin in a way I can't explain, *and I don't have to.* I am going to spend forever with him. I want you to find that person who is meant to be with you. I'm not it, Lucas. We tried. Maybe it's Jessie. But I'd seriously think about that. She's kind of crazy, and I know you know that. I don't want her to hurt you, and I don't want to hurt you, I truly don't. I would love nothing more than to come home to Blue Valley and see you happy." Tears begin to fall. "Please be okay, Lucas."

Collin squeezes my hand. "She's had enough. I've had enough. I don't like you even a little, but you look to have had enough, too. We have two options here, Links. We can walk out there, fill out paperwork, and my lawyers will hang your ass—"

"Collin," I whisper-plea.

"—or you can stay the hell away from her and accept that she and I love each other and are getting married. And I can promise you, if you so much as harm a hair on her head, I will not regret what I do to you. Are you ready?"

"It wasn't his fault, Collin."

He ignores me. "I need an answer."

"I wasn't trying to hurt her. She just told you that, asshole, and I would never hurt her. But if she ever says the words, I'll wipe the floor with your ass and show her what she's missing. I love her, and whatever it is you've done to mess with her head will wear off someday. So, you do whatever it is you need to do; I really don't give a fuck."

Lucas looks away from him, and his eyes soften as he looks at me. "Tessa, I love you, baby. When you need me, call. I'm not going anywhere. I love you so fucking much. We can call it even, all right? We can start over with a clean slate."

I turn so he can't see my hurt. It has to confuse him. Hell, it has me. "Lucas, please stop. Be safe." I walk out the door.

Landon follows me out, looking a mess as he asks, "You're okay?"

"Yes, Landon. Are you?"

"No." He shakes his head. "He's this way because of me. He loves you, and because of what I have shown him, he's hurt you, and now he's lost you."

"I know I am exactly where I'm supposed to be. He'll be all right. He's a very smart man. Please tell the girls I love them. And please keep him busy and safe. Be there for him. I need to live my life now."

I look up at Collin, hug him, and whisper, "Collin, I'm sorry."

He kisses the top of my head, lifts my chin, takes in my eyes, and gives me his. In them are his forgiveness and concern. "We're done here. I don't want to ever revisit this, do you understand that?"

I nod.

"Now, you can make a decision about what we do about this, or I can. Whatever you need."

"There's only one thing to do, Collin—the right thing."

"You're one hundred percent sure he'll not hurt you?"

"He would never physically hurt me, Collin."

After filling out the paperwork to drop the charges, I look at the officer. "Let him go now, please."

"Yes, ma'am," the officer says, looking at Collin and waiting for his nod of approval.

I sigh. "Let's get the hell out of here."

Once outside, he picks me up, throws me over his shoulder, and smacks my ass. "That's for leaving today and not telling me what the hell was going on."

Deserved … and oddly enjoyed.

He smacks my ass again, and I gasp out, "What was that for?"

"I wanted to hear that little moan you let out the first time. It made me a little hard, Tessa, and today, that won't be wasted and going down the drain."

I smile into his chest and whisper, "Don't do it again."

Beginning of Forever

Chapter Thirty-Four

Collin

S tanding at the front of the church, hands deep in my pockets, I stand alone. There are a number of people, *associates*, I could have called upon to be at my side, but that would be hypocritical.

In the past, during my time in the military, I was in one wedding. I took my promise to support their marriage seriously, and when he cheated on his wife, a sweet young woman, I was not happy. Took a call to Pastor Lou to calm me down enough so I didn't beat his ass down. After that, I made every excuse in the book to never be in another.

I don't like broken promises.

And, although I am not a superstitious man, I did not want anyone standing with me when I commit my life to her. Tessa chose to follow suit. She does, however, have a bachelorette outing planned. I booked a spa day for all but one of her former choices to fill that role. Her mother took that spot, as well she should.

Yesterday, they were supposed to go to get fitted for the dresses that Tessa picked out and bought for them to walk down the aisle and sit in the front row. Obviously, that plan took a turn. But, with enough money, you can make things happen. The local bridal boutique did their magic today, and the local stylist worked on the women's hair and makeup, and after Tessa's little trip to the Justice Department, she joined them.

I watch them walk down the aisle, all dressed in navy blue, and I'm sure they look stunning, but my eyes stay focused on the doors, for her.

The thought of my past beliefs, that I will never be allowed love, have been banished, the ingrained idea that I didn't deserve to love this way, decimated. The wall that kept everyone safe from me, *and me from them*, torn down all by the woman standing with her arm linked through her father's, who was, no doubt, created for me to love.

She looks from him to me. My bride isn't nervous like one would think; she's a beaming beauty. There is no evidence of the broken-hearted girl who just walked away from a man she was once in love with. Tessa Ross looks at me like there is no one else in the entire world. Her smile is brighter than the sun that shone high in the sky today, *our wedding day*. She is glowing, and that erases any worry that today, because of the happenings, was not the right day. Watching her walk to me, I know there is zero doubt. She is walking toward me without reservations.

ive. God, thank you for his smile. I love his smile, the kind he's giving me now, the one that reaches his eyes and radiates warmth of *true love* through my body, my mind, my heart, my soul.

Four. Closer now, his eyes twinkle in the light that breaks through the stained-glass windows of the church where I first met him many years ago.

Three. He looks amazing. His dark gray suit fits his strong, solid body perfectly, as does everything he wears.

Two. Halfway there, I watch as he adjusts his light blue tie that matches the seriously amazing undergarments he chose for me to wear. I wiggle my butt, just enough, hoping he catches on. He laughs, and I know that, on the worst days, that sound will be an automatic mood enhancer.

One. "Who gives this woman to be with this man?" Pastor Lou asks.

When Dad says, "Her mother and I do," Collin looks up and mouths, "*God.*"

Dad leans forward and whispers to Collin, "We don't want her back."

Staring at me, Collin smiles. "That's good, because I'd never give her back."

I lightly elbow Dad, and he chuckles as he wraps me in a big old Dad hug then takes my hand and gives it to Collin with a warning, "Don't hurt her."

"Never."

Dad further warns, "We have a lot of land. No one would ever find—"

I interrupt with a well-timed foot stomp. "Are you two about done?"

He kisses my cheek then moves to sit with Mom.

Staring into his eyes, I feel so calm, so at ease, so much at peace, and his mirror the same.

The church isn't full, but the people in attendance fill my heart and will undoubtedly do the same for his, with time. They are family, connected in the heart, held together with love.

Our vows are as traditional as they can get. He softly strokes my thumb with his as he repeats his vows, his eyes piercing into my soul as he speaks.

I give exactly that back to him, with mine, but my hands move to his lapel, and I step in closer, just to ensure it.

When Pastor Lou is about to announce us man and wife, Collin shakes his head, and I swear his cheeks pinken. "I need to say one more thing, sorry."

"Go ahead." Pastor Lou smiles.

"Tessa Ross, from you, I finally know what it is to feel love. My every emotion is within your control. Your smile brightens my heart. Your kiss, I feel throughout my body, *my soul*. I'm drawn to your scent, your eyes, your touch, *your heart*. I have never dreamed that I could feel this way *ever*. I never even knew I wanted it." He takes my face in his hands as a tear slides down. "I thought you were a dream, Tessa. For years, I thought you were an angel. Now I know the truth. You are. I'll love you always. This is my promise to all who love you, to you, and to God."

Wrapping my hands around his wrists, words fall from my heart. "My dreams were not of angels, but of the opposite. I often wondered why I no longer had revealing dreams. My hope was always to have someone to share the details with. Someone who is my best friend, and someone

I can completely trust to hold my heart. I came here to escape and to find myself again. I was asking for God's help. I wasn't searching; I was led here.

"From that first day on the beach, I felt your touch and wanted desperately to ignore what it did to me. You weren't a dream or a fleeting desire; you are a gift from God to me, to my heart. I exist for you. I belong *to* you, I always have, and I *always will*. This is my promise to all these people who also get to love you, *to you*, and to God."

"You may kiss your bride … again."

Collin slides his hands down the insanely beautiful silk gown that *he picked out for me*, digging his fingers into my hips as he pulls me toward him.

He touches his lips to my forehead gently then travel sweetly down to the tip of my nose, to the side of my face, as he cups my chin and smiles. Our lips both slightly open as they touch. It's tender. It's perfect. It's us.

With his forehead pressed against mine, he kisses me again, caressing his thumb along the side of my cheek as he grabs the back of my neck and pulls me into him, head to heart.

"Ladies and gentlemen, it's my honor and brings me immense pleasure to introduce to you Dr. and Mrs. Collin Abraham," Pastor Lou announces as everyone claps.

"Shall we, Mrs. Abraham?" Collin kisses my neck and wraps his arm around my waist.

"I love you, Collin."

"I've always loved you. That will never stop." He seals his promise with a kiss, and then we walk, husband and wife, down the aisle to the fellowship hall.

After pictures, hugs, laughter, a seafood buffet, and fellowship, Collin pulls me aside. "I have something to show you."

"Right now?" I wiggle my brows, and he laughs.

"Oh, Mrs. Abraham, not yet." He squeezes my waist. "My wedding gift to both of us."

He leads me back to the sanctuary, and I pull away. "Can't return me already."

Catching my hand, he chuckles, and then we walk to the right and down the side aisle.

He then turns me toward the window and wraps his arms around me from behind. "For us."

I run my hand over the different hues of blue that make up the stained-glass window that Collin has replaced one of the old windows with.

In Loving Memory
Of our Beloved
Ann

"It's … beautiful. Collin, it's so incredibly beautiful." I turn and hug him, crying softly on his shoulder. "I love you so much."

"And I you. You are my love, my life, and now you, Tessa, are my wife. You've made me the happiest man in the world today. And I've made you cry on your wedding day. I'll certainly make up for that later."

"They're happy tears. I'm sure that's the sweetest thing anyone has ever done for me."

"Without her, I never would've met you. I owe her a lot more than just a window. I did that for us, Mrs. Abraham. Your family, those in the past and those watching us from over there." He nods to all of them looking in on us. "They made you who you are. And you have shown me the only love I've ever known. I'll take care of your heart, mind, soul, and body forever. It's more than love, Tessa. I treasure you. I adore you. I'll show you that until my last breath."

"My God, could you be any more perfect?" I kiss him.

"I don't deserve you, but I'll spend the rest of my life trying my hardest to prove to you that you're my world from now until the day you take your last breath and mine with it."

He kisses me breathless then steps back.

"Just to be clear, I'm still good with you making up for—"

Laughing, he grabs my hand and pulls me toward *our* family. "We need to eat cake and get out of here. I want to start taking care of your body as soon as possible."

So, we eat cake as Pastor Lou presents us with a black and white poster-sized photo of our first kiss.

After everyone heads back to the beach house, we head to the hotel where we attempted to stay a week ago.

Collin

I carry her over the threshold and into the hotel suite. Then I set her on her feet as I kick the door shut.

I wrap my hands around the side of her neck, lifting her chin with my thumbs, and my stunningly beautiful wife blurts out, "I'm nervous."

I hide my amusement, laying lips to her long, sexy neck. "You look beautiful in this dress, like I imagined you would." Then I kiss her ear, the top of her head, and turn her back to me as I walk her over to the windows over-looking the ocean.

I begin the task of slowly untying the bodice, *a selfish gift to myself*, and kiss her shoulder. "So much better than my imagination."

She reaches over her shoulder and runs her fingers over my scalp. *God how I love that.*

"How am I ever going to decide where to lick you first?"

His breath hits my back, and I bite my lip to stifle the noise creeping up my throat as the dress, this beautiful dress, falls to the floor.

He runs his hands down my sides and rests them on my hips as he glides his lips along my skin, moving from hip to hip then down my rear.

I feel his tongue trace the crack of my ass, not deep but still *there*, as he licks all the way to the base of my spine, sending shivers up my body.

"I don't know if I can practice restraint with you, Tessa. I want to touch you everywhere, taste you, make love to you, and fuck you." He unhooks my strapless bra, and it falls to the floor.

"Please," I whimper.

"Tell me where to begin, beautiful. Tell me there is no end."

"Never," I whimper as he kisses up my back to my neck, turning me, kissing my shoulder, across my collarbone, to my breasts. He cups one, licks across my nipple, pinching the other between his fingers, tugging at it while he sucks the other into his hot mouth.

Hands in his hair, I arch into him.

"You taste so damn good. I need more." He begins moving down my belly, covering it with light kisses until he reaches my panties, slowly pulling them the rest of the way down so I can step out of them.

With one strong hand, he cups my breast, rolling his fingers over my nipple and pulling, as he grips my ankle with his other hand. He lifts it to remove one heel and tosses it to the side, then lifts my leg to rest over his shoulder. With hips on my inner thigh, I grab his hair to steady the sway when my knees weaken.

He releases my breast, lifts my other ankle, and removes that heel as he takes my other breast and performs the same magic. Then, standing full height, he steps to me, pressing my back against the wall of windows as he kisses me.

Hungry mouth to hungry mouth, hands shaking with anticipation, I push his suit jacket off one shoulder then the next. I then work on his tie, his buttons and belt, and when he breaks our kiss, he steps back to look over my body.

"You are stunning. Better than I could have imagined," he says as he unbuttons his pants, and they drop to the floor.

Reaching for my hand, he steps out of them, pulls me close, swoops me up, and then walks us into the bedroom. The soft glow of candles light the room as he lays me on the bed then lays beside me.

He cups the side of my face and kisses me as he moves his other hand slowly down my body, and I do the same.

I caress his seriously impressive hardness as he slides a finger between my folds, both moaning into each other's mouths. He begins circling his fingers around the tender ache before breaking the seal of our lips and kissing down my body, eyes never leaving mine.

He blows gently on my heat before parting me with his tongue. Unable to keep still, he lifts my legs so my feet rest on his back, and then places his hands on my hips and soon, too soon, sends me into an orgasm so intense that I nearly forget to breathe.

He moves to my belly, kissing gently, and then at my breasts, he almost sends me over again.

Lips to mine, he reaches to the nightstand and grabs a condom, tears open the package, and swiftly rolls it on. And no, I shouldn't care that every move is stealth-like, including the orgasms that come out of nowhere, and the effects lasting longer than I can wrap my brain around. *Not that I'm thinking at all*, but, like seriously, I want to *see him*.

Before I have a chance to speak, his lips are on mine, his cock being nudged between my legs and … "Oh God," I whimper.

"You are so tight and wet, beautiful. *So wet for me*," he growls against my mouth as he enters slowly, *un-stealth-like*, stretching me beyond comprehension, and doing it so completely that I am full, *too full*. Then he begins to sway, hitting my G … *H, I, J* … okay, all the spots, and it's … *heaven*.

"Oh God." I dig into his shoulders and hang on, because there is a slight chance wherever he sends me, *whatever galaxy he sends me to*, I'll never return.

He dips his head to my breast, sucking a nipple into his mouth, teeth scraping, causing pleasure to spread, intensifying the burn between my legs as he thrusts in deep, *deeper*.

"Collin," I whimper.

He skates his hand down my side until he is cupping my knee, spreading me wider until he's rooted. He pivots his hips, and the friction … *delectable*.

"That's better," Collin growls between his clenched teeth.

"I love you," I gasp. "God … I love you so much."

He pulls out slowly then presses in slower yet. "Tell me again, Tessa."

"I love you!" I cry out, feeling every part of me igniting. "Oh God, *oh God, Collin*. I love you." I lift my head to bury it in his chest, and he leans back.

Blue eyes on fire, he groans, "Look at me. Look what you do to me."

I watch his face as he moves in and out of me faster, deeper, until I cry out my next orgasm.

I feel him jerk almost violently inside of me as he comes.

"Love you. *Good Christ*, love you so damn much. Forever mine."

Body dropping, laying on me, we pant and kiss while trying to catch our breaths. Then he rolls over, pulling me with him. "I love you, Tessa Abraham."

"I love you, Collin Abraham."

He folds his body up, effortlessly, with me now on his lap, then rolls to deposit me on my back again. I clench around him, wanting to keep him right there. His eyes roll back slightly.

"Tessa."

"Don't take it out. Stay."

He laughs. "Every part of you shows me love. Your vagina even hugs me."

I clench again, and he groans.

"Yeah, like that. So sexy. I need you again, and that means I need to change this condom, or we'll have a mess."

He pulls out swiftly, causing me to gasp and my knees to clench together.

He sits, back to me, on the edge of the bed, and I know this is my chance.

I move to my knees, my chin on his shoulder, and look down

Stunning, thick, heavy, long, perfectly proportioned, like seriously beautiful.

"What are you doing?"

I flop back. "And on the eighth day, God created Collin Abraham's penis."

He whips his head around and looks at me, face unreadable.

"It's a work of art."

He tilts his head to the side.

"Good move taking me stealthy. Had I seen it first, I may have run."

He then breaks out in laughter and turns his body to me.

"You want to lay there and discuss my penis, or can I have you, my stunning wife, *my everything*, again?"

"We'll table the discussion on how aesthetically pleasing your dick is for a later time. But I was actually thinking how much I would like to have you this time." I push him down, take the condom from his hand, and toss it. "Without this."

I wet my lips and lean in to kiss his chest as he pushes up and leans against the headboard.

I pull the blanket around me.

"Lose the blanket, Tessa," he says in a soft yet authoritative voice.

I let the blanket fall and take a deep breath. Then I whisper against his chest as I kiss lower and lower, "You can't watch me."

"I can't look away." He leans over and pulls me onto his lap. "I love *you*. I want *you*. That can wait."

"I need my lips on you, just as much as you needed yours on me."

I kiss him, moving down his neck, licking, tasting his skin, then moving down his chest, his nipple, then the next. I glance up and see his eyes, deep and dark with desire. His full lips curl softly, and I close my eyes as I move back up to his mouth.

He reaches for the condom that I tossed, and I take it from him, opening it as I kiss down his insanely gorgeous body. Then I take his hard, large shaft in my hand and watch as his head falls back. A growl escapes when I stroke him gently, his nostrils flare, jaw clenching as he bites down hard, lips separating and his teeth slightly baring.

It's so raw, his response, animalistically so.

Turned on by his show of emotion to physical pleasure, I kiss down his hard-toned abs to the finely manscaped area just above his hard, thick shaft. His V, so naturally given, causes my mouth to water as I lick and nip the sensitive skin, making my way to his inner thigh and suck.

"Fuck!" he sputters.

Using my tongue, I skim across his erection to his left inner thigh, where I suck his flesh again. His cock twitches, and I make my way back to it.

I stroke him lightly while caressing the broad tip with my tongue and am rewarded with a small bead of cum. I lap at it, loving the taste of him. Then I sheath my lips and suck as low as I can go while still stroking him.

"Tessa," slips out, followed by a deep, guttural sound.

I move one hand to cup his balls as I continue sucking his length.

He raises his knees, feet firmly planted on the bed, as I lick and suck *my husband's* incredible dick.

"Dammit," he growls, grabs the headboard behind him, and then thrusts his hips forward.

I accommodate as much of him as I can but manage to gag a little.

He sputters, "Sorry, damn, you suck me so good."

Turned on by how he reacts to me, my belly burns, pushing me to take him deeper, lick lower, suck on his balls, one and then the other, as he mutters an incomprehensible variety of curses before growling, "I need you, dammit."

I take him deeper, suck harder, and shake my head in the negative.

"You need to stop before I come." I hear the headboard creak loudly.

But I continue.

It doesn't take long before the first hot, thick burst fills my mouth, and I barely swallow it down before the next, and the next. The last proceeds a guttural groan and my name.

When he's finished, I push up on my knees, and he pants out, "My God," as he reaches down and pulls me up.

I giggle as I wrap my arms around him.

As if he can sense I'm close to coming undone just by the friction between us, he brings my hand to his mouth, sucks on a finger, and then moves our hands lower, between my legs.

I start to pull my hand away when he whispers, "No." Then he guides my finger around my clit until I *almost* come. However, he lifts my hand to his mouth and sucks on our fingers. "You taste divine."

With his free hand, he spreads my legs, opening me wide, as he kisses my neck. He then pulls me between his strong legs and hooks my ankles around him, spreading me even wider.

I look up to ask him what he's doing when he takes my lips as he drags our hands down my body, and together, we rub the ache, causing it to catch fire, and then he slides a finger inside of me and, within seconds, I come.

Still kissing me, he pulls the blanket up around us.

"That was … um—"

"You have no idea the effect you have on me, Tessa Abraham. Hell, I didn't know the extent of it until now."

"Touché, Dr. Abraham." I turn as I yawn and rest my head against my spot on his chest.

"A brief rest?"

"Yes, please." I curl into his arms and drift off to sleep.

Beautiful

Chapter Thirty-Five

Collin

I wake to Tessa draped over me body, both of us still completely naked. I hold her tighter and rub my hand up her back, which is a bad move on my part because it wakes my dick that is now and forever changed.

I look at the clock. It's almost midnight, and it's been one insane day. She needs sleep, and I need to calm the addict between my legs.

When I feel her stir, I whisper, "Shh …" until I feel her relax again.

I try to fall asleep, like her, but watching her creamy white tits and rose bud nipples rise and fall with each precious breath, I just can't.

My dick is now hard, and I'm not sure there is a damn thing I can do. And to a man like me, one who practices restraint on a daily basis, it's maddening.

I smash my eyes shut, hoping that will help, but it doesn't. This is seriously torture.

When I open them, she is looking up at me.

"Hi."

I smile, but it's guarded. Who the hell knows how she feels about waking to this?

She wiggles against my erection and giggles. "Did you miss me?"

"My apologies. That's … embarrassing."

She sits up and looks down at my erection. "There is nothing to be embarrassed about. It's quite amazing, actually."

I attempt to explain, "Your tits were rubbing all over me, and little moans escaped your mouth, and I could do nothing to stop it from happening. Again, I am sorry."

She looks down at my dick. "I think you like me." She wraps her hand around it. "I think I like you, too, which is perfect, because you're mine." She looks back up at me and smiles. "I'm pretty sure we are married, right? That wasn't just a dream?"

"We're definitely married." I take her hand and kiss her ring.

"The way I see it, what's mine is yours, and if you wake up and want what's yours, you should take it. I mean, you are wasting all that, and that is definitely not something you should ever waste."

"Let me clarify what you just said. Anytime?"

"Yes, please. Unless, of course, I say no, or we have fought, or—"

I pull her onto my lap. "I love you, Mrs. Abraham."

"Not as much as I am loving you right now." She reaches between us and brings my dick to her warmth.

"You're sure you want this?" I ask as I flip her onto her back.

She grins. "*I do.*"

I awake and look down. His head is on one breast, his hand is holding the other, and his knee is between my legs, pressing snuggly against my bare crotch. Smiling, I bite my lip and try to stifle a giggle, as not to wake him.

He blinks and looks up at me, allowing his eyes to adjust to the light, and then they widen. "Oh God, Tessa, I'm sorry." He moves quickly away.

I lean over and press a kiss to his lips. "No other way I want to wake up for the rest of our lives." I kiss him again. "But I do have to use the bathroom."

Standing in front of the mirror, I search for the change, and I know that it may not be visible to anyone else, but it is to me. It's huge. It's a smile without being forced, a heart that doesn't feel heavy. Instead, it's floating on a cloud of happiness and love.

It's the old me, with some seriously fucked-up hair and raccoon eyes, yet still the old me, all grown up and only caring a little bit that I look like hell.

I wrap a towel around me, start the shower, and then I head back to brush my teeth.

In the mirror, I see the door open and him peeking in.

"Are you okay in here?"

I set my toothbrush down and walk over, opening the door wider. "Everything's fine. Better than fine. Are you okay?"

He runs his hand through his hair and asks, "So, you were serious last night about whenever I wanted you?"

I step back and nod, looking him all sorts of over. Then I turn, drop the towel, and step into the shower. I glance to the mirror and see him looking me over as he grabs his toothbrush and squirts some paste on it.

"So, that means I can join you in the shower?"

"Yes, please." I turn and step under the water, automatically shampooing my hair.

I hear a growl as he reaches over me to grab a washcloth and the body soap. Once my hair is shampooed, he pushes my hair to the side and washes my neck, my back, and then moves me under the water to rinse it all away. He then turns me around and hands me the washcloth before bending his neck to the side.

"Here first."

God, *oh God*, how I love him.

We slowly and thoroughly touch, caress, and wash each other's bodies. Bodies we now know in the Biblical sense, bodies made for each other, bodies that please each other, bodies that *love each other*, and bodies that ... desire each other's.

Bodies washed and rinsed, his erection heavy against my belly, I reach down and gently stroke him.

"I'm not done with you yet, beautiful." He turns me around, hot water beating down against my chest as he runs his hands up my sides and kisses my neck. Against it, he whispers, "Hands on the wall, Mrs. Abraham."

I look over my shoulder as I do as he requests, anticipating him entering me from behind. He pushes my feet apart with his, spreading me wider to accommodate him. Then he moves forward, pressing his lips and torso against me so I bend slightly. "So beautiful."

Hand between my legs, he rubs a finger against me,

inside me, easily finding my sweet spot. Already turned on, I begin to close my legs around his touch, seeking an orgasm.

"No, Tessa, not yet," he whispers against my neck.

I moan in protest, "Collin."

A dark, throaty chuckle vibrating against my skin as I feel him skim his finger down the crack of my ass, and my cheeks clench around it.

He wraps his arm around my waist, sliding his fingers down further, pressing on the ball of nerves as I feel his tongue slide down my spine, between my cheeks, growling as he licks me, then licks lower, pressing into my pussy, devouring me from behind.

"Collin, I'm going to—"

Mouth leaving me, he stands, holds my hips, and rubs his cock against my opening, and then he fills me. Hand at my neck, he pulls me back, upturning my head, and kisses me as he moves in and out of me until I come, crying out his name into his mouth.

"I can't get enough of you," he growls as he pulls out, lifts me, and then carries me, soaking wet, to the bed, kissing my neck and laying me down.

He grabs a condom and rolls it on. "You are going to tell me when you have had enough. God, what are you doing to me?" He kisses my lips hard then moves down my neck. "Ridiculous how badly I need you. No fucking self-control. Your smell, your taste …" His lips vibrate down my body as he stammers about his need for me, which opens the flood gates, so I am nearly ready to come again.

And I do … as soon as he pushes inside me and makes love to me.

When we finish, he lifts himself up and kisses me softly on the lips.

"I'm going to end up killing you," he scolds himself.

"Hmm … Death by fucking. I can think of worse ways to go."

"I love you, Tessa Abraham." Collin smiles as he rolls off me, pulls off the condom, and then deposits it along with the others, in the garbage beside the bed. Then he rolls to his side. "Let me hold you now."

"We're soaked."

"No other way I want you."

W hen I awake, he is dressed and packing our bags. I sit up and stretch.

He drops the pants he was holding and looks rather annoyed as he walks over and kisses me. "Good morning again, Mrs. Abraham."

"Morning. Where are we going?"

"Catered brunch at the beach with your family."

"Our family," I correct.

He smiles. "Our family."

"Time to get to brunch?"

"Eleven a.m."

"And what time is it now?" I ask, wrapping the sheet around me and sliding off the bed.

"Ten thirty."

"Oh my God, I have to get ready." I sigh in disappointment.

"You look—"

"Why did you look aggravated when I woke? Did I do something wrong?"

"No, Tessa. I, however, seem to be unable to retain control of my desire when it comes to you. I apologize and won't ask so much of you."

I step to him and grab his face. "Don't work too hard

at it. I've never felt so good in my life. You are amazing. I love you. Please don't let that stop."

"You're sure?"

I laugh. "Very."

"We should get going?" he asks.

"I need to get dressed." I walk to my bag.

"There's a dress in the closet ready. And Tessa, we need to stop at a drug store. We've run out of condoms."

I open the closet and see another dress that my husband has bought for me, and yes, it's blue.

Blue Valley

Chapter Thirty-Six

Collin

*W*e spend the next few days in bed, and then we decide to head to Blue Valley where I would get to know her—our—family better. I promised her father not to keep her away, and I am a man of my word.

I book us flights, and she's a little irritated by this, which seems odd to me, but I quickly find out that she hates flying. I inform her that needs to change.

When we arrive at the farmhouse, no one is home.

After playing a bit with our girl, she asks, "What would you like to do?"

"I think I would like to get to know more about my wife. You know, outside of the bedroom."

We both laugh. *God, how I love her laugh,* even more than I love the fact that I am laughing and can't recall any time I've done that until I met her.

"Have a seat and prepare for the murky years."

I sit and wait as she walks to a bookshelf and grabs a pile of photo albums, setting them on the floor in front of us.

We look through album after album, her life in a book. I can see how close they are; Jade and her especially. Alex, Ryan, and Jade's brothers, who passed away, best of friends, and then she pulls out one from her senior year.

"Okay, so, senior year, there was a school closing nearby. And this is Tommy. He and Lucas, his best friend, came to Blue Valley."

Just the utterance of his name makes my blood boil.

"He and Jade dated, and he was wonderful. He, uh … died in a car accident when Sadi, Lucas's ex-girlfriend, was pregnant, which was after she faked a pregnancy to break us up. And then, because Lucas is an idiot, he had sex with her and got her pregnant for real." She shrugs after telling me, which I already heard before, but she was drunk at the time, so maybe she doesn't remember.

"Anyway, that was after Toby and Ann. Then, psycho Sadi birthed a stillborn and said horrible shit about me. He chose to believe her, because I started a relationship with Ben, my friend when I was a mess. I told you about him. He has been in my life forever. His dad and my dad are friends. He means a lot to me, Collin, but that's it—friends.

"So, one night, Lucas made Tommy and Jade come watch Ben's band, and I behaved badly on stage, singing with Ben to hurt Lucas, or get over him, or both—I don't know. Anyway, we were going home, and well, the main part is we came upon the accident, and he got me through that loss, even knowing that I would end up back with Lucas to take care of him."

"That's a lot, Tessa."

"Banner senior year," she jokes then begins again.

"Jade didn't know she was pregnant and found out that night in the hospital. Tommy's parents threatened to take the baby from her. So, Ryan was friends with the twins, Jade's brothers, and, well, he loved her and married her before the baby was born, and they are amazing together. Little Luke, named after Lucas, is my godson, and Lucas's, and so are Riley and Jackson, the two children that Jade and Ryan have together. Do we need a break?"

I shake my head and pull her a bit closer.

"All that happened, and Lucas and I, well, we got back together. I moved in with Lucas when he attended SU on a football scholarship. It was a choice I made because I found out I was pregnant."

I try my best not to react.

"I miscarried."

"I'm sorry."

She shakes her head. "Things were never good for more than a few months at a time. I know it wouldn't have been easy for a child to be raised in a toxic relationship. Anyway"—she rolls her eyes— "then, when he was drafted, nothing was okay." She flips a page. "Last-ditch effort to keep me in a shit relationship was him building a house on land that he had bought from my father, which I have since bought back some of the land and signed off the house, with the agreement that my family gets first dibs on buying it back if he ever sold it. Should I stop?"

"Drafted?"

"By the Jets."

"Hold on. Your ex was a pro football player?"

She nods then keeps going, like it's no big deal. "And he is currently with the 49ers but is screwing that up pretty spectacularly. He got hurt pretty bad during pre-season, so who knows if he'll go back? Before I met you, he said he was going to go back to work for his father, because life was better then."

"Okay." I move to sit up and get some things straight. "I thought this was just some hometown, punk-ass kid."

"He is."

"Tessa, it doesn't seem that way."

She crosses her arms. "Then let me explain how much of a punk-ass he is. When he went to meet with San Francisco, he and I fought because he wanted me to go with him, and I refused to go because I didn't want to miss my final. I surprised him by flying out that night, after my final. I got a hotel key and went in, and he was screwing some woman. That was when things *really* fell apart. He also messed around on me at SU and always promised to change." She stops talking and looks at me. "Collin, are you questioning why I'm not with him?"

I speak too quickly. "No, Tessa. I just didn't think my competition was as accomplished or the depth of the history I'm up against."

Brow raising slowly, she stands. "I'm going to shower." She takes a few steps, but then she stops. "I was under the assumption our marriage meant as much to you as it does to me. This is *not* a competition."

"Tessa ..." I start to stand.

She holds out her hand. "Stop. I'm not hiding anything."

After she goes in, I get up and walk to the door. I try to turn the handle, but ...

She locked me out.

And it hurts. But what hurts more is knowing my reaction caused that.

When she comes out, I set down the album, the one of her as a baby, and she walks past me and up the stairs.

I decide to shower, and I leave the door unlocked. Then I dress and walk upstairs. She's not in her room.

I walk outside and see her with Leia, and then I see John waving me over.

The first thing he asks is, "How's my girl?"

"She's upset with me right now."

John laughs. "What did you do?"

"I questioned her about her punk-ass——" I stop. "I apologize, but I didn't know Lucas was a pro football player."

We stand and watch as she and Leia take off for a run.

"She's angry, trying to work through something." John nods

"This is one hell of a honeymoon."

John pats my back. "Fix it."

"How?"

"You'll figure it out."

That I will.

"John, in two weeks, I'm going to Ecuador for work. I want her to go with me as long as things are worked out and security has everything wrapped up. Do you have any reservations about that?"

"None."

"All right, then I'll talk to Tessa about it as soon as we've worked out our issue."

———

I stay outside and wait for her, and when she walks past me, I reach out and pull her into my arms. "I don't doubt how I feel about you, about us. I just hope you don't, Tessa."

"I want nothing more than to spend forever with you. I said I do. I don't know how much more I can say about it."

"I believe you. And I probably should have looked into him myself. I didn't strictly because there was a good possibility I'd find him and—"

She laughs, as if I'm joking. I'm not.

"You have nothing to worry about, and I need you to believe that."

"I do."

She smiles. "I like those two words."

I lean down and kiss her, and then we break apart when a car pulls into the driveway.

I wrap my arm around her waist and ask, "Who is this?"

"Landon," she mumbles, and Leia growls as he gets out of the sports car.

"Perfect." I force a laugh.

He walks right up to us and doesn't waste any time. "Collin, Tessa, I'm here to thank you for not pressing charges."

Tessa looks up at me as I respond. "My wife doesn't believe he would hurt her, and I trust her. Therefore, he wasn't guilty. Now, if he continues to come uninvited, there will be consequences."

"He's hurting but knows he did it to himself." Landon looks at Tessa.

"Are you going to stay with him?" she asks.

"I am for a couple days. I'll see what Audrianna thinks about coming up."

"He *is* going to need someone, Landon. It's not okay for him to be alone now, do you understand?"

I interject, "Excuse me. Have either of you ever thought that he needs to figure it out for himself?"

"He's basically been alone all his life, taking care of himself. An absent father, addict mother, he didn't fare very well. He needs his family." Eyes narrowed, Tessa defends her ex while looking directly into Lardon's eyes.

I interject, "If he doesn't learn to do it for himself, nothing is going to change for him. You care about him, but by not letting him do that, you're not doing him any good. He's an adult now, regardless of what has happened to him. He needs to be allowed time to become one. I'm not pretending I know everything, but you don't teach someone something, and then continue to do it for them." I look at Landon. "But you don't stop being a parent—or rather start—either."

Landon looks at both of us, clearly annoyed, as John walks over.

"You two certainly are a perfect match," Landon says then looks at John. "Pretty smart kids, huh?"

John nods.

"I have it for a couple days, but John, he would like to talk with you and Maggie. You've all been his family here, and he truly cared about you all."

"Anytime," John said.

"Thanks again. I'll certainly miss your spunk, Tessa," Landon says as he leaves.

John huffs as he pats Tessa and me on the back then walks back toward the shop.

Once he's far enough away, I ask the burning question, "Are you angry at me?"

"Yes."

"You were a kid trying to teach him. You understand that. You even said it."

"Yes, but that's not why I'm angry. I'm mad because you doubted me earlier. And from experience, doubt hurts relationships. I don't want that for either of us. I don't want us to fail, Collin."

"Failure is not an option. And unlike the jock, I'm a

very fast learner. I will own that I am reactive. I'll attempt to tame that. You need to own your past, though, beautiful, and realize that everything in it made you the woman I am so in love with. To the point that I am dealing with the likes of Landon Links." I reach out my hands, and she takes them. "I love you."

"I love you, too. We have to also be in love with us, too."

I pull her against me. "I am."

———

This is all new, a learning opportunity, and I am here for that exact reason—to learn about the woman I will be spending the rest of my life with and gain a deeper understanding of her wants and needs, just as she will be doing with me.

God help us both.

Sitting at dinner, I also learn that she will, in fact, be a handful. Oddly, that works for me. Challenge appeals to me, in more ways than one.

I sit on the edge of her childhood bed, showered and ready for more opportunities to get to know my wife.

When her eyes open, I lean down and kiss her cheek. "Good morning."

Sighing contently, she rolls to her side and wraps her arms around me.

"You fell asleep on me last night."

"It's just weird being here in my parents' house." She tips her head up and pushes out her lips for a kiss, which I gladly give her.

"Good to hear. How do you feel about taking off for a while?" I ask as I pull her up onto my lap.

"Where are we going?" she asks, kissing my neck.

I quickly pull her sleep tee up and palm one of her breasts. "It's a surprise."

"I don't like surprises." She pulls my shirt up and over my head.

"You will." I lay her down as she drags my Henley off and kiss full, supple breast as I pull her panties down.

"Collin, not here," she says as she unbuttons my jeans and shoves them down, along with my boxers.

"Okay." I move off the bed, lift her legs, and pull her panties off, leaving her legs on my shoulders and lining my dick up against her hot, wet opening, *raw*.

As I slide into her, she reaches up and grabs my hips. "I said, not here."

"I'm trained to know the difference between a lie and the truth, Mrs. Abraham, and you weren't telling the truth."

She curls up and grabs my hair, pulling me down onto her. I thrust in deep, and she moans, nearly making me come.

I press my lips to hers. "Shh …"

She laughs. "Are you crazy?"

"You better hold on and try to be quiet." I nip at the soft skin of her neck and thrust in and out slow.

I feel her tighten around me and can't believe she's already nearly there. I am loving it because I know I'll give her at least one more before I can't hold back.

Her body goes stiff, and she pushes me. "Collin, stop."

"What's wrong?"

"I'm not on any type of birth control." The way her eyes dance when she speaks, I know exactly what she wants, and she's not alone.

"You want children, right?"

"Yes, but we can wait until you're ready and—"

"I'm ready if you are. Say the words, beautiful."

She grins from ear to ear and tries to cover it with her hands over her face. "Yes."

I let her legs fall and wrap my arms around her to move her back up so her head rests on the pillows. "Let's do it."

Holding her face in my hands, I go deep and hard. "Tell me what you want—boy or girl?"

"Surprise me," she whimpers as I pull her up and sit back as she comes. I grip her hips and begin to move her as she contracts around me so tightly with me so deep. "So good."

Draped around me, I lean us forward, pull out, and then flip her to her belly and thrust in. "Need you to come with me, beautiful. We do this together."

"Again?" she whimpers.

"Together."

Head to my chest, we lay, trying to catch our breaths, when she looks up and asks, still breathless, "So, what is it going to be?"

I move her to the side, grab one of the several pillows, lift her hot little ass up, and then push the pillow under it to elevate her hips. "A surprise." I kiss her then move off the bed. "Don't move for about ten minutes."

She laughs. "Where are you going?"

"I can't stay in here and watch you like that for ten minutes. I'm already getting hard again."

"What?" She laughs again.

"I never wanted kids, didn't want there to be even the slightest chance it could happen. I just went raw for the first time in my life, just came inside of you. I have zero chance of not being back in that same spot if I come any closer. A seventy percent chance if I don't leave now." So, I turn and walk out, needing that distance.

She laughs as I nearly jump down the stairs. "I love you!"

After cleaning up, shaving, brushing, and flossing, all while looking at the clock every thirty seconds, she walks in, perfect nose in the air. She walks to the toilet and sits.

"What are you doing, Mrs. Abraham?"

She shrugs. "Going to the bathroom."

"With me in here?" I ask, amused.

"Will that bother you?"

"I don't know really?" I smile and lean against the counter. "Go ahead. Let's see."

"Get out." She throws toilet paper at me. "Now I can't."

I wink. "You'll have to eventually."

"No, I won't." She starts to stand.

Laughing, I leave her to it.

When I walk into the kitchen, Alex is standing at the sink.

"Good God, are you two about done?"

I cringe at the thought of him hearing us. "Oh, I'm so sorry. I didn't know anyone was home."

Tessa walks into the room and starts laugh.

I give her a *hush* look.

"We're so sorry."

"Tessa, what the hell was he doing to you up there?" Alex asks, and I want to crawl under the table. "All the times I've walked into your old place, you never sounded like *that*. Are you okay? Did he hurt you?"

Laughing, she looks at me, and seeing my face is no doubt as red as a beet, she laughs even harder. "Do you want to tell him, Collin?"

"No, not really." I look at her like she's lost her damn mind

Apparently, choosing to spare me, she looks at Alex. "You mean to tell me that Phoebe doesn't sound like that?"

"She's still alive, isn't she?" Alex replies dramatically.

"You need to unleash on your wife, Alex," She nudges me. "Tell him, Collin, what you were doing to me."

"Tessa, this is uncomfortable for your brother and me," I scold her.

"Sorry." She smiles. "Alex, he and I were having sex." She leans in and whispers, "The best sex I've ever had." Then she walks out of the room.

"I apologize for my wife's—"

"You may as well not even start, or that's all you'll be doing," he jokes, and I feel a bit of relief.

A very little bit.

Honeymoon

Chapter Thirty-Seven

Tessa

e head to Alex and Phoebe's to help her. Aka, steal Remington time, which happens to be a fight because my husband—God, I love saying that —is also a baby hog.

While Phoebe and I freeze breast milk—because, as Alex told me, she's a little obsessive about pumping for fear of drying up—Collin sits and rocks Remington, staring down at him with a soft protectiveness that makes me melt.

"You better give him a baby soon," Phoebe whispers. "He's supposed to be a daddy. Look at him."

Once we finish filling half the freezer, I ask her to come to their room in their apartment and somehow get her to lay down, something Alex asked me to do because she's exhausted, and I tell her that we're going away, somewhere for an unknown amount of time, and I promise to practice a lot.

We talk, and I tell her too much. Then she falls asleep, and I cook her and Alex dinner.

When Alex gets home, he wakes her up with white roses in hand. Then they eat by candlelight while I sit between Collin's legs on the couch, holding Remington and feeding him his first bottle. After that, we head to Ryan and Jade's, a stark contrast to the calm at Alex and Phoebe's. The house is chaos and cookies, the kids bouncing off the walls, and Jade bounces with them as they dance in the living room and don't even hear us come in. I look up at Collin, seeing he is perfectly relaxed and amused, and totally not put off.

Luke is the first to see us. He bolts to me and immediately asks, "Where is Uncle Lucas?"

"I'm not sure, Lukie, but I want you to meet someone who is very special to me, okay?"

He nods.

"This is Collin. He's my husband."

"You're not marrying Uncle Lucas?" he asks, confused

I bend down so we're eyeball to eyeball. "No, that didn't work out, buddy, but Lucas loves you, and so do I. And you're going to love Collin someday, too."

"So, there's more people to love? That's not a bad thing"—he nudges me—"baby."

I can't help but laugh.

Jade walks over. "What's so funny?"

"Me," Lukie announces. "I called her baby, like Uncle Lucas does."

I look up at Collin, who rolls his eyes.

"Sorry," I whisper.

"No need to be." He kisses my cheek.

"So"—Jade hooks her arm through Collin's and drags

him into the house—"Collin, how was she? You never called."

"Very quiet," he deadpans then looks back at me and winks.

"Hey, I brought pizza," Ryan announces as he walks in.

Jade laughs. "You two want to stay for dinner?"

"We would love to, but we're actually going to take off for a while," I say, picking up Jackson.

"Where and how long?" Jade asks.

Collin smiles at me. "We can stay. We leave in the morning, and the location is a surprise."

"Well, Collin, I would ask you to call me when you get there, but you've disappointed me already." Jade fake pouts.

"I'll make sure you're not disappointed before you fall asleep tonight, Jade," Ryan whispers in her ear as he kisses her cheek.

While eating, Ryan and Collin talk about Ryan's work and they continue talking while Jade and I clean up, I then hear him tell Collin what Lucas has done for him and Jade.

"He isn't a bad friend, but he's obviously a mess of a boyfriend. I'm glad she has you. You got a good one. Be good to her, Collin. She deserves nothing less."

His reply is totally Collin Abraham. "I don't like him because he could have killed her that day. I don't doubt that he became a good person. How could he not be after spending four to five years with her? I'll never hurt her intentionally," he assures Ryan. "You all need to let him grow up and figure that out himself, or he'll be lost forever. She cares for him, and I don't want to see her beating herself up because he can't function without her. You're a good man, Ryan, and you have a beautiful home and family, not because of him, but because of what you've done."

"Not going to tell you how I knew Lucas wasn't the one, but I did." Jade frowns. "Tommy told me I was wrong, but I am going to tell you that I know Collin is. He's perfect for you, and you for him."

At the door, Lukie hugs Collin then steps back and laughs. "Goodbye, Collin. Be nice to my baby."

Collin's lips turn up. "I will. You be good for your mommy and daddy." He then holds his hand up, and Lukie high-fives him.

"Deal."

W hen we walk into the airport, it's still dark. I let go of his hand when he gives me the plane ticket then watch as he flexes the one I was holding.

"Did I hurt you?"

"You've got one hell of a grip, Mrs. Abraham." He nods to the ticket. "You've attempted to bribe me with every sexual favor under the sun, expect for anal, to get this information out of me."

I laugh. "Because I hate surprises."

He leans in close to my ear. "So, anal is still—"

"Oh my God, what is it with anal?" I smack at him with the ticket, and his eyes light with pure entertainment, and his laugh … God, his laugh is a song, and I want to make that happen forever.

"Beautiful, open the damn ticket and stop looking at me like that." His smile is all soft.

"Okay, okay." I pull the ticket out and see "*Hawaii*."

"Just you, me, and the ocean."

I shove my arms under his, pull him tight against me, and look up. "I love you."

When he holds his arm up high, I look up to see he's

holding his phone, and the camera is pointed to the window.

I giggle. "What are you doing?"

"Pictures were never a thing in my life, but I know how much they mean to you, and I want to make sure we have decades of our life in pictures for you, too. So, I'm capturing our reflections in the window. Then"—he kisses my cheek and takes the picture—"I'm going to start my own photo album of you. Smile, Mrs. Abraham."

He refuses to pose for me as our flight is called, and then he sends a text to my parents, Jade, and Phoebe, telling them we're off.

As we walk down the bridge, he asks, "Have you ever had sex on an airplane?"

"Have you?" I ask in return

"Not while in flight."

B y the time we land, I am exhausted and mildly embarrassed, because there was no way possible that the flight attendant didn't catch on to what was going on a mile high in the sky. My knees are sore from bending over the airplane's bathroom sink as he slammed into me every hour or so. I lost count. They also hurt from being slammed against the walls as I rode him on the closed toilet seat. He antagonized me by telling me not to try to keep up, but there was no way in hell I wasn't going to give it my all.

"Are you tired, beautiful?" He kisses my hand.

"Exhausted." I smile.

"I can't wait to have you on every surface in the bungalow."

"Why not a hotel?"

"You're loud," he whispers.

I shrug. "Your fault."

"When do you menstruate?" he asks, as if the conversation didn't just veer left, and I laugh. "What?"

I giggle. "Menstruate is such a technical term."

His lips curve up. "Well, when?"

"Two and a half weeks ago."

"Perfect." He squeezes my hand. "We are going to have fun, Tessa Abraham."

"I don't doubt that at all." I lean into him as we touch down.

We stay on Mauna Lani Bay, in a private bungalow, with a private pool and a round-the-clock butler service. It's beautiful.

It faces the ocean, and we swim with turtles as big as Leia, and dolphins. We go snorkeling, hiking, and cliff-diving, which is epic. We talk about our families and our dreams for our own the future.

He doesn't touch his phone the entire time we are there, but I know that, every night I go to the bathroom, he would call home. And we make love all day, every day.

To accommodate this, Collin dismissed the butler, asking him only to come when we are out. I am sure that this was caused because of the ordeal with Alex, and he's now scarred for life.

Collin is funny, and charming, and loves me. I don't care about his past because it molded the perfect man who is now my husband.

When I do think about Lucas, I no longer feel like it's my duty to make things right for him, but I desperately pray he will be. Even though I use the words "care for him," without love, I wouldn't care, and I know I will love him forever. But my love for Collin is the strongest that I have ever felt in my life. There is no doubt or jealousy. Although I have not had to be away from him for long, I just know when I am, it will be all right.

The day before we leave, he gets serious and asks that we talk. So, we do.

"When we get back, I have to be in Ecuador for two weeks. I have asked your father if it's all right for you to come with me, and he said that it is as long as it is with you."

"I would love to, but I have to start working sometime."

"My wife doesn't have to work."

I scowl, and he nods.

"Okay, that's important to you."

Old worries creep in, possible mistakes I made. "Yes, actually, it is, but I want to be with you."

He studies me for a minute, and I wonder if he sees it —the insecurity.

"Let me explain my work. When create villages in the middle of nowhere, we help them set up housing and structures. But it's much more than that. Tomás and the group you saw on the deck help them learn about security and we train them to be able to sustain and maintain the village and the communities that they help build so that they are vested and have learned to maintain it with little help when we leave. And we always leave with the hope they will teach others how to do the same thing.

"What funds the majority of this is our health program. I have a group of doctors and nurses; the majority are interns. They give immunizations, medications, and perform field surgeries, if available and necessary. But they also focus on teaching women how to take care of themselves and their children, while the men focus on security and learning how to build and farm, to ensure they can provide the necessities for their village."

"Dr. Abraham, I'm going to need two hearts for all this love I have for you."

His lips curve up, and then he returns to serious. "You're a nurse, Tessa. We could work beside each other almost every day, doing great things for people who truly have no idea that life can be anything else but surviving while living in poverty, filth, and fear."

I close my eyes and thank God for my husband.

"Do you have any questions?"

"A couple."

He sits down across the table. "Okay, shoot."

"You truly are amazing."

"That wasn't a question, but I am glad you think so." He reaches across the table and takes my hands.

"How long do these trips take?"

"Well, my part has always been a month or more, but I've found a reason to put a little faith in my people. This trip will last about two weeks. A small group stays with the villages until they're settled, and again we stay involved in some capacity."

"Is there private housing?" I grin.

He laughs. "No, but there will be."

"When can I start?"

He stands and rounds the table. Then he pulls me up, taking my face in his hands. "Thank you." He gives me a quick kiss then asks. "All right, now, where do we set up home base?"

"Where do you want to?"

"Where will you be happiest?"

"Wherever we are," I answer honestly.

"All right, I have an idea." He steps back and waves to the chair, and I sit. He rounds the table and sits back down across from me. Then he immediately begins with excitement in his eyes. "The place we ate lunch after you tried to kill me—you know, the hay barn fiasco—there used to be a structure there that burnt down, right?"

"Yes. Doe Camp."

He looks confused, so I explain about the camp and the fire, and that Lucas's house bordered it, but from a great distance.

"Do you think your father would sell us the land? And, if so, would you like to build there?" he asks.

Unable to contain myself, I jump up and rush to sit on his lap. "Yes! But, are you okay with that?"

"I wouldn't have asked if I weren't."

Future Plans

Chapter Thirty-Eight

Collin

I phoned John while Tessa was sleeping to discuss the land that Tessa seems to love so much. He agreed to the sale of the land, as long as the same agreement was reached that Lucas and Tessa had come up with, which was, if something happened, the Ross family had the first option to purchase it back. I assured him that wasn't necessary and asked that it all be put in Tessa's name and her name alone.

W e are by the barn while Tessa enthusiastically tells her parents about the honeymoon when I see Tomás pull in.

"Will you excuse me a moment?" I ask, giving Tessa a kiss on the cheek before walking away.

As I get closer, I see his brows are knit.

"Talk to me, Tomás."

"We're not ready for civilians yet, sir."

"Unbelievable," I grumble.

"It will be in two weeks. There is nothing more I can do to speed up the process. We knew this might be a problem. I can go back, if you'd like," Tomás offers.

"Tomás, what did you do to my husband? He's been perfectly happy until you arrived," she calls from behind me. At my side, she wraps her arm around my waist. "What's wrong, Collin?"

"Thank you for coming to my rescue, but I do need a few minutes with Tomás. I'll be in, in just a few minutes."

She studies me for a minute then nods. "Come in happy?"

"Yes, ma'am." I wink.

A fter my conversation with Tomás, I set to find her, and do so while she is sitting on the deck.

She looks up. "Is everything all right?"

"No, it's going to be another three weeks before we're ready for civilians."

"All right."

"Tessa, this is not what I want, but I have to be there."

"I can go back to the Cape and wait for you."

"Why would you do that? Your family is here." Then it hits me. "You're worried about Lucas."

"No, I'm worried that you'll be worried about him. I love you, Collin, and—"

I pull her up, take her seat, and pull her onto my lap. "I know that, and I'm not worried about you and him. My concern is that you don't believe me when I tell you that. I trust in what we have. My concern is that you'll be resentful of the places that may take me away from you from time to time, and I want you to truly love what we do."

"I knew this before we got married. I just can't wait until I can go with you, *be with you*."

"You're going to be busy. You have a house to design. I want to be in it by Christmas."

She sits straight up and looks at me. "That's in two months!"

We spend the next week planning for two weeks apart. During that time, we return to the Cape, and I remind her of all the places I said I wanted her, and she reminds me of how perfect we are for each other.

We spend an afternoon importing important dates into my calendar to ensure I don't miss birthdays, anniversaries, or anything that's important to her. We spend another afternoon going over her wish list for a home, and it takes forever to get anything out of her, aside from "a nice kitchen." My list is only a bit longer. I want two things, other than whatever she can dream of—a security room below our home and living quarters above the garage for when we have visitors that aren't family and staff.

We fly back the day before I am slated to leave and

spend the afternoon with Jake, John, and Maggie. Then, after we eat dinner, we relax in the living room, on the couch, with Leia, who has missed her terribly, sitting pretty between us.

W hen we arrive at the airport hotel, for the second time, I find myself resentful of the life I chose to build, caused by something that was never a choice. It was, for lack of a logical explanation, as Pastor Lou has explained, *divine intervention*.

Until Tessa, I would have overthought this, questioned it, but we have been brought together so many times, and the feelings brought with those moments need not be soiled by logic.

I would have preferred to leave her sleeping in bed when I left, but she insisted on us getting a room at the airport hotel, and did so stomping her foot. I looked at John while this happened, and he simply chuckled, telling me what I needed to know, that stomp is an exclamation point, an *end of,* and she deserved a win after my delay in her look into what our life would be. So, now, I'll be leaving her here instead of leaving her safely at home, with her parents. *I feel there is a lesson in this, too.*

I push the hair from her face and watch as her eyelashes flutter open.

"Sorry, I fell asleep."

"Don't be sorry. You're tired. Let's get checked in and get you into bed." I kiss her forehead.

Entering the room, I set the bag on the floor as Tessa walks to the bathroom.

I grab the toiletry bag and this night's attire—a navy-blue, silk nightgown. It will look beautiful on her. But

433

looking at her now, in a tee-shirt and panties, standing there, washing her face, I know there isn't anything that wouldn't.

Side by side, we brush our teeth.

When she giggles, I glance at her. "Mrs. Abraham, what is so amusing?"

Tessa sets her toothbrush down, takes mine and sets it down next to hers, and then she takes my face, stroking the tips of her nails over the stubble that's grown on my face.

I should have shaved.

"I like this."

"Really?" I grip her hips.

"Really." She leans in for a kiss as I lift her up and set her on the counter.

She grips the bottom of my shirt then lifts it up, pulling it off and dropping it on the floor. Then she skims her fingertips over the sparse hairs that lay across my chest, following the trail down my torso, igniting a fire inside of me that has yet to be tamed, every damn time she touches me.

"I like this, too." She licks her lips as she pushes me back then slides off the counter. She unbuckles my belt and unbuttons my pants. "These are nice but need to go."

After I get rid of her shirt, she pushes my pants and boxers down. Then she unsnaps her bra, and I start to reach for her, but she brushes my hand away and pushes me back a few steps.

Her eyes take me in, desire burning in the blue, as she steps forward and uncrosses my arms that *I didn't even realize I crossed them.*

I feel her lips touch my neck, down my collarbone … Stepping back, eyes work from my face, all the way down to my cock, as she cups her breasts, pinches her nipples, and tugs at them as she steps into me again.

I reach for her, and she shakes her head. "No."

Taking my wrists, she lowers them to my sides and kisses down to my abs, hips. And the way she kisses them … *good God*.

Hand wrapped around my cock, *or hers*—I forget who it belongs to anymore, me or her—she licks up the underside, and every muscle in my body tightens as she looks up at me.

"Tessa, *fuck*," I hiss as I twist her thick, blonde waves around my hand and pull it back so I can watch her work what is undoubtedly hers.

With each upward thrust, she sucks hard on my head before she digs her fingers into my hips, and I pull out slowly, so damn slow, and not because I'm greedy and want her on her knees, but because I see the need in her eyes to give this to me.

Hands on her tits, I pinch at her nipples, tugging them, when she cups her hands around mine, lifts higher on her knees, and encloses my dick in them, mouth still on my head.

I rock into them, leaving her enough of me to suck. Her hands free, she cups my sack, gently rolling and caressing them, causing them to burn for her.

"Beautiful, you need to stop."

She doesn't.

Mouth wide open, she milks my dick until the first burst of cum hits her open mouth. She wraps her lips around my cock and swallows everything I give her.

She pulls me out as my last shot surges through me like an aftershock, hitting her perfect tits. After she licks me clean, I drag my dick through my cum like a brush to canvas.

I pull her off her knees and turn her to face the mirror.

She smiles when she sees what I've done, and then she looks over her shoulder at me. "We need a shower."

"I made a masterpiece, and you want to wash it away?"

"Should we take a picture?" she asks, trying not to smile.

"Yeah," I groan.

After I take the picture, I run a bath. Tessa adds oils and bubble bath, and I step in, sit down, and hold my hand out for her.

She steps in and begins to sit when I wrap my hand around her ankle. She stops.

After resting her foot on the edge of the tub, I pull her to me. "Hands on the wall, beautiful."

Nose buried between her legs, I inhale the scent I love more than lilac—*my wife's arousal.*

Fingers gripping her ass, I pull her close enough to taste, and that's exactly what I do.

Licking, sucking, drinking her in, I don't stop until she fists my hair so hard that my scalp tingles and cries out my name.

I stand, line us up, and slide in, and I do it deeply.

"I could live on you alone, Mrs. Abraham."

"I don't think," she whimpers, "I can stand."

Arm wrapped around her waist, I pull almost all the way out. "I got you."

Groaning into her neck, I feed myself into her slowly, inch by inch.

Once we've both come, I turn her around and take her lips.

"Let's finish up our bath and get you into bed."

"No, I don't want to," she whispers.

When I laugh, she tenses up. I lift her chin and ask, "What's going—" I stop when I see her eyes filled with tears. "Tessa, did I hurt you? God, I am so sorry. I—"

"No, I just don't want you to go." Tears roll down her cheeks.

My heart starts racing as I wipe away her tears. "Okay, I can try to figure something out. Please don't cry, Tessa. I love you. Please don't—"

"No!" she snaps, shocking me. Then she starts to laugh and cry.

"What can I do, Tessa. Just tell me. Please, tell me," I beg.

Shaking her head, she starts, "I'm being ridiculous! I want you in me again, and I know you have to go, and I'm going to miss you." She links her fingers behind my neck and pulls herself up, wrapping her legs around me.

"Tessa?"

"I have problems."

I wait for her to elaborate as she buries her face in my neck and she reaches between us, lining us up.

When she doesn't say anything, I tell her, "I hope this doesn't upset you. And just so you're aware, if you need me to stay, I will figure it out. I don't think that's your problem, though, Tessa. Don't get me wrong, making love to you, that connection with you is amazing. Never in my life have I felt—" I stop and reword when I realize what it is that is bothering her. And no, with my dick now hard again and inside her thinking of that punk isn't ideal, but there it is.

"I can't get enough of you in any way. It's you, all of you. My life, my body, my heart is all yours. You need to remember that I'm not him. I would die before I allowed hurt to come to you, let alone do it to you myself. I'll never do anything to make you not trust that you are part of me, connected in body or otherwise. I will never ..." I lift her chin, but she keeps her eyes closed. "Look at me, Tessa. I will never hurt you. That is not an idle promise and as real as needing air in my lungs to survive."

Tessa's tears fall harder as she hugs me even tighter, with every part of her beautiful body. "I love you. I'm sorry."

"I know, Tessa, I know that." One arm under her, I turn on the shower and hold her as I wash her.

"You lied to me." She stomps.

"It was necessary."

"I do not need a new car."

"These are the safest vehicles on the market." I point at my printout. "And you need to keep in mind we are going to have a family. Pick which one you would like."

"I have the Jeep."

"I think it's time to retire it. It's just a vehicle. You still have memories of Toby."

She shakes her head and pushes the paper away. "I don't care. You choose."

"I want you to have what you like."

"You choose. The only thing I want is navy-blue, like the Jeep, and—"

"Four-wheel drive. That driveway is going to be a beast in the winter."

She finally smiles. "A beast, huh?"

"Why does that amuse you?"

"You … you growl"—she giggles—"like a beast."

"I what?"

"You growl when, well, you know." She shrugs.

"That's your fault. Beyond my control."

"Did I embarrass you by saying that?"

"Your body responds nicely to that sound. Not embarrassed at all. We will, however, need to christen that vehicle you just ..." I look down at my pants. I'm getting hard. "Fuck, you drive me mad."

She laughs. "See? You growl, just like that."

I look behind me to ensure no one is looking then rub my hand across her chest. Her nipples tighten immediately. "Like that."

"So, have you made a decision?" The salesman walks into the office, and she glares at me.

I kiss her quickly then get out, walk around, and open her door.

We christened her navy-blue Range Rover in the parking garage of Hancock airport.

Girl Time

Chapter Thirty-Nine

*I*t took a few days before I dragged my sorry sad behind off the couch where I sat with a brand-new notebook and took notes when Collin and I talked on the phone and text messaged ideas back and forth. I have never missed anyone as much as I miss him, ever. But, on Sunday, Mom is adamant I go to church, so I do.

After church, I go to Jade's for lunch.

We eat and as we are sitting on the couch, watching a slideshow of my honeymoon, I hear, "Did you have a good time, Tessa?"

Lucas.

"Yes." I grab the remote to turn it off.

"Don't stop on my account. Jessie and I would love to see your pictures." He says this with complete sarcasm as he walks past the coffee table and grabs the remote from my hand. Then he and Jessie sit together on the loveseat.

"I don't think this is a good time for this, Lucas," Jade snarls at him.

"It's fine. Hello, Jessie."

She sincerely starts to say, "I'm sorry about the festival. I was—"

"I accept your—"

"Apology. She accepts your apology," Lucas cuts me off after I cut her off, while animatedly mocking me. "So, where did you go?"

"Hawaii, on Mauna Lani Bay."

The pictures roll, and I realize that, no matter how much I love my husband, and always will, none of me wants to hurt Lucas, and none of me wants to hurt Collin, either, which means not keeping the fact Lucas is here from him.

"You look happy," he says with a horrible mix of anger and pain in his voice.

"I am."

I excuse myself and walk into the other room to call Collin. Thankfully, he answers.

"Hey, I miss you."

"I miss you, beautiful. What's going on? Are you having fun with Jade?" he asks.

"I am. Listen, Lucas and Jessie just walked in. If you want me to leave, I will, but they are actually watching our honeymoon slideshow with Jade as we speak. And, by the way, should it freak me out that you take pictures of me when I sleep?"

"Tessa, go turn that off now," he insists.

"Okay, I'm sorry." I hurry into the living room and see myself asleep by our private pool, sunbathing topless.

I run to the TV and hit the power button. "Collin!"

"Sorry, beautiful." He laughs.

"You're ... bad," I whisper.

"I trust you, Tessa, but if he steps out of line ." He pauses then laughs. "Forget it. Jade's there, right?"

"Yes." I laugh, too, as I look at her.

"Call me when you leave? I love you."

"I love you, too." I hang up the phone, feeling my face burning.

Jade laughs. "Nice pictures."

"I'm sorry. I didn't know." I shake my head as Jade grabs a pillow to cover her face as she laughs hysterically at my embarrassment.

"Where is your husband, Tessa?" Lucas asks, trying to hide his anger.

"In Ecuador."

"Why?"

"On business."

He raises a brow. "So soon? How do you feel about that?"

"I miss him," I answer resolutely. "But it's all right."

"Can I talk to you alone for a minute?"

I look at Jessie. "Are you all right with that?"

"Sure." Jessie shrugs and continues leafing through a *Sports Illustrated* magazine, no doubt looking for her next man.

We walk into the kitchen, and Lucas asks, "Can we go upstairs for just a couple minutes?"

"No, Lucas."

"Then outside by the pool?" He doesn't wait for me to answer, so I follow him out.

When he turns, I see hurt and anger in his eyes as he asks, "Are you really going to stay with him?"

"I love him, I married him, and I trust him completely." I cross my arms over my chest. "When I fell in love with him and said yes to his proposal, it had nothing to do with any hurt feelings or the desire to cause you pain. I'm so sorry, but you have moved on, and so have I. I still want you to be okay." I stop when he turns his back to me. "Lucas, are you hurting? Or am I wasting my breath?"

He turns and looks at me. "Do you really have to ask? I'm fucking bleeding out here, Tessa."

My eyes immediately burn. "What do you need from me?"

"Tessa, don't you cry."

When he reaches to wipe away my tears, I step back and slap them away. "I don't want you to hurt."

"I don't know how I'm supposed to feel. Hurt that you chose him over me. Pissed at you for not loving me after you promised forever."

I always will.

"Pissed at myself for doing this to us."

I'm not. Not anymore. Not after Collin.

"Pissed you can't forgive me."

I have. I'm standing right here. Right. Here.

"I feel numb, Tessa, like my heart will never be whole again."

Please, please, allow it to be.

"But if you're happy, truly happy, and he doesn't hurt you, and he takes *care of you* like I couldn't, then …" He hugs me.

I don't hate it.

"I'm happy for you."

"Thank you." I pat his back then step away.

"Do you still love me?"

"Why do you need to know that?"

"Because, through everything, regardless of how I acted or what I did to ruin us, I have always loved you, and I always will. You're it for me. It's the only thing I know is real. You're married and look happy, but fuck, baby, I love you, anyway."

Unable to look into his eyes, especially when he's giving me everything from his, I look up at the sky. *Blue.* "It breaks my heart still to feel like I can't help you through this, and not because of any other reason than I do love you. But it's a different love than I feel for Collin. I don't know how to explain it. I wish I could, and I'm sorry if that hurts."

"So, although I feel this way, and even though I know I will never stop, and never, without a doubt I know, I never fucking will, you stand here, saying you love two people. That doesn't make sense, Tessa."

"It does. It's in different ways, I guess. Like family? I would lie down and die for the people I love, and I would do anything for them. You're part of that family of people I would do anything for. And I know you, Lucas. I know you'd do anything for me. But I'm deeply in love with Collin. It's something I've never felt before. Very spiritual. Like he was put here for me and me for him. He knows how I feel about you, and he understands."

"Yeah right," he huffs.

"He does, Lucas, and I trust him. I know that, in time, we can all be friends."

His jaw tightens, and he shakes his head. "Not to open wounds here, Tessa, but the only other man in your life that I was okay with was Toby. You thought you loved him, and you realized it was me. How is this different?"

"It just is. He—"

"How do you think he would feel about that?" he cuts me off.

"He would be happy for me."

He rolls his eyes. "How do you know that?"

"Collin served with him, and he was at the funeral. After everyone left that day and I sat sobbing at his grave, he was the man in uniform who appeared from the woods and handed me a tissue. And I think I told you that already. Maybe you just don't remember."

"It's all jumbled together"—he looks around, lost, broken, hurt— "seeing you with someone else, and not like Toby or Ben. It's different."

I don't reply, because he's right; it *is* different.

Understanding shows in his eyes. "I guess I have nothing more. I want you to be happy, but all this happenstance shit feels put on."

"It's not."

"Well, I now understand what you mean by you needing me to be okay, because I worry about you all the fucking time. If he hurts you—"

"He would never. You would really like him. I wouldn't ever expect him to become your best friend, but you would really like him. I mean, if you tried."

"Is that what you want me to do?"

Yes.

"I just want it to be okay for you, me, everyone we love."

He pulls his hat down over his eyes.

"How are you and Jessie? Is she possibly the one?"

He lets out a breath and shakes his head. "No … but she's fine for now."

"How are you going to find the right person if you can't be alone for any length of time?"

"Well, hello, pot meet kettle," he pokes fun at me, and when we both laugh, I feel … hopeful. "I'll try, Tessa. Just …" He shrugs. "I love you. I know what I've done, but I

445

need you to know that, if you ever … Fuck, this sucks. I love you, baby. You said you were put here for him and, well, that's how I feel about you." I open my mouth to reply, but he cuts me off. "I don't want to talk about it anymore, all right? I just need you to know that, if things don't work out with him, I would stop at nothing to make sure you knew my love for you is and always has been *eternal*." He hugs me. "Friends, baby?"

I elbow him then step back and look him over. "What else is going on? You still seem off to me. Is your mom all right?"

He scrubs a hand over his face and nods. "She's good. I came here today because I have to lay Ryan off for a few months, and I don't want to. The only other option is for him to go on the road for the winter, and I don't want that for him or his family. Sorry, it's not your problem."

"No, but I think I have a solution."

"What's up, *T. Ross*?" He shoves his hands in his pockets. "Or whatever your last name is?"

He knows, but I remind him. "It's Abraham. And we're going to build a house here. Collin wants it done by Christmas."

"He can do it. I'll help." He shrugs then shakes his head. "No, I won't. But he built our place, and he did it very quickly while working full-time for my dad."

"Will it bother you?"

"No, of course not. Where are you building?"

I look away. "We're kind of going to be neighbors."

"Does your husband know that?" He laughs.

"Yes."

"You're building at the pond, aren't you?"

I nod. "Yes, we are."

Lucas smirks. "Does your husband know you and I have *been* in that pond?"

I roll my eyes. "You're an idiot."

Ryan and Luke walk through the gate right then, and Luke jets to me.

He lifts his chin then hugs me. "Hey, baby."

Laughing, I give him a giant hug.

"That's my line, little man." Lucas scoops him up.

"Everything okay, Tessa?" Ryan asks as we all walk in, Jade conveniently in the kitchen where she had no doubt been watching us.

"Yes." I hug Jade. "I'm going to head home, but Ryan, will you call me later?"

He nods.

Lucas lifts his chin. "Goodbye, Mrs. Abraham."

I do not say goodbye to Jessie.

S itting on the couch, petting Leia, I tell Collin about everything that was said, pretty much verbatim, and then I get excited when I tell him about Ryan getting laid off and Lucas's idea.

He says nothing. *Not one thing.*

My excitement deflates.

"Are you, um … okay with all that?"

"I told you I was jealous, Tessa, so no, I'm not okay with you being that friendly with him. I'm perfectly fine with Ryan building our home if you think he is capable of doing so. I would like to discuss some things with him, so please give him my number and ask that he calls me. I have to go. I will see you in a week. Do you think you can behave for that long?"

Pissed, I snap, "You knew we'd be in the same circles at times. And, by the way, *Collin*, I didn't fuck him. I helped him close a door I closed months ago. Goodbye."

I wait for the tears, but they don't come. Neither does the fear that I ruined us.

God, I love him.

I continue to sit, looking at my phone, willing him to call me back, and when he doesn't, I refuse to stew. I have shit to do.

I call Jade and ask her to give Collin's number to Ryan, and to please call him soon.

———

The next morning, when Collin texts me, I ignore him and focus on my notebook entitled "*Dream Home/Dream Life.*"

Standing at the sink, trying to figure out what to make for lunch, because nothing sounds appealing, I see Tomás pull in and immediately feel sick with worry. When I see the large, thick envelope he's holding, that worry changes to bile rising in my throat as he walks to the front door.

No one uses the front door.

I open the door, and he hands me the manila envelope. "Papers to sign, ma'am."

No, no, no, I think as I take the envelope and pull out a packet.

"Thank God," I sigh as I step back inside. "Come in. I'll get a pen."

The papers are for the land transfer.

"Are you all right, ma'am?"

"It's Tessa, Tomás." I sit down and point to the chair across from me. He doesn't sit. "I thought he was divorcing me."

"No, ma'am. He loves you. Try to take it easy on him."

I nod as I flip through and sign the rest of the areas requested then hand it back.

"Do you need anything?"

"I should probably call him."

"Yes, I think you should."

In seconds, he's gone.

"Hello, Tessa," Collin answers, voice even, *cold*. I manage a quiet, "Hi."

Silence.

"I'm sorry," we both say in unison then laugh.

"So, you didn't divorce me," I joke.

"Pardon me?" he asks.

"Tomás shows up with papers for me to sign, and I—"

"That's never going to happen," he states.

"Good," I whisper. "I love you, Collin. I'll see you Monday, right?"

"Absolutely. So, get some rest. I'm going to book a room. I don't want to disturb anyone."

"We could meet at the Cape."

"No. I have a meeting with Ryan to finalize the plans. But that does sound good. Maybe we'll head east after we get the ball rolling on the house. I love you, beautiful."

Saturday, I help prepare for Luke's fifth birthday, and it is just now that I realize how out of shape I am, or is it that people in general are exhausting? I settle on both.

Activities outside of cooking while Jade bakes include a bouncy house and a creepy clown. And speaking of creeps, Landon shows up, but that's okay because he is accompanied by Audrianna and the girls, who give me huge hugs and don't act like it's weird at all, which, just sayin', that in itself is weird. But that's what we, a small group of people from Blue Valley Class of '93, became.

I glance over and see Ryan, who used to always be so quiet, who became a man strong enough to be a dad and get married while still in high school, and Lucas, the only D1 athlete turned pro from Blue Valley High, and did so surrounded by tragic events. A dream that most people would have given up on while trying to heal. The two of them became unlikely friends, and are now best friends, grilling hot dogs and little sliders for the kids, to celebrate a boy's, whom they both love, birth. Jessie, well, she's looking at a magazine, of course, paying zero attention to anyone.

I hear Jade calling everyone for lunch and slide out of the rocking chair, where I am rocking with Riley May, who dives for Uncle Jack with zero warning. Thankfully, he's used to this.

I walk over and grab a plate as Phoebe waves to me, smiling. I smile and wave back, and then she laughs and points. I follow her line of fire, and when I see him, I immediately rush to him and jump into his arms.

"Surprise." Collin kisses my lips then the top of my head as I squeeze him tighter.

"God, I missed you."

"Time to eat, love birds!" Jade yells, and I see her wink at Collin. "See? I can keep a secret!"

"Did you book a room?" he asks Jade as she walks over and hands us both a plate.

She nods.

He kisses the side of my head then whispers, "It better not be far from here. I want you now."

Plates full, we walk to a table and sit.

"I'm so glad you came home early."

Collin winks. "Luke is family."

"Steak or chicken?" Lucas, who is now standing in front of us with a platter of meat, asks.

"Steak, please." Collin gives him a tight nod.

Lucas flops a hunk of steak on his plate.

"Thank you."

Lucas doesn't bother asking me; he simple drops a chicken breast on my plate then walks away.

"You two don't mind if we sit here? It really is the only place left." Jessie sits across from us without waiting for an answer.

Collin rolls his eyes slightly. "That's fine."

I push my food around, and Collin forks up some potatoes and feeds me a bite. As soon as it hits my stomach, I want to hurl. When he holds up a forkful of chicken, I shake my head.

"What's wrong with the chicken, Mrs. Abraham?" Lucas asks, sitting next to Jessie.

"It's fine. I'm just not hungry."

Lucas smirks, and Jessie stands, asking, "Would anyone like a drink?"

"Sure. Do you two want anything? Beer or wine?" Lucas asks, looking at me.

"We'll have water," Collin answers. "Is that okay?"

"Yes. Thank you, Jessie." Okay, maybe she's what is souring my stomach.

Collin picks up the fork. "You need to eat something."

I cover my mouth, and Lucas stands. "Congratulations, Collin."

I glance at Collin, who looks like he wants to kill Lucas, who then reaches across the table and messes up my hair. Collin drops his napkin and starts to stand. I grab his hand as Lucas walks away.

"I warned him not a hair on your head," Collin sneers.

"He's trying. Please be nice." I stand and head into the

house, praying I make it to the bathroom before I throw up.

When we walk in, Lucas is standing at the counter, smiling like he knows a secret.

He does.

I glare at him while I hurry into the bathroom.

"You're pushing it," Collin snarls at him.

"You better go tend to your wife. She's going to be a lot of fun," I hear as I throw up. "Go get her, man … unless you want me to go help her out."

"Collin!" I yell right before I throw up again.

As he's crouched down behind me, rubbing my back, I lean back against him, "Can we get out of here?"

After I rinse my mouth, he takes my hand, and we walk out.

I look at Lucas.

His eyes soften as he looks at me. "It'll be different this time, Te—"

Collin stops and points at him, his finger an inch from his face. "You *will* learn you place."

"I don't want your wife, man. But fuck up once, just once …" Lucas walks out, shaking his head as he exits out the front door before he slams it and yells, "Fuck!"

Collin turns, and I stop him. "Can we leave, please?"

"Yes," he snaps, and then we leave through the garage. "We'll come back for your vehicle."

In his SUV, I turn and take his hand. "I need to stop at the store, and then home to grab some things."

"Of course. Are you—"

"I'm good." I smile and sit back.

Silence.

As we enter town, I point to the drug store. "Here is good."

He pulls up front and parks. "I'll go in and—"

"No, I will. Alone."

"Fine."

I reach over and take his chin. "I want to kiss you, but I have puke breath. And you better be nice to me, grumpy. I'll be back in a couple minutes."

Welcome Home

Chapter Forty

Collin

She's sick and pissed at me. He's lucky to be breathing. These two thoughts cloud the fact that I just flew over ten hours to get to her after no sleep for the past seventy-two hours so that I could do so, and I'm irritable as hell.

What was she thinking? I think to myself, throwing off my seat belt, realizing that I should have just gone in with her, held her hand, even if she's pissed at me. I'm unsure, though, how she expected me to react to the cocky meathead who has now forced his input into our home. And yes, this thought is also irrational, because it was actually Ryan, a childhood friend now family, and I already overthought the hell out of that and realized it was, in fact, the right thing to do. The fact he knew what the hell he was doing, the icing on the cake.

"*It won't be like last time,*" I mimic his words and actually want to cuff myself for being so childish.

I open the door and step out, muttering, "Damn right it won't be like last time. This is a home, not a fucking place to keep a woman while I dick around."

As I round the front of the vehicle, she walks out, smiling, yet still a bit green.

My wife confuses the hell out of me.

I open the door, and she slides in with a sweet as pie, "Thank you."

When I start the vehicle, she turns on the radio then laughs as she turns up the volume and starts to sing along as I pull onto the street.

It's that song about the cowboy.

She pushes up the console and slides over, buckling quickly as she sings to me. Sings to *me.*

Still humming the tune as we walk into the farmhouse, I wrap my arm around her from behind and pull her close.

"Could you give me a minute? I need to brush my teeth."

I flop down on the couch, throw myself back like a spoiled child, and grumble as Leia hops on the couch, nudges my hand, and I pet her. "Sorry, girl."

After several minutes have passed, I have finally had enough and stand. "Tessa, please get out here."

The bathroom door cracks open, and she peeks out. "Give me two more minutes."

Her face is no longer green. She's actually pink, and her blue eyes are sparkling.

I reach in and push her gently back so I can open the door and step in. She hugs me and laughs.

I lean back, push her hair from her face, and then rest a hand on her forehead. "Are you feeling all right? Are you menst—I mean, do you have your period?"

She pushes up on her toes and whispers, "How about you come check it out for yourself?"

I feel like this is a test—her seeing how far I'll take it— which seems a bit off.

"You do realize I would have kissed you even after you threw up, right? There are no boundaries between us, Tessa. None."

Smiling, she steps back, pulls her dress over her head, and drops it. Then she unhooks her bra and lets it fall.

"I'm not cool with you kissing me and me tasting like vomit. Other than that, I'm good with no boundaries."

"All right then." I step to her.

She steps back, looks left, and then … she starts crying.

"Tessa Abraham, you need to tell me what's wrong."

Wiping away her tears, she smiles. "Have I told you how much I love my new last name?"

"Beautiful—"

"Collin," she whispers, smiling, and then nods toward the counter. "Not a thing in the world is wrong."

I look at the counter and see four long, plastic strips lined up, all displaying plus signs.

I grab her in my arms and lift her up. Lips against hers, I laugh. "We're going to have a baby."

Tessa laughs against my lips, too, digging her fingers into my hair, and repeats, "We're going to have a baby."

L ying in her childhood bedroom, her head to my chest, after making love to her slowly and easily, she sighs contently. "I missed you so much."

I look down at her and push back a wave of blonde silk. "Are you ready for all this?"

"Mmhmm. As long as we figure out how to never go

two weeks without each other again, I'll be fine. Right now, I'm tired."

My mind races with how to make that possible, but I am determined to do so.

"Do you mind if we lay down before we head to the hotel?"

"I'm a little tired myself." I move her to sit up then grab her a tee-shirt and myself some shorts when I notice her tits have grown. "That little bastard."

She laughs. "Excuse me?"

"Links, he knew. Your breasts have grown." I bend down and fight the urge to mark them. Instead, I kiss one, and then the other.

She arches against me. "It was the chicken. I got sick when I tried to eat chicken … last time."

Last time. Dammit, I should have insisted on testing. I never want to put her through that hell.

"Collin, it's going to be different this time," she says, trying to soothe me when I should be doing the soothing.

"I assure you it will." I kiss her, pull her up, and grab the tee before I end up inside her again so soon. Putting it over her head, I then step into a pair of boxers, oddly placed on her nightstand. "I just hope he doesn't tell anyone. I want to wait a bit. I'll call him and tell him to keep his damn mouth shut."

"No." She laughs. "Unless you can do it nicely."

I slide in next to her. "Fine."

She points to her bag on the tiny nightstand made of crates. "It's in there."

I find his contact and hit *send*.

Jessie answers.

"This is Collin Abraham. May I please speak to Lucas?"

"Just a sec," she says in what I assume she feels is her sultry voice. Sounds a lot more like desperation.

He doesn't say hello; he simply asks, "Am I right?"

"This is Collin. We would like it to be kept quiet."

"Understood," he clips. "Anything else?"

"Yes. I need to ask you how you knew."

Lucas laughs. "You really want to know?"

"Yes."

"All right, but you asked, which means you don't get to be an asshole when I give you the truth."

"What are you doing?" Tessa barely whispers.

He continues, "The girls were the first sign, then the chicken." He pauses. "Just so you know, Collin, she is going to be nasty at times, and you better be able to handle it. She doesn't mean anything by it."

"Just so you know, Links," I spat, and Tessa flops to her back and crosses her arms.

"Go ahead, man. I'm all ears." Lucas laughs antagonistically.

I grit out, "We appreciate you keeping it quiet."

"It's not for you. It's for her. She already lost one, and it nearly broke her. Go easy on her," he warns. Then he switches gears. "I hear we're going to be neighbors. Do you hunt?" Lucas laughs.

"No, but if you want to go with me, I can make an exception."

"Oh my God, stop," Tessa says, rolling to her side and giving me her back.

Lucas laughs again. "No thanks, but all the guys—her family and friends—get together the weekend before deer season. And, since the camp burnt down—by the way, ask your wife about her incredibly stupid move that night—it's at my house. You're welcome to come. Just trying to be *neighborly*. Tell Tessa she better cook still. Nice chat, *Mr. Ross*." The bastard hangs up.

She rolls to her side, facing me.

"He's very"—I pause— "annoying."

She raises a shoulder and rolls her eyes. "Hard to hate him, huh?"

"No, not at all," I state.

"I love you." She kisses me quickly.

"What happened with the camp?"

She tells me all about her trying to put out a fire that could have easily cost her, her life.

"Don't you ever put yourself at risk like that again, Tessa. Got it?"

She puts her hand on her belly. "Okay."

I place mine over hers. "And I'll make sure that we never spend two weeks apart."

After she falls asleep, I need to clear my head, remove the anger he caused, so I take Leia for a quick run.

When I walk back into the house and head for the bathroom, she's walking out, wrapped in a towel. "Where did you go?"

"For a run." I kiss her then grab the towel off her and walk in. "Get in here."

"You're very bossy." She laughs as she steps in.

Hate-free and ready for love, I grab her up and kiss her.

"Collin, stop please." She grabs the towel and attempts to wrap herself as she runs to the toilet and throws up again. When she's finished, she sits back on her heels and covers her face. "Sorry. It's going to be a long few weeks. We should have waited."

She looks back at me and apparently sees my disappointment in myself for not having thought she may not be ready.

She flushes the toilet. "You're mad at me?"

"No. I just wished you'd told me you weren't ready." I wrap her fallen towel around her.

She shakes her head. "I didn't expect to feel this way again."

Then I see it. Concern, confusion, and then fear.

"What if it's the same?"

"Tessa, it's not." I pull her up and ready her toothbrush. "You need to believe that. No stress, please."

A fter the first trip into *his* garage, I am questioning my sanity as I carry yet another crockpot of food in.

"Are you sure you made enough?" Alex jokes as he follows us with a third.

"I hope so." Tessa laughs then beelines it toward Phoebe and takes Remington. "Go eat; I've got him."

"You sure?" she asks.

"Like ten million percent sure." Tessa laughs as she walks toward me. "Don't you dare try to steal him from me."

"Wouldn't dare," I say, wrapping my arm over her shoulders and looking down at him. "Your aunt tells me this is a big deal, Remington—your first season."

He looks at Tessa, as if he knows she's supposed to confirm.

"Hello, beautiful boy." Tessa leans down and kisses his cheek. "Tell Uncle Collin it's huge."

I watch her interaction and fall further in love with the story, the one of us. The one that has no lulls, no filler, no waiting, knowing that my wife is going to be an amazing mother, and that I will match that in the way I father our child, hopefully many.

"You totally want to steal him from me." She laughs.

I don't deny this. I find it soothing to hold a life that is pure and knows only love, all while hoping that's all they'll ever know. And, if not, I hope that they one day find their prize as I have found mine.

"Fine, but only because I know you'll give him back, and my family will not call me horribly inaccurate names, like baby hog, if I share." She smirks.

Holding him against my chest, I rub his back. "You're going to be a good man, Remington Ross."

Aside from Tessa'a scent, the one of a baby is incredibly soothing, I think as I watch Tessa fills two plates then brings them to a table nearby and sets them down.

"How does that feel?"

"Very comfortable," I respond as I sit beside her.

She holds out her hands. "Gimme. You eat."

"I think your family may be on to—"

"Hush." She takes him and cradles him in her arms.

Forking up some of her cooking, I ask, "How are you feeling today?"

"Good, actually." She smiles at Remington then looks up at me, eyes … hungry. "I've been neglecting you, haven't I?"

"Shh …" I close my eyes and sit back.

"We're going to have to do something about that." She kisses Remington's head and stands.

I watch as she walks to Phoebe and hands her back Remington, and then she hurries back to me.

She winks, "I left something at the farm."

"I assure you—"

"Take a hint, Abraham," she cuts me off as she covers

our plates. "Your wife is starving, *and not for food*."

———————

I did enough research to know that morning sickness isn't just a morning thing, and that it comes and goes at its own leisure. So, when she's feeling well, there is no way I'm not going to follow her lead, which is exactly what I am doing now as I jump out of the vehicle and haul tail behind her.

In the kitchen, she tosses off her shirt and throws it at me, walking backward slowly. I catch it, clear the distance, and take her lips.

She breaks the seal of our lips, turns, and rushes to the stairs.

Rounding the corner, I hear, "Hey, girl ... or girls," and see some asshole hug my shirtless wife, who laughs as she steps back and grabs a blanket off the back of her father's recliner.

"Ben," she says as she covers herself.

He laughs. "You sure are happy to see me." When his eyes meet mine, he chuckles. "You're not, though." He extends his hand. "Hey. Collin, I'm assuming. I'm Tessa's friend, Ben, and would like to personally thank you for getting her away from that asshole."

"You just won points, Ben. I've missed your face." She hugs him again quickly.

Ben, again, laughs. "Your husband didn't. So, you two want to take me up to jock itches Foe Camp? I'm sure the three of us walking in would make his day."

Okay, so maybe I will grow fond of this Ben character.

I look at Tessa then back at Ben and explain, "I'm being cordial."

"Great. Then you'll have fun watching me piss him

off." Ben grins.

"It's not my place anymore." Her smile falters, and she looks toward the bathroom as she continues, "I can't save your ass, Ben." She then sprints to the bathroom.

"Tess, what the hell?" Ben rushes in behind her, and now I'm not liking him all that much anymore.

I walk in to see him rubbing her back. "Already, Tess?"

I clear my throat. "I got this."

"Of course." He moves out of my way, just in time, too, saving himself from being thrown. "When are you two expecting?"

And now the thought renders. I pull her hair back as she hurls again. "She may just have a stomach bug."

"Yeah right, she's throwing up, *and* the girls, they're huge." He laughs.

I glare at him.

"Sorry, man, they ran right into me." He doesn't stop laughing.

"Good God, Ben." Tessa sits back and wipes her face with the tissues I handed her. "Collin, I'm sorry."

Ben, who is still in the damn bathroom with us, asks, "For what? He's a lucky guy. I'll go out and give you a few minutes, but we need to get up there." Heading out, *finally*, he calls back. "Pull up your big girl pants, Tess. It's time to have some fun."

"If you hate me, I understand." She stands up and hits the sink. I hand her a washcloth and then load her toothbrush with paste. When she finishes cleaning up, she asks, "You mad at me?"

"No, of course not. Just a bit overwhelming." I hold out my hand, and she takes it.

"We should go back to the Cape."

"Oh, we will. But let's take care of your buddy, Ben."

"Collin, I'm—"

"The vows are written *for better or worse*. Lucas is in the worse category, and we're handling it. Ben is yet to be determined."

When we walk out of the bathroom, I nearly trip over Ben. "File me under better right now and be prepared to move me under best." He smirks. "Now, let's go have some fun."

When we walk in, Ryan is the first to see us, and he tries his best not to laugh. For a brief second, it pisses me off. But that second passes when I see Lucas turn fifteen shades of red, with a fake as hell smile and eyes looking borderline psychopathic when he sees Ben Sawyer. I look back at Ryan, who laughs as he shakes his head and holds up a beer in mock toast.

Jade giggles from behind me. "Are you having fun yet?"

"Yes." I wrap my arm around Tessa's shoulders.

"Hey, *Benji*, welcome back," Lucas quips.

"You miss me, Links?" Ben rubs his hands together, enjoying this.

Tessa looks up at me. "See all the fun you missed out on by not being an overindulged adolescent?"

"Ours will not act like this." I kiss the top of her head.

Maggie whisks Tessa away and I make my way over to Alex and Ben, who are polishing their shotguns.

"You like guns?" Ben asks.

"I respect guns, yes."

He gets a glimmer of mischief in his eyes. "Do you hunt?"

Lucas walks up, saying, "No, but he offered to make an exception to go out with me."

I catch him raising a brow at my wife, as if he's tattling

on me. I lift a shoulder, and she rolls her eyes.

"Well, if you two go out, I want to go, too." Ben leans in. "Just so you know, Links, I'm on his side."

"This is going to be a fun weekend." Lucas gives the crowd an exaggerated smile.

Jade laughs. "Not much different than field hockey games in high school."

Tessa appears at my side. "Who wants to play cards?"

"I do," Ben and Lucas say at the same time.

"Anyone else?" Tessa looks at me, pleading with her eyes. "All right, wonderful! Collin is in."

I guess I'm in, I think as she drags me to a table and whispers, "Do you know how to play pitch?"

"No."

"Perfect. You're my partner." Then she looks at the two of them. "And you two can play together."

She explains the game and tells me to just bid two if no one else already has, because she's pretty sure the two we're playing against would attempt to outbid me, which would put them in the negative.

"I'm not sure I love that strategy, but I am sure I will do pretty much anything to just start and finish this game."

As Tessa suspected, that is exactly what they do. With each hand, Jade is at the table with drinks.

After I've had a few, I ask Jade, "Are you enjoying this?"

"I am." She laughs. "Tessa, you need a drink."

She acts as if she doesn't hear her and ends the game by laying down the Ace of Spades.

"Best two out of three?" Lucas asks.

"No, thank you." Tessa stands. "Collin, are you ready to go?"

"You can't go yet." Jade pouts. "How often do I get out with my husband? Stay with me, Tessa."

"No, I can't."

Jade gives her a scrutinizing look.

Tessa laughs. "Do you see my husband? You're getting him drunk."

Jade winks. "You'll thank me for it tomorrow."

It isn't often I get intoxicated, but Tessa isn't wrong. I have had a bit too much to drink.

I curl a finger toward my wife, who looks amused as she walks over. I take her hand and pull her down onto my lap.

"Are you tired, Tessa?" I press my forehead to hers and glide my fingertips down her soft cheek.

"A little, but at least I'm not sick." She wiggles her bottom against me as she gets comfortable and asks, "Is this too much for you?"

"No, not something I think I could do every weekend, but I enjoy watching you in your natural habitat."

"My what?" She giggles.

"How you manage those around you and do so with your brand of love. You compartmentalize everyone in such a way that it's its own form of art. It's you. It's beautiful."

She kisses my cheek. "I think someone has had too much to drink."

"I may have, but Mrs. Abraham, you have a way of making people feel special. I'm sure you're a wonderful nurse. Isn't anyone else I would choose to be by my side to help me heal." I kiss her cheek. "You've done it already. I love you."

"You're seriously too much to handle clothed." She starts to stand.

"Tessa, don't get up."

She wiggles her butt against me discreetly, and I close my eyes as she asks, "Why? You did."

"Please just sit still and be quiet."

And she does, so quiet that she falls asleep, curled

into me.

My nose in her hair, I kiss her cheek softly, so as not to wake her, and close my eyes.

When I hear soft giggling in the background, I open them to see Phoebe and Jade, along with Maggie and Cassie smiling at us. I also catch Lucas, hat pulled down, acting as if he's involved in the conversation surrounding him, but he's not. He's … hurting, and down deep, I feel sorry for him. Sorry that he lost someone so precious that he feels it. And, as much as I want to hate him, I'm sure he hates himself more than I possibly ever could right now.

When our eyes meet, he nods once, pushes off the barstool that he's sitting on, and walks to the door that I assume leads to the home he built for her. I'm guessing, right about now, he wishes he had also made it, and its contents, his home, too.

When she wakes, she smiles softly. "I fell asleep on you?"

"Again."

"Would you like a drink or something to eat?" she asks.

"I would love water, but I can get it. You sit here." I lift her up as I stand then set her back down.

I grab two bottles of water from the fridge, walk back to her, squat down, and open one for her before handing it to her. "You're going to drink this while I get you some-thing to eat."

She drinks her water as I make her a plate of vegeta-bles and hard cheeses. Sitting back down and putting her back in my lap, I feed them to her. She seems especially fond of the grape tomatoes. "Mmm … so good," was the hint.

I mindlessly rub a carrot stick across her lips. "I can't wait until you can keep something down."

"Me either." She bites a carrot and smirks. "I love

you."

"When do you think Jade is going to let us out of here?"

"Never," she jokes.

"Maybe I can talk to Ryan now, and we can get back to the Cape for a few days."

"I don't think that is going to happen anytime this weekend." Tessa nods toward Ryan, who is shot gunning a beer.

"I never understood that." I shake my head, and she giggles silently. "You've done that, haven't you?"

She nods.

"Is my wife a lush?"

"Only when she's pissed off." Lucas reappears and walks past us.

I feel my lip curl, and she laughs, which is a bit funny.

"Are you ready?" I sneer.

"Yes," she says, uncurling her legs. "Keys, please."

"Should we ask Ben if he needs a ride back?"

"Probably."

Ben declines. It's obvious that he is having too much fun messing with Lucas. He did ask if we would come get him when Lucas finally got sick of his shit and kicked him out.

We agreed. That's when Ben glances down at Tessa's belly.

She and I look at each other, then around the room.

"Collin, if one of those two spills the beans, I will feel even worse that they knew before my family than I already do."

"I completely agree with you."

"Why didn't you say something?"

"Tessa, you have been sick for a week; I wasn't going to upset you further."

"They're all here now, and tomorrow, the rest of the hunting crew will be here." She shrugs, "Will you?"

I nod as I look around again. "I will. And after tonight, and seeing how much this tradition means to you, I want to build a camp, because this is incredibly uncomfortable. We can pick a spot, all right?"

Eyes shimmering, she nods. "Of course." She then walks over, turns down the radio, and nods to me.

"Excuse me." I clear my throat. "Tessa and I have an announcement to make. It will only take a minute."

Everyone quiets.

"We wanted to let you all in on a little secret that was kind of brought to light a week ago. It was our intention to wait a while. However, two young men actually figured it out without being told. One actually knew before we did. Thank you, Lucas." I'm not sure why I thanked him, but in that, he seems a little more … at ease. "It seems that my wife's breasts are as fascinating to them as they are to me." I look at Ben. "By the way, they are mine now, but I will share them."

"Oh my God, Collin." She covers her face as a slight gasp fills the room.

My bad.

"With our future children only," I explain.

The room around us now fills with an *aw* …

"We feel it's a bit early but want those closest to Tessa, *and now me*, to know that we've just found out that Tessa is pregnant."

And then the applause.

"You do know we really aren't getting out of here anytime soon now, right?" she says as everyone comes to congratulate us.

"I knew something was up." Jade hugs her while poking me in the chest. "I'm pissed you didn't tell me first."

Home(s)

Chapter Forty-One

Tessa

$\mathcal{W}$ hile meeting with Ryan, as he looks over the blueprints that Collin had an architect draw up, he asks, "If you don't mind me asking, why the rooms in the basement? You could save a lot of money and finish it later if—"

"Thanks, but we will need them. It'll be less of a mess if it's done during the construction. I would prefer not to deal with dust and noise in the months to come." Collin places his hand on my belly as an explanation, without sharing that it is a way for him to feel safe and to ensure our child is, as well. "How long do you think this will take?"

"I know it could be done on your timeline, but it will cost a lot more for the amount of men I'll need to make it happen," Ryan says, looking over the massive house that is too big in my opinion, but he insists on bedrooms for my parents and at least one spare for Kendall when she's home from college, and full bathrooms for each room.

"On this project, time sets precedence over expense. Any future projects will be different," Collin tells him.

When Collin walks him to the door and shakes his hand, I hear him say, "Spare no expense."

Ryan looks at me, no doubt waiting for me to wig out like I did when Lucas made extravagant gestures, but I don't. Collin needs this in order to feel safe, and there is no way I would argue the cost of that.

And then his phone rings.

"On my way, Jade." Ryan says as he walks out.

We leave for the Cape the next day, Leia's first flight. I no longer hate flying.

When we walk into his house, he carries me over the threshold and asks, "Are you still feeling all right?" His eyes are dark and hooded, I know he's happy to be back in a house in which the walls don't talk.

Sliding out of his arms, feet on the floor, I step closer and look up. "Actually, I'm a little tired but very, *very* hungry."

"You don't have to do that, Tessa," he says when I push him down on the couch and sink to my knees between his legs.

"That wasn't very convincing."

"You want to take off your shirt, please?" he asks.

I push up on my knees, pull mine over my head, and he does the same with his.

"Your chest, so incredibly hot." I kiss it then move down. "Body, fire." I lick down his treasure trail, and his body tenses. I love his body, and no, this is not the time to think about why or how, but seriously, it's broad but not too hard until he tenses, and then it's Miller time.

What the hell is wrong with me?

"How about that bra?"

I reach behind me and unsnap my bra, without issue.

"Beautiful," he says as he reaches down and pulls me back to standing.

"What are you doing?" I smack his hand away and start to bend back down, but he hooks his thumbs in my leggings and shimmies them down.

"You better take those off, too," he says leaning forward and kissing my belly.

"Collin, you might want to sit back, shush up, and enjoy."

I unbutton his pants, reach in, and grab his insanely beautiful cock. Then I drop to my knees and suck him deep.

"God, Tessa," he *growls*.

For the next few days, we focus on me learning the business, and I begin digging to find government grant money in all the areas of the world that he helps. And I can't even allow myself to let the feelings about my husband's extreme generosity penetrate because his dream is to grow this movement even larger, and I am going to do all I can to help make that his reality.

He's funding most of it from a bank account that

makes no sense, but I don't ask where the money comes from because that would be a slap to the face of a man whose generosity is insurmountable. And yeah, I know he spends an hour a day playing with stocks, and what I saw yesterday was a fifty-thousand-dollar profit, so he's obviously, basically … a damn genius.

Still, I need to do my part.

In the evenings, after checking in with the detective at the Cape to make sure his mother is still under lock, — *something he doesn't know I'm aware that he does*— he watches the news and takes notes, which I thought was funny, but now I know why. I also laughed when I considered how women tell men to think with their big brains, meaning their little brain is in their dicks. My husband's big brain isn't big; its ginormous, as is his dick. When he asked me why I was laughing, and I saw a bit of an insecurity in his eyes, I told him about my own scientific theory, and he simply shook his head.

I'm also already starting to feel a bit anxious about the fact he hasn't traveled in weeks and know he's going to be heading back to South America after the holidays. I was supposed to go with him, but now he is adamant that we will make that decision together after my first doctor's appointment. I pointed out to him that we had already made that decision, and my pregnancy should have no bearing on it. The next day, I overheard him talking to Tomás about resorts that were secure near the Ecuadorian village. We had our first big fight after that. He wanted me to stay at the resort and travel to and from the site, and I told him that, if this was my life, my work, I will not be sitting at a resort, being pampered like a trophy wife. He acted as if I had not spoken a word, like it was no big deal, that I was just throwing a tantrum. It was then I started a job search. When he found out, *he* threw a tantrum.

By the end of the night, we both did what married couples are supposed to do—we compromised. I agreed that I would not take a job until after my appointment, and he agreed that if everything was okay, and assured me that he knew it was, we would revisit the discussion.

While I spend my days researching available grants, he's writing another paper. In the evenings, we eat dinner, watch the news, make love, shower, and then go to bed. At night, when he thinks I'm asleep, he is at his computer in his office, working on security details that he obviously does not want me to know about. I assume it's his way of ensuring I will be accompanying him to South America. There was one conversation I overheard, in which he stated, "She watches *Bambi* and cries at the beginning of every deer season. The less she sees, the less she'll worry."

As far as the life growing inside of me, my pregnancy is a dream. The morning sickness is now just in the morning and does not always result in me throwing up. The day he catches me in the bathroom, standing sideways, looking at my profile in the mirror, rubbing the nonexistent bump, he steps in, wraps his arms around me, places his large hands over my smaller ones, and rubs it, too.

Seriously, how did I get so lucky?

The next day, a package is delivered. When we open it, the box is full of classic children's books.

"You did this, didn't you?"

"With assistance. I called Maggie and asked the titles of your favorite books when you were a little girl."

I look up at him, ready to ask what his favorites were, then quickly close my mouth.

Each night, I read to my belly, but I do it for my husband, too. And, while I read, he plays classical music softly in the background.

The books? Epic. The music? *Not so much.* My husband is tactically brainwashing our child to like boring music. Operation I love Rock N Roll begins.

When the lights go out, and his calming music sweeps through the system, I pop in earplugs and set my Walkman next to my belly, on the side opposite him, and play hours of all my favorites on low so that he can't hear it, but high enough that, at least, it drowns out that boring shit, *well hopefully*.

Sex is amazing because my husband's skill and knowledge of the female anatomy is almost disturbing, but I refuse to go down that path, so I decide it's disturbing in the best way. But he was being … cautious. Too cautious. So, I devised another tactical plan and Operation Sneak Attack began. Those nights, I rode my husband as wild as I wanted, and he did not complain.

Then one night he decided to get in on the action and surprise me with his own sneak attack.

He rubs my body as he starts working his mouth at my neck, slowly making his way down.

Then, when he jumps, I jump. And, when the lights come on, I ask, "What's wrong?"

His face splits into a grin, and he laughs, but I can't hear him. I start to think something is terribly wrong and rub my ears.

Yeah, busted.

And I'm further busted when he discovers the Walkman and headphones at my side.

I hid those for nearly three weeks!

He retaliates the next night by turning the volume up a

bit more. So, those nights, I lay in bed, exhausted, making up inappropriate lyrics to all those wordless songs in hopes it causes him to turn it off, but it has quite the opposite effect. It turns my husband … on.

We are so happy. No nights do I lay awake, hurt. No time do I ever feel that he wants anyone but me. I never wonder when this will end. I know to my core we will be together forever.

That doesn't mean that I never think about Lucas; just brief moments wondering if he's okay. Or wondering if I'm the one who messed up, that if I had just given up on my dreams and followed him around, would we have been this happy. I know it's stupid to even think. The answer was no from the minute I saw him, and the reason lays beside me. But I truly pray he can stop carrying that burden and not block the love of another, because all people—*except Collin's mother*—deserves love like this.

When those thoughts swarm my brain, I snuggle up next to my husband a little closer and thank God even more for him, but I also pray Lucas will find his *true love*.

I never in my life want to be touched or loved by anyone else. Collin is not just the sun and the moon, but ever heavenly piece in-between. He is the person I want to share every secret dream and desire with.

We have fun and laugh together every day. We pick out everything for our new home, from flooring to the guest towels in the bathroom together. Okay, I pick them out, and he writes them in my—our dream house notebook and agree to everything except the one time I pretend to be in love with a hot pink room to prove my theory that he doesn't care, that he's just pretending for me. He cares. He totally cares.

Sex is mind blowing, but I finally realize that it isn't all about sex. Good sex comes from a good connection. When you are full—truly filled with the knowledge of your partner, trust, and respect—you really can't ever go wrong. I even consider breaking my *butt rules* after the baby is born. I will deny him nothing *ever*, and I know—God, how I know—he feels the same.

We went home for Thanksgiving, but I had to promise not to go to the house. I did almost break said promise, but then Mom busted me on an attempted escape when he had to go into Syracuse to file some sort of paperwork.

Pissed me off, too. I had it all planned.

Collin

The house is finished a week before expected, and Tessa is none the wiser. The notebook, her dream house, is becoming a reality. I want it all furnished when she walks into not just a house, but our home.

Jade has been in the house a dozen times with Ryan, sending pictures to my email to share with Tessa. I explained that would not happen and that this was a surprise for her. Then I enlisted her help. She was quickly becoming a daily call. I trust her enough that she has my black card and has been ordering things from the book as I email her lists almost daily.

While in my office, working as Tessa sleeps, I receive an email from her, notifying me that the living room furniture is being delivered tomorrow morning and asking if she could please set up the nursery.

I type out: *Thank you for all your help. We'll be in town tomorrow.*

I completely avoid the nursery conversation.

Tomás left the vehicle at the airport, ready for our arrival. Tessa is under the impression that there's a problem with the construction that needs my attention. The truth is I have watched her dream, written down all the things she loves, and took great pleasure in her excitement.

The living room furniture she wants took a bit longer to come in due to the fact everything we looked at she mentioned wanting to be big enough for her family to snuggle up on for movie nights. I want it bigger for other reasons. Therefore, it was necessary to special order a handcrafted and custom-made leather couch to fit the room and to fulfill her vision. That and the bedroom are the only two rooms that I made changes to. I know she will love them.

Pulling into town, she's excited to see her family and begs that I allow her to see the house, even though it's not finished.

We pull into the farmhouse driveway to drop Leia off. Then head to our home.

Home.

"Where do you want to go first, Tessa?"

She wags her brows. "Our bedroom floor."

Pulling down the long drive, she sees the house for the

first time. Seven thousand square feet of indoor, "wide open spaces." Everything she asked for and so much more.

She covers her mouth with her hands and screams gleefully into them.

"You think we should turn back and grab some blankets for that bedroom floor, Mrs. Abraham?"

"No, but could you drive faster?" she asks, bouncing up and down and clapping her hands.

Beautiful.

Standing at the back door, I punch in the code then sweep her off her feet. "You ready?"

"Collin, open the door," she growls.

Both laughing, I turn the handle, push open the door, and then I carry my wife inside her home for the first time.

"What? How? Oh my God!" She kisses my face, leaving her eyes open and taking it all in.

I had caved and showed her some of the pictures of the rooms before any of them were painted, of the kitchen with cupboards but no countertops and definitely not the curtains she fell in love with in the *Country Living* magazine.

Tears running down her face, she runs into the kitchen and smooths her hand down the white quartz countertop. Then she bends over and opens the cherry wood cupboard doors, holding her hands over her heart when she sees the cupboards are full. Full of food, full of the dishes that she mentioned she loved, glassware, and all the cooking and baking sets that she pointed out.

"I cannot believe you did this." She turns from the wall of appliances, all made for a professional kitchen, and walks to the island with seating for seven on the opposite side, an island big enough to bake, as she explained, "all the Christmas cookies," and then into the family room.

"That couch!" she cries. "Oh my God, that couch!

How did you get it out of my head? How did you get it through the door?" She laughs. "It is absolutely beautiful."

She skips into the massive room, arms extended, and turns in a circle as she takes it all in. Then she hurries to the mantel above the stone-faced fireplace and runs her hand down it. The beam is from one of the barns that they tore down to put up a new metal building. Our wedding picture sits proudly on top.

"Jade's touch." I smile as I open the refrigerator door, grab the bottle of sparkling cider, and then grab two glasses out of the cupboard. I twist open the top, pour some bubbly into each glass, set the bottle down, and leave the glasses on the counter as I walk toward her outstretched hand.

She smiles as she wipes away the tears, tears of happiness, as she looks at the pillows, so many pillows, which she tried to explain why they were necessary, yet I still don't understand it, *at all*.

We head to the right and into the dining room, which is separated from the kitchen and family room with only an arch to distinguish that, where a sixteen-foot table sits, with two long benches on the sides and two oversized chairs at each end. The table is wide enough for two chairs at each end if necessary. She said she didn't like the idea of a formal dining room, but it would come in handy when we hosted, 'every freaking holiday I can get away with hosting'.

We head to the front of the house. French doors with glass lead to a smaller living room with a wood stove for "in-home date nights" or Saturday morning cartoons. The couch and two chairs match the leather in the living room but are significantly smaller.

Beyond that room, through a door, is our home office that runs from front to back and has its own bathroom, and the stairs that lead to the 'bat cave,' as she calls it, which is separate from the basement.

"You noticed everything, paid attention to what I loved, wrote it all down." She grabs the pillow that says '*Hers*' off her desk chair and hugs it. "Even the pillows."

I hold out my hand that she has long since dropped in her excitement and clapping. "Shall we head upstairs?"

"We shall." She grabs my hand and pulls me toward her, wrapping an arm around my neck and kissing me, mouth hot, sweet, and hungry.

We walk up the stairs and stand at the door. Our master is in the center of the hall and at the top of the stairs so no one can get to the other bedrooms without passing by it, including teenagers who may act like their mother and attempt to sneak out when they get a wild hair up their behinds. And no, my wife doesn't know that's why; I simply told her it's more convenient.

I scoop her up. "Now, here's where I hope I don't ever disappoint you." I then open one of the double doors leading into the master suite.

"I know it's not what you picked out, but I thought it would be perfect for us." I kiss her then set her on her feet so she can do her exploring.

She walks around the massive four poster bed that nearly reaches the top of the cathedral ceilings. There's a television above the electric fireplace, a chaise lounge, and two nightstands with lamps.

When she is in the master closet, I hurry down and grab the glasses of sparkling cider, come back up to set them on one of the nightstands.

"You know this is almost as big as the bedroom I shared with my sisters, right?" She peeks her head out. "And the amount of clothes, shoes, and handbags you've stocked up in here … more than I'll ever wear."

"Come with me." I hold out my hand, and she takes it.

We walk into the master bath that I designed, and she takes it all in—the clawfoot soaking tub, the double tiled shower with his and her sides, and a rain shower in the middle.

"We have warm water." I kiss her hand.

"I don't even know where to start, Collin."

"How about the bedroom floor?"

We walk out, and I grab the glasses, sitting in the middle of the floor, her next to me. I hand her a glass and hold mine up. "To you, my first and last kiss."

We clink glasses, and she smiles. "To you, my first, my last, and my one true love."

I take a sip then set the glass down on the dark wood floor. "The floor or the bed?"

"The bed, please." She stands up, sets her glass on the nightstand, and then climbs on the bed and lies on her back.

I pull off her little sweater-looking boots—*Uggs*—and toss them onto the floor before grabbing her slouchy socks and pulling them off, as well. Then I hook my thumbs under the waistband of her butter-soft leggings that hug every muscle and curve of her hot, sexy body and make sure to take them without removing her panties, because I have other plans for them.

One leg over my shoulder, I lean in and take her underpants between my teeth. I pull one side down, and then the other side. I set her legs down to remove them completely then step between them and rub my hands up her sides, pushing her shirt up, exposing her tits. "Damn, Tessa." I unclasp her front clasp, and her tits spill out. "We spend too much damn time in the dark. God, you're even more beautiful."

"You make me that way."

My cock jerks at her words.

I lean down and taste her nipple, causing it to bud. I blow across it to see it tighten even more. Then I take it in my mouth, inhaling her scent as I taste her skin.

"Take those clothes off. I need to touch you."

I lift my arms as she pulls my shirt up and drags it over my head before tossing it.

She runs her hands down my body as I take her mouth, sliding our tongues against one another's as she unbuttons me and removes my pants.

Her hands now at my wrists, she runs them up my arms, over my shoulders, stalling and squeezing them, before running them up my neck and gripping my hair. She then sits up, leaning across my body, sucking on my lip until she has me on my back, one hand gripping my cock. She moves to sit on me and begins sliding my dick between her slick, hot folds, using her other hand on my chest to steady herself.

"Beautiful," I hiss as she rubs against me, my head nudging her clit.

"Sit back and enjoy," she moans as she rocks.

I clasp my hands behind my head and watch her take me inside her, slow, hot, soaked, *all mine.*

She arches back and grabs her shirt.

"You cover up, and I will tie your sexy body to this bed," I hiss out as she slides forward, taking me in deeper.

She grips her breasts and whimpers.

I sit up and pull her against me. Then I flip her onto her back and thrust deeply into her as I catch something shiny out of the corner of my eye.

Her phone. She's reaching for her phone.

Seated to the root, I roll my hips as I grab it. Then I set the pace, the one that makes her come within seconds, and when she does, she does it squeezing her tits, and I take a picture

Legs wrapped around me, she whimpers, "Busted."

She curls up and kisses me, and I again end up on my back, and she rides me wildly.

In the light of day, seeing her like this, it undoes me.

"Gonna, come for you, beautiful."

And when I do, she snaps her own picture.

Laughing, I grab for the phone, but she holds it tightly to her chest, rolls off of me, and heads to the bathroom.

Chapter Forty-Two

S itting on the toilet, peeing, I look at the pictures of my sexy as sin angel of a husband and, for the zillionth time, thank God for him. Then I flip and see the one he took of me.

Oh no, no, no, no. I'm already looking huge, and I am seriously ugly when I come.

I wipe and flush, hurry to the mirror, and it's the first time I have visibly noticed how big my boobs have gotten. I then cast my eyes down and see my belly. "Oh my God."

After using the bathroom, I wash my hands and notice the scale. When I step on it, I see that I've gained twelve pounds already.

Collin walks in, and I jump off of it. Then I see it—the concern in his eyes—and it pisses me off.

"Did you do this on purpose?" I demand.

"What, Tessa?"

"This." I kick at the scale, and it slides across the marble floor. "Dammit!" I attempt to grab my foot but lose my balance briefly.

He catches me, "Did you hurt yourself?"

"Yes! Get that damn thing out of here." I wiggle away from him and out of the room, needing clothes to cover myself.

I rush into the closet and see all the clothes that he's bought and know none of them will fit right, nor hide the fact that I'm getting fat already.

I walk across the closet floor, grab one of his sweat-shirts, and throw it on as I head out to find my underwear and leggings, which are the only things I have been wearing lately.

He walks out of the bathroom, rubbing one hand over his head, looking amused, holding the scale in his other. "You want—"

"Throw it out." I climb in the bed.

When I wake, he is holding me.

"Are you hungry?"

"Very funny," I huff as I sit up.

He sits up, too, asking, "Tessa, what is going on?"

"Don't play stupid; you're not, so just don't."

"Tessa—"

I slide off the bed, and as soon as my feet hit the floor, I walk to the bathroom, telling him, "You don't have a scale at your Cape house. You think I'm getting fat, fill me in; don't be passive aggressive. Just say, *hey, you're getting fat*."

I close the door behind me, sit on the floor, and … cry.

The door opens moments later.

"Just don't, okay?" I wipe away the tears.

He sits beside me. "There should be no doubt in your mind that I don't think you're the most beautiful woman on the planet."

"But fat, so you put a scale—"

"I had a scale at my—*our* place on the Cape, and my set broke. I hadn't replaced them. I don't think you're fat; I think you're beautiful." He starts to put his arm around me, but I stand. Then he says, "It would be unhealthy if you didn't gain weight while you're pregnant. And just saying, love isn't weighed by the poud."

I look over my shoulder at him. "Has my ass gotten bigger?"

"What?" he says and looks … amused, which angers me.

"It did last time. Lucas even had the balls to tell me my ass had grown, so just tell me: is my ass bigger?"

He slowly stands as he raises one brow. "So, because he made you feel insecure, I am being called a li—" He stops and shakes his head. "No, Tessa, your butt has not gotten big, and I will do all I can to erase the shit he did to your head, but you have to work with me to do the same." He turns and begins to walk out. "I'm going to guess we're going to have company very shortly, so please get your beautiful ass out here and stop being ridiculous."

Ridiculous? I think as I stomp toward him. "He wasn't being an ass, Collin. He liked it bigger. He wanted it. I was asking you to tell me if you put the scale in here so that I'd realize I was getting fat."

"Tessa, I'm unsure of how you expect me to react to that news, or confessional, or possibly a hint that you may be missing Lucas and all the fun he was, but I'm borderline pissed off right now, and we just got here three hours ago."

"You started this!" I point at the scale. "I don't miss him, and you're an asshole."

When he turns to look at me, he's not borderline pissed anymore. He's livid. He walks to me and grips my biceps, leans down so we're eye to eye, and says in a calm that doesn't match his demeanor, "I bought a scale, Tessa. I bought many things for you, and you're being." He snaps his mouth shut, grabs the back of my neck, and kisses my forehead

Who does that when they're fighting? Who!

Then he turns and walks toward the door.

Collin Abraham does.

I burst into tears and climb on the bed. "Don't do that!"

He turns and calmly asks, "Don't do what, Tessa?"

I grab a pillow and scream into it then flop back and look at the ceiling. "Don't be mad at me. Please just ... Please don't be mad at me."

Again, calmly, he states, "You're mad at me."

"No, I'm pregnant, and fat, and tired, and I am being a mean, nasty bitch," I throw myself back. "I'm sorry I suck!"

I hear him walk across the floor, and then he sits next to me on the bed. "You're not fat, and I'm sure you're tired, so please do not confuse your past to your here and now."

Not my forever anymore? What have I done?

He takes my hand and brushes his lips across the back. "And don't ever be sorry that you suck. I kind of like that about you."

I open my eyes and see he's no longer angry. "Collin, I've gained twelve pounds."

"And do you know what tomorrow is?" He lies back beside me.

"No."

"Our three-month anniversary. Our first full day in our house. Your doctor appointment." He rubs his hand over my belly. "And you're going to be in your second trimester. Life is good. It is better than good; it is perfect. So you've gained twelve pounds? You're supposed to gain weight. And if you haven't noticed, I'm a breast man, so forgive me if I haven't noticed a change in your backside."

I roll to my side and wrap my arms around him. "I'm sorry I'm acting horrible. I'm sorry I ruined—"

"You haven't ruined anything."

"I have. Can we start this again?"

"You haven't, but yeah, let's start again." He rolls to his side, and I search his eyes for any damage I may have caused, but as he lifts my shirt and kisses my belly, I realize Collin says what he means and means what he says. "You have the best and most beautiful womb in the house."

I cover my face and try not to laugh. "What is wrong with you?"

He kisses my belly, again.

About an hour later, *our* family and all the kids show up, bringing Leia with them, and Collin gives them the tour. They are amazed by what he has done to surprise me, and I praise him right along with them, staying glued to his side, still feeling ashamed over how I acted.

He knows how I feel, too. I can tell. And he thoroughly enjoys the making up part, and *my ginormous boobs.*

"We have some lab results that are a bit concerning, but not alarming."

I squeeze Collins's hand, and he rubs his thumb across the back of mine as she continues.

"Your HCG levels are elevated, so we would like to do an ultrasound to see exactly what is going on in there."

I look up at him and see a slight smile form.

Watching the screen, I smile at Collin and notice he now seems concerned, but I'm not. Not one bit.

He looks at me, and I smile at him. "Does everything look all right?"

"Yes." He nods as my heart swells. He looks back at the radiologist. "Please tell me I'm not seeing things."

"No, you're not." She smiles.

"Twins?" Collin asks.

"Are you going to be okay?" I ask, feeling my lips begin to quiver but don't fight my tears, *my happy tears*.

He puts his hand on that spot, below his heart, and when he whispers, "*Beautiful*," that's when the dam breaks.

The doctor comes in to talk with us, asks if we have questions, and Collin asks a lot about activity and travel. The doctor okays our travel plans but suggests I stay close to home at five months.

We go out to lunch and do some shopping before going home.

While he's checking his email, I go upstairs and into the room that will be their nursery with a notebook and pencil. I sit on the ground and start sketching out different layouts for two cribs.

When he finds me, he walks behind me, stretches his legs around me, and rests his chin on my shoulder. Kissing my neck, he asks, "Do you have it all figured out yet?"

"No, not until we find out what they are." I reach back and run my nails lightly over his scalp. "How about you? Are you overwhelmed by this?"

"Not at all. And you seem happy. Quiet but happy. I'm sure everything is going to be fine. Better than fine." He kisses my neck. "Are you sure you still want to go to South America?"

"Yes, if you're going, so am I."

"Do you think we should make some calls and let your family in on our news?" he asks.

"What do you think?"

"That's up to you. I just think they may be a little more concerned with our travel plans. Maybe we could keep it between us until we're there?"

"I agree. Not just because of them, but because this is perfect and beautiful, and I want to enjoy it —you and I alone— for now."

C hristmas came, and he indulged my overzealous decorating ideas, and even helped bake and frost cookies. We hosted Christmas dinner at our house, and I caught myself wondering how different this must be for him than his past Christmases. He no longer talks about his past, always looking toward the future.

He flew to the Cape for a few days, —work and upcoming trial prep— and I stayed home since we would be leaving on the third of January for South America, and he wanted me to spend as much time with my family as I could before we left. And that worked out fine, because he was going to be busy.

Chapter Forty-Three

That first morning alone in the house, with each Christmas decoration I take down, my emotions heat up, and by the time I'm done, they are slowly coming to a boil.

When I pull into Jade and Ryan's, they boil over.

At my text request, not wanting the kids to see me upset, Jade meets me in the garage.

"Tessa, what is going on?" She hugs me.

"The kids—"

"Luke, and Riley are at the store with Ryan. Jackson is napping."

So, I let the strangled sob escape and, with it, words as we walk into the house.

"I love my husband with everything I am, but I miss Lucas. What the hell is wrong with me?" I don't wait for

492

her to answer. "I've felt guilty about being happy since we went to camp at his house. I don't know how he felt about us being there, but a few hours ago, it hit me that it was incredibly insensitive and—"

"Tessa, I don't think we should talk about this right now," Jade whispers.

"I need to know that he's happy and okay. I should hate him, right? I should—"

"Tessa, he's—"

"Don't tell me he's okay unless you know he is. And don't lie. Just tell—"

"You could always call and ask yourself."

And then Jade's warnings and the look on her face all makes sense.

"Shit."

Lucas laughs.

"Okay, both of you, couch," Jade demands.

"I need to go. Sorry." I turn to walk right out the damn door.

"Oh no, you don't. Have a seat." Lucas grabs my hand and pulls me behind him and into the living room.

Pulling my hand away and using my sleeve to wipe my face, and stand while I explain, "Look, this isn't what I came here for, and I'm sorry."

Jade takes my shoulders and directs me to sit. "It's perfectly normal to miss and worry about someone you spent so much of your life with. It doesn't mean there is anything wrong with you." She points at Lucas. "And the fact that you never ask is far more than I can say for Lucas. He misses and worries about you too."

"Nice, Jade." Lucas sighs in aggravation.

She ignores him. "But he knows you're happy and safe, and married and pregnant ... Holy shit, you're getting big already."

I glare at her. "Thanks for pointing that out."

"Well, I didn't notice your baby curves at Christmas. You were wearing a—"

"Muumuu?" I spit.

"You trying to piss her off?" Lucas asks.

"She had on a dress and a cardigan," Jade tells him then looks back at me.

"Own those curves. Ryan loves my squishy belly so much he keeps getting me knocked up."

"You're not squishy," I defend her belly as if it's my own.

"I have three kids; it's squishy." She rolls her eyes. "And I earned it. Wouldn't change it for the world."

"All right, back to missing me," Lucas says, and we both roll our eyes at him. He chuckles then asks, "How is everything going? You're just past the scary part, right?"

"Yes, and things are perfect—the house, the pregnancy, my husband, my sex life, my work. Everything is perfect."

"So, what's the problem? You miss being treated like shit?" he asks.

"No, Lucas, not at all. I miss knowing you're okay." I turn and look at him, tears pricking my eyes.

"I'm great. My sex life, however, hasn't been the same in quite some time." He winks.

"My concerns lie with everything else. You, your family. Jessie wasn't at camp, and I don't want you to be lonely. Football; are you healed? Are you going back? Your birthday. Where did you spend Christmas? When are you going to find your person, the one who makes everything you've gone through make sense? I want you …" I shake my head. "No, I *need* you to be happy, Lucas. You deserve that."

"You can call any time you think I'm lonely, Tessa." He

smiles, but there is still gray clouding the green. "I'm better than I was when you first met me. Little steps."

"How are the girls and your parents? Audrianna?"

"Pretty perfect." Lucas smiles. "Spent a few weeks there after Camp. Thanks for asking."

There's something in the way he smiles, a sadness that causes me worry. When he sees that I see it, he hugs me and whispers, "You worry too much about me. It's gonna send the wrong message, and I've just accepted the friendship thing. And I realized that maybe you were right and that's the way it should have been, *Mrs. Abraham.*"

Oh God, I think as I squeeze him then pull away and stand. "Okay, I need to go."

"You feel better?" Lucas asks.

"Yes. In a way, but I feel bad for all of this," I admit. "And I know it'll probably hurt him."

"Don't tell him. It's not a big deal. We can have secrets, Tessa, you and I. It's not like I dragged you upstairs and fu—"

"Lucas!"

"What?" He laughs.

"We share everything, even the not so pleasant things, and I know I would be angry with him."

"Do you know all about his past relationships?" he asks.

"I don't need to. I know that he would never cheat on me. I know that I trust him one hundred percent. He's amazing."

"Then, why do you miss me, Tessa?" he asks, and not in a dick way.

"Because I'm stupid."

He laughs as I hug Jade, and then … I leave.

When I see him coming down the hill, I run upstairs, strip down, jump in bed, grab the giant blue bow from the nightstand, peel off the film, and slap it against my belly.

After Jade's spiel on her love of her *squishy curves*, I couldn't agree with her more. I delved a little deeper into my issue, and it had nothing to do with pregnancy weight; it had everything to do with the weight of the depression I fell into … after Jenny, *the hoe*, did what hoes are intended to do—unearthed the issue.

Lucas allowed her into our home that day, trying, in his own way, to fit in with his team, so she's not the only one I blame for that kick in the ass toward that dark time.

And I know—God, how I know—Collin is not one who feels the need to fit in, nor would he love me any less if —when—I get a squishy belly.

And, as if on cue, he walks into the bedroom and drops his bag on the floor as he walks toward me, pulling his shirt off over his head.

"I've missed you."

"I see that." He unbuckles his belt, undoes his jeans, and pushes them to the floor with a *thud*. "You look beautiful." He then kisses my belly, right below the bow. "Daddy's home, babies."

Daddy's home.

Gah … I love that.

I run my hands up his thick, strong arms, over his broad, sturdy shoulders, and through his thick, silky hair as I hook my leg around him, maneuvering him on his back and kiss my way down his insanely amazing chest, down his treasure trail, and run my tongue with a featherlight touch down his shaft, and lavish in the way it twitches then falls heavily against his abs.

He pushes up on his elbows, twists my hair, and pulls it to the side as he watches me with lust-filled eyes go down on him.

Through clenched teeth, he hisses, "Amazing." Then he growls and says, "I don't deserve you."

I push aside the guilt that sprouts up by those words and give him less than he deserves—*my everything*.

After he comes, I curl up beside him.

"Give me thirty seconds and—"

"I'm good right here." I wrap my arms around him and lay my head on his chest.

"What's wrong, beautiful?" he asks as he runs his hand up my spine.

I take in a deep breath then exhale. "I have to tell you something, and I think you're going to be angry."

"I could never be angry at you." He brings us up to a seated position. "All right, talk to me."

In one breath, I tell him every detail about what happened when I went to Jade's. Then I don't take another, waiting for him to speak.

He stands without saying a word, and I still hold my breath, punishing myself until it is necessary, knowing he isn't talking anytime soon when I hear the shower start.

After throwing the bow across the room, I throw on my bra and panties, grab a flannel shirt and a pair of sweats, and dress quickly. Hands shaking and heart racing, I wait.

When he walks out of the bathroom, fully dressed, I close my eyes.

"I'll be back. Then we can figure out what we are going to do about this mess that you seem to be trying to make."

"Where are you going?" I yell to his back.

"Don't worry about it."

"Fine, I won't worry. Just like I've not worried about

your past relationships, yet I tell you everything about mine. At least I tell you!" I yell. "And I trust in us enough to let you leave for days, even weeks, without knowing anything of what you do or saying a word."

"Maybe that's because I have nothing to hide, Tessa, but you obviously have unresolved feelings, *wife!*" he yells before he walks out.

When I hear him tear down the driveway, I call Jade, now worried that I just caused problems for Lucas, and he can't handle that.

"Lucas headed back to Jersey five minutes after you left here. And Ryan is here if he comes. He'll deal with it. But Tessa, you need to stop. Collin loves you, and you love him. Lucas is fine. If he ever needs you, I promise I'll let you know. But don't ruin this."

Don't ruin this.

Now I feel guilty that he felt he had to run from his house.

- I'm going to stay at my parents' for a couple of days. This is your home, and I know you have a lot to do before the trip. I don't know what else to say, Collin, except that I love you … Tessa

---

I walk into an empty house with Leia, which seems to be more often than not these days. Then I walk upstairs and head to my bed, rubbing my belly. "It'll be okay, little ones. It will be okay."

I lie in bed and forbid myself to cry. Leia is snug against me as I fall asleep.

I wake to use the bathroom and, while washing my hands, I hear my phone ringing upstairs. I rush out and quickly stop when I see him standing in the living room, closing his phone.

He holds out my phone. "You left your phone on the bed."

I reach out and take it, lip quivering. "Thanks."

"You need to come home."

"No."

"Tessa, you hurt me. I reacted badly. Come home."

"Do you still love me?"

This pisses him off, and I know this when he yells, "Of course!"

"But you're still mad?"

"Even more so now," he admits.

"Then I want to give you your space." I turn to walk upstairs, because now I am going to cry.

He walks in minutes later and demands, "Now I'm pissed, and if you don't come home, Tessa—"

"What, Collin?"

He turns, walks out, and bounds down the stairs. At the bottom, I hear him say, "It will break me."

I quickly toss off my nightshirt and throw on clothes, and while running down the stairs, I hear him pull out. "Come on, Leia."

He's not home when I pull in, and he's not answering his phone an hour later.

I grab a couple of blankets and a pillow out of the linen closet and head into the nursery, where I make a bed on the floor and lie there in the dark until I fall asleep.

I wake up to him picking me up.

"Collin, I'm sorry."

"I know," he says, walking us to our room where he deposits me on the bed and covers me.

When he turns to leave, I whisper, "Please don't go."

He stops at the threshold, and I watch his back expand as he takes a deep breath.

"Please," I whisper again.

He turns and walks toward the bed. Still not looking at me, he sits on his side of the bed and removes his shoes before lying back.

Arms crossed over his chest, he stares at the ceiling, and I roll to my side and hug him. When he doesn't move, I take his arms and uncross them, rest my head on his heart, and then I take his arm and wrap it around me.

W hen I wake, Collin is in the shower, and I brazenly get up and get in with him. "Good morning."

I get a clipped, "Morning."

No eyes, not a glance, as he grabs his towel, passes it over his hair once, before stepping out and wrapping it around his waist.

Hands over my belly, I stand under the shower. "Life lessons keep coming even at your mom's age, babies. I apologize in advance for whatever mistakes I am bound to make, but I promise, no matter the ones you may make," I whisper, "especially if you take after me"—I rub my belly again—"I'll love you." I pause to change the next part, "No matter what."

After I shower, blow-dry my hair, and dress in jeans that will probably not fit by tomorrow and a thermal that is so tight on my boobs that he won't be able to ignore them, I head down and make breakfast.

Eggs, toast, and bacon plated, I head to the office and set his beside him at his desk.

"Thank you."

I sit at my desk, which he set up so that we could face one another—*I wonder if he's regretting this now*—and eat my toast while I boot up my computer.

The first thing I do is check my email, and when I see that the World Health Organization has still not replied to my grant recipient, I send another.

When the house phone rings, we both start to stand.

"I'll get it," I say as I head toward the kitchen.

After my call, I peek into the office. "Phoebe has a doctor's appointment, so Remington is coming to visit for a few hours."

"Okay," he says, and he does this *without looking up*.

I spend a good hour playing on my hands and knees, chasing Remington around as he army crawls around the family room. We sing and dance—well, I do with him in my arms—and then I make lunch with Remington in my arms; nothing fancy—shredded chicken breast, Collin's on a roll, with a salad.

"Let's take this to the boss man, and then your mommy's schedule says you get lunch, too." I smooch his head, and he giggles.

When I walk in and set Collin's lunch in front of him, he again doesn't look up and simply says, "Thank you."

"You're welcome," I say in a mocking tone.

When Collin brings his dish out, I am snuggling with Remington as he sleeps against my chest.

He walks over and stands in front of me.

I don't look up.

"You're tired. Let me take him so you can rest."

"I'm not going to see him for a few weeks." *If I'm even still going.* "I want to hold him. You can sit with us if you want."

"It's unsafe to sleep holding a baby. I can take him."

"No, thank you, but feel free to sit with us. You know … just in case I fall asleep."

Uncharted

Chapter Forty-Four

Collin

ot understanding how to do this, this … fighting has been an enormous obstacle.

Did I overreact? I do not know. I said what I felt then needed space to try to tame the anger, caused by jealousy, from her interaction and feelings for Lucas. To figure out how to do that, I took the space.

When I returned, she was gone.

She left me. She left us.

She messaged me, telling me that this was my home, so I went to get her to bring her to our home. She wanted to give me my space, *my space*, meaning here, the house she dreamed up, and I with her, even though I hadn't dared to dream of this my entire life… *until her.*

I didn't come back here. I was on 81, driving home,

when I heard a fucking song, the one with words that fucked me up enough to come back.

"*I don't want to close my eyes, don't want to fall asleep 'cause I miss you, babe, and I don't want to miss a thing.*"

Whoever wrote the words to that song needs to be slapped.

I drove back to the farm, but she wasn't there, and when I saw her vehicle here, at home, I felt hope that I wouldn't be that kid, the one who sat alone because he literally smelled. I felt hope that it wasn't a cruel joke, and I would never be that kid who fought every day of his life to survive. I had hope that I wouldn't be just a guy who was loved by Tessa, amongst the others.

I had hope.

And hope crumbled when I found her in the room our children will be sleeping in while I looked through a window and mourned the life I should have never dreamed.

My stomach is in knots, and I have felt numb for hours now.

After listening to her play with Remington, singing with him and feeding him, I couldn't take it anymore.

And then I finally looked at her, and I saw she wasn't faring any better. She's exhausted.

Now, nodding off and leaning against me, I situate my leg behind her and pull her so if she falls asleep, she can do it holding a little bit of happiness.

She yawns. "Okay, I am tired. You should take him."

"I've got him." I wrap my arms around her and hold my hand over hers. The burn has returned and nearly takes my breath away, but I manage. "Get some sleep."

When she looks up at me, her lips tremble. "I'm sorry, Collin."

"Me, too."

I watch the clock tick, and that fucking song plays on repeat in my head, taunting me.

When the door opens, I look back and see Phoebe put her fingers over her lips as she walks over and reaches in her large bag to pull out her camera and take a picture.

Smiling, she puts the camera back, sets her bag on the ground, and then sits on the sectional. "Don't wake her up. She needs her sleep. Pregnancy is exhausting."

I nod.

"How's she doing?"

"She and the babies are good."

"What did you just say?" she whispers, facial features morphing into a mock scream.

"Nothing."

She arches a brow.

"I was supposed to——"

She waves it off, sits back, and curls her legs behind her.

"I talked to Jade yesterday. I know what happened."

I start to look away, and she reaches out and touches my arm.

"I assure you it was not her intention to hurt you, Collin. She loves you. I can promise you she doesn't like to hurt anyone, and you're not just anyone; you're her husband. And, in case you weren't aware, Lucas tried to wife that since senior year, and she always pushed it off, delayed it every chance she had. She knew." She holds her hand over her chest, and then she points to me. "She knew he wasn't the one because, deep down, that little girl with the blue bow was waiting for you. She just needs to figure out how to not care so much, to not worry about others' hurt. But between you and me, I hope she doesn't change who she is." She looks down at her hands and asks, "Has she told you about my past?"

I shake my head.

"How about Ryan, or Becca, or Lucas?"

"I know some," I admit. Because after the whole pro football player reveal, I did some digging.

"Probably about Lucas, but not the rest of us." She looks past me and at Tessa, smiling softly. "She always says it's not my story to tell." She looks back at me. "The entire time she was with him, with all the things that he did to break her heart, she didn't stop being kind. She made Alex promise to be his friend, Collin, because she knew he needed one. She never said the words, but I assume, with as many times as his mother almost OD'd, she probably worried he'd take that route, especially after Tommy died. She doesn't want him back, Collin; she just wants him to be happy and to have love in his life."

She sighs loudly and shakes her head. "All the hell she went through, she chose not to burden anyone with it, because she didn't want to share her hurt with anyone. So, her telling you tells me she thinks you're like Jesus or something." She scrunches up her nose. "Maybe not Jesus, but something strong enough to handle her. And she's strong, Collin, but not invincible. She tells you everything—her thoughts, her feelings. And when she trusts in your love so deeply that she even tells you when she thinks she may have hurt you and admits to it? That, Collin, is incredibly special."

She's quiet a moment, and then she starts again. "My father shot my mother then turned the gun on himself in front of me." This I knew. "I moved from abusive foster home to abusive foster home until I came here. I told no one about the abuse. I just made sure I was not allowed to stay." She smiles and shakes her head. "She never told her brother about the problems I had until I was ready to do it myself. She's loyal and as trustworthy as they come. Don't be mad at her or piss on her leg, marking her as yours; be her partner, her friend, her protector, be her whatever, and her everything, but accept her for who she is, because I know she's incredibly special, and she chose you because I know she thinks you are, too."

Tessa starts to move, and when she opens her eyes, she's disoriented. She looks over her shoulder at me and sees Phoebe out of the corner of her eye.

"I'm sorry. How long was I out?" she whispers so as to not disturb Remington.

"Not long," Phoebe says as she slides off the couch and moves to take Remington.

"Long enough for me to screw up, though," I admit.

"Why? What happened?" Tessa asks in concern.

"When she asked how you were, I told her that you and the babies were doing great."

Phoebe shrugs. "I won't tell."

"I know. I love you."

"What are you two doing tomorrow night for New Year's Eve?" Phoebe asks as she stands.

"I haven't even thought about it. We always just." She stops.

"It's Lucas's birthday"—Phoebe shrugs— "so we've always celebrated both."

"Well, time to make new traditions." Tessa nods sharply. "Why don't we think about it and call you later, and we'll make a plan. I think he's going to wake up and want some of his mommy's juice," Tessa says as she walks to the car seat.

"I'll get that," Phoebe says, and I follow her out to her car.

Once Phoebe has gotten the seat in the car, she looks up at me. "One more thing?"

I nod.

"Might be a hard time of the year for her. She, um …
well, she had a pregnancy that ended."

"I know."

"But, do you know when?"

I shake my head.

"New Year's Day. So, maybe that's why she's
concerned about Lucas. He's lost three."

"Christ," I grumble.

"Take it easy on our girl, Dr. Abraham?" she asks,
reaching for her door.

I beat her to it. "While we're bonding and sharing, I
need to confess that I looked into you." When her smile
falls, I look at her curiously. "I am sensing I don't know the
entirety of your history, as minors our records are sealed,
but what I uncovered is that you are an only child, and
your parents owned a property in—"

"I want nothing to do with it, which is what I've told
their sleaze-ball lawyer since I turned eighteen."

"Can I offer some advice?"

She slides into the driver's seat. "Sure."

"Sell it."

"I've told him to sell it and donate the money to charity, but he says." She stops and looks up at me. "You run a
charity; you take it."

"More advice?"

She shakes her head. "Alex is the only one who knows,
and he wants nothing to do with it, either. We're making
our own way."

"Would you be all right with me looking into some
options and discussing them with Alex?"

"I'd rather it burn to the ground."

"I can probably make sure that happens," I answer
honestly, and when she looks at me oddly, I realize this isn't
normal.

She then laughs. "Oh, you're not joking?"

I shake my head.

A slow smile creeps up. "Let me think about it say, like, next year?"

Smiling, I step back.

"And Collin, no one else knows, and I don't want anyone to think of me as any other Phoebe than the one I was meant to be."

I wink. "Not my story to tell."

"I knew I loved you."

Something strange washes over me—warmth.

She grins. "And you'll love me, too, when you realize it's okay, too."

When I walk in, Tessa's doing the dishes.

"I wish you would let me get someone to come in and take care of the house."

"No, thank you. It takes all of five minutes to rinse dishes and put them in the dishwasher. I think I can manage. Besides, it gives me something to do other than walk around here, feeling like." She stops and turns on the dishwasher before walking to the office. "Never mind."

When I walk in, she's sitting at her desk, smiling at the screen. I place a plate of veggies and some of the shredded chicken on pita bread in front of her.

"Thank you."

I walk over and sit at my desk. "You look pleased."

"I am. I've been working on this for a month. I'll forward it to you." I watch her tap away on her keyboard, and then she sits back, still smiling at her screen before she stands up, grabs the plate, and walks out the door.

When I get the email from my wife, I click it to open.

Then I skim the correspondence from the WHO and am shocked and seriously amazed that they have not only given us a grant but a sizable one.

When I click back and follow the chain of emails from the first, I can't help but smile.

I get up and make my way out to the kitchen where she's sweeping, music playing in the background.

"Tessa."

She looks up as I walk to her.

"I'm impressed. Do you know how many people you just helped by getting that grant? I'm not just talking about our upcoming trip; I am talking about the entirety of our organizational reach. We have tried for years to get this. Congratulations." I wrap her in a hug.

"Thank you," she says, pulling away slowly. "Persistence."

I watch as she walks over and sweeps up the Cheerios that Remington must have dropped, and Leia didn't find, into the dustpan.

"Where did you put the scale?"

"In the garage," I answer cautiously. "Why?"

"I want it back," she says, heading to the back door.

I follow her. "Perhaps you should just check your weight at appointments."

She huffs.

"I will get it for you."

She shakes her head. "No, I can do it myself."

I follow her into the garage and point to where it lays beside the garbage. She scoops it up. I reach out to carry the scale for her, but she holds it tightly against her, walking through the wet snow and into the house. Then she kicks off her slipper boots and heads up the stairs. I wait in the bedroom for her to come out.

When she walks out, I ask, "Are you going to nap?"

"Are you going to stop following me around, being … I don't know, helpful?" she accuses me as if I've committed a crime, and I have to look away so I don't laugh.

I shake my head. "No."

She turns and climbs into bed. "Then yes, I'm going to sleep so that I don't have to look at you and feel like shit about stupid—"

"Tessa"—I climb in next to her— "I don't understand what it is you're going through, but I know that I may have overreacted. This is new to me. I'm sorry I made you feel bad. I—"

"Collin," she sighs as she shakes her head. "I need to sleep. I'm sure these babies have enough to deal with right now, like growing limbs and developing organs. I need them happy, and I'm happy when I sleep."

"This was an apology, Tessa, not a way to make you feel worse. Again, I'm sorry, but before you go to sleep, I want to clarify something. This is not my house; it's *our* home. Either of us need space, there are several places for that to happen. And you never sleep on a floor again. You have a bed. There are other beds in our home. And to be honest, seeing you like that made me feel like a monster. Like." I stop right before divulging that we had mattresses on floors as beds, and it triggered me. "You're not a dog. I have zero intentions of divorcing you, and before you even think about it, I can assure you that you have zero chances of divorcing me."

"I don't want a divorce." Her lip trembles. "I love you."

I lie back and pat my chest where her head belongs. "I'm not going anywhere. This must stop now. I love you. Go to sleep."

She wraps her arms around me and rests her head on my chest. "Please, just tell me what you need from me. Tell me so I don't mess this up."

"I need you to be you, the person I love. I need you to continue talking to me about everything, regardless of what it is. I hope you never stop. I just need time to adjust, to learn your heart. We're married, Tessa Ann Abraham. We love each other, and I don't want you to change. I just want you to be a little less angry. I promise I'll be the same."

She pushes her hand up my shirt, a trail of heat following in its rise to my heart, branding it deeper.

Inhaling her scent, feeling her body relax against mine, feeling … whole again as she drifts to sleep, I fight my own exhaustion, no longer pushing away the words and emotions caused by that song playing over and over in my head.

Eyes closed, rubbing up and down her back softly, slowly, I feel her jerk, and then gasp.

"Tessa?" I try to hold her still, but she rolls to her back, lifts her shirt, and takes my hand.

"Butterfly wings." She holds my hand on her belly. "They're moving. Do you feel that, Collin? Our babies are moving."

I roll to my side and look down into her smiling eyes, clear as the sky, bright as the sun, and under my touch, I feel it—our children.

I nod and feel my eyes start to heat with enough emotion that I have to clear my throat in order to reply. "I do. They like you happy and rested. And so do I."

Her eyes instantly moisten, and I lean down and brush my nose against hers before pulling up her shirt and laying lips to her belly. "Hello, babies, this is your daddy. I'm going to make sure your mommy is happy out here. And I'm sure everything is beautiful in there—"

"Maybe you should check it out," she interrupts.

I glance up into heated blues. "If they are moving, I think they will feel, well, us moving."

She runs her hands through my hair and fists it in the back. "If you seriously think they will remember, you're crazy." She laughs then arches her brow. "If you think I'm going to wait months for that, you're clinically insane."

"It freaks me out a bit; however—"

"Fine, go buy me toys then." She rolls her eyes and then to her side, giving me her back.

"Are you ... serious?"

She lifts a shoulder. "Maybe."

"In the past few days, you have mentioned your beautiful ass and now toys. Am I missing something here? Is that something you want?" I watch her shoulders shake a bit and realize she's laughing. "Or are you trying to drive me over the edge?"

"I'm definitely trying to drive you over the edge." She sits up and smiles at me. "I have to look at you every day; the least you could do is put out."

"Beg," I whisper.

She scowls as she crosses her arms. "Nope."

"You will be." I roll off the bed and begin undressing. "I'm going to shower."

"Fine, have fun in there," she says, amusement clear in her voice.

I turn around and watch as she removes her jeans and her panties.

"Would you do me a favor first?"

"Sure," I say, feeling my cock begin to swell.

"Throw these in the hamper; they need to be washed. For some reason, they are a bit damp." She flings them at me.

"Really?" I laugh as they nearly hit me in the face, and

then I scold myself for not allowing it. I miss the smell of her need.

She slides off the bed, throws off her shirt, and unclasps her bra. "I don't want to be a burden." She bends over, ass in the air, and says, "I can do it. I shouldn't have asked."

"Get in bed, Tessa." A low rumble accompanies the demand.

"What, Collin?" she asks as she picks up every article of clothing off the floor with the obvious intention of further turning me on. Then she heads out into the hall and toward the laundry room.

Standing there, fully and painfully aroused, I hear the washing machine start and the pitter patter of Tessa's sexy little feet coming back down the hall.

"Hey, do you want a drink?" she asks while passing our bedroom, completely nude.

"No. Could you get in here?"

"No, I'm hungry. Take your shower."

Gripping my cock, I walk out into the hallway and watch as she streaks down the stairs. I head down after her.

I find her bent over, grabbing ice cream out of the freezer.

"Would you like a sundae?"

Hand now stroking my cock, I shake my head as I watch her scoop ice cream into a bowl, grab whipped cream from the refrigerator, and basically jerk it off before spraying it on top of the ice cream.

After setting two spoons in the bowl, she looks at me and smiles, making sure she does not look down. "Let's watch mindless TV."

She sets the bowl on the coffee table, grabs one of the many throw blankets off the back of our leather sectional, and lays it out over a portion of the couch. Then she grabs another blanket and moves around some of the throw pillows before sitting down, covering her gloriously naked body and patting the spot beside her. "Eat with me?"

Using one of the spoons, she scoops up some of the whipped cream as I sit, and then she smears it on my nose. I like where this is heading. She then kisses it off of me, and I take her lips as I pull the blanket down, exposing her beautiful breasts. Then I reach beside me and grab the can of whipped cream that I brought along. I pull back, give the can a few good jerks, and squirt it in the most strategic places—her nipples. I lean in and lick them clean before going back and sucking them, causing them to harden in my mouth.

As I am focused on tasting her, I feel her move and look to my right to see her hand wrapped around the whipped cream right before it disappears between us where she following my lead and covering my dick.

I remove the bowl from her free hand, set it on the floor, and she takes that opportunity to take me in her mouth.

After my cock becomes dairy free, I gently push her back. "As good as that feels, I owe you."

We make love on our couch before eating ice cream soup, and then we do it again.

"So, what do you want to do tomorrow night?" she asks. "More of that," I say, pulling her naked body tighter against me as we spoon in front of the fire, watching the news. "I suppose we could invite your family out to dinner before we resume living room couch activity."

"Okay, but then New Year's day here?"

"Sounds perfect."

We walk into the lakeside restaurant just outside of Blue Valley and sit with her family, who have already ordered appetizers. I find the conversation to be quite nice, as everyone is sharing the things they would like to accomplish next year. The atmosphere is also lovely, with a string quartet playing and people dancing on the small, wooden dance floor.

Tessa somehow finds it amusing, so between appetizers and dinner, I make my wife dance with me. She also laughs when I point out that there are no words to the music we're dancing to. To this, she begins making up her own ... of course.

Her words are extremely inappropriate, highly erotic, and I'm getting hard in the middle of a dance floor, surrounded by couples who are likely older than Maggie and John.

"Unless you want to skip dinner, you better stop that now."

She barks out a laugh as she looks beyond me. "It's as if you will this to happen, Dr. Abraham."

I turn my head and notice Kendall, Molly, Phoebe, Sarah and Jake walking toward us, smiling as they whisper to each other. Alex lags behind, rolling his eyes.

When they all start to dance, Tessa throws her head back, laughing from her belly. It is only then do I notice they're doing a slow version of the Macarena.

She looks down between us. "You good now? Ready to turn this place up?"

To that, I kiss the top of her head and wave my hand

out toward her family, and it isn't until she turns around that she spots me bee-lining it toward her parents.

John and Maggie laugh as I sit with them and soon, so am I as we watch them all act foolishly, doing the monkey, the electric slide, and then a dance I've never seen, but it's obvious they all know them.

"Can't take those damn kids anywhere still, huh, Mags?" John laughs.

When dinner comes, they make their way back to us, all laughing because they managed to get several of the older people to join in with them.

"You are going to have to start participating in this, you know, Dr. Abraham."

I wink. "I'm not sure I could keep up."

The place is filling up, and it's nearing nine o'clock.

When the hostess brings a couple to sit at the table beside ours, I am taking a sip of bourbon when I hear a familiar chuckle.

"Hello, Ross family."

They all say hello as I attempt not to choke.

Tessa smiles. "Happy birthday, Lucas."

"Thanks, Tessa," he says, and then ... "I'd love for you all to meet Ashley."

Ashes

Chapter Forty-Five

Tessa

udrianna's little sister is stunning, which I noticed in pictures, but none of them did her justice. Her hair is perfectly blown out in soft waves, her skin is like porcelain, and makeup flawless. *Jade is going to love her.* She's shorter than I thought she'd be, and her figure? Lucas is an ass man, and she has plenty of that.

As I stand and step around the table, I hold out my hand and glance at Lucas, who holds up four fingers. I have to bite back a laugh, which isn't hard when I see his eyes, clear and bright, and his smile, everything it always was during good times, but something more.

She's it. I know it, and I love it for him.

"Nice to meet you, Ashley. I've heard a lot about you."

I shake her hand. Lucas dated her years ago, before we met. She was one of his original twelve, *his dirty dozen*.

"I feel like I already know you. The entire Links family is very fond of you." She smiles, further evidence that she is absolutely perfect for him—her teeth are seriously perfect.

"Yeah, well, I'm fond of them, too." I reach back and hold my hand out for Collin.

He sets his napkin on the table, stands, and walks to me.

"Congratulations on your marriage. Landon won't admit it, but I think he admires your husband. Collin, right?" she asks.

"Pleased to meet you." He shakes her hand.

"Well, Ash, their dinner's probably getting cold—"

"Lucas, if you two want to join us, feel free," Dad offers.

Lucas glances at Collin, and I see the smirk threatening when he moves from him to Dad. "Thanks, John. We're going to let you guys eat, though. We haven't ordered yet."

Maggie smiles. "Well, stop over tomorrow, both of you. We're all going to be there."

"All right, we'll definitely try." Lucas takes Ashley's hand, and they head to their table.

"Maggie, Tessa and Collin are having all of us over tomorrow, dear," John says softly.

She covers her mouth. "Oh, my I forgot. I feel awful."

"Tessa." I look at Collin, who continues, "Are you're all right with them coming over to our place? We did go to his."

"Only if you are." I know I must look confused.

Collin stands and walks over to their table, and in-between annoying, non-lyrical songs, I hear him say,

"Lucas, we're actually hosting dinner tomorrow at two. We would like it if you both came over."

Lucas laughs.

Seriously, Lucas?

I cringe as Collin just stands there, and I swear, if Lucas isn't nice, I'm going to kick his freaking ass.

"Oh, you're serious?" Lucas asks, seriously thinking Collin was being a dick.

My husband is not a dick.

Lucas then looks at Ashley. "Is that okay with you, Ash?"

"Sure." She smiles up at Collin. "Thank you."

"All right, thanks, Collin. We'll be there. What should we bring?" Lucas asks.

"Tessa and Maggie have it all covered. Enjoy your meal." Collin walks away.

Walking into the house, I admit, "You surprised me tonight, Collin."

"It's a new year." He kisses the back of my head then quietly says, "Maggie looked like she was going to cry."

He helps me with my coat, and I look at the clock. "It's eleven fifty-four, Collin Abraham. We have five minutes to get naked and be up in that big, old bed."

"I'll meet you up there." He pats my ass, which is totally unexpected, and a turn-on.

I hustle upstairs and throw my dress off as I hurry to the bathroom, pee, brush my teeth, wash up a bit, and then run to the bed. As I'm diving in, he walks into the room, looking way too calm, cool, and collected, with two champagne flutes of sparkling grape juice in one hand. He sets them on the nightstand as he shrugs off his sports coat, unbuttons his shirt, tosses it, and begins to unbutton his jeans.

"You're picking up bad habits." I point to the clothes on the floor as he steps out of his jeans and pulls off his socks.

"You're provoking them with naked laundry days."

He starts to climb in, and I hold my hand up, stopping him. "Lose the boxers, big guy."

He does, and he looks … delicious. And I'm starving.

I push up on my knees and wrap my arms around him, kissing his lips then whispering, "I love you."

He flips me to my back, grabs the remote, and turns on the TV as the countdown begins.

"You are going to love me more in five …" He rubs his hand lightly across my chest. "Four …" He rubs down my belly. "Three …" He rubs gently between my legs. "Two …" He positions himself on top of me, "One." He kisses me as he enters me slowly.

"Good morning, beautiful." He kisses me awake. "I wanna show you something."

"I would prefer feeling something." I open my eyes as I roll to my back. "What's with the clothes?"

"Come on." He chuckles, holding up my robe.

Holding my hand, he opens the nursery door and turns on the lights. We walk into the nursery, and I see the most beautiful, round canopy cribs set up in the middle of the room, both cherry wood draped in white.

"Oh, Collin, they're beautiful." I hurry to them, dragging him behind me, and run my hand over the wood. "They're perfect." I turn and hug him.

He kisses my head. "I am glad you like them. You know we leave in two days. Phoebe already knows, so I think it's appropriate we tell them, and I think it would make them almost as happy as we are."

"I agree." I turn and lean back against him, bringing his hands to rest on my belly. "I have never seen anything so beautiful. Well, besides their very handsome—no, hot—daddy."

His silent chuckle vibrates against my back.

"The way they sit in the center of the room makes my heart smile." I look up at him. "You know they're going to be the center of our world. Very symbolic."

"You're the center of mine now. I hope you know that will never change. I love you, and I'll love them no less, but no more."

Everything is ready as the family starts rolling in. Drinks are served, appetizers are getting eaten, and all is good.

When the doorbell rings, I head to the door and open it. Leia growls behind me as I step back and wave Lucas and Ashley in.

"Well, hello, dog. Still mean as ever, huh?"

I hold out my hands. "I'll take your coats and that bag."

They take off their coats and boots, and I hang them up. He does not, however, give me the bag.

When he walks in, he looks around. "This place is amazing. Ryan, you do great work," Lucas says as he shakes Ryan's hand.

"Tessa, did you decorate?" he asks.

"She actually designed most of it," Collin answers.

"Collin actually did all the decorating." I laugh as I run my hand over my belly mindlessly and catch him looking at it. "Yes, it's big."

"It's perfect." Collin winks at me. "How about a drink?"

Hot daddy is a gracious host.

After dinner, we are all sitting in the family room and talking when Collin stands and pulls me up by his side. "Ready?" he asks, eyes dancing.

I smile and nod.

"We would like to thank you all for coming to our very first New Year's Day party. Things will be a little different next year." He lays his hand on my belly. "Each of you mean a lot to us, and we know any children we have will feel the same. We finished up the nursery early this morning, and—"

"He did. I was sleeping off my sparkling grape juice hangover."

Collin smiles. "We'd love to show it to you."

He lets go of my hand and reaches out to Mom. "Mom and Grandma first."

"Where do sisters rank here?" Kendall laughs, and so does everyone else.

At the top of the stairs, I nod to the door. "Mom, you go first."

Mom reacts as I knew she would. She hugs me and begins crying. "You're having twins, Tessa?"

"Yes, we are. We can find out in a couple months what

they are, but there are definitely two." I look over my shoulder at Collin "Are we going to find out?"

"That's up to you. I already know."

"No, you don't." I laugh, and he winks as he nods. I shake my head. "It's a surprise, remember?"

"No, I'm pretty sure."

I look downstairs at my big brother and grin. "Alex, do you have a guess?"

Alex rolls his eyes. "I'm trying to forget that day."

———

D ownstairs, I watch Lucas grab the bag that he carried in and walk up to Collin.

"Collin, can I have a minute?" he asks.

Ashley and I look at each other and, for some reason, we both laugh nervously as they exit the room. But, while they're gone, we somehow migrate to each other.

I whisper, "You have any idea what this is about?"

"Whatever's in the bag, I suppose," she says.

And we both stay like that until Collin walks out and over to me.

"Lucas would like a minute."

I look at Ashley, who smiles. "He said he needed to talk to you about something."

I look at Collin, who kisses the top of my head then nods to Ashley. "Let's you and I get a drink."

"Collin?"

"We're good, beautiful."

When I walk into the living room, Lucas is going through a pile of records. Laughing, he sets them down then turns around and sees me. "Opposites in the music department, huh?" He walks over and sits on the couch, patting the spot next to him.

I sit.

"You did your whole goodbye thing on the bridge, and I don't want mine to be like that, so I'm warning you now, you try to kiss me, I'll yell like a little bitch for your husband."

"Shut up." I laugh, and so does he.

"Should have listened to you and not made it harder on you or me." He gives me puppy dog eyes, and I roll mine, cross my arms, and sit back. He laughs.

"So, here's the thing, I'm not going back to football, not this season, maybe not next, so—"

"I'm sorry, Lucas."

He shakes his head. "I knew it wasn't a career I'd retire from. All my goals have been achieved, so I'm good no matter what happens." He reaches up to pull down a hat, but there is none. He chuckles again. "So" —he leans forward, elbows on his knees as he looks up at me—"you were right. He is yours, Tessa Ross. Put here for you. From what I see, he treats you really good. Spent some time between Camp and now refusing to believe it until I looked around and my eyes landed on Ash."

I smile. "She's your *one*."

"Yeah, she is," he says in such a sweet and soft voice that I get chills.

We look at each other, and every good memory of us evaporates in a soft goodbye. I smile at him.

He leans back, crosses his arms, and speaks. "I'm going to move to New Jersey. Dad bid on some much bigger jobs in the City, and I need to be there. Ash works in the City for some senator, and we're going to give it a go. I'll be selling the house. I'm going to tell your family so they can decide what they want to do."

"Okay."

"I asked your husband to let me tell you first, because it never felt like mine."

"I know. He told me you wanted to talk to me." I avoid the why it didn't feel like his, because this is the goodbye that I had hoped for, instead of the angst. I will give that to him, even if he didn't give it to me.

"What's wrong?"

I shrug. "Blue Valley is your home, too." Tears fill my eyes.

"Now, don't do that, Tessa. You'll get us both in trouble."

"Okay." I nod then ask, "Does she make you happy?"

He looks down. "Yes, very."

"Good. I'm so glad."

"Who would have thought, Tessa? Less than a year ago, we were a mess, and here we are."

"I guess this is what was supposed to be."

"You think so?" he asks.

I nod. "I'm happy for you. You always said it was—"

"Different with her than the others." He smiles. "My way of dealing with my daddy issues. You know ... screwing his girlfriend's baby sister. But there was always mutual respect."

"Good, Lucas."

"Just weird, my dad and her sister are married." He laughs.

I grin. "Maybe you should consider moving. I hear that's acceptable in some parts south of the Mason-Dixon line."

He smiles. "Not funny, ba—Tessa."

"I'm just joking. I'm very happy for you. And, by the way, she didn't even try to kick my ass. I think she is actually sane."

We sit quietly for a few minutes, and then he shakes his

head. "When I sold the house, I kept some acreage next to it, and just bought more land next to Ryan and Jade. If I have a family, I want them raised around here."

"That's great. Maybe our kids will be friends someday." I laugh.

"I'm sure they will be. I'm in no hurry. That kind of still scares me, you know." He looks down. "Today's a rough day, but not so bad as it was, huh?"

Tears immediately fall. "I know, Lucas. I'm sorry if this was hard for you today. God, I'm so sorry."

He wipes away my tears.

"You will make a great daddy someday. You deserve that."

"Thanks, baby. Who knows? Maybe you'll have a girl, and I'll have a boy, and—"

"I'll move far away."

We both laugh.

"Or maybe I'll have a boy, and you'll have a girl. Have you met my husband?"

"Okay"—he smirks—"now it's not so funny."

"I want you to know, Lucas Links, I will always love you, *anyway*, like I do my family." I wipe away more tears as I stand.

"I feel the same, Tessa." He steps to me and hugs me. And again, I don't hate it. We're going to be friends, him and I … anyway. He steps back and smiles. "Your belly just kicked me."

"I think they were saying close enough."

He grabs my face and brushes away my tears, and no, I don't hate that, either.

"You ready to go back in there?"

"I'll be out in a minute, okay?" I nod.

"You going to be okay? Happy?"

"We're both going to be fine. Better than fine. And I

am happy. And now you are, too. Doesn't feel like such a waste, you know?"

He cocks his head to the side, and I shake my head.

"These hormones are kicking my ass. I just need a few minutes. I'm going to the bathroom. Be out in a minute."

Behind closed doors, I sit on the cold bathroom floor and cry, because I'm overwhelmed and don't want anyone to see me. I'm not sure if I'm happy or sad. I do one hundred percent know that my husband is supposed to be mine, and he's amazing. He invited them here today and, for that, I couldn't possibly love him more.

And Lucas, well … I know I am right that we are meant to be friends. Regardless of what has gone on between us, I will always love him … anyway. People break up every day and walk away, never looking back, but because of who Collin is and who I always knew Lucas could be, I had the love of my life and the boy who taught me how to be loved. It hurts that he still feels the same pain I do, but I wouldn't change it. He will be happy with Ashley, and I pray that they will be as happy as Collin and I are.

A knock on the door has me reaching for toilet paper to wipe my tears and blow my stupid nose.

Shaking his head, Collin asks, "Are you all right?"

I blow out a breath and look up at him. "Yes … no. Four years ago today, I lost a baby."

"Is that what he wanted to say to you? He upset you on purpose?" Collin snaps.

"No! God, no. I remembered it. I wasn't excited about my pregnancy with him until a few weeks before I lost the baby. He was happy and wonderful then … one of the few times." I laugh.

Collin looks confused.

"He lost a couple, and one of his crazy ex-girlfriends

had an abortion behind his back, and then a stillborn. He doesn't think he deserves to be a father, Collin."

"He needs to leave. He shouldn't be laying this on you. I'm done with being—"

I jump up and grab the back of his shirt. "It wasn't him. It was me! *I* brought it up. He simply told me he was selling the house and that he was very happy with Ashley. I'm happy for him. He mentioned moving here and raising his family and, well … I said he deserved to be a father. He'll be a good father, he will, and he doesn't believe he deserves it. He wasn't looking for pity. It's me, dammit. I hate to see him hurt. Not just him—you, my family." I wave my hand to him. "You because of me right now. I need people to be happy, dammit!"

He inhales a deep breath as he looks me over, and then exhales before asking, "Is this the pregnancy causing this emotional outburst?"

I laugh and wipe my eyes. "The emotional shit, no. The outburst … also probably no."

He smiles as he shakes his head. "Should we stay in here all night and hope they all get the hint and leave, or do you think you can keep it together?"

"You did *not* just say that to me?" I glare at him.

"Yes, I did," he says matter-of-factly.

"Collin …" I stop.

"Beautiful, crazy wife," he growls.

I look down, trying not to laugh, and a smile spreads across his face.

I pop a hand on my hip. "I'm not crazy."

"Right …" He chuckles.

"God, you drive me …"

"Where do I drive you?" he asks, all cute-like as he steps toward me.

I put my nose in the air and cross my arms.

"Say it, Tessa."

I have to turn my back to him so I don't laugh.

"Say it," he insists, hands on my hips.

"Nope."

"I will then." He turns me and pulls me against him, his voice booming as he says, "Crazy."

"You're not funny."

"I am." He kisses my neck.

"Nope, but you *are* very hot." I laugh.

"And I'm yours, Tessa, always." He kisses my ear and whispers, "Even when you act like a crazy woman."

I laugh. "And I'm yours."

"Let's go … Sybil."

I step back and pout some more.

Laughing, he picks me up and carries me out the door, smacking my ass. "That's mine later."

And that's when I see Ashley and Jade waiting for the bathroom.

Collin chuckles when he sees them and slowly lowers me to the floor.

"Please excuse my wife. She is kind of—"

"Crazy?" Jade laughs.

Collin leaves the room, amused.

I look at Ashely. "Sorry."

"I wasn't trying to listen to your conversation, but—"

"You were very loud, Tessa." Jade laughs, cutting Ashley off.

"He loves you. I'm over the moon happy for him and you. I just worry, and I know I shouldn't. It's not my place. Sorry." I yawn. "And sorry about that, too."

"You tired, Tessa?" Jade asks.

"God, this has been an exhausting day." I yawn again.

"You want him to be happy, and you think I am the one to do that?" Ashley asks.

"I do. And if that upsets or hurts you, I'm sorry."

Ashley laughs. *She has a good laugh.* "Why would that upset me, Tessa?"

"I don't know," I sigh. "But I'm not going to promise you ass play in order for you to get over any stupid, jealous notions that might be constructed in your head."

"What the *hell* is going on in here?" Lucas laughs as he walks into the room.

Jade, Ashley, and I burst out laughing and can't stop.

The rest of the night, we all have fun. Ashley is just like her sister, and Lucas and her seem comfortable together. Before the night ends, it becomes obvious that Lucas has spoken to Dad when Dad announces he will be buying the house, and Alex and Phoebe will move to the farm after his graduation.

W e lie in bed, in each other's arms.
"Was all that too much for you, Tessa?" Collin asks as he rubs my back.

"It was perfect. Why? Do you want to go again?" I kiss his chest.

"Well, sure, but I was talking about the Lucas situation."

"No, I think it's wonderful. She seems amazing, and he truly looks happy. I'm very happy for them. Are you all right?"

"Let's see … your ex is moving and has someone else, and your parents will be our neighbors, not him. Yes, I think it is a perfect start to the new year."

"I love you so much, Collin. You're more than I could ever dream possible."

"Well, they really weren't all that big of shoes to fill," Collin jokes.

"Silly man, you never even had to worry. It almost makes me crazy that you even thought that way."

"This is still all new territory, Tessa. Your world is much different from what I'm used to." He laughs. "But, in two days, you're going to see exactly what I mean. I just hope you can handle it."

"I can't wait," I say as I move on top of him. "But for now …"

Too Much

Chapter Forty-Six

Collin

Walking out of the airport and onto the street, I raise my hand to hail a cab, which is best because one of our vehicles picking us up draws too much attention.

When I see that we're being watched, I look down at Tessa, who is wide-eyed and obviously disturbed by her destitute surroundings.

"Sunglasses, now," I demand, but as she reaches into her purse, we're surrounded by children begging for food.

"Hungry, Miss, hungry," they say as she grabs her wallet and begins handing out bills.

"Tessa, let's go *now*." I open the door and just about have to toss her in.

I watch as hands hit the windows while I give the address to the driver in his native language.

"Collin, what are we doing here. They need us. Did you see them? They're hungry and just children." Her hands shake when I take them in mine.

"It was a long day. We are going to eat, and shower, and rest. Tomorrow, we head up the mountain. But you can't give them money. There are people watching children like them." I stop, knowing she cannot handle what could happen to a kid who is spotted with any type of currency. "We talked about this on flight. This isn't the US." I sigh as I watch her look at me like I'm some sort of monster. "This wasn't a good idea."

"Collin, I'm sorry. I'll do better. I promise. I'll get better."

I pull her under my arm and press my lips to the top of her head. "You will." *Or this is done.*

Walking into the hotel, I keep her glued to me, head pressed to my chest, big Jackie O sunglasses covering her eyes to shield their emotions as we check in. I continue keeping it there until we're inside our room.

Guilt floods me when I have long since closed the door and she's yet to move away.

"Is this all right?" I ask, and she finally looks up and around.

"Yes, it's nice." She moves to sit at the edge of the bed. "You're upset with me?"

"No, Tessa. Worried that this is going to be too much. Worried that you won't say no and that bringing you here may put a target on your back." I sit beside her and sigh.

"What I love about you most may cause you to be in harm's way. I just didn't consider that before we came."

She shakes her head, lip quivering, as she says, "Just tell me what to do. I can handle this, I promise."

I stroke her cheek. "Let's shower and go eat."

We leave the comforts of the resort at daybreak and meet up with an ex-Navy Seal associate, Enzo, to start the two-hour trek up the mountain in a Jeep, hoping that the early start will help us beat the majority of the heat.

"Who's on our six?" I ask as I settle in next to Tessa.

"Sonny and Kanan, sir," Enzo answers as Rourke slides into the passenger seat.

"Up ahead?" I ask.

"Diesel and Tank."

Rourke looks back at me. "It's a good day to climb a mountain, sir."

"Glad to hear it." I nod then look at Tessa as I grab a bottle of water out of the bag. "Drink, please."

With a hint of sarcasm, she says, "Yes, sir."

I wrap my arm around her. "Enzo, Rourke, this is my wife, Tessa."

"Nice to meet you, ma'am," they both say.

She holds up her water. "Cheers."

To that, they both laugh as she looks up at me and smiles. Then, as Rourke hands back my weapon, her smile slowly falls.

"Necessary?" she whispers.

"Never unprepared."

T wo hours later, we approach the village, incident-free.

I watch her as her eyes climb the security wall and rest on the razor wire laying across the entirety of the perimeter's top.

"Early phases here. Less intimidating inside," I assure her.

Klause walks out as the gate opens and hands me my bag, which contains a walkie, portable video monitor, and files updating me on the progress of the Ecuador project.

"Welcome, Mrs. Abraham." He nods.

"Thanks," she says sweetly.

He looks at me. "I'm heading east to—"

"Safe travels." I nod.

I look at Tessa as the Jeep pulls in. "Klause is—"

"One of the fab five from—"

"Yes," I interrupt her disclosure of our home location, another thing I failed to prep her for.

She tilts her head and understanding sets in. My wife is intuitive.

"You ready for all this?" I squeeze her hand.

Looking up as we pull in, she sees the armed guards in the tower. "Is all that necessary?"

"Yes, especially in early stages. The South African village is vastly different. It was for all intents and purposes, our project's prototype."

"How long has it been in operation?" she asks.

"Two years."

"So, this is all fairly new?"

"It is. However, in essence, it started for many of us as soon as boots touched ground."

"Some things you can't unsee," Enzo adds.

"And some things, the US government stirs up while

politic-ing, and then checks out. You can take the soldier out of the sand, but sometimes that solider can't shake the fucking sand," Rourke adds.

"Language," Enzo snaps.

"Sorry, ma'am," Rourke mumbles.

Tessa laughs. "I'm not politic-ing, I'm not the queen, and I can assure you that I'm not a ma'am. I have used that word a few times in my life. It's all good."

Her good nature and natural ability to make people feel at ease is an outstanding quality she holds. However … "Let me remind you all, if we ignore the hierarchy of authority, we compromise our safety. If safety is compromised, then the reason we're here—to help assist in them becoming a heathy and thriving village—will not happen."

"Sir, yes, sir," they both say.

She gives my hand a squeeze, and I look over at her. "Sorry."

"You're not a mind reader, Mrs. Abraham. I should have better prepared you."

"Luckily for you, I'm a quick learner," she says as she takes in the steel buildings, and then through another gated area leading to a large area of the village, where kids are playing baseball with some of the ex-military personnel, and not just US military; men from all over the world are vetted to join our efforts. Only a few, who have seen action, do not seek some sort of absolution from what they were made to do when they swore an oath to a country that used them as pawns in their game of power and control, hidden under a blanket that they call freedom. All good men who, like me, want to protect and serve.

The Jeep comes to a stop in front of the medical building. I hop out and extend my hand.

As she steps out, I ask, "How are you feeling?"

Walking into the building and looking around, she simply says, "Overwhelmed, but ready to work."

I let go of her hand. "I'd like to show you around. Are you up for it?"

"I just sat in a truck for two hours." She smiles as she looks me over. "Are you up for it?"

We walk around the medical slash first-aid building. Then I show her where the food and supplies are stored. I introduce her to Mick, the armed man guarding the food and supplies, who also happens to be in charge of everything that comes in and out.

"Mick, this is Tessa, my wife. She has full access, understood?"

"Yes, sir."

I show her the rest of the village, introducing her to the key contacts and, as we near the end of our *brief tour*, I look down at my watch and notice we've been at it for three hours.

"You ready to rest?"

"No, we can continue, but I do need a bathroom." She reaches for my hand, but I reluctantly pull it away.

"This will be just as hard for me as it is for you, but while here, we should keep it professional."

"Okay," she replies, but it's clear in her beautiful blue eyes that she does not understand. "There is one part of the tour you did not give. What is in the gated area we drove through?"

"That's where I spend most of my time. The village is under twenty-four-hour surveillance. We will gate the medical facility by the end of the week, so you'll feel safe there. Until then, I'll have someone with you when I'm not."

"So, you won't be with me?"

"The medical facility will operate six hours a day, but

until it's gated, we will only open it for four hours or in emergency situations. I will be there with you most of the time."

"And, what will we do the rest of the day?" she asks, still looking around.

I point. "We'll be in that gated area. I'll be doing some training there. That's also where our living quarters are. You'll be able to use the internet and do whatever you want in our quarters."

"Okay," she said. "Am I going with you for training?"

"No, Tessa, that area is restricted."

We walk to the gate, and the door is opened. I point left, and we head that way. "The brick building houses our quarters."

I look at Diesel, who is closing the gate behind us. "We're going to our living quarters. If anyone needs me, let me know."

Punching the code into the keypad, I warn her, "This is not like home, Tessa." With a loud *click*, the system is disarmed, and I push the door open.

We walk down a long corridor, pass several doors, and come to the end. I punch in another code, open the door, flip the light switch, and wave her in. "Home sweet home."

As she looks around, I give her the rundown. "Our bedroom and bathroom are through that door. No one else has access. No one is allowed. I hope you feel safe."

She walks through the door into the bedroom, where there is a bed, an armoire, and two nightstands. The bathroom has a shower, toilet, and sink.

"Our things are in the foyer. I'll go get them." I smile as I walk out to give her a minute to adjust to her surroundings. When I return, she's standing, arms crossed as if she's hugging herself. "Tessa, you have said little of anything since we arrived."

"I'm just trying to take it all in."

"Let's debrief. Tell me what's bothering you."

"Nothing."

"I'm not convinced."

She shakes her head. "I'm very sorry, sir."

"Does that bother you?"

"No, it's kind of hot … sir." She smirks.

"We okay?" I step toward her.

"Of course." She steps into me, and I wrap my arms around her. She laughs. "I think we should keep this professional, sir."

"Oh, I understand now. That's what's bothering you."

"No, I get it. How you explained it …" She looks down. "Okay, yes, it bothers me. I wasn't trying to jump you out there; I was trying to hold your hand."

I walk to the bed, sit down, and pull her next to me. "They don't see me like you do, and it is better that way."

"All right, so I can't hold my husband's hand, or kiss him, or grab him here"—she grabs my dick, and none too lightly, I might add—"any time I want?"

"For obvious reasons, you grabbing me here"—I place my hand over hers—"should always be in private." I lean in to kiss her, but she backs away and stands.

Nose in the air, she walks into the bathroom. "It's going to be a very long two weeks."

I chuckle. "Get out here."

She walks out and opens a bag.

"What are you looking for, beautiful?"

"Toiletries. I need to use the bathroom and freshen up a bit." She finds them quickly, but as I am walking toward her, she brushes past me and heads to the bathroom.

I knew this would be difficult and, like me with trying to understand the emotional aspect of our relationship, she is now trying to understand the professional aspect. I will be patient, because no part of me wants to leave her home, raising our children, and be apart from them for weeks at a time.

Walking into the bathroom, she asks, "Sir, will you let me know the codes so that I can come and go when I'm given permission … sir."

"Of course, Tessa. You're not a prisoner here." I look around our living quarters and realize why it may seem that way to her and decide we need to do some decorating when given a chance. Until then, fresh air and under-standing will help her adjust.

"Let's you and I get out of here." I open the door.

"Where are we going, sir?"

"Tessa, stop."

"No, sir, I am going to keep this very professional," she says with a smile playing on her lips, which eases the discomfort in my chest, my heart.

"You're going to drive me crazy," I whisper.

In a tone clearly intent on mimicking mine, she looks up at me, eyebrows drawn, and says, "Two weeks. We can be professional, can't we, sir? I mean, you could order me to drop to my knees right here and take you in my—"

"Please stop torturing me," I growl out as we walk into the courtyard, which uncommonly runs around the perimeter of the housing, an added barrier of protection to those inside.

"Yes, sir. I'm so sorry. Maybe you should bend me over your knee and spank me for being so insubordinate."

I laugh. "You're impossibly frustrating."

She smiles as she looks down. "You're holding my hand."

I run my thumb over the back of her hand. "Yes, I am."

Reality Check

Chapter Forty-Seven

Tessa

he next week, I followed his rules … mostly. He stayed with me, only occasionally leaving when he received a call. He even started kissing me on the cheek before he left me to work in the clinic. The woman who helped me smiled each time and, although I can't understand her, we seem to communicate better and better every day. I vowed to myself that I would learn Spanish. When I told Collin this, he reminded me how many variations of the language I would need to learn, yet he still thought it was a good idea.

Tonight, before sunset, we walk into our home away from home, and he lies down to rest with me. This is something we do before dinner each day. When I fall asleep, I know he will head to the training building, and when I wake, I will work to find even more grants for vaccines that we receive every day and that are unavailable to people who need it just as badly. My goal is to hit up drug companies … big pharm—God knows they make enough money —to donate to impoverished areas such as this.

After sending a dozen emails, I plan to find a way to increase supplies needed so that we can bring even more people to this safe environment in the middle of a country that, to the best of my knowledge, through research, is extremely unsafe, especially for women and children.

Today, my curiosity gets the best of me, and the fact I'm missing him even more, so I leave the housing area and go to find my husband to drag him to dinner.

Outside, I pass a guard, one whose name is lost to me because there are so many that come and go that I can't keep them all straight, not yet. anyway. Sadly, maybe not ever. From what I'm understanding, as soon as Ecuador is up and running itself, we will probably not be visiting again because our time is best served constructing other locations. Collin promises I can help him scout at some point in our future.

Collin isn't in the near vicinity, so I continue to head toward the training center.

The guard looks shocked as I approach, and it irks me.

"I need to see Dr. Abraham."

He glowers at me.

"I would advise that you take me to him. He'll be upset if you didn't."

To this, he opens the door immediately, and we walk in. The fact that these men are intimidated by my husband is laughable. He's a big teddy bear once you get past his tough exterior. It surprises me that they don't see that. What other kind of man would do something like this?

We walk into the steel building that resembles an airport hangar. All around the open area are men training. There are dozens of weight benches outlining the perimeter of the building, and the center has mats where hand to hand combat exercises are taking place. I will not lie; I would not hate to see my husband sparring right now. I'm also not disappointed that he is not one of the many, many … many men training.

We pass by the area and into another setup with many different obstacle courses, climbing walls, beams, and makeshift buildings. It makes me seriously want to jump in and train myself, but this isn't some funhouse I can pay ten bucks to shoot laser guns for fun and then leave; this is the real deal.

I rub my hand over my belly and remember why that is not possible at this moment, anyway. However, it's certainly not going to stop me from pressing my husband to allow it after our babies are born.

We come to the end of the building, where there is a door, and then we walk through it. I see empty desks that I will assume are used by the men training right now. I follow the guard through another door that leads to a stairway.

At the bottom of the stairs, I look around and notice it's a much larger version of the basement room in Collin's Cape home and also what the room in our basement in Blue Valley is beginning to resemble—computer screens, conference tables with blueprints, and a large desk sitting on a platform raised slightly higher than those around it. Behind that desk, my husband immediately sees me.

"I'll call you back later, Tomás."

He hangs up the phone and walks toward me. "Is everything all right?"

"Yes, sir." The guard salutes him. "Your wife insisted she see you."

"You're dismissed," Collin barks at him.

He then sweeps his eyes over me, as if to check for an injury. "Are you okay?"

"Yes, you were late, and I, uh … I had some ideas that I wanted to talk to you about."

"And it could not have waited?"

I shrug. "I guess."

"You aren't supposed to be in here. We've talked about this." His voice becomes extremely cold.

"*You* talked about it," I correct him.

He shakes his head and takes my hand, quickly walking toward the door. "All right, let's go back, and we can discuss it in our quarters."

"What is this all about?"

"Tessa, let's go back."

I pull my hand away and sit at the conference table. "Why can't we discuss it here?"

He looks at me with obvious annoyance, and it pisses me off.

"Fine, but if you intend to keep things from me, then—"

"Then what?" he snaps.

I stand up and walk to the door, hearing his heavy boots following behind. He doesn't stop at the door, or on the stairs, or as we walk through the training area, where I again take everything in, making sure he sees I am not affected by this. I'm no fucking flower; I understand why we're here. Sadly, he's missing the point that we are here.

I hoof it back to the living quarters, punch in the code, open the metal door, and head down the hall, where I again punch in the code, and open another door.

Inside, once the door is closed, he asks "What did you need to talk to me about?"

"I just wanted to see you."

"You couldn't have called?" he asks.

I turn and look up at him, squaring my shoulders. "No, I wanted to see you. If I wanted to talk, I would have called, thus the use of the word *see*."

He narrows his eyes. "You wanted to see what was in that building."

"Of course, I want to know what you do when you're not with me. I sit in here for what seems like forever, alone, while you're in there doing whatever it is you're doing. Should I apologize for missing you? Should I train myself not to miss you?" I throw a hand up when he starts to talk and continue, "Never mind. I'm tired. I'm going to sleep."

I lie down and hear him sigh before the bed buckles under his weight. "In that building, we train young men to defend themselves and others. They're trained by men who have left the service of their country and joined us. There are checks and balances that ensure the safety and well-being of the village's residents. However, the men, both local and ex-military, have lived under extreme circumstances, Tessa. I'm not saying that they are dangerous, but I'm not saying they are not if triggered, and we have yet to learn their triggers.

"That building is off limits to women and children for their own safety and the safety of the men who are doing drills that could possibly trigger them, in hopes it desensitizes them, as well as readies them for any situation that may arise in the coming days, months, years. There are psychiatrists that fly in from time to time. We have telecommunication ability in both English and native languages for these men to speak to therapists, which we insist upon. Our primary objective here is to empower the local people, but in a very fortunate turn of events, we realized that it also helps our heroes without homes, without family, without a mission, or a purpose.

"That building, Tessa, brings together men who speak different languages, to build a team, camaraderie, and give them a purpose. In South Africa, we learned that—," he stresses, "and it was a beautiful turn of events. They need that time, that training, those moments of learning together, from each other, and with each other in order to meet the primary objective. These men are healing as they heal communities. And they do this while teaching the local men about our countries, which most of them hate, despise, blame for their impoverished lives. This delusion they've learned from drug lords as a recruitment tactic. Here, they learn differently.

"The areas that are unrestricted, the men amongst the women and children, we have some sort of intelligence information on them, or they have wives and families living amongst us, and they know how important our mission is. But there are many of them who have not had that. Whose mothers do not differ from mine. Whose bright shining light of hope, future paths all lead toward drug lords. But, for some reason, they wanted better, and they came here. We give them the opportunity for change.

"Outside these walls, men are not kind; they are on drugs and angry. They rape and kill women and children for a dollar or a fix, or to save a life of someone they do love, or they see it as an only chance to survive. If we can give them knowledge and power, they can defend themselves against the guerrillas and drug lords. The room you saw me in helps us to see the areas most desperately in need, to look for the children of some of the women here who are missing, to see movement that helps us to ensure that we keep everyone here safe.

"At times, these men come to check in on loved ones they've had to leave in order to survive with the hope that they can help save them. The armed personnel are people who we trust and have enough information on, to know that we can.

"Over the next few years, we hope to have built a strong enough team that can outnumber, and yes, outgun if necessary, those who wish to rape, kill, or traffic the innocent lives we want to protect. The difference in what we do and what governments around the world promise, and fail to do, is we will actually leave. We will make no play for power, monetary gain, or markers owed. The trust we build allows us to build relationships that are stronger than fear because we remove it and breed hope."

Now sitting up and listening to my husband, I am further in awe of him, but he's also missing something. "What about teaching the women how to defend themselves? They should have that opportunity, as well. They raise the future of their prospective countries. And, by no means am I trying to undermine the wonderful things you're doing, but hasn't our country done this before and failed? Haven't they trained men who have then come against us? What if the key to all this, the lesson, is that women, the ones raising their children, the ones feeding them, molding their minds, their hearts, should also be seen as strong? Not just seen but actually be strong. And why is it I can't be in there when you're in there?"

"You're right, in a sense." He nods. "We can work on a program when we get home, if you want to. But our programs outline mission statement is much different from those that train terrorists. I've been there, in Iraq, where we built an army of rebels and left them to fail. In Somalia, where we leave our own to get dragged through the streets.

"What you're involved in outside of that building teaches more than weaponry. We are helping them become self- sufficient, teaching them how to sustain what we start after we leave, to become independent from the cartels, war lords, and guerrilla forces here. But, without the other, they can't protect themselves. I'm not disagreeing with you, but that building is not a place you need to be.

"I can take care of you. I know how you feel about hunting, never wanting something or someone to hurt. And I saw your reaction to me being handed a gun on our way here. I don't want that part of this to touch you." The hurt and anger still looms in his eyes, but it has softened.

"I … I feel like you think I'm doubting you."

"Isn't that's exactly what you're doing?"

"No, I am questioning what I don't know and don't understand. What you're keeping from me. Have you ever heard the term *ignorance is bliss*? Well, it has the opposite effect on me. It pisses me off."

"Well, have you ever heard the term *curiosity killed the cat*? Some of those men came from the gangs we are trying to stop. And you're safe in here." He jabs his finger into the mattress. "But you clearly don't trust me enough to sit still. What if one of them …?" He stops and stands. "We're not doing this." He walks to the door and punches in the code. "We are done and going home. I'll make arrangements. Do you think you can stay safely in the parameters you've been given access to for an hour so I can get you the hell out of here?"

"Fuck you," I hiss in a whisper.

He whirls around. "Excuse me?"

I lie down and cover my head with the blanket.

"Tessa!" He storms over to the bed and pulls the covers off my head.

"Leave me alone!" I pull them back.

"Tessa, dammit, talk to me." He places his hand on my back.

I wiggle it off as I get up and quickly make my way to the bathroom.

I hate that he is upset with me, but more than that, I hate that he thinks I am not extremely proud of what he is doing. *I mean, who does things like this?*

My husband.

I blow my nose as I pee then wash my hands and face before hurrying back out, where I find him sitting on the edge of the bed, hand just under his heart, as he looks up at me, slowly releasing a held breath.

"You're gonna hear me out, okay?"

He nods.

"I'm not a weak person, nor am I untrustworthy or stupid, Collin. I tell you everything there is to know about me. I can't have secrets in my life. I have huge trust issues from my previous relationship. I have opened up to you, trusted you, and loved you with all that I am because of who I believe you to be. I haven't asked about your past and love that I don't worry about things like that with you. You opened yourself up to me, exposing everything, which made me trust you that much more. It made me feel like your partner and your equal, not someone taking the backseat, waiting, just waiting, on the damn sidelines. If you can't handle me here, I need to do more for me to feel whole."

"Tessa …" he begins.

I shake my head. "This whole thing hurts. Maybe I went about it the wrong way. I'm not perfect like you."

"I'm not—"

"I apologize if you think I doubt you," I cut him off again, "or the wonderful things you do for people, because I don't. I just wanted to know—no, I needed to understand. My God, Collin, do you not remember that I was in the mix when Catherine turned up?"

He closes his eyes.

"I'm strong. I can handle anything you come with, especially because it comes with you. Now please accept my apology and do whatever it is you need to do—kick me out, lock me up—"

"I'd never do—"

"I'm exhausted and need to rest and be alone for a while; calm my mind, which bothers me because this whole thing started because I was lonely in here, alone and missing you." I crawl up in bed and cover myself.

"Tessa, I—"

"No. Please, Collin, understand this is not to hurt you. I'm tired, really very tired." I curl up, cover up, and hug the blanket, because I'm seriously exhausted.

When I wake up, I'm thirsty as hell and have to pee —neither urge less strong—so I hop up, rush to the bathroom, stop to grab a bottle of water, and pee while downing the entire bottle.

After washing my hands, I run them over my belly. "Okay, you two, playtime is over. Back to bed, yeah?"

When I come out, I see Collin sitting in the chair in the corner, hand to heart, and he starts to stand.

"Don't, please." I crawl in bed.

"Please talk to me," he whispers, kneeling next to the bed.

"What time is it?"

He pushes a fallen strand of hair away from my face. "Eight. I have dinner."

"I'm not hungry." I turn to my side and tuck the blanket under my chin.

"Tessa, please."

Sitting up and turning to look at him, I say, "Collin, I really am just tired. I'm sorry about all this."

"Don't be. It was me," he starts.

"I want to sleep, okay? Can this wait, please?"

Pushing up on his knees, he gently takes my face in his hands. "We need to talk about this, but I'll let you rest. I love you."

"Thank you." I close my eyes and a tear falls.

He wipes it away, and I lie down, begging God to let me sleep through this … this … hurt.

When I wake again, he's still kneeling beside the bed, head resting on the mattress, eyes closed, looking peaceful. I glance up at the clock and see that it's been two hours.

I hate that he has been like this for that long. I hope that he hasn't, but I can't bring myself to wake him up, not when he looks so peaceful; not angry, or hurt, or betrayed like I made him feel.

I do this—watch him sleep—until the two little ones inside of my belly begin treating my bladder like a trampoline. Then I quietly and carefully start to slide off the bed and whisper, "I love you so much," to their daddy.

When he jumps and looks at me, even in the dim lit room I can see fear in his eyes, frightened like an animal about to be attacked, and it breaks my heart. I move to him, wrap my arms around him, and he wraps his around me. Then, out of nowhere, I start crying.

He cups my face and tips it up so our eyes meet. "Are you okay?"

I sniff back my tears. "I have to go to the bathroom."

Collin closes his eyes and lets out a breath.

I turn and rush to the bathroom, push down my shorts, plop my behind on the toilet, and exhale a pleasurable, "Oh my God."

He walks in as I flush. "What is it, Tessa?" He looks around the room, completely confusing me. Being Collin, he catches on to my confusion and answers my unspoken question. "Oh my God what?"

To this, I try to hold back a smile.

"Please, are you okay?"

"Yes." I dry my hands.

"Please tell me what that meant then, Tessa," he asks as if he urgently needs an answer, like our lives might depend on it.

"I don't think now is a great time to answer that question." I shake my head as I walk out. "Let's sleep. Please, can we … sleep."

"Whatever you want." He grabs my hand and turns me to face him. "I. Love. You."

"I love you, Collin. I love you, too." I hug him.

He hugs me back then pulls the covers back down, helps me in, drops his pants, pulls off his shirt, and crawls into bed next to me, holding me tightly against him.

"I'll let you sleep, but please tell me what you were thinking about in the bathroom, please."

"It's really not important right now. I can't fight anymore today, please."

"I want you to get whatever it was off your chest before you fall asleep. You were crying in your sleep earlier because I upset you. I want you to get it out now. I don't want to hear you cry again. Please, beautiful, just tell me."

I let out a deep breath and sit up, knowing if I expect he answers every question, I do the same. "I won't ever lie to you. I will always tell you the truth, and if I answer, you'll be mad and for no reason. It's stupid."

He sits up. "I won't be. Just tell me the truth."

"Okay, fine. It's stupid and means nothing. I had to go to the bathroom for a long time. I chose to watch you sleep. You looked peaceful, not like earlier, and I wanted to be in that moment, that peace, with you. I couldn't take it anymore, so I finally got up, and the pressure was horrendous. When I finally peed, it felt so good.

"When I was younger, I asked Lucas what it felt like for a man when he came, and he told me when you have to pee really bad and finally do. I never understood what he meant, and ... well, I kind of get it now. Are we going to fight again?"

"Was our fight so awful that you miss him?"

I shake my head. "No, Collin, it was worse than I've ever felt with anything I ever went through with him. I hurt you today. This had nothing to do with Lucas, but you insisted on an answer. I feel awful, and I'm so angry at myself for making you mad or felt I was questioning or doubting how much I respect you and your work, how much I adore and love you. But we can't keep going at it like this. I don't think it's good for them. So, please, Collin, can we please not fight now? Can we table any discussion for whenever you're getting me out of here?"

"You'll go when I go, but yes, we can."

After I get into bed, he shuts off the light. We settle in and, as the tension begins to ebb, he sighs.

I raise my head from his chest and look at him in the blackness of night.

"He's wrong, you know. That's not what it feels like," Collin whispers.

"Sorry?" I whisper back and snuggle against him.

"There is heat that starts in your groin, and it builds and moves to your testicles like liquid fire without a burn … just heat. It slowly moves down your shaft as you harden. It tingles inside. Pressure, heat, and a titillation inside until you release. When you release, its mindless pleasure that takes over your entire body.

"When I come inside you, it's almost spiritual, like I am sharing energy with you, giving you my pleasure. I had never not used a condom until you. It doesn't feel like the need to take a piss, Tessa. It's amazing. I am not mad, so no apology necessary." His lips press to the top of my head. "I love you. Goodnight."

Sweet son of sensual desire, and lord of my already full womb, I inwardly convulse as my core begins to burn and exhaustion fades.

"Are you okay?" he asks.

"Mmhmm …"

"I love you." He rolls to his side and kisses my cheek so sweetly and so softly, but the need filling me from his description comes out in a breath held too long, wrapped in a moan.

He leans back down and kisses my lips so … teasingly, and I arch into him.

He lightly runs his fingertips up my spine, and a need-filled whimper escapes and is met by his whispered, "Beautiful."

In the dark, his lips meet mine. Hungry, I bite down on his lower lip, and he hisses.

"Sorry, dammit, sorry," I whisper, brushing my lips against his, feeling incredibly embarrassed.

He kisses my lips softly then pulls away, whispering, "Can I help you out?"

His face in my hands, my lips on his, I attempt to climb on him, but he stops me.

"Need to get you ready, beautiful."

"All set," I rasp out as I reach between us and find him hard and ready.

His breath hot against my skin, he groans, "Tell me what it feels like, Tessa."

"Oh God, I need you," I whimper as I rub him against my wet heat.

"Tell me," he demands, keeping himself from me.

"Dammit, Collin," I whine then blurt out, "Like I need a Q-tip. Like I have been camping for a month, and I need to clean my ears. That there is an itch and … Please, Collin, I need …" I stop when I feel his body shake against mine and squeeze his dick. "Not funny."

I release him and try to release the pressure myself, but he takes my hands and pins them to the mattress. Then he sears my skin with his lips, moving from my cheek, down my neck, across my collarbone, skips my freaking breasts, and heads right to my belly. He moves to my thigh, runs his tongue flat against my pelvic bone, and then blows his hot breath against my throbbing clit.

"Collin," I beg.

"You need me, Tessa, as much as I need you." He licks up my thigh, causing me to shudder everywhere. "You don't want to come until I am deep inside you." Lick. "You want to feel me fill you with my cock. Your reward? My cum." Lick. "You need me just as badly as I need you," he growls as he licks me from front, all the way back. And he does it again and again until my orgasm rips through me as he moves and thrusts all the way inside of me fully.

Unable to keep as quiet as I have the entire time we've been here, I cry out his name and swear I hear it echo through the brick walls of our home away from home. And he doesn't stop; he continues long after I can no longer meet him thrust for thrust.

"Reward," I pant. "Give it to me."

When he comes, he does it so hard that I feel every jerk, twitch, drop of his cum bursting inside of me. And when he pulls out, I feel his slick cock drag across my thigh until I'm empty.

He falls beside me and takes my hand, kissing each finger, and then holds it against his pounding heart.

"Q-tips?" he husks out.

I sink my fingers into his muscular chest. "Cleaning my ears with a Q-tip. A buildup of pressure and heat. I pull it out and, Oh God."

He laughs.

"Then, when you're inside of me, I feel full and all that pressure peaks until it finally has nowhere else to radiate other than throughout all of me."

"Okay, no more talk. I'm exhausted and getting hard again. I love you. Goodnight," he breathes softly.

"Q-tips, dark chocolate, a pedicure, your smile that can cause tremors to rock not just my body but my world." I yawn. "I love you."

Collin growls and rolls away from me and onto his stomach. "Goodnight, Tessa."

I wake to Collin sitting on the edge of the bed, looking at me.

"Good morning, beautiful," he says with soft caution.

I sit up and move to him, hugging him and whispering, "Good morning."

"I've been thinking, and I know you need to feel you can take care of yourself, so maybe you would like to learn about the guns we work with at our sites."

"You want to teach me to shoot?" I try to keep my amusement at bay.

Face set in determination, he nods. "If you want to learn, I would love to teach you."

"If I'm a good student and learn quickly, can I maybe go with you occasionally while you train?"

He laughs. "Sure, Tessa."

You're going to regret that, Doc.

"Can we go now?"

He looks at his watch. "Yes, actually. It's perfect timing. Get dressed."

I know he remembers me telling him that my dad likes guns, so I'm not sure if he's patronizing me or ... Yeah, he's patronizing me. But I am loving it—him teaching me how to load, unload, ensuring I am learning each of the weapons, which are not all of them, but I have no interest in automatic weapons, so I give him that win, as he is giving me this.

When he teaches me how to hold it and how to aim, I play a role that I have never once in my life played—the airhead. And Collin being Collin, I'm sure he catches that, too.

As he wraps his arms around me to teach me how to handle the pistol, I lean against him to distract him. Then he finally steps back, gently strokes the side of my face, and steps away.

"All right, if this makes you uncomfortable, you can stop, okay?"

"We still have a deal, right?"

"Of course," he says.

Aiming at the target, I tell him, "I could never kill an animal, and I know it's because I've never been that hungry, so no judgment, but I really like guns." Then I shoot and hit the target, dead center, and keep shooting until the magazine is empty.

I remove the clip, set the gun down, and then I remove my ear protecting headphones. Raising my hand in the air victoriously, I turn and see his slightly shocked and smug, hot as hell mug.

"Always loved shooting Sunday evenings with the boys."

He steps to me, and I step to the side. "Say it."

"It." He lunges toward me, and I laugh.

"Say I win."

"You win," he says, lifting me up with one arm and leaving the building.

Walking past the guard at the door, carrying me, he mutters. "Take care of the weapons, Diesel."

He chuckles. "Yes, sir."

"Are you mad at me?" I wiggle in an attempt to escape as we pass by several groups of men.

"No," he says, setting me down at the door to the residence building then punching in the code. Opening the door, he drags me inside.

"Slightly irritated?" I ask, trying to keep up with hot daddy long legs.

He says nothing as he makes his way to our door and enters the code.

Inside, he shuts the door and turns to me. "That was … Fuck, beautiful." He pulls off his shirt and points to the bed.

Laughing, I hop on the mattress and begin unbuttoning

my shirt. Apparently, I'm too slow because he rips it open, sending buttons flying … everywhere.

"If that makes you hot, I can't wait to show you what I can do with a bow."

The rest of the week, I work on setting up a charting system and taking pictures of each of the residents to attach to each folder so that a language barrier doesn't cause any incidents, such as double immunizations, and to start a health baseline of everyone who lives here. So far, the population is two hundred, and that's including the thirty men inside the compound training to become protectors of the residents.

Alejandra, the girl who works at the medical center, we learned to communicate and are teaching each other words in our native language. She is only seventeen and smart as a whip. I emailed Mom and asked her to send me some things for her—clothes, books, snacks, and also lollipops and stickers to bribe the kids who hated coming in here, because hey, it works in America.

Even though she's only seventeen, she shows the most interest in learning and gaining knowledge. I asked Collin that we officially make her the "office manager" before we leave, and he agreed. I will tell her when the package arrives, right before we head back.

The day before that happened, he came to me and asked me to offer her tuition for nursing school if she trained others to do what she was doing for a year and promised to come back and help out when needed.

I cried, but not as much as she did when I gave her the care package and had Rourke translate Collin's offer.

The night before we left, Collin and I stayed up late,

making sure things were all set, and when we left, I cried into his chest.

At the airport, I stayed close and had to will myself not to scoop up every kid who begged for food or money. And when we were alone, he hugged me tight and said, "We can't fix an infection with a Band-Aid, but we can continue hoping to change one life at a time and praying they'll do the same."

Birthday

Chapter Forty-Eight

Tessa

ravel slowed as my belly grew, and for the next few months, we stayed here, in Blue Valley, surrounded by everyone who just left after celebrating Collin's birthday.

Busy trying to clean up, I ignore my cramps so that the afterparty, just him and me … and my enormous belly, can happen before exhaustion hits me, as it does every night at around seven.

Yep, I became that girl. Can't stay awake long enough to see the sunset half the time, but tonight, cramps and exhaustion be dammed, I am going to ride my husband like I own him … and I totally do, just as much as he owns me.

From upstairs, Collin yells, "It's six forty-five, beautiful; we've got a good fifteen minutes before you're asleep."

Laughing, I bend down to pick up a lone Cheerio when I feel hot liquid gush down my legs. After placing paper towels on the floor to soak up the yuck, and deciding not to bend and clean up my mess, I look at Leia. "That's not a treat." Then I waddle my ass up the stairs.

Naked, hard and ready, my husband, the birthday boy, is sprawled out like a whore's buffet on our big, old bed, and I have to stop to take him in.

He laughs. "You coming in, beautiful?"

I smile and nod. "You can't touch me."

He laughs. "That's one hell of a way to end my favorite birthday so far."

I rub my hand over my belly. "I think you have a couple more gifts on their way."

He cocks his head to the side like an adorable, confused puppy.

"Surprise!" I smile. "My water just broke. I'm going to take a shower, and then we're going to the hospital."

"You're being serious," he states as I grab the belt to my wrap dress and pull it open.

"Yes, very."

He springs off the bed, and I watch as his erection wilts as he gets closer, asking, "What can I do?"

"Get dressed and get the bags that are in the closet. I'll be done in a minute." I walk toward the bathroom as I call over my shoulder, "Any guesses yet?"

"Two babies," he snaps.

I look back, seeing him look around as if he's lost in his own house, which makes me laugh.

"Tessa, how can you be so unbelievably calm right now?"

"I have you, and we're all going to be fine. Now please

go get dressed. The last thing I want to see right now is a frowning penis."

"This is not the time to make jokes."

Walking to the shower, I giggle. "It's not a joke. I literally watched your dick go limp. Saddest thing I've ever seen."

I start the shower.

Lying in the hospital bed, we wait for Dr. Brown.

When he walks in, he asks, "How are you two feeling?"

"Great." I squeeze Collin's hand. Total lie. It freaking hurts.

He looks over the tape. "Your contractions are right on top of each other. How long have you been having them?"

"Since about noon. My water broke an hour ago, and this—"

"Since noon, Tessa?" Collin asks. "Why didn't you tell me?"

"It's your birthday. I wanted you to have a nice time. Until now, they've been perf—" I stop when a contraction begins and hold my breath.

"Breathe, beautiful," Collin whispers.

When it ends, I exhale. "Perfectly fine."

Dr. Brown pulls on his gloves. "Let's check you out."

I look at Collin, expecting him to be agitated, but he's not. *Because he's a grown man*, I remind myself.

Dr. Brown smiles as he removes his gloves. "You are nine centimeters dilated, Tessa. You're going to have these babies very soon."

"Collin, could you text my parents?"

He looks … frozen.

I squeeze his hand. "You're a doctor; you can handle this."

"I wish I could take your place," he whispers.

"Well, that isn't going to happen since they're inside of me."

"Do you want your mom in here?"

"No, just you and I—yyyouch." I squeeze his hand through a contraction. "Sorry."

"Don't be," he says, flexing his hand then sending a text.

"The window for an epidural is closed, but would you like a little something for pain?" Dr. Brown asks.

"No, thank you." I close my eyes. "Just going to nap through contractions."

"Tessa, if you're hurting, please take something. I don't want to see you in pain."

"Dr. Brown, could you get my husband something? I think this is going to be a little rough on him." I open one eye to see Collin shaking his head. "So, I'm guessing boys."

"Are you concerned about them being early?"

"They have been in my belly for long enough. They will be perfect."

At eleven fifty p.m., our first child is born, a beautiful boy with brown, curly hair and big, blue eyes, weighing seven pounds and two ounces, measuring twenty inches long, and arrives all pink and perfect.

Then I labor into the next day before our second son is born. He is six pounds ten ounces, twenty-one inches long, and just as perfect. His hair is a little lighter, and his eyes are exactly the same blue as his brother's.

Collin and I both cry after each of their births, and

when asked their names, we laugh, because it's not something we've really discussed, not with all the travel.

"There is a waiting room full, and it's past visiting hours," Dr. Brown informs us. "But if they come and go quickly, I'll look the other way."

For the next hour, they begin coming in. Mom and Dad first, followed by Molly, who says she'll bring Sydney by when we get settled in at home. Then comes Alex and Phoebe, with Remington asleep in a baby sling attached to Alex, and Kendall, Jake, and Sarah. After they leave, Jade and Ryan pop in, but they do so briefly and give us lots of love. The last person to come in is Tomás. Apparently, he has been pacing the halls the entire time.

"Congratulations, sir and—"

"You come at me with *ma'am*, I'm going to get up and kick your ass, Tomás." I narrow my eyes. "And I will bleed all—"

He curses under his breath in Spanish, and I laugh.

"He's not caved to calling me Collin in all the years I've known him, Tessa. You might as well surrender."

"We have two boys who will not grow up hearing a man who has our backs, and will have theirs if need be, calling you sir." I look at Tomás. "You're family to him, and now me and our sons. Please, I'm asking you, call me Tessa."

"Congratulations …" he pauses, and I swear he may explode as he says, "Tessa."

I look down at our firstborn lying across my lap. "This is Uncle Tomás." I look at our second born. "He's going to be a very important part of your lives."

When I look up at him, I see that what I just said means something to him, and I know he sees that it does to both Collin and me, too.

"Changing lives already, little men."

Once alone, Collin holds baby two as I get baby one to latch on easily. Then, when he's in a booby-juice-induced coma, I take baby two and do the same as Collin burps him.

"You need to rest, beautiful."

"I don't want them to be taken to the nursery. I want them to stay here. I actually just want to go home with my three favorite boys and lay in our bed for weeks, holding you all." Tears fill my eyes.

"They can stay in here, but you're going to rest. But, before that, maybe we could name them so Jade stops messaging me suggestions."

I smile. "Do you have any ideas?"

"I think their middle names should be Ross," he suggests.

"Matthew and Mark? The first two books of the New Testament?"

"Prominent names, but Luke follows that."

Hurt, I shake my head. "My godson's name is Luke, like the Bible, not Lucas."

"Matthew and Mark would be fine."

I shake my head. "I knew I'd name my firstborn after the boy I met at the Cape, so I'd really like his name to by Collin John?" I say it like a question.

He puffs his chest out a bit with pride before saying, "I really like Matthew." He looks at him. "Matthew Ross?"

"I like it. Collin John and Matthew Ross. Are we sure?"

"I like them both. I think they're perfect."

"Matthew means gift from God, and Collin, you were a gift from God, and these two are, as well."

"Yeah, that works."

I crash after we name the babies and sleep nearly eight hours. When I wake, I do so to a table full of flowers. Amongst them is a small lilac bush. Yellow roses and white daisies are from Lucas and Ashley with a card attached that reads:

Congratulations on the birth of your sons.

LYA,

Lucas and Ashley.

White roses and blue carnations are from Ben.

Two boys to occupy the two girls (joking, Collin).

I'm thrilled for you both.

Love ya,

Ben

Collin read the cards, and I can't help but laugh.

"I clearly understand Ben's, but what does *LYA* mean?"

I answer without thinking as I rub my nose across the top of Collin John's little waves. "Love you, anyway."

"Oh."

"Sorry," I say, handing Collin to … Collin and taking Matthew.

Once he's attached, I look down at him. "Your daddy needs to stop asking silly questions if he doesn't want the answer. Tell him, Matthew. Say, 'Daddy, Mommy loves you forever, so stop pouting because it makes Mommy want to bite that bottom lip, and one thing will lead to another and, well, you don't want Mommy frustrated, do you? No, of course not.'"

Collin smiles. "CJ, tell Mommy it's fine and remind her that she still has a beautiful mouth that seems to be in working order."

We both laugh as he leans over and kisses me.

Two days later, we, the Abraham family of four, head home.

When we walk in, the counters are littered with flowers, food, and gifts.

"I am so glad to be home." I smile as I look around, and then I look down at the sleeping babies, one carrier in each of my husband's hands. "Welcome home, little men."

The next two weeks are crazy. Our little men eat every two hours, sleep, pee and poop, are little lovers and love snuggles, and they rarely cry.

I spend my time, unattached to one of them, cleaning and, it seems, constantly refusing my husband's request to having outside help … other than family when they drop in.

When I wake, Collin wakes. When one is feeding, Collin is getting me a drink or snack, and burping whoever last. He is much better at it than I am. Aside from my three men, the most beautiful thing is that we never fight once, and it has been five weeks.

We seriously make a great team.

Lying in bed, I look at the clock and see it's seven a.m., not that it would matter if it were seven p.m.—it's all the same anymore—but what is not the same is Collin's hair.

"Sweetheart?"

He looks at me oddly.

"I get it's the first time I've called you that, but I am trying out nicknames I can actually call you in front of our kids."

His lips twitch up, and CJ burps.

"My point is, you, um … you need a haircut."

He shakes his head, and his waves fall into his eyes. "What? This shaggy look isn't working for you?"

"It works." I lick my lips as I lie back and look up at the celling.

"Tessa"—he stands to put CJ in the bassinet beside his sleeping brother—"we have a few weeks; don't look at me like that."

"Don't tell me what to do." I roll to my side and openly gawk at him.

He flops back and runs both hands through his hair, and I take that opportunity to lean over and take him in my mouth.

Collin lets out a deep groan. "Not fair to you."

I don't care, and I express this by going down in a big way. And when it ends way quicker than expected, I look up at him, expecting him to be questioning his manhood.

"Thanks, wife." He pulls me up and kisses me.

"Anytime, husband. Just ask."

W eek six, and we're both like the walking dead. And this isn't because Mom isn't constantly here to help; it's because, when she's here, I love watching her fuss over them and take a million pictures. Therefore, I do not take the opportunity to sleep, and if I don't sleep, neither does Collin, even when I tell him it's okay to.

When he turns from the open fridge with my cell phone in his hand, he shakes his head. "We need help here, just for a few weeks. A housekeeper, someone to do the shopping or laundry—anything. Just … something."

"No nanny," I say, looking down at Matthew.

"I agree, but a housekeeper, please. I miss you. I know it sounds insane, but if your mom wasn't here, making lists of supplies we need and doing the shopping, she might be able to relax and enjoy them. And if you weren't obsessively bleaching our home"—he laughs—"we might be able to eat a meal together at a leisurely pace or go get our hair cut."

"Fine, but only a few hours, a couple days a week, and not on weekends."

He steeples his hands and looks up, thanking God, not me. "Thank you."

"But they don't take care of the boys."

"Okay, I agree. Our responsibility."

"Our blessing," I coo at CJ, who's lying next us on the couch. Then I look up. "Can we go running together when they nap?"

"Yes."

"Okay, and maybe I can start dancing again." I grin.

"We are doing this so we can rest, right?" he asks, picking up CJ and pulling me against him.

"Yep, and maybe dance."

H is old housekeeper, Joan, is here the next morning. He hugs her—I repeat, he *hugs* her—and she laughs.

"Happy to see me, Dr. Abraham?"

"Ecstatic."

Collin showing spontaneous affection to someone other than me is new.

"Changing lives," I whisper to Matthew as we walk into the kitchen and let them know we are present.

"Wow, that was fast." I smile.

"Sorry, Tessa, but I've been so tired." He walks over and pops a kiss to my cheek and then Matthew's. "CJ awake?"

"Nope, just this little man." I smile down at him as I

walk over and extended my hand. "Hi, Joan. I'm Tessa, and this is Matthew."

I like her immediately. She's in her fifties, petite, has soft, kind eyes, and has worked for Collin for years. Together, we talk to Joan a bit. Then, as I feed Matthew, Collin shows her the apartment above the garage so she can settle in.

"Is your mom coming over today?" he asks as he walks back into the house and follows me up the stairs, just in time for me to hand him Matthew to finish burping him while I grab my sleepy little man to feed in order to keep their schedules close.

"Yes, for a few hours. I should call her and tell her not to bother."

"Tessa, Joan is here, so there are two of them. We haven't left the house in weeks. Come with me to get a haircut and let me take you to lunch."

I agree, knowing this must be hard for him. He spent all his life going nonstop and not having to answer to anyone.

Two weeks later, the fair is in town, and Collin talks me into taking the kids to the parade. I have been adamant about no one touching them, in fear they'll get sick.

"They may actually like being out of the confines of our home," he poked fun at me. "Besides, we have yet to use that double stroller."

"Fine."

Okay, reality check, I've lost all the weight I gained but ten pounds, and yes, that's great, but I am seriously squishy.

This also means putting on clothes, which messes with my head.

So, I wear shorts that will not allow me to eat even a French fry and will probably leave me looking as if I tattooed a belt to my waist; a tank top so at least one part of my body, the one I hid when I was not ready to become a woman, that I like almost as much as my husband does, shows a bit; and cover all that with a long, thin, white linen shirt.

"You look beautiful," he says, looking over my reflection as he walks into the bathroom where I am applying a couple swipes of mascara.

"I feel just the opposite."

"Maybe you'll feel better when you're out of the house."

W alking down the sidewalk with Kendall, I avoid eye contact with everyone we pass by, and this is totally because I do not want anyone to approach me and think they can touch my little men, who are wide awake and looking totally adorable in their little matching navy bibs and overall short sets with little GAP tees.

And the minute I do look up, to the sound of my name, my eyes meet … Sadi Black.

"Tessa Ross, look at you." She throws her arms around me and hugs me. "Amazing."

When I hear Kendall whisper, "Lithium," I can't help but laugh, even though it's rude. I manage to play it off like I'm excited to see her, which isn't hard when I see a little girl next to her.

"Your daughter is beautiful."

She peers into the stroller and squeals, "Two boys? Lucas must be proud."

Well hell, I think, and then I correct her. "They aren't Lucas's. Just wasn't meant to be."

"Oh, I'm sorry. He really loved you."

I steer the conversation away from Lucas and point to my husband. "Sadi, this is my husband, Collin. Collin, this is Sadi Black."

"Nice to meet you." She holds up her hand.

"Likewise." He smiles, politely of course, but I can already tell he's not impressed.

Sadi smiles at me. "So, what is Lucas doing?"

"He's living in New Jersey and is with Ashley. He was at our house for New Year's, but that's the last I have talked to him. I'm sure he is doing great, though. And, how are you doing?"

"Great, happy, still in love." She beams.

"It looks good on you, Sadi."

When we walk away, Collin whispers in my ear, "Pretend pregnancy, Lucas's ex who tried to assault you every chance she got?"

I laugh. "Yep, sure is."

"Why did you talk to her?"

"Why not? It was high school. She was hurt. I'm way past that, and I forgave her." I smile.

Collin smiles back and shakes his head.

We then see Jade, Ryan, and the kids.

"What's going on?" Ryan chuckles. "You got her out of the house?"

"I did. She just doesn't want anyone touching her little men." He laughs as he watches Jade do just that. "Except for Jade, apparently."

"She's practically pulled mine from my vagina, so ..." She shrugs as she snuggles Matthew.

Collin wraps his arms around me. "You going to be all right?"

I look up at him. "Yes, actually."

As my husband lays his lips to mine, I hear, "Look at you four," from behind us.

Lucas.

Collin sighs, and I whisper, "Be nice."

"New year, beautiful." He kisses my cheek then gives me a slight nudge, permission … a blessing. God, I love my man.

When the girls appear, they hug me the same as they always did, and I love that.

"You're seriously this old now?"

"You had two babies," Ally jokes, "so, yeah."

"What are their names?" Alexandra asks.

"Jade has Matthew Ross. He was born right after"—I lean in to pick up CJ—"Collin John, but we call him CJ."

"They are beautiful." Lucas smiles as he looks at Matthew.

"They're pretty perfect," I say, feeling so at peace it's insane. "Thank you."

"May I hold him?" Lucas asks.

Collin laughs. "If you can pry him out of her hands."

I scowl at him, and he winks.

"Go ahead."

As Lucas holds our son, I look into unclouded, crystal clear, brilliant, happy green eyes.

He's … happy.

"You look like your dad, CJ." He smiles at Collin as he ask, "Are they always this quiet?"

"They're wonderful babies," he answers.

Jade hands me Matthew.

"This is Matthew Ross. Can you say hi to the Links family?" I ask as I turn him to face him toward them.

"Matthew Ross, you look exactly like your mommy. Gonna be weird when you grow facial hair," Lucas jokes as he hands CJ to Collin then reaches out for Matthew, who begins kicking. "Little guy, I'm cool. No need to kick me away." Lucas laughs as he takes him.

"He kicks his feet when he's happy," Collin explains, which is truly a gift to Lucas. I know that, and so does Lucas.

And again, God, I love my husband. That was such an act of kindness, forgiveness, and truce all rolled into seven words.

I look away from Collin for fear I will combust right here and see Audrianna, Ashley, and Landon walking toward us.

"They're precious," Audri says as she hugs me. "May I?"

Collin gently hands CJ to her, and she hugs him. "Hello, little one."

Then I notice how Ashley is looking at Lucas's reaction to Matthew and whisper to Jade, "They're going to make beautiful babies."

She winks at me.

"Do you two sleep?" Lucas asks Collin.

"We do now. For what, Tess? Three or four hours a night?"

"Yes, thank God. It was two," I admit.

"You don't have help?" Landon asks.

"She finally agreed, after weeks of no sleep, to allow me to hire a housekeeper, so at least we can get a few minutes alone. But no nanny. They're ours," Collin says proudly.

"Have you told them the news, Lucas?" Landon asks.

"Not yet, Dad. We just ran into them." Lucas chuckles and looks at Collin. "Ash and I are getting married."

I immediately smile at Ashley and hug her. "I'm so happy for you, both of you." Then, because he's holding Matthew, I give Lucas a quick peck on the cheek and ask, "When?"

"Two months. Invitations went out today. You guys are invited, but I understand if you have your hands full." Lucas then looks at me. "You are really happy for me, aren't you?"

"Yes, of course."

"Well, thank you. I don't think I deserve that after the way I reacted to your pending nuptials, but now, looking at these two, not gonna lie, never been happier for you." Lucas laughs nervously.

"We both accepted—"

"My apology," Lucas cuts Collin off with a laugh. Then he looks at Matthew. "You, little dudes, are going to have manners coming out your ears." He then looks at Collin then me. "Thank you, both."

Breaking what could have been an awkward, where-do-we-go-from-here silence, Jade clears her throat. "So, tomorrow night, Adam's band is playing again, Tessa. Do you think maybe you and Collin would like to meet us at the big fair for a couple hours?"

"No, we don't have a sitter." I look at Collin, pleading with my eyes that he has my back.

"I'll come up. I'd love to hang out with the boys," Kendall offers.

"So, it's all set then," Jade says smugly.

CJ starts to get agitated, and Jade, who took him from Audri, hands him immediately to me.

"What's wrong, my love?" I ask, and he turns toward me, beginning to nuzzle into me. "We have to go."

"All right, nice to see you all." Collin takes Matthew

and sets him in the stroller then takes CJ from me. "Not going to work over here, little guy."

———

With his arm wrapped around me, we walk through the entrance to the fairgrounds to watch Adam's band.

"Are you going to make it three hours?" he asks.

I start freaking out. "Two. We said *two* hours."

To this, his lips twitch up.

"Collin, please, I don't like this."

"Okay, beautiful, I won't tease you. But will you try to have a good time?"

"Yes, but I need some incentive."

He shrugs. "I guess I could let you go down on me."

This catches me totally off guard, and I laugh. "Oh, you will, will you? I was thinking maybe you would dance with me."

He rolls his eyes in jest. "Fine."

Walking toward the crowd by the bandstand, I see Jade wave to us. When we get to her, she looks at Collin and hands him a beer and a wine slushy.

He hands me the slushy. "Pump and dump?"

Jade snort-laughs, telling me she's already had a couple. "They sleep better if you don't."

"Is she being serious?" he whispers in my ear.

Sucking some of the delicious slushy through the straw, I shake my head.

"Thank God. I was going to have to change my opinion of her." Collin scowls.

I reach up, grab the back of his neck, and pull him down for a kiss. "I love you. Dance with me."

"Of course."

I finish my drink as Adam finishes Pearl Jam's "Wishlist" and begins "Higher" by Creed, Although it's not slow, per se, my husband dances with me as I sing to him. I send a thank you up to the Good Lord for making a man who is more than I ever could have imagined.

When the song switches, his fingers flex on my hips, and he pulls me closer. I have to step back and look up at him, because I could have sworn I heard my husband, the king of lyric-less music, singing along to Aerosmith's "I Don't Wanna Miss A Thing."

"Are you singing?" I ask incredulously.

He rolls his eyes and pulls me close again.

As the band takes a break, we walk toward the crowd, and I see Jade pointing to me. Then, over the mic, I hear Adam.

"Tessa Ross."

Jade whispers to him.

"Sorry, Tessa *Abraham*. You got five minutes."

Adam hops off the stage and heads to us, hugging me and shaking Collin's hand.

"I haven't done this in forever. I'm not going up there."

"Why aren't you singing?" he asks me but glares at Collin.

Jade hands Collin a beer, which I intercept and toss back before answering, "I've been a little busy. We have twin babies at home."

Laughing, Jade hands Collin my slushie, and he hands it to me.

Knowing I'm not getting out of this, I decide screw it and begin drinking that down, too, as I watch Collin's jaw drop.

I give him an, *I'm sorry* look, and he laughs.

"You're fine. There's enough in the freezer to feed an entire village."

And I shove the thing at Jade and squeeze the sides of my head

"Are you okay?" Collin asks.

"Brain freeze," I whine. "Don't let me drink anymore."

"Okay. Are you going to sing?"

"No."

"But you want to," he states.

"Of course she wants to," Jade said. "And she will." Jade hands me back my drink, and I start sucking it down slower this time.

He slowly shakes his head.

When it's finished, I hand him the empty, and he takes it. "Thank you."

Adam calls me up, and I push up on my toes to give him a kiss. "Changed my mind."

"I knew you would." He winks.

Collin smiles as I sing the same song I did almost a year ago, "Cowboy Take Me Away" by the Dixie Chicks, and then I choose Sara Evans' "I Could Not Ask For More." When I'm done, I give Adam a hug and thank him.

"One more?" he asks.

"Not tonight. I need to get home to my boys."

"Congrats, Tess." He winks as I head down the stairs. Then I run to Collin and jump in his arms.

"Did you have fun?" he asks, smiling, and I nod. "You're amazing."

Then I blurt out, "I want a piano."

"You play?"

"Not well, but I'd like to try again."

Adam's band plays "Slide" by the Goo Goo Dolls.

"*I wanna wake up where you are,*" I sing along as I drag him back out. "*I won't say anything at all, so why don't you slide.*"

I dance, and I do it for him.

"I want you tonight," I whisper in his ear.

"We have to wait," he says then growls.

I start to sing again. "*Put your arms around me. What you feel is what you are, and what you are is beautiful. Wanna get married, run away.*"

As he holds me close, I whisper it again, "I want you tonight. And I'm fine."

He smiles tightly. "Yes, you are, but we're waiting."

He's determined to "follow the rules," and I know it, so I stomp my foot and pull away. When I turn, I hear his laugh and see Lucas and Ashley standing with Jade and Ryan. When my eyes hit his, we both start laughing.

Collin grabs me and turns me toward him. Then he lifts me and tosses me over his shoulder, smacking my ass as we walk past everyone. "We're going home. Thanks, we had fun."

"I think that's the same position she was in the first night we met you." Jade laughs, and I flip her off as he hauls me away then grab two handfuls of his ass.

He lowers me to my feet. "You're going to make this impossible."

I laugh. "I want to sing another song."

"I bet you do." He waves his hand back to the bandstand. "Lead the way."

When I get to Jade, I take her beer and slam it before walking to the stage as Adam and his band start another song, "My Own Worst Enemy," and I see Lucas walking away and toward Ashley, giving her that heart-stopping, Lucas Links, happy, playful smile as he sings to her. He requested it, and I can't help but bust up laughing as Jade and Phoebe, who must have just gotten here, hurry toward me, and we dance, and sing, and laugh ... just like we used to.

When Adam calls me up again, I whisper my song choice in his ear, and he chuckles.

Mic in the stand, I look only at my husband and sing "Whenever, Wherever" by Shakira as my buzz takes hold, and I shake my hips and ass as I sing.

Halfway through the song, he approaches the stage and stands there, looking me over as I sing to him, dance for him, and God, it feels good.

When the song ends, I yell, "You better catch me," and then I jump off the stage, laughing as I whisper, "You can avoid the baby shoot, but there are other places that you could go."

"Did she just say *baby shoot*?" Phoebe laughs her ass off.

I grin. "Take me to bed, cowboy."

Chapter Forty-Nine

Collin

CJ's and Matthew's checkups went impeccably. They're growing and developing as they should, and at a rapid pace. Both our sons are in the ninety-fifth percentile in weight and height.

The pediatrician suggested we supplement one bottle before bed with formula, because they started eating more frequently and, although Tessa is doing great, they may need more.

Since the change, they are now sleeping five hours straight every night in their cribs. That move was difficult, but we managed.

Tessa's appointment was just as good. She could resume "regular activities" as soon as she felt up to it.

After the appointment, we come home and she breast-feeds our "little men" and, as per their norm, they fall asleep. Once they are down, and we are out of their room, we look at each other, and she starts to laugh, which makes me laugh.

"I don't understand why I'm so nervous."

"Tessa, realistically, when is the last time you went six weeks without sex?"

"I don't know," she said. "A year ago?"

Why I ask questions that I do not want the answers to is beyond me, so I simply say, "Oh."

"And, how about you?"

Obviously, she's no different in that sense, but in the what she is referring to, she's not just different; she's everything.

"Before you, I never felt the need to keep track."

She looks up and whispers, "You are so much better at this than—"

I kiss her quiet as I run my hand up her side and over, cupping her breast.

She pulls away. "Can we do this on the bed, please?"

"Uh-huh." I kiss her again as I move us to our bedroom.

Standing at the foot of the bed, mouth to hers, I slide a finger into her waistband and slowly move lower. When I feel her soft curls—natural—she inhales a sharp breath and holds it.

I pull my hand up, reach behind her, and cup her ass, lifting her onto the bed. "This okay?"

"Yes."

"I've missed you, beautiful," I say against her lips, bending and leaning as I kiss her until she's lying on her back. I trail kisses down her neck and am about to kiss her breasts when she scoots up.

"I need a shower." She slides to the side of the bed and

off. "And maybe, you know, leave the boobs alone, because you may get a mouthful."

Sighing, I follow her into the bathroom as I strip off my clothes, leaving them where they fall.

When I get there, she's stepping into the shower and starting the water.

Stepping in, she looks at me and steps back, retreating until her back hits the shower wall.

"This is happening." I bend to my knees as water beats against my back, and I look up at her as I lift her leg over my shoulder, kiss her hip bone, move across it, and slice her open with my tongue.

"Oh God," she says as she grips my hair, and I lick her deeper.

"Collin, stop, please," Tessa whimpers.

Pulling my tongue out of her, I ask, "Do you really want me to?"

She closes her eyes and nods. "Let's go to the bed." Then she opens her eyes and says. "Let's do this."

Soaked, I stand and pick her up, mouth crashing against hers, and walk across the floor from the bathroom to our bed.

When I set her down, she scampers back.

"What's wrong?"

"I am afraid it's going to hurt."

"Valid fear." I move up the bed and lay on my side, facing her. "So, we go slowly."

I lean in to kiss her, and she leans back. "I am not trying to be a pain, but just let's do this." She lies flat on her back and rolls her head, eyes locking on mine. "Just get on me and do me."

Biting back a laugh, I take her seriously beautiful face and kiss her. "I'm not going to just get on you and do you."

She closes her eyes and sighs as she smiles a bit. "Okay."

I move to position myself above her and resume kissing down her neck, avoiding her breasts, not that I care if we have a milk mishap, but she does, so I avoid one of my favorite parts of her body and position myself above her.

Reaching between us, I rub the tip of my cock up and down her seam, and then, when I start to push in a bit, she clenches her knees at my sides.

"I need to feel your warmth, beautiful." I kiss her neck. "I love you so much. Feel me, Tessa. Let me make you—"

Again, she starts to retreat, saying, "You need to put a condom on."

"I'm not sure I'll actually need one," I joke.

"I'm sorry," she says, closing her eyes.

"Don't be. We can work at this all day. Hell, take a couple days. I have no problem with that. Nothing I want to do more than you."

I grab a condom off the nightstand and rip it open. Then I roll it on and notice her watching me. "All yours, Tessa, whenever you want it." I stroke myself a few times as she watches.

She swallows hard before saying, "Now, please." She spreads wide enough to accommodate me and links her fingers behind my neck, pulling me down into a kiss.

I brush my lips across hers as the tip of my cock nestles in her warmth. "You're shaking."

"Don't stop, please. I'm fine. Nervous, but fine. Does it feel the same?"

"Of course. Hot, wet, tight, real fucking tight," I groan. "So good. But if you want to stop, we can." I stay right there, hand raised and ready to knock on heaven's door as she begins rocking her hips.

Kissing her neck, I follow her lead, and when I am

inside, almost fully, I slide a hand between us and rub her clit.

She whimpers against my neck, and then, she moves.

W hen we've both finished, she sits up. "Sorry."

"What?" I ask, annoyed, even though I know where she's going.

"That couldn't have been enjoyable for you."

Pulling off the condom, I tie it off and hold it up. "I beg to differ."

Smiling, she lies back, and I head to the bathroom to take care of the condom.

When I return to see her on her belly, elbows against the mattress and looking at me, I get hard instantly.

"Try that again?" she asks coyly.

By round three, she's back to normal again.

"Fucking beautiful," I growl out my third release.

W ithin a week, the boys are sleeping six hours every night, without either waking, and eating a lot more. We moved to supplementing formula for two feedings.

Maggie insists on coming up one night a week, and we go out to dinner, or shopping, or parking by the pond and making love. As much as we try not to talk about the boys, conversation always leads there.

Since the birth of our sons, I have written two articles that were published in the past eight weeks, and Tessa is working on grants again during their two naps that last between an hour and a half and three hours.

I will be flying out again in a week, but I'll stay only one week. While I'm gone, Joan will be there more. I was ready to fight for that, but Tessa didn't argue.

"We were in survival mode," she said one night, and she was dead ass serious, and I couldn't help but laugh, thankful she found humor in it too.

Leaving them later that week was incredibly difficult. While I was gone, we video conferenced at least twice a day. It was hell not being there, even though I knew they were safe. Catherine was not a threat behind bars.

On day three, I had a piano delivered, and she was ecstatic. Tessa is bound and determined to master it so that she can one day teach our sons, who she said love it when she plays.

Our lives are perfect. Better than perfect, actually.

So perfect that I was the one to breach the wedding invitation topic, and we agreed to go. I'm not sure she realizes it, but the wedding date is exactly the same date we finally met … again.

I will be visiting a new site in Haiti that week, and we maneuver that I will fly into Newark and meet her in Jersey.

Tessa and her family all ride together, Joan and Tomás following, as they will stay the day of the wedding then take Leia back to the Cape with them. Tomás will be picking up me from the airport, and Joan will watch the kids while we attend the ceremony.

Sitting in a pew with my entire family, I keep checking the time and trying to do it so that Ryan, the best man, and Alex, a groomsman, don't notice I'm seriously worried. But I am.

I know Ashley looks beautiful, and Lucas … well, he's Lucas, so he looks amazing. And I know the ceremony is amazing, but I don't pay one bit of attention to it, because this is unlike Collin. He's late, and he hasn't messaged.

After Mr. and Mrs. Lucas Links are announced and they exit, I stand and, instead of watching the bride and groom, I focus on Tomás, who is supposed to be bringing Collin here … to me.

I send him a text.

- Where is my husband?

He reads it and motions for me to head down the side aisle, so I do, nearly running.

When I get closer to him, I see he is … not okay.

"Tessa, there has been an accident."

The first words out of my mouth are, "Is he okay?"

He doesn't say anything, and I feel … faint.

Until we walk back down the aisle, I notice nothing but my wife, *my Ash.* The woman who literally saved me from myself over the past few months. But something finally does catch my eyes.

Tessa and her husband's friend, —or whatever the fuck he is— is holding her up.

"Lucas, focus," my father snips as I watch John and Maggie, who just hugged my wife and me, hurry toward her. "Then go see what's going on."

W hen Ash and I walk down the hall toward her room after Alex informed me that Collin's convoy was ambushed while leaving the village and they lost communication, I feel the tension.

"Not what I thought we'd be doing after saying I do, Mrs. Links, but—"

"She's our friend. Well, your and—"

"Ours."

"Yeah." Ash nods.

"You look damn fine, Ashley Links," I say, trying to ease any discord that she may feel.

She blushes and smiles. "I'll look the same after we check on Tessa."

"I know you will." I wink, and then we walk into the room, where everyone is focused on Tessa, who is holding her two sons and crying softly until Leia growls at me.

Tessa looks up, arms full of babies. "Sorry about this. I—"

"We're just here for support," I say as I sit down on the edge of the bed.

"You need to get back downstairs." She forces a smile. "This is your wedding day."

Fuck, fuck, fuck, I think and nod. "I know, but you need me now."

"No, Ashley needs you. My boys need me." She plays it off like she's being funny, and I am two seconds from … *No. No, I'm not.*

Then hell apparently freezes over because Leia lays her head on my lap.

Tessa and I both look at each other, shocked.

Maggie takes Collin John, and Kendall takes Matthew when Tessa starts to shake.

"I'm fine," she snaps then shakes her head as she pulls her knees to her chest. "I'm sorry. I am so—"

I move to her and hug her. "Everything's going to be okay, Tessa."

Then move the fuck away because she's right; this is mine and Ashley's wedding day.

I stand and pet Leia as I walk over to Ash.

Without me saying a word she whispers, "They wont miss us downstairs for awhile Lucas. It's okay that we stay."

We do, for half an hour before Tomás leaves, and then another hour until I finally look at Ash and say, "We need to go."

She shakes her head, "It's okay."

I leave her side and walk over to Alex. "We'll be back. But we want to know the minute he calls, okay?"

Hand in hand, Ashley and I walk down the hall. I glance over at her and see tears.

"Ash …" I shake my head.

"Are you sure this is what you want?"

"Yes, Mrs. Links." I kiss her and hold her perfect face in my hands. "Do me a favor?"

She nods.

I kiss her again. "I need a couple seconds to get my shit together before we go down and celebrate us. And Ash, I told you that once those words were said—*I do*—there is no going back. So, seriously, just a few—"

She nods. "Of course. I need to run to our room to use the bathroom."

"I'll be up in two."

I hit the button for her then kiss her like a man kisses his wife, one whom he loves.

When the door shuts, I hear a sob rip down the hall. Tessa.

I crouch down and lean against the wall. "Get it together, man. Get it fucking together."

"You need some help standing up?" I hear a familiar voice and look up.

Laughing, I hug—yes, hug—Collin Abraham. "I've never been so happy to see your face in my life."

He stands stiff as a board, and I can't help but laugh some more.

"Let's go."

At their door, I bang on it and throw it open. "Get in there. I'm going to find my wife."

Collin

"Thank God," John prays as he hugs me.

I pat his back, eyes locked with hers as she looks up.

"Everything okay, beautiful?" I ask.

She jumps up and dives off the bed, and I catch her.

"You're okay!"

"Sorry I'm late. I missed my flight." I hug her tightly, maybe too tightly, but I needed this just as much as she does.

Kissing my cheek a dozen times, she says, "I don't know what I'd do without you."

I sit on the bed, situate her between my legs, and hold her. "You'd be strong. You'd live for you and for the kids, Tessa. But I have to tell you, I'm not going anywhere for a very long time."

"Promise me, Collin." She starts crying again.

Holding her, looking at our sons, I promise her.

W hen she wakes up, we are finally alone.

"Collin … I don't know what I would have done." Tessa starts crying again as she lifts my shirt, looking me over. "You're okay. You're really—"

I flip her to her back. "I need to feel you."

A fter making love, we shower.

Stepping out, I ask, "You think we should go down to the reception?"

"It's probably over by now."

"Let's go see. I've been dreaming about you in that dress. Navy blue silk is going to look stunning on you."

When we walk in, everyone still in attendance turns and looks at us, but I simply lead her to the dance floor, where we dance, and no one, not one other person is in this room but her and me.

We don't leave the dance floor until the band ends for the night and when Tessa excuses herself to use the restroom.

Tessa

W hen I walk into the bathroom, Ashley is coming out of a stall, reaching over her head and fighting with her zipper.

I move quickly to her and help her pull it the rest of the way up.

"Thank you, Tessa."

"Of course. And hey, I'm sorry about all that. I didn't even get a chance to tell you how absolutely beautiful you look."

Ashley hugs me, and I can tell she's been celebrating, as she should be. "It wasn't your fault, and thank you." She washes her hands as she continues talking. "You know, we're going to be breaking ground up by Jade and Ryan's soon."

"That's great. Are you excited?"

"I am, but a bit nervous. It's a small town, and I won't know a lot of people." She shrugs as she applies lipstick.

"Well, Jade will be right next door; she will keep you more than entertained. And … I hope you and I can be friends."

She turns and looks at me. "It doesn't bother you at all, does it? Me and Lucas?"

"No, I love Collin, and I do love your husband, but not in the way that is disrespectful to you. But, if it bothers you, I can stop being so friendly."

"No, it doesn't bother me at all. He has changed because of you. Landon changed, my sister changed, his mother changed. I am grateful that he knew you. And I trust him. I know that may sound weird to you, but I do."

"He is definitely different with you, Ashley Links. It's like he's finally comfortable in his own skin. As far as changes in all those people you mentioned … Lucas was ready to change, and he changed them. It wasn't me. It was your husband." I point to the bathroom. "We can do a girl chat soon. I have to pee, and it's your wedding night. Don't you think you should get out there?"

When I come out and she's waiting, I can't help but smile as I wash my hands.

"You ready to get back out there?" I ask.

"Yep." She links her arm through mine, and we walk out together.

"Are you two going to have babies?"

She shrugs. "I hope so. He seems a bit nervous about it."

"He will be a good daddy."

"You think so?" Lucas asks as he wraps his arms around Ashley from behind.

"Yes, I do," I say. "So don't be a jackass."

"You ready?" Collin asks as he approaches.

My eyes fill unexpectedly. "Are you?"

"When are you going to stop crying when you look at me?" He hugs me.

"Collin, I would have died. Do you understand that?" I cry.

"I know you may think that, but as I said, our sons would need you, and you would have been strong for them, Tessa." He wipes my tears. "As I said before, I'm not going anywhere, beautiful."

U pstairs, the boys are awake. He holds them both and watches them as I get ready to nurse. After they are fed and burped, we lay them in the portable cribs and sit on the bed.

"A year ago today, Tessa, I saw you … again, and my life changed. I feel blessed. You have given me the world, one I never even thought I wanted or deserved. Thank you."

"I hope you know that, without you, I wouldn't have ever been happy or full, or have ever felt true love, the love I feel every time I look at you. I'm blessed to have you, and I thank God every day for you."

He hugs me tight, so tight that I feel him hard against me.

I kiss him and whisper, "Can you get a condom?"

W e wake to the beautiful sounds of our now fourteen-week-old bundles of joy, get them fed and ready, and then join our family for brunch.

We all watch as Lucas and Ashley walk in, looking exhausted. Jade giggles, and I can't help but laugh, and neither can Phoebe.

"Good morning." Lucas nods to all of us as he pulls out Ashley's chair.

"Good morning."

After we all eat, our little men start getting fussy.

"They need you." Collin winks at me.

I pick CJ up from the stroller as I stand. "Thank you for the invitation. It was a beautiful ceremony. We're going to take off."

"We'll see you in a couple days?" Jade asks.

"Yes, I'll have the house ready for you all."

"Are we going out on the boat, Collin?" Jade winks.

W e walk into the house, and Leia starts barking. Collin holds up his finger, and she sits. He sets the twins' carriers in the living room then lets Leia out. They are fast asleep, and he doesn't want to wake them. He isn't alone.

I look around and see that Joan, a freaking saint, has stocked the fridge and pantry for us. Then I turn and watch as he walks toward me.

"Their first time here."

"Uh-huh." Collin kisses my cheek.

"We need to set up the room for them."

"Already done." He kisses my neck.

"Show me?"

"You first." He smiles as he pulls my shirt over my head and tosses it.

I pull his up and kiss his chest. "I love you."

"I love you. And right now, I need you." Collin pulls me into the bedroom.

I make quick work of unbuttoning his pants and kneeling in front of him as I pull them down, take him in my mouth, and start giving him the kind of head a woman gives the man she loves after she thought she lost him.

"All right, you need to stop."

Mouth full of him, I shake my head.

"Tessa," he growls. His idea of a warning is more an aphrodisiac and throws my need to suck him off into hyper mode.

"You're amazing," he groans as he comes.

A fter a couple fun days with family at the Cape, they head back, and we follow a few days behind in order to make it to Remington's birthday. The entire family is there, Ashley and Lucas included. And they are seriously in love.

Remington is toddling and looks exactly like Alex. And my husband, he found his family, his people. He even caves to calling Mom, Mom.

One year ... and we don't let a moment pass that we are not aware of each other's every move. We are past the getting to know each other's quirks phase, and all defenses are down. There is never any disrespect to one another, and I know—God, how I know—that he will always and forever have my back.

Camp

Chapter Fifty

Tessa

A week before hunting season, the cabin is finally finished. Ryan has done the work between his full-time job, life with kids, and a wife who is still as in love with him as the day they were married.

Ashley messaged me and asked if it would be all right if they came.

My response:

- You'd better be here!

L eia begins tap dancing on the floor and whining, telling me that Collin is home while I'm in the kitchen and the boys are busy playing on the floor.

I look at the clock and see it's two hours before
schedule

I run and dive into his arms. "You weren't supposed to be here for another two hours, and we were going to pick you up."

When I look into his eyes, the world ... well, it stops.

Regardless of how long it has been since I last saw him —be it an hour or ten days, but never more—I always feel like I should pinch myself to make sure I'm not dreaming. He is the man of my dreams, although I have never dreamt of him. Collin far surpasses any expectations I had of a husband, lover, partner, or friend. I know why. It's because he is a gift to me from God. God gave me more than I could have possibly hoped for.

He gave me Collin.

"I changed my plans. After the last time, I think it's best that you do not know what flight I'm on." He kisses me neck. "Less to worry about."

I step back a touch. "Collin, that's not all right. I need to know where you are. Would you like it if I did that?"

He looks frustrated. "No, I guess not. I just don't want you to worry again. I told Tomás."

"Well, you didn't tell me."

"Okay, I'm sorry. I get it. I won't do it again. Don't be angry at me." He pulls me back into his arms tightly.

Our sons start gibbering, and I can't remain irritated.

"They hear you. Go play with them while I cook."

"Where's Joan?"

"I gave her the day off. We planned to come get you, and everything would have been done around here—"

"She would have cooked," he says, picking up Matthew.

"I like to cook." I pick up CJ and kiss the top of his head. "Almost feeding time at the zoo."

"Still mad at me?" he asks when we walk out of the nursery after putting them down for bed.

"I wasn't mad." I walk into the bedroom and head straight to the bathroom, because I had planned to be showered and looking good when he returned. "I need to shower."

I feel the back of my shirt lift, and then he pulls it over my head. "Me, too."

"I feel nasty. I haven't had you in days. You should give me a few minutes. I would like to shave my legs."

"You have two minutes." He kisses the back of my neck. "Then I'm coming in."

In the shower, I quickly scrub the most important parts then shave my legs and pits.

As I'm shampooing my hair, I hear him come in. Seconds later, he's in the shower with me.

"Can I help?"

"Yes." I turn to him and kneel then grab his hard cock. "Massage the shampoo in, and I will work on this."

He groans, "Will you ever let me go first?"

I shrug.

The next day, we have the boy's well visits, both get shots, and both are still in the ninetieth percentile for weight and height. They will start on solid foods tomorrow.

As they sleep, Joan stays in the house while Collin and I are at Camp. I had a room built off the back and hung a sign above the door. "*DOE CAMP.*"

"That's our designated area," I tell him. "Only little boys allowed, and you. No hunters."

He kisses me. "Do you think we should break it in?"

"If you do it quickly and you're prepared," I say as I pull my shirt over my head.

"Sounds good." He steps out of his pants. "But later, it won't be." He grabs me from behind and bends me over the counter. "Hold on, beautiful," he groans as he thrusts into me, a little rougher than usual. And each time I cry out his name, he moves faster and harder. Then, when he reaches around my waist and strokes my clit, I come, and he follows seconds later.

As I grin and say, "Nice, Dr. Abraham," the door flies open, and Alex walks in then turns right around.

"Good God, do you two ever stop?" Alex yells as he walks right back out the door.

Collin's eyes widen, and I laugh.

"We better get dressed."

K endall comes in with a bottle of wine. "Can you drink with me?"

"I can have a glass or two after I feed the boys, right?" I ask Collin.

He whispers in my ear, "Just don't fall asleep on me tonight."

I whisper back, "If I do, you can take it anytime you want."

Handing me a glass of sweet red, Kendall holds up hers, and I hold up mine. As we tap them together, I say, "To Doe Camp."

Well, my tastes have certainly changed, I think. *Gross.*

José and Kendall split ways a while back. He wanted more than she was willing to give while in school, and she has a wanderlust heart, so traveling around the world while on break from pharmacy school— the most recent was a trip to Ireland—is now the love of her life. They never did any more than kiss, but she cared for him, and I assume, times like this, while away from school and not traveling, she misses having someone.

Grabbing a water, I look toward the door of what is now deer camp, and Ben walks, taps off his boots, and looks up at me, smiling as he comes over.

I give him a quick hug then drag him behind me to the room we deemed Doe Camp. "You have to meet my little men, Ben."

Kendall stands up, looks at Ben, and lifts her chin. "Hey."

"Hi, Kendall." He picks up Matthew and smiles. "You look like a Ross, little guy. Tessa, he looks like you." He glances at CJ. "And you're all Daddy. You'll like me way more than he does, though." Ben laughs, and then CJ laughs.

He looks at Collin. "See? He likes me."

I put the boys down for a nap and, as we exit the room, Kendall stumbles and Ben grabs her.

"Uh-oh, someone has had too much to drink." He looks at me. "When did she get old enough to drink?"

"Two years ago, jackass." Kendall pulls away.

"She's going through some things," I excuse her … behavior, and do so trying not to laugh.

"Sorry. Ben, right? Not jackass," Kendall smarts.

"Jackass is fine." Ben winks, and I swear Kendall blushes, or maybe it's the alcohol.

The four of us play cards, laugh, and sing … Well, Collin doesn't sing but hangs in there.

"You good?" I whisper.

"I don't think I could handle that all the time," he whispers his admittance.

When the boys wake, we take them back to the house, feed them some cereal for the first time, bathe them, and then rock them to sleep. Joan comes over, and then we hop on the Gator and head back to camp to rejoin everyone.

As we're standing around, the door opens and Lucas and Ashley walk in.

Ben laughs out. "Hey, look, Lucas is here … with his wife."

"Hello, Ben. This is Ashley," Lucas says with no hidden amount of sarcasm. "Ash, this is Ben."

Ashley bites her lip to stop a laugh then says, "Ben, I have heard a lot about you. Nice to put a face to the name."

"Don't believe a word. I'm a good guy." Ben winks at her to annoy Lucas.

A bit later, Kendall and Ben are singing and dancing when Lucas looks at me and shakes his head. Then, as he walks by, he says, "This is not okay."

"He's a good guy. Give him a break."

"Tessa, you haven't drunk with me yet," Kendall slurs.

"I'll sing with you."

And so we do. We sing along to Van Morrison. "Brown Eyed Girl" becomes brown eyed squirrel and "Moon-dance," moon walk, and then I make Collin dance with me to "Crazy Love."

"You're getting drunk, aren't you?"

"If I have to deal with this, you bet your ass I am." He kisses me.

"Slow down. I don't want *you* to fall asleep on me."

He cups the back of my head and deepens the kiss. I moan as his tongue strokes mine.

Pulling back, I whisper, "You taste damn good. You need to stop."

"You don't mean that." He kisses me again, just like that.

"No, but I think Kendall is going to need us here for a bit." I nod toward Kendall as she stumbles back to Doe Camp.

He presses his forehead to mine. "All right, but we're not through with this."

When we walk back to the room that is now officially Doe Camp, even during deer season, we find Kendall sitting on the floor, laughing as all the older guys have either left or gone upstairs. Alex, Phoebe, Jade, Ryan, Lucas, Ashley, and Ben trickle into the room where we all sit and enjoy the Kendall show.

She flops back on the floor and looks at the ceiling. "I'm not good at this drinking business."

"It's genetic." Alex elbows me.

"So, your sister says she wants to go hunting in the morning. I offered to teach her." Ben grins at me.

"She isn't a very good shot." I laugh because it's true.

Ben lifts a shoulder. "I can teach her."

Kendall rolls to her stomach, rests her chin on her hands, and looks at him. "Yes, you can." She then starts to giggle.

"You can't be serious?" Lucas snaps.

"Why?" Ben asks.

"You fucked around with her sister!"

Ben smirks. "No, actually … we never fucked, Lucas."

"Lucas, really, you're going to criticize him about sisters?" I shoot back.

Lucas hisses, "Tessa, you sucked his—"

Collin raises his hands in the air. "I wasn't around then, but this I never heard."

"Well, there isn't much to tell." Ben chuckles, and I snort-laugh.

Lucas keeps on. "Only because you got pulled over by the cop you passed when she was—"

"Yeah, that was funny shit, huh, Tess?"

"No, actually, it wasn't. You basically told the cop what I was doing, and he gave you an *atta boy*."

"You did what?" Kendall asks.

"Nothing you need to know. Go back to sleep or La La Land"

"You were such a ho." Kendall snort-laughs.

"No, she wasn't," Ben defends me. "She was just dealing with an asshole. She was a good girl, and high, I think."

Lucas laughs. "Pissed, if I remember correctly."

"Shut up, Lucas." I laugh then look at Collin. "Are you okay?"

"Tessa, the more they talk, the more I realize how lucky you are," Collin says, serious as the day is long.

Everyone, including me, laughs, except Lucas and Ben.

I kiss him. "I love you."

"I know." He winks.

"Who needs a drink?" Ben stands up, laughing to himself, and then walks out without waiting for a response.

When he comes back in, he hands out drinks.

I hold my hand up. "All set."

Laughing, he points at Lucas then Collin. "You two are both idiots."

"Ben," I gasp.

"I'm overstepping here, but your wife"—he looks at Lucas—"can't even stand the sight of alcohol right now. I don't know what the girls looked like before, but they're pretty damn big. Bigger than the pictures on your Six Degrees page."

He then turns and looks at me. "You haven't drank. And no disrespect, Collin, but those two boys should have drained them down a bit over the past almost five months, and they're huge." Ben points to Ashley then me. "Are you two pregnant?"

"No!" Ashley and I both exclaim at the same time.

"Okay." Ben shrugs as he sits down and smiles smugly.

"What are you? The fucking pregnancy police?" Lucas snaps at him.

"Nope, I just know boobs. They're my favorite things in the world." Ben chuckles. "The booze was just obvious."

I look at Collin, and he at me. I then look at Lucas and Ashley, who are both deep in thought.

Then Ashley cuts her eyes to me and stands. "Tessa, can you take me downtown? I don't know my way yet, and I need to grab a few things."

"Sure, nobody else around here can drive." I stand. "You need anything, Collin?"

"Yes. But I can wait."

Ashley and I return from the drug store and stop at the house. While she uses the bathroom, I check on the boys, who are both sleeping happily.

As soon as my feet hit the bottom step, Ashley says, "Your turn."

When I finish, we both sit at the island and watch the clock. When the egg timer goes off, we both jump up.

Outside the bathroom door, I grab her hand. "Ready?"

"I think so."

***

When we walk into camp, Ben grins. "So, was I right?"

"About what?" Collin and Lucas both ask.

I crook a finger at Collin, and Ashley holds her hand out for Lucas.

When we leave Doe Camp, I hear Ben laugh.

***

At the Gator, Ashley grabs the bag and asks nervously, "Which one was yours?"

"I don't know, but I don't think it really matters much."

When I look up at Collin, I see he's caught on. I expect him to be shocked, because I was until I pinpointed the moment, but he's not. He reaches out, takes my hand, and pulls me into his arms.

Ear against his pounding heart, I look at Ashley and Lucas and see he's confused. And when she hands him the stick, he looks at it then pulls her into a seriously sweet embrace, his chin on her head as he whispers, "Love you, Ash." And I see he's worried.

"It will be different this time," I tell him.

"But she's going to be a real pain in the ass." Collin chuckles, using the same line Lucas used when he figured out I was pregnant with the boys.

He looks down at Ashley and kisses her. "Thank you." She kisses him back, and then he asks, "Are we good?"

"Yes, we are. So are they."

He looks over at us.

Obviously, Lucas missed that I'm knocked up again, because he laughs. "No way?"

"Yes way." I laugh.

Collin lets go and waves toward Lucas. Then my drunk and seriously amazing husband hugs Ashley. "Congratulations."

Lucas and I step toward each other and give each other a quick hug.

Collin laughs. "You're going to have a girl, Links."

"That shit's not funny, Abraham."

"Yeah, it is. I have two boys, fifty-fifty chance I'll have three. It's really funny."

I elbow Collin. "And our boys are going to treat whoever they end up with just like their daddy treats me."

Lucas and Collin are laughing and joking with one another when I notice Ashley is clearly worried.

I hug her. "Your wedding was quite eventful."

"I guess so."

"What's wrong?"

"Just nervous about how he is going to act," Ashley whispers.

"Are you kidding me? He'll be the best he's ever been. I can almost guarantee it. Take full advantage." I squeeze her a bit tighter.

When we walk back into camp, everyone is laughing and chatting.

Ben looks up. "So, Jade and Phoebe have something to share."

Phoebe grins. "Pregnant."

"Pretty sure I am, too," Jade says, looking exhausted.

Ben winks at me. "You happy?"

"Exhausted, but yes, very happy." I look up and smile at Collin.

"You're done breastfeeding. I want those back for a few months. I miss them."

"Oh my God, be quiet." I cover his mouth, and his brows shoot up. "Tomorrow, when you're sober, you'll be happy I did that."

"You should try breast milk. It's good stuff," Ryan interjects.

He nips at my hand, and I pull it back. "I have twins. I can't take away from them."

"You haven't even tried it?" Ben asks.

Collin scrubs a hand over his face, leans back, and looks at the celling. "We have an entire freezer full of the stuff. Liquid gold. Tastes amazing, like—"

"All right chatty, you're going to be aggravated that you were so talkative tonight."

"Chatty?" Alex laughs. "What does that make you? Screamy?" Alex asks, referring, I suppose, to this afternoon.

Collin nuzzles into my neck and chuckles as I scowl at my brother.

"Phoebe … I'm sorry if my brother doesn't make you scream."

"Oh, he does." Phoebe sighs.

"Phoebe," Alex warns.

"Oh, Alex, leave her alone," Phoebe warns, "or you can sleep on the couch tonight."

We all laugh.

I look down at the floor and see Kendall out cold. She missed the whole thing. "I think we need to get Kendall back to our place."

"I can get her." Ben wags his brows.

I point at myself as I climb off Collin's lap. "I shoot well. Remember that tomorrow."

Collin stands then scoops up Kendall.

"Hey, where is Ben?" Kendall laughs as she wraps her arms around Collin's neck.

"I will see you in the morning, Miss Ross," Ben calls to her as we walk out.

Kendall giggles. "Maybe … maybe not."

In The Name

Chapter Fifty-One

Tessa

Collin and I spent the holidays with family, but our first Christmas morning was just me and my men. That night, I sat and played piano for a while, at his request.

Pushing my hair over my shoulder as he sits, straddling the bench and looking at me, he asks, "Why don't you sing anymore?"

"I'm still making music, just with my hands and not my voice."

He places sheet music on the piano. "When I get back from my next trip, I want you to sing while you play this for me."

Aerosmith's "I Don't Want To Miss A Thing."

While he's away, when the boys sleep, that's what I do.

I learn the song that I'm now pretty sure he sang to me at the fair, and every damn time, I cry, because I miss just one thing—him.

Collin is now traveling alone for a week every month. I hate it, and he hates it, but we know what he has started is so important. And I don't feel as if I'm not a part of it. In fact, I know bringing in money with grants, searching for donations, and working on finding less expensive suppliers is an important part. I am working, and I am able to do so while taking care of two amazing little men.

By spring, I am exhausted all the time, and he starts to get worried, so he cuts his trip short and surprises me by being at the OBGYN office when I walk in. And me, being exhausted and emotional, I cry.

As I lie on the table, him holding my hand, he asks, "What's your guess?"

I run my hand over my belly. "Girl. I feel different."

"I think so, too."

During the exam, we find out we are right. We're having a sweet little girl.

"Now I can start her nursery." I smile, looking at the sonogram.

"Whatever you want is yours." He hugs me, kisses my cheek, then leans back. "But when you speak to Ashley, I want to make sure they think we are having a boy."

I laugh. "We have two; isn't that enough worry?"

Collin doesn't laugh; he simply shakes his head.

"You're leaving me again." My lip wobbles.

"Hey." He wraps his arms around me tightly. "Just for a week. But, beautiful, we can figure something else out if it's too much."

"No, you love your work."

"I love all this more."

"Our plan is going to change. The traveling with the boys, that's going to have to be pushed ahead."

"We'll see. But say the word, Tessa, and I'll figure it out."

I sigh. "Well, let's see, we could work at a hospital and be away from them for forty plus hours a week, or do what you love. My mom saw my dad less, and they ended up splitting up. We're fine. Just estrogen overload, I think."

After I get myself together, we take the boys to the park and play. Then we bathe them and watch them crawl around the house as we cook them dinner, feed them, and rock them to sleep.

Just like every time he leaves, Mom and Dad come over to watch the boys so we can go on a date. But tonight, when we come home, the boys are awake and crying. Both have low-grade fevers due to teething.

Tylenol is served, holding and rocking commences, and soon, they are asleep. Finally, we both drag ourselves to bed and pass out.

I wake to him kissing me and look at the clock. "It's two in the morning."

"I know," he says, kissing lower as he pushes up my nightgown.

"Sneak attack?"

"Mmmhmm ..." He rolls me to my side, pulls my knee over his hip, and then slide his fingers inside of me, and I moan as he readies me. Then he slides slowly inside me, and I clench around him as I whimper.

The next morning, I make breakfast as he finishes up getting things ready for his trip.

When he walks down, he's carrying two handsome little men, dressed and ready for the day.

I smile. "Good morning."

"You look very happy this morning." Collin winks as he sets the boys down then walks over to me.

"I woke up very happy—twice."

"Did you get enough sleep?" Collin asks before kissing my neck.

"No, I'll sleep tonight." I turn to flip the omelet and gasp. "Oh, Collin, look."

Matthew has pulled himself up and is cruising.

"Video camera." I point to where I keep it handy.

"Got it."

"Come on, Matthew." I kneel down and hold my hands out, and he takes three steps before falling on his butt. Collin and I both cheer and clap.

He grins big.

"Did you get it?" I ask.

"Yes, I did. CJ, my man, your younger brother is showing you up." Collin sets the camera down and holds his fingers out for him. "Come on, buddy."

CJ just looks at his hands then up at him.

Collin laughs. "Not going to happen, huh?"

"Tell Dada when you are ready," I coo.

"Dada," CJ chants.

I grab the camera, laughing. "At their own pace."

"CJ will be telling Matthew what to do in no time." Collin chuckles.

At ten months, Matthew has taken his first steps, and CJ is starting to talk.

"I don't want to miss a thing."

I look at Collin and see sorrow in his eyes. Setting the camera down, I walk over and hug him. "Whatever you need, we'll figure it out."

The boys go down for their morning nap, and so do Collin and I. Two out of four actually sleep, and it's not us.

***

When Mom and Dad come over to watch them again so I can take Collin to the airport, we tell them the news, that we're having a girl.

"Third child and a girl, Tessa?" Dad laughs. "Have fun with that. You, Jade, and Aunt Josie. Keep that in mind."

I laugh. "Thanks a lot, Dad."

He kisses my cheek, still chuckling. "Oh, and by the way, Troy's in love again. Gonna get married this summer. Best mark your calendar."

"He and Carmen back together?" I ask, grabbing my purse.

"No, new girl he met at college. Her name's Emma," Mom says, giving Collin then me a hug before we walk out the door.

***

"You know it gets harder to leave you guys every time. It's supposed to get easier."

I squeeze his hand. "I'm sorry, Collin."

"It's not your fault, Tessa. My choice."

"Well, another year, and we can all go together. Dependent on the places you travel, of course. But you do get to choose, right?"

"The whole team chooses, but I could try to sway it." Collin smiles. "So maybe … Forget it. I have a week to try to figure it out."

W hen I walk into the house, Mom walks up and hugs me. "Is it easier to say goodbye now?"

"No, and it's getting harder for him, which makes it worse." I give her a squeeze. "How were my babies tonight?"

"The Tylenol you gave them before you left worked."

"Would you like—"

"You need to head up to bed. You look exhausted."

After they leave, I lock up, and that's exactly what I do. I head up and crawl into the full-sized bed that Collin set up in their room so I can sleep with them when I needed to, and tonight, I need to.

W hen he calls, I wake up, and so does CJ.

"Hello," I whisper as I pick CJ up, hoping he doesn't wake Matthew.

"Hello. Are you in the boys' room?"

CJ starts babbling *Dada*, and Collin laughs.

"Come here, buddy. You're going to wake up your brother." And that's exactly what happens, but he doesn't cry. Matthew just starts babbling *Dada*, too.

"Okay, let's go you." I drop the phone when I start to pick him up then laugh as I grab it. "Sorry."

"Was that Matthew?"

"Yes, and you didn't miss it."

"Can you put me on speaker?"

"Yes, just give me a second." I set the phone next to the rocker, grab their pacifiers, and set them beside it, too. Then I grab Matthew and head over to try to get them settled down again. It takes a while because Collin talks to them as they look at the screen like it's magical.

"You need to sleep," Collin says softly.

"I will. Their teeth are probably bothering them." I yawn as I rock them. "How was your flight?"

Collin chuckles. "Interesting."

"What does that mean?"

"Remember the girl from the first day we met?"

"How can I forget?"

"She is a flight attendant and was on the flight. It was very uncomfortable."

"Oh."

"Are you jealous?" he asks, and the amusement in his voice ticks me off.

"Should I be?" I snap quietly.

He laughs. "No."

"It's not funny."

"I get to rub elbows with your ex several times a year. I was on a six-hour flight with her, and you're jealous."

"I know how much you like airplanes," I grumble.

"I like you on airplanes," he says with a smile in his voice.

"Great."

"Tessa, I love you."

"You, too," I snip, and he chuckles again. "You know it's not that funny."

"I'm sorry," he says, now at least trying to mask his amusement.

"No, you're not, but let me tell you why you should be. My ass has been pregnant for almost two years, hormones raging, puking, exhausted, and you all fine-looking and … well … just you. So if you get jealous over them, you're a jackass. I'm mad now and tired, and I'm going to sleep. I'm glad you're there safe. Are you in for the night or are you traveling more?"

"Tessa, don't be mad. I'm sorry."

"I accept your apology, but sorry doesn't always make it better. Are you in for the night?"

"No, I'm going to the village. I slept on the plane," he says softly.

"Well, let me know when you get there, please. Say goodnight to Daddy. Collin, you're on speaker. Tell them goodnight."

"Goodnight, boys. Please tell Mommy that I am sorry I upset her. I love you all. Goodnight."

"We love you." My voice catches.

"Tessa, don't," he whispers.

"Sorry, I'm just tired. We will call you tomorrow. Please text me and let me know when you get to the village."

"I love you."

"We love you. Be safe. Goodnight."

Once the boys are asleep, I lay them down then reply to his text, telling him to sleep well. Then … I crash.

D ad comes up the next day and rototills the garden, as I asked. The boys play in the little fenced-in area that he put up earlier that morning, and Leia does circles around the perimeter as if she's keeping the prisoners inside it.

"Thanks, Dad." I hug him.

"You really going to plant this whole thing?"

"Yep. I have a week before Collin comes home, and I want to be busy."

"All right. Just don't do it all in one day. If you need help, give us a call." Then he walks over and plays with the boys while I get to work.

A little while later, my cell rang.

"Hello, Collin."

"Hello, Tessa. You sound better. Did you get any sleep?"

"Yes, I did. I'm sorry about last night."

"So am I."

"Listen, I shouldn't have been rude to you. I know we love each other, and I also want you to tell me things like that. So, by being bitchy, you second-guessed yourself, and that was wrong on my part. Thank you for telling me. That said, the boys are playing with Grandpa John right now. He came here very early this morning and made a surprise for them."

"I love you so damn much, Tessa," he says, as if it physically hurts, and then he takes a deep breath. "What did Grandpa make?"

"He fenced in a small area for them to play in."

"Tell him what else you made me do," Dad yells.

"What else, Tessa?"

"You'll see when you get home. It's really no big deal."

"But you won't tell me?"

"No, not yet." I walk over to the fence and hit speaker. "Hey, boys, Daddy is on the phone. Say, hi Dada."

They both babble *dada*, and my dad chuckles.

"Hi, baby boys. I miss you." And boy, do I feel those words.

"You're going to make me cry if you keep sounding like that."

"They're getting so big so fast."

After the call, I set to planting. I plant pumpkin and sunflower seeds, and lots of them, because I wanted amazing summer and fall pictures of my little loves surrounded by them. Then I plant zucchini, squash, cucumber, and tomatoes. After that, I feed the boys lunch, and then they take a nap, and so do I.

When I wake up, I am sore and laugh, thinking I'm getting too old for this.

The four of us—Jade, Ashley, Phoebe and I—get together that night to exchange prego info at Doe Camp, and we all bring a dish.

The information? Phoebe is having boys, Ashley, and I are having girls, and Jade's baby is being very uncooperative. I am secretly shocked that Lucas is even capable of creating a girl. He's the king of finishing doggy-style. Of course, I don't mention that.

We eat as the kids, older and younger, play near the pond. Phoebe and I take a ton of pictures, and Jade suggests we do a maternity shoot.

"What's that?" Ashley asks.

"Hot prego pictures." Jade wags her brows. "That's how I told Ryan about baby two. Tessa's idea."

We plan to meet the next night.

The next day, I finish the garden and am exhausted again, but when the boys sleep, I start researching ideas about places in the US that we may be able to help. I find several and write all my ideas down. I want to focus on healthcare and women and children empowerment. I spend several hours on it and even apply for some grants. I want to see the response I get before mentioning it to Collin. Then I call him.

"Hello, Tessa."

"Hello, Collin. Are you tired?"

"I am actually. It's been kind of hectic here."

"You're safe, right?"

"Yes, I am."

"Then go to sleep and call me later. I want you rested when I see you in five days."

"Really? Why?" he asks, sounding more upbeat.

"Because I miss you very much," I tease.

"I'm missing you, too."

"So, we got together and exchanged baby news tonight."

"And?"

"Phoebe is having a boy, Jade's bundle is not showing the goods, but she is thinking boy, and Ashley, and I are having girls."

"Lots of Ross boys." He laughs.

"And little princesses for them to all look after. By the way, what do you think of a white crib, like the one you picked out for the boys?"

"I like it. Antique white?" he asks.

"More like a worn white. I want her room to have a beachy, Cape vibe. Does that make sense?"

"Perfect sense. Will you let me work on that?"

"Sure."

"So, you miss me *very much* still?"

"Uh-huh." I grin, knowing where this is leading.

We spend an hour on the phone, and he seems much happier when we end the call.

Jade, Phoebe, Ashley and I do the photo shoot as Joan feeds the kids. It's fun. Hell, even Ashley loosens up.

I then run into camp and grabbed the *"Doe Camp"* sign. We stand in a line and bare our bellies. Jade, Ashley, and I wear pink camo ribbons with a bow wrapped around our bellies, and Phoebe wears a green camo. We set up the tripod and do shots of us together. Then the girls and I go to the house, where Joan has the kids watching TV. Remington is asleep on Lukie's lap, Riley and Jackson are asleep on the couch, and CJ and Matthew sleep on Joan's lap. I must have taken a whole roll of film.

After they all leave, the boys wake. I ask Joan to take the film to the city to the one-hour photo lab before they close. Then I bathe the boys and feed them a snack, hoping to get them back on schedule, since it's already passed their bedtime.

When I put them down and they fall asleep, I basically army crawl out of the room so I didn't wake them and head downstairs, seeing that Joan has left the envelope of pictures on the island.

I scoop them up and head to my desk. I message the girls that I have the pics, and they all must be super excited about it because they all message back, they're on their way.

Within twenty minutes, we're pouring over pics when I hear someone walking toward the office, and I stand.

Kendall walks in. "Whatcha doing?"

"Come see." I wave her in.

"They're amazing," Kendall says as we look through the pictures. "You should do Christmas cards from Doe Camp to all the hunters, or open season invites."

We all agree.

"So, what are you doing here, really?"

"Well, I kind of wanted to talk to you."

It hits me like a ton of bricks. "Ben?"

Kendall blushes. "Yep."

"You didn't …?"

"No, ho." Kendall laughs. "But I … Well, he and I really like each other, and I want to go visit him on my next trip. So, how do you feel about that?"

"Kendall, I love Ben, and I love you. The thing with him was high school and a long time ago, like a hundred years almost. I would love for you two to be together." I smile. "His idea of what relationships should be is perfect. Well, back then, anyway. And you, Kendall, would never be bored. He is absolutely perfect for you and you for him."

"So, what would you say if he and I became boyfriend and girlfriend?" Kendall asks, turning even more red.

"I would say I am so happy for both of you," I tell her as I hug her.

Ben peeks around the door. "Safe to come in?"

"Yes, Ben. I've missed your face." I hop up and hurry over to him, grabbing his cheeks then hugging him.

"So, you're giving us your blessing?"

"Yes, and a warning. If you ever hurt her, I will shoot you through the heart. Oh, and she and you can both wait, right?"

"Tessa, you were banging Lucas for years and look how that turned out, I think I can wait," Kendall says.

My jaw drops.

"Oh God, Ashley ... I'm so sorry. Tessa, I'm sorry."

"You had sex with Lucas?" Ashley asks, sounding surprised.

"Ashley, I'm sorry," I play along.

"Kendall," Ben scolds her.

"Don't scold her!" I snap at him.

Ben laughs. "Don't yell at me, Tess."

Then I start laughing so hard I cry. Sitting down, I get a cramp and hug my belly.

"Everything okay, Tess?" Ben asks.

"Yeah, I think so. I just need to sit for a minute." I grab my phone to time what feels an awful lot like contractions.

"Tessa, is everything okay?" Jade asks. "Because I'm overdue, and if you go before me, I'll freak out."

"No, I'm sure it's fine." But I am not. Not at all.

"All right, you need to go to the damn hospital," Ben says. "Kendall, I don't do babies yet. Can you?"

"Ben, I'm fine. I could use some water, though. I think I just overdid it today."

I then look at Phoebe. "Can you please call Mom?"

I am totally not fine and freaking out, but there are four of us, and if they start, I will likely lose my shit.

M y blood pressure is elevated and, yep, I am having contractions.

"Dad, could you give me my phone, please? It's in my bag."

"Are you going to call Collin?"

"I'm going to check on the boys. *I'll* call him if I need to."

But as I look down to call Kendall to check on the boys, my phone rings. Collin.

"Hello, Collin, how are you?"

"I'm good. How are you, beautiful?"

"Well, I want you to listen and not freak out, okay?"

I proceed to tell him where I am and that I don't know anything yet, but as soon as the doctor comes in, I will put him on speaker and he will know when I do.

"I'll wait. Who is there with you?" he asks calmly.

"Mom and Dad."

"Are you all right?" he asks just as calmly.

"Scared," answer him before turning to my parents.

"Mom, could you give me a minute alone, please?"

Mom nods, and then she and Dad leave the room.

"Sorry. I have some good news. Kendall and Ben are dating."

"That's great," Collin says, and I hear him slamming drawers.

"Collin, this could be nothing. Stop packing."

"Okay."

But it's not okay, and he is still packing.

When the doctor comes in, I put the phone on speaker.

"You're showing signs of pre-eclampsia. Although there was no protein in your urine, your blood pressure is high. We're going to keep you in the hospital and continue to check your urine for a few more hours. You'll then be home and on bed rest until you deliver."

"Dr. Brown, this is Collin. I would like you to keep my wife in the hospital until I come and pick her up. She's stubborn and bedrest won't work unless someone ties her ass down. If that's a problem in regard to insurance not covering it, I don't give a fuck. I'll pay for it.

"Tessa, keep your ass in bed, and I'll be there as soon as I can. I'll call Joan and give her instructions." I hear a door slam.

"Dr. Brown, is there any way that I caused this to happen?" I ask, knowing the answer.

"No, it just sometimes happens."

"Did you hear that, Collin? I didn't do this!" I yell.

"Regardless, I'll be picking you up," he snaps.

"Like hell you will. I'm going home as soon as I can. I'm so pissed at you right now. Have a safe trip … Hopefully, it's a full-service fucking flight!" I end the call.

"Tessa, you need to calm down," Dr. Brown instructs. "Blood pressure, remember? I'm going to give you some meds for your blood pressure, and then you are going to get some rest."

"No, I want to go home," I say then begin to cry.

Mom and Dad walk in.

"Tessa, don't cry." Mom hugs me.

"I'm so mad, Mom. He thinks it's my fault."

"No, honey … I'm sure he's just scared," she says soothingly.

"Well, that's great. What does he think? That I'm having a great time here?"

My phone rings, but I ignore his call and toss it on the bed.

Mom pushes the phone back toward me. "Tessa, he needs to know what is going on."

"No, he needs to be supportive, and I need to calm down, and that certainly isn't helping."

The nurse comes in and pushes meds into my IV, and I immediately feel the effect.

"Nice," I sigh out. "Mom, I'm going to be super high. Please go take care of my little men. I need them to see you if they wake up. Ben will have them bouncing off the walls."

"She's asleep now. Yes, you heard right. She is pretty out of it," Dad says into his phone, and I know it's Collin.

I begin to try to get up.

"Tessa, don't do that," Dad says, holding my hand.

"Daddy, please take me home. I'm going home. I'll sign whatever I need to."

Then I fall asleep again.

When I wake up, I rub my eyes and try to stand.

"Hello, Tessa."

At hearing his voice, I close my eyes and lie back.

"Hello. How was your flight?"

"It was fine. How are you feeling?" he asks, lying on the bed next to me and pulling me closer.

"Great. How are the boys?"

"Your mom said they are still asleep. Apparently, Ben played with them until they passed out." Collin rubs his nose across my cheek.

"Good. When can I go home?"

"Dr. Brown will be back in about two hours from now, and we'll find out then." He kisses my forehead.

I turn away and lie on my side, giving him my back. I hear him take a deep breath and release it slowly.

"Tessa, I was scared. I was a long way away from you, and I wanted to make sure you were all right. I'm sorry I upset you, but I'm not going to apologize that I wanted you here until I knew you were going to be all right. So, I'm sorry … sort of."

"I *sort of* accept your apology."

"Then please move back over here."

"I wouldn't want my blood pressure to rise. Then you might feel it's your fault."

"Tessa, come here." He turns me to face him.

Lip quivering, I admit, "I'm scared."

"Me, too. Me, too. Please rest, Tessa."

We eventually went home, and Collin took care of me, the boys, and Leia while I was on bed rest and could not be active any more than one hour a day. That hour, I used to shower and play with my boys. It's hell but necessary to keep our little one safe and in my belly for as long as possible.

My blood pressure spiked thirty-six weeks, and everything indicated that our little girl was ready to meet the world.

Collin and I went to the hospital that day, and I was put on a Pitocin drip and my water was broken. Then it hit me hard after only two hours. My contractions were one on top of the other, but I was not dilating fast. Collin rubbed my back and tried to soothe me. He did everything he could think of, but I was in pain.

"Tessa, it's all right to get something to relax you, or to stop the pain," he said several times throughout the day.

I didn't talk much at all. I concentrated on breathing and focusing through the pain. It was nine hours straight until I was finally dilated eight centimeters. When he went to the bathroom was when I finally broke down and cried.

"Tessa, don't you think that enough is enough? You're tired," Collin says trying to remain calm as he rubs my back.

I just shake my head.

An hour later, I ask him to get the doctor.

Dr. Brown comes in and checks me. I am finally ten centimeters dilated after twelve hours of grueling labor.

I push for an hour straight, and then I cry like I never have before when our daughter is born.

She has blonde, curly hair and big, blue eyes. She weighs six pounds seven ounces and is nineteen and three-quarter inches long. She is beautiful, her lips full and lovely. She looks like our Matthew, but softer. No other girl in the world will be as loved and protected as she will be.

"I love you girls so much," Collin whispers as a tear rolls down his face.

Harper Ann Abraham is here. She is safe and healthy. However, my blood pressure is still dangerously high, and I have to stay in labor and delivery when they take Harper to the nursery. I sob, knowing that I won't be able to keep her with us for her first night. Harper hasn't even latched on.

Collin holds me until the sleep medicine kicks in, and as I am falling asleep, he promises me that he will stay with her in the nursery for the entire night, as soon as he knows that I'm okay.

T he next morning, I wake up, and he looks exhausted. "You should go home and sleep."

"Good morning." He kisses me softly. "I'm not going anywhere. Harper is doing very well, you're going to be moved—your blood pressure is down—and your parents are going to be bringing the boys up as soon as I give them the word."

"I didn't see them much yesterday."

"Tessa, they're fine, you're fine, and our little girl is perfect. Don't be sad."

"And, how are you?"

"Much better now." He brushes his lips across my knuckles. "Would you please rest?"

"If you do."

Two days later, we go home.

Over the next two weeks, I am overwhelmed with company and Collin constantly asking me if I am all right.

"I'm going to take a walk. Alone."

I walk to the pond with Leia, sit on the dock, and look over the water. I am happy with my life. So happy, in fact, but I feel an emptiness inside me that I have never felt. I have no idea why, but I know that's extremely upsetting. I sit and cry for a long time, holding my knees and rocking myself

When I hear the Gator, I wipe the tears off my face as the engine stops. Then I turn to see Collin walking toward me. He looks as if he's wondering what's going on, as if it's hurting him to see me hurting. I wish he hadn't come, because I have no answers.

Sitting next to me, he looks over the water. "I'm not sure what's going on, beautiful, but for the past few days, you've been very distant."

I bury my face in my knees.

"I feel kind of helpless right now. I want to make this better for you, because I love you so much more than I did the first time I saw you. And Tessa, that's saying a lot. I love you more than the day I saw you dancing in the rain, which was the first time I told you I loved you. So, whatever it is, beautiful, you gotta tell me, because I need to fix it for you."

I don't even know what to tell him, because I don't know what my problem is. "If I knew, I would tell you. I promise." I turn my head and look at him. He's smiling.

"You ready to go back?"

"No." I lean into him and wrap my arms around his waist.

He rubs my back when, all of a sudden, raindrops begin to fall from the sky. He stands up and holds out his hands. I take them. Then he pulls me up and twirls me around before setting me on my feet. He then raises his hands in the air and yells into the sky, "Tessa, I love you!"

Laughing I hold raise my hands too. "I love you."

We leave the Gator and walk back to the house in the rain.

When we walk back in, arm in arm, we have more company.

Laughing, we head upstairs to change and come back down just as Harper wakes up.

I scoop up my little angel and take her into the family room to feed her.

Sitting there, I listen to Ben and Kendall talk about trip plans, and Jade and Ryan are warming up the dinner that they brought.

Looking down at my sweet girl, I hear Alex and Phoebe come in, and then I hear Lucas and Ashley, too.

"All those people out there are family, Miss Harper."

I hear Leia growl then Lucas say, "Seriously, dog? I thought we were friends now." Then he laughs. "Much better, dog."

"Did you like your book, Collin?" Jade asks.

"I have no idea what you're talking about," Collin says in confusion.

"Tessa didn't give it to you yet? Oops, sorry." Jade laughs, and I smile down at our girl.

Walking out to the other room, I say, "We've been a little busy. The book might have slipped my mind."

Collin has the boys at the table. He turns and looks at me then winks. "Yeah, a little."

"Have you two decided on a name?" I ask Ashley.

"No, it is a little hard coming up with a girl's name with Lucas," Ashley says, clearly annoyed.

He pulls his hat down, and I can't help but laugh inside.

"You never banged a Harper, did you, Collin?" I ask.

"I don't *bang*, Tessa, and no."

"Bang!" CJ yells.

Everyone laughs, and then he and Matthew start chanting, "Bang, bang, bang …"

"You boys will not be doing that, either."

"I don't know, Tessa; looks like Lucas's little girl will be the only one in town they aren't related to," Collin says to annoy Lucas. And then he looks at Ashley. "I apologize."

"That would be fine with me," she says. Then Lucas looks at her, eyes narrowed. "What do you expect, Lucas?"

"She'll be a good girl," Lucas says.

To that, I laugh.

"This is not funny." Lucas scowls at me then says, "Maybe she'll like Harper."

I shrug then look at Ashley. "Let's help you figure this out, Ashley."

Ashley sighs. "Please do."

"All right, no Maria, no Chantal, no Amy, no Leah, no Sally, no Tina or Tammy, no Carly, no Madison, no Sadi, no Jessie, no Ashley, no Jenny or Tessa, and I'm not sure about the football groupies or San Francisco. What was her name?" I ask.

"Tipper," Lucas mumbles, looking down.

I laugh. "I think that's about it."

"How do you know all their names? I just got a number." Ashley rolls her eyes.

"Oh, I had the pleasure of meeting *all* of them, actually. Now that we have met, all were crazy, except you. I got beat up by how many, Lucas?"

"Four," he grumbles.

"Yes, and three were in the same hour."

"*The* three?" she asks.

"Yes."

"Did you try to help her?"

"She took care of it herself. She's very mean," Lucas throws me under the bus.

Collin pulls out a chair for me next to the boys, and I sit. He rubs my back and kisses Harper's little head.

"I think you should consider an A name; isn't that your thing? You and your sister and the girls are all A names, right?" I ask then pepper kisses to the side of Harper's head.

"Ava," Ashley whispers.

"Ava?" Lucas asks.

"Yes. Why?" Ashley scowls.

"No, I like it. Ava Links." He stands then walks over to her and hugs her. "I like it, but when we have a boy, it has to be an L name."

"Agreed. Ava it is." Ashley sinks into his arms.

After getting word that Catherine will be serving a life sentence, I decide, why not add to the reasons to celebrate? So, I show Collin the responses I am receiving about starting an organization right here in the United States. He is amazed, and then we set to work hard to get it off the ground.

The boys are now jabbering a lot, walking, and Collin and I are falling even more in love with our little men.

They are gentle with Harper, and it reminds me of him and the way he is with me.

We have been married less than two years, together less than two years, and I feel more comfortable, loved, secure, respected, and desired than I ever imagined at any time in my life that I would be.

True Love

Epilogue

Tessa

_W_e work on breaking through the political barriers in the States for the next year, and Collin is as frustrated as I am. Why it is made nearly impossible is beyond me, but Collin tells me that this is why he went outside the country to begin with. Now, however, he is determined not to give up. He'll fight with all he has.

When Harper is one and the boys are almost two, we take our first trip out of the country. Collin decided we would go back to South America so that I can see what has become of it.

The village has flourished. They are self-sufficient. The girl, Alejandra, who we sent to college, completed her degree in less than a year and is now in charge of the clinic. She is so grateful to us for the opportunity, and she's now helping others realize what they can do with a little help. It isn't about money; it's about the effort.

When we tuck the kids in that first night, I snuggle up to him.

"I get it."

"I know, beautiful." He kisses me.

"I want to do what we planned before. I want our kids to see all this and understand that what we have is a blessing and—"

"I know that, too, because I know you, beautiful. I know you."

"Thank you for exposing me to all this."

We make each other better people. I now treasure what family truly can be. My heart, all four chambers, are fuller than I ever thought possible.

He lifts my shirt above my head and tosses it to the ground. "Thank God they're mine again."

I pull his off and kiss where his hand still rests when he's overwhelmed with our love … true love. Then I kiss down his belly and smile up at him.

He slowly shakes his head from side to side as he lifts me up and kisses my lips. Then he tricks me by flipping me to my back.

I laugh. "No fair."

"Shh …" He nods toward the three portable cribs around the now even more cramped quarters.

He then moves his hand down my belly and under my panties. Within seconds, I am thinking of nothing else but us. Not only the physical ecstasy I feel every time we become one, but the unbreakable bond between two people who love each other truly and deeply. Two people whose delight is truly in loving one another. Whose bliss is in watching their children grow, whose joy come from knowing that, no matter what they came from or where they are going, it's each other who matters the most in this life.

We are blessed.

The End

Want more from Blue Valley
HERE'S A TASTE

Kendall

*O*ut of all the things I love about the 90's, music tops the list.

What do Sinéad O'Connor, The Cranberries, Van Morrison, and one of the biggest rock and roll bands of all time—U2—have in common, aside from me being a super fangirl?

Talent and style?

Yes … but also no.

The answer is: some of my all-time favorite bands, singers, and songwriters hail from the city that I'll be spending three more glorious days and nights submerged in.

Dublin.

Even though our group tour is planned around exploring the history, architecture, and castles in Ireland

and Dublin is just one stop, this small-ish city is rich in musical history.

Did I know this before I booked my trip with the same July travel partners I've had since I graduated high school six years ago?

No.

But I researched it, and even though this travel group is not at all interested in rock and roll, I am.

Today, when we finished our tour of St. Patrick's Cathedral, a street band was playing in a local park that we happened to be walking through. We all stopped to listen for a beat. I dropped a couple Irish pounds, or punt Éireannach, in the open guitar case beside them.

One of the folks near them handed me two tickets to a freaking U2 concert at Whelan's! I, of course, googled and found out it was, in fact, a place where live music is played.

And now, as I stand and look in the mirror, I'm kind of freaking out and minutes from deciding that I will just pop my headphones on and listen to U2 in the comfort of my cozy room at the Skylon Hotel tonight.

Flopping back on my bed, I hit my iPod, close my eyes, and hit shuffle, hoping to find my answer via lyrical guidance or assistance.

Weird?

Yes.

I mean, how many people use their iPod like a pre-teen would a magic 8-ball?

Probably just me, but it hasn't steered me wrong yet.

As Dad would say, "*If it's not broke, no sense in fixing it.*"

Proof the random shuffle is accurate?

When I broke things off with Jòse, my first real boyfriend because he wanted a long-distance relationship and I knew ... from secondhand heartbreak ... that it would never work, Fleetwood Mac told me via random shuffle to "Go Your Own Way," so I did.

Two weeks later, I decided Fleetwood Mac and the random shuffle could suck it. I missed having a boyfriend. I was sure I missed us. I would tell him that he had been right when he said, even if he was traveling around the United States playing football, we could make it work. But when I called him, he was true to his character. José told me that he had slept with someone. He then told me it was just a one-night stand and that she had bailed in the middle of the night. That was when I realized how right Fleetwood Mac and the "random shuffle" were. And true to my demons, caused not by my love life but those created by my older sister's, Tessa's, heartbreaks, as well as my parents, I bowed out.

No thank you. Not for me. No way.

Love isn't for the faint of heart and, well … I'm trying to overcome my aversion to my heart fainting like a myotonic goat whenever I feel like maybe "he could be the one," that I should allow myself to feel heartbreak first-hand … again. So, I go to the source of all my best decisions—the random shuffle—and I bow out gracefully.

Again? you ask.

It wasn't José who caused my first heartache; it was the boy who picked a thorn from my finger when I was far too young to remember. But for some sadistic reason, that moment has been allowed to stay etched in my memory ever since.

"Don't be afraid of picking roses; just be careful." Then he kissed my finger, and I kissed his cheek.

My tiny little, pre-k heart had been sent into the biggest tizzy it had ever experienced and has never been the same.

"Ben Sawyer," I sigh his name while looking at the ceiling. He was the one boy in a herd of many who hung out on the family farm from time to time. And he … well *he* made my little girl self—weak in the knees.

Until he and my sister dated briefly, and then that one-dimensional romantic bubble burst.

I hit *play*.

When the sound of the keys begin then the tambourine, guitar, and drums all work together to create the epic interlude of the song by my favorite rock band, U2, that was featured in my all-time favorite movie, *Runaway Bride*, I smile to myself as I accept the fate of the random shuffle.

"I have climbed the highest mountains, I have run through the fields, only to be with you, only to be with you."

As faint a heart as I carry inside the walls of my chest, as many hearts I have seen break before my very eyes, and not only seen but felt, I still believe in love. I know that somewhere in this great, big world that I have traveled over the past six years that one day, I will, in fact, find *"what I'm looking for."*

A t ten o'clock at night … alone in a strange city, I make possibly the bravest move in all my traveling journeys, maybe even my entire life, as I step outside the Skylon.

Pathetic, I know, but it is what it is.

And what it is, is being a typical, twenty-four-year-old college student in a foreign land, wanting to act the part for once.

My traveling companions for the last six summers, Jay, his wife Debbie, and Minister Maureen, or Moe, as we call her, wouldn't be interested in going, and there was a great possibility that they would tell my parents. So, here I stand, free tickets in hand.

"Look at the state 'o you," I hear from behind me and turn to see our guide, a local woman about my age, Dana. "You looks to suffer from a double dose of original sin."

"Oh. Is it bad?" I look down at my outfit. A baby blue, jersey, cotton tank dress that's not overly revealing, especially since I have a denim jacket on, paired with white high-top Chucks, but it's certainly much different than what she saw me wearing today.

"'Tis only a stepmother would blame you."

I have no idea if that's good or bad, but stepmothers are often referred to as a protagonist, so I'm guessing it's okay.

"Ye on the tod?"

"Your accent, coupled with words that just don't seem right together, have me a *wee bit* confused."

She laughs as she says, "You going it alone?"

"It?"

"Out alone?"

I nod. "Just for a little while."

"Unguided?"

I again nod.

"Ye looks to be twice cursed by Adam's slipup."

What in the hell? I ask myself.

"I'm worried about'cha, lass."

I hold up my U2 tickets. "I'm just going to a concert. Taking a cab from here to there."

"Two tickets, I see."

"Would you like to come?"

Her eyes light up. "Aye. Two people shorten the road. Where we headed?"

"Whelan's." I smile.

On our way, Dana, who is a beautiful, fair-skinned redhead —totally looks like what you would imagine an Irish person to look like—tells me, if I'm going to be going out alone, I need to know everything not to do while in Ireland.

"Never look for leprechauns. They're evil, like cats."

Cats? I think.

She continues, "Never ask for directions in Kerry; you won't get a proper answer. Never refer to Ireland as part of the British Isles. Never forget to buy a round."

I mentally take in all the information as she continues.

"Don't mention the civil war. Don't argue with a cab driver. And do not talk politics."

"Okay." I nod.

The cab pulls up in front of the venue, and I'm struck funny by how small it is.

After paying the driver, I slide out behind Dana. "This looks so small compared to the images I saw on the internet. I can't believe U2 is playing in such a small venue."

She snatches the tickets and looks at them, grins, then barks out, "U2 covers, lass."

I snatch them back and look closer. "Well, hell."

When she swings the door open, I smile, not caring one bit when I hear the words of "One" by U2.

"It's the Murphey Brothers." Dana grins then repeats, "The Murphey Brothers!"

After showing our tickets to the giant man at the door, also with red hair, I follow Dana to the bar.

"First round's on me," I yell to her over the music.

"Four pints of Guinness," she yells to the bartender.

So, Guinness, it is.

I hand cash over her shoulder to the bartender who winks. Good-looking man, with a thick head of hair, matching copper beard, and twinkling green eyes.

"Keep the change." I smile as I take the two pints from Dana.

"Stay close, lass," she yells as she leads the way through the crowd.

Standing on a balcony, overlooking the crowd, I watch people dance and sing along to a couple of U2's lesser-known songs in the US, but they seem to know every word.

Three songs in, I watch as the crowd below goes wild as bagpipes begin.

This isn't U2. It's clearly an original "Murphey Brothers."

"Do you dance, lass?" Dana asks before slamming back one of the two pints in her hand.

"After a few drinks, I do." I hold up my half-finished pint then follow suit.

"This is the song that got our boys signed with a label. Songwriter is from the US," she yells before holding her full pint up. "Sláinte."

I wipe my lips with the back of my hand then hold up my full pint. "Sláinte."

Smiling eyes meet mine as we have a sort of chugging contest, which ends up being no contest at all since Dana finishes first while I need a breather between halves.

Once I finish, Dana nods, and I follow.

As we pass another bar, she stops. "My round."

"I'm good," I yell over the crowd.

Apparently, she doesn't hear me because, when she turns, she hands me two shot glasses.

Normally, while on an international vacation, I have a two-drink limit, but I'm immersed in music, feeling quite buzzed already, and I have a personal guide who looks to be having a great time.

"Sláinte," I say before tossing one back.

Four songs and four drinks in, I'm feeling nothing but

absorbed in a country that I already know, down deep, I'll be returning to.

With my jean jacket tied around my waist, hands in the air, I find myself singing along to the chorus of a Murphey Brothers' original in no time.

When the song ends, another doesn't immediately begin like the last ones. Instead, the lead singer announces something in a breathy verse of words that I can't quite decipher, as the sexy guitarist moves to front and center stage.

I whip my head toward Dana who laughs out, "The songwriter's taking over. Heard good things about him; never witnessed."

As soon as I hear the very familiar mix of keys, tambourine, and guitar begin, I turn toward the stage, which my back has been to the entire time so that I could take in the locals who I immediately felt one with.

"He's a looker, aye?"

Through fog, smoke, and lights, I see a messy mop of curls from under a black baseball cap and five days of stubble covering the square jaw of this tall, very well-built man holding a guitar, with full, sexy lips inches from the mic, delivering velvet in words that have always soothed my wanderlust soul.

"*I have climbed the highest mountains …*"

I sway with the crowd, hands above my head, eyes closed, and sing along at the top of my lungs, "*But I still haven't found what I'm looking for.*"

I open my eyes as he swings the guitar behind him, removes the mic from the stand, and sings as he shields his eyes, bends forward, and seemingly searches the crowd as he holds out the mic and we all sing, "*And I still haven't found what I'm looking for.*"

Through the entire song, he plays the crowd like I've

never experienced at a concert before. Possibly, it's the more intimate arena that has my body, mind, and soul on high alert. Yet, all my surroundings seem to be in a haze as my attention falls on the songwriter behind the blur of lights and smoke.

When he's positioned in front of Dana and me, I see him smile briefly, and then he points toward me ... us ... oh hell, I have no idea which one of us, or if he's even pointing in anyone's general direction. And it matters not one bit, because *damn, damn, damn.*

Click Here To Read Now

Books by MJ Fields
MJ FIELDS

THE LEGACY SERIES FAMILY OF BOOKS
(Recommended reading order)
The Blue Valley series
Blue Love
New Love
Sad Love
True Love

Blue Valley series spin offs

The Way We Fell
(Kendalls story)
Coming in 2022
The Way We Met
(Phoebe's Story)
The Way We Love
(Jade's Story)

Coming in 2022
Wrapped In Silk

Wrapped In Armor
Wrapped In Us

Stained
Forged
Merged

Love You Anyways

THE STEEL WORLDS
(Recommended reading order)
The Men of Steel Series
Jase
Cyrus
Zandor
Xavier
Forever Family
Raising Steel
Or get the
Men Of Steel complete box set

The Ties of Steel Series
Abe
Dominic
Eroe
Sabato
Or get the
Ties of Steel complete box set

The Rockers of Steel Series
Memphis Black
Finn Beckett
River James
Billy Jeffers

or get the
Rockers of Steel complete box set

The Match Duet
Match This!
ImPerfectly Matched!
or get the
complete duet

The Steel Country Series
Hammered
Destroyed
Wasted
or get the
Steel Country complete box set

Tied in Steel series
Valentina
Paige
Gia
or get the
Tied in Steel complete box set

Steel Crew
(Generation 2)
Tagged Steel
Branded Steel
Laced Steel
Justified Steel
Tricked Steel
Busted Steel
Smashed Steel
Marked Steel
Maxed Steel

The Norfolk Series
Irons
Shadows
Titan

Timeless Love series
Unraveled
Deserving Me
Hearts So Big
Couture Love

The Caldwell Brothers Series
(co-written w/ Chelsea Camaron)
Hendrix
Morrison
Jagger
Visibly Broken
Use Me

Holiday Springs
(co-written w/ Jessica Ruben)
The Broody Brit: For Christmas
The Irresistible Irishman: For St. Patrick's Day

Standalones
Offensive Rebound

About the Author

MJ Fields is a USA Today bestselling author of contemporary and new adult romance novels. She lives in New York with her daughter and smoochie faced Newfie, Theo.
When she's not locked away in the cave, she enjoys spending time with her family, listening to live music, watching theatre, singing off key, dancing to her own beat, listening to audio books, and reading— of course.

Forever Steel!

Join MJ's mailing list:
https://mjfieldsbooks.com/newsletter

Thank you

The end of another series, an amazing group of badass
women to thank!
Thank you …
Cover designer, Amy at Q Designs
Editor, Kris at C&D Editing
Proofer, Asli Arif Fratarcangeli
Proofer, CeCe Perez
Beta boss, and new member of the team, Brittni.
Sister from another mister, and legacy series historian,
Jamie.
My merch queen and forever friend, Diane.
My Street Crew, sounding board, book lovers, and friends.
My friend, almost daily call, right hand, sounding board,
kick in the ass when needed, cheerleader, and PR ,
Autumn
To my reader group; that has grown,
OG Crew, thank you for helping steer the ship while I am
in the cave.
Those new to crew…I promise you, this is 'just the tip'

To Miss A, (we got this) and love you… more <3
You all are the amazing, and I am blessed to have you all in
my life.
So much love…anyway,
MJ

Made in the USA
Coppell, TX
08 June 2022

78607134R00363